"Not just good, but important. A haunting shot across the bow of the worst the Internet has to offer. A stunning and electric debut."

— **DONNY CATES** —

(*GOD COUNTRY, Redneck, Thanos*)

"Good science fiction is about the human condition. Forcing you to look at yourself and society through a different lens. *NO. 1 WITH A BULLET* is that good science fiction."

— **ERICA HENDERSON** —

(*The Unbeatable Squirrel Girl, Jughead*)

"Unsettling and all too real, *NO. 1 WITH A BULLET* takes the comforts of every day and turns them into sharp knives and heavy stones."

— **CHRISTOPHER SEBELA** —

(*SHANGHAI RED, Crowded, High Crimes*)

"A masterful blend of message and sensation, *NO. 1 WITH A BULLET* reveals the other side of our bare-all culture and dangerous double standards."

— **VITA AYALA** —

(*The Wilds, Submerged, Rebirth: Supergirl*)

"A cross-genre of Elmore Leonard crime and David Lynch unease, *NO. 1 WITH A BULLET* is a strange and vibrant slice of modern day horror."

— **STEVE ORLANDO** —

(*CRUDE, The Unexpected, Midnighter*)

"*NO. 1 WITH A BULLET* takes our fears about cyber security and throws them right in our awed faces. No p@$$W0rD will save you when 'he' comes 'round."

— **ERICA SCHULTZ** —

(*Charmed, M3, Swords of Sorrow*)

SOMEWHERE IN THE HOLLYWOOD HILLS.

ONE MONTH AGO.

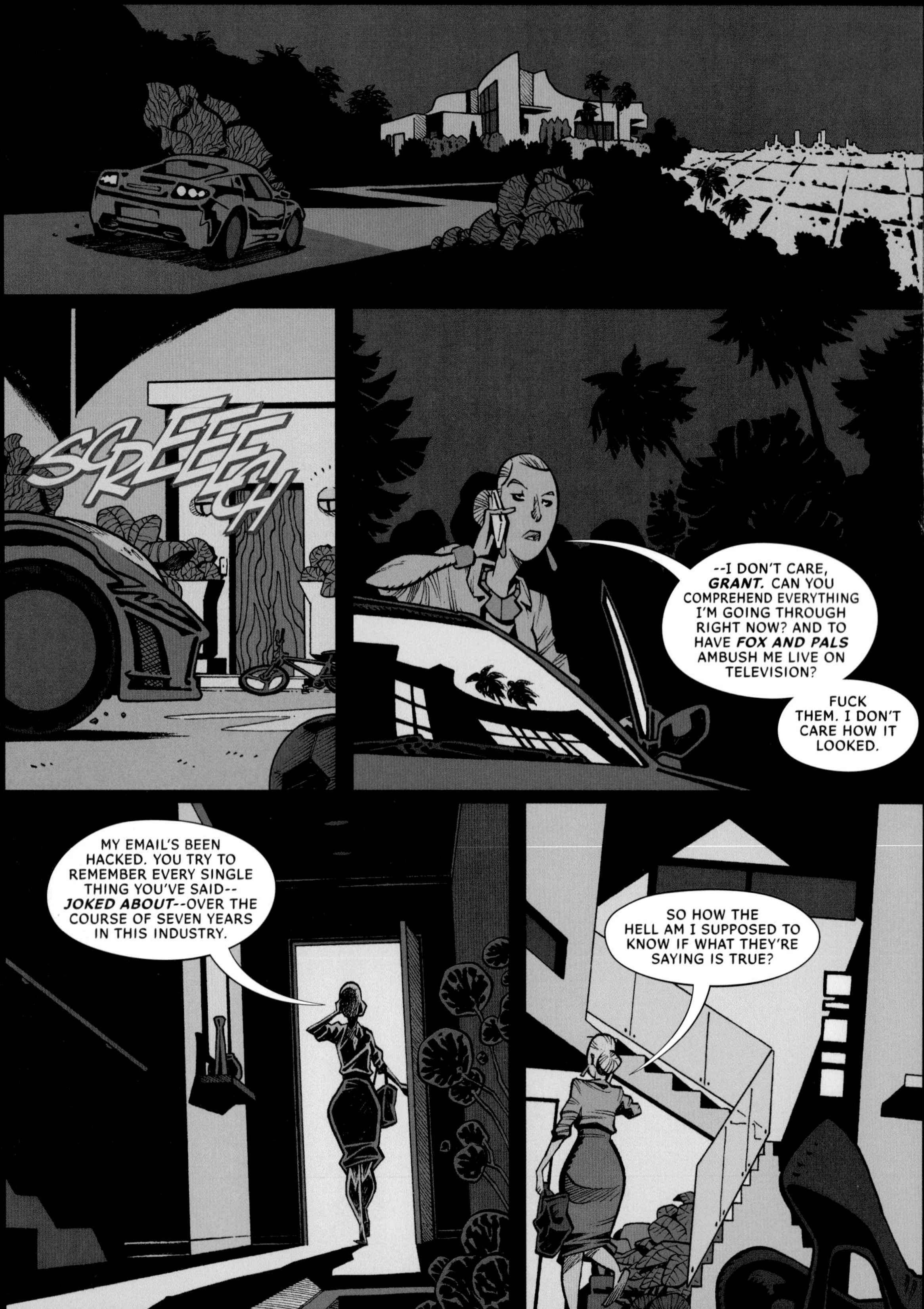
SCREEEECH
--I DON'T CARE, GRANT. CAN YOU COMPREHEND EVERYTHING I'M GOING THROUGH RIGHT NOW? AND TO HAVE FOX AND PALS AMBUSH ME LIVE ON TELEVISION?
FUCK THEM. I DON'T CARE HOW IT LOOKED.
MY EMAIL'S BEEN HACKED. YOU TRY TO REMEMBER EVERY SINGLE THING YOU'VE SAID-- JOKED ABOUT--OVER THE COURSE OF SEVEN YEARS IN THIS INDUSTRY.
SO HOW THE HELL AM I SUPPOSED TO KNOW IF WHAT THEY'RE SAYING IS TRUE?

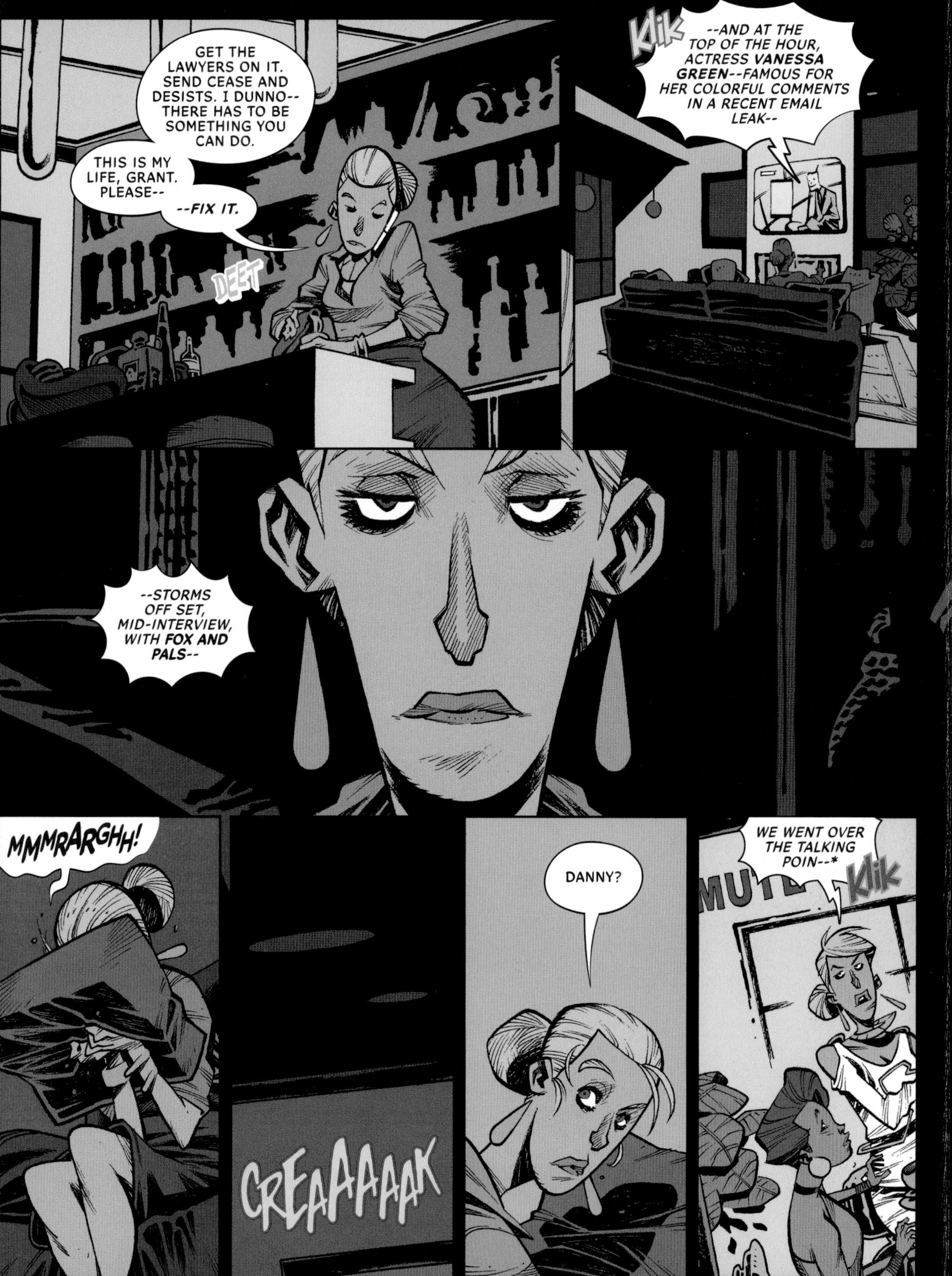
GET THE LAWYERS ON IT. SEND CEASE AND DESISTS. I DUNNO-- THERE HAS TO BE SOMETHING YOU CAN DO.
THIS IS MY LIFE, GRANT. PLEASE--
--FIX IT.
DEET
KLIK
--AND AT THE TOP OF THE HOUR, ACTRESS VANESSA GREEN--FAMOUS FOR HER COLORFUL COMMENTS IN A RECENT EMAIL LEAK--
--STORMS OFF SET, MID-INTERVIEW, WITH FOX AND PALS--
MMMRARGHH!
CREAAAAAK
DANNY?
WE WENT OVER THE TALKING POIN--*
KLIK

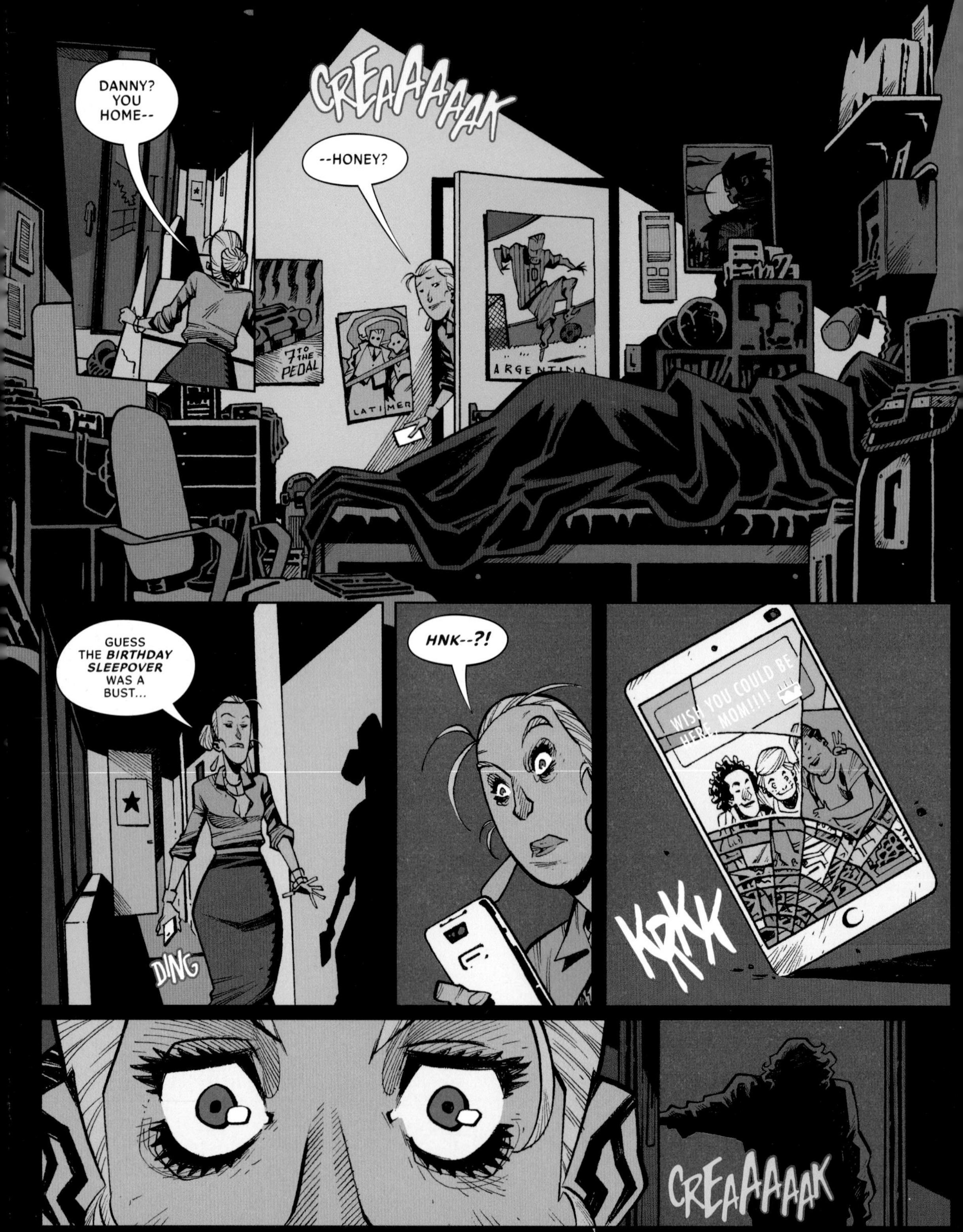
CREAAAAAAK
DANNY? YOU HOME--
--HONEY?
7 TO THE PEDAL
LATIMER
ARGENTINA
GUESS THE *BIRTHDAY SLEEPOVER* WAS A BUST...
DING
HNK--?!
WISH YOU COULD BE HERE, MOM!!!!
KRKK
CREAAAAAK

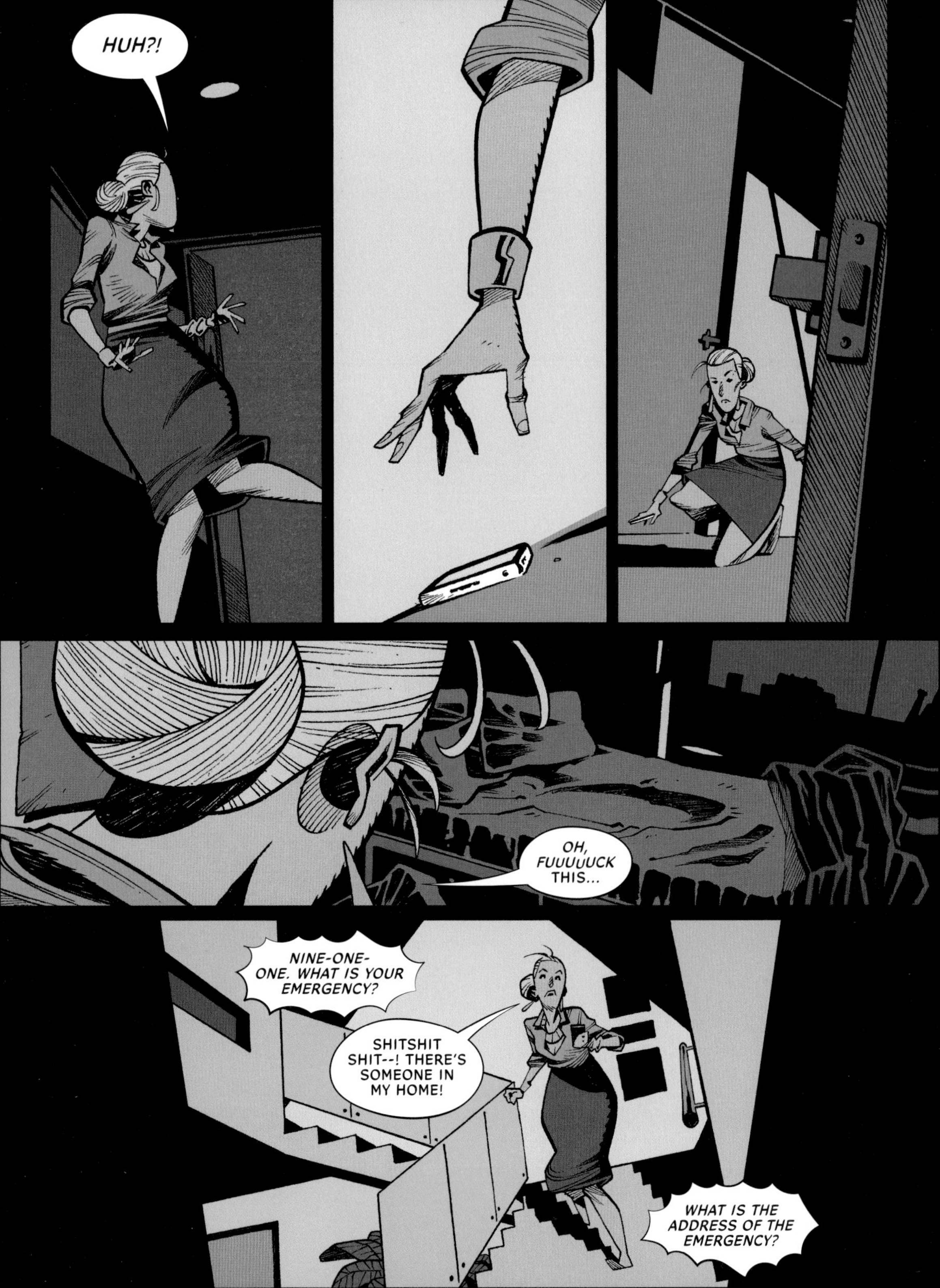
HUH?!
OH, FUUUUUCK THIS...
NINE-ONE-ONE. WHAT IS YOUR EMERGENCY?
SHITSHIT SHIT--! THERE'S SOMEONE IN MY HOME!
WHAT IS THE ADDRESS OF THE EMERGENCY?

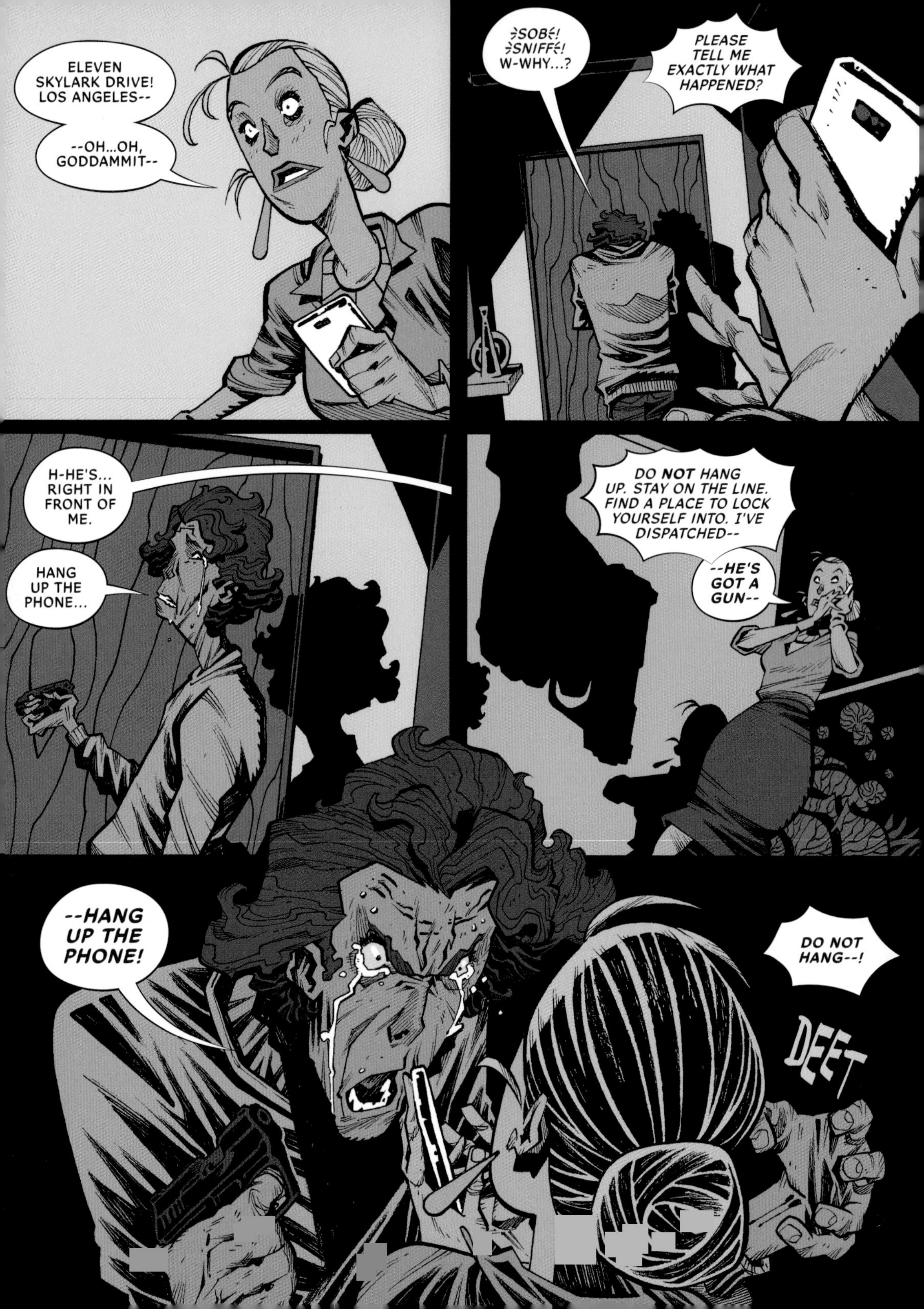
ELEVEN SKYLARK DRIVE! LOS ANGELES--
--OH...OH, GODDAMMIT--
SOB! SNIFF! W-WHY...?
PLEASE TELL ME EXACTLY WHAT HAPPENED?
H-HE'S... RIGHT IN FRONT OF ME.
HANG UP THE PHONE...
DO **NOT** HANG UP. STAY ON THE LINE. FIND A PLACE TO LOCK YOURSELF INTO. I'VE DISPATCHED--
--HE'S GOT A GUN--
--HANG UP THE PHONE!
DO NOT HANG--!
DEET

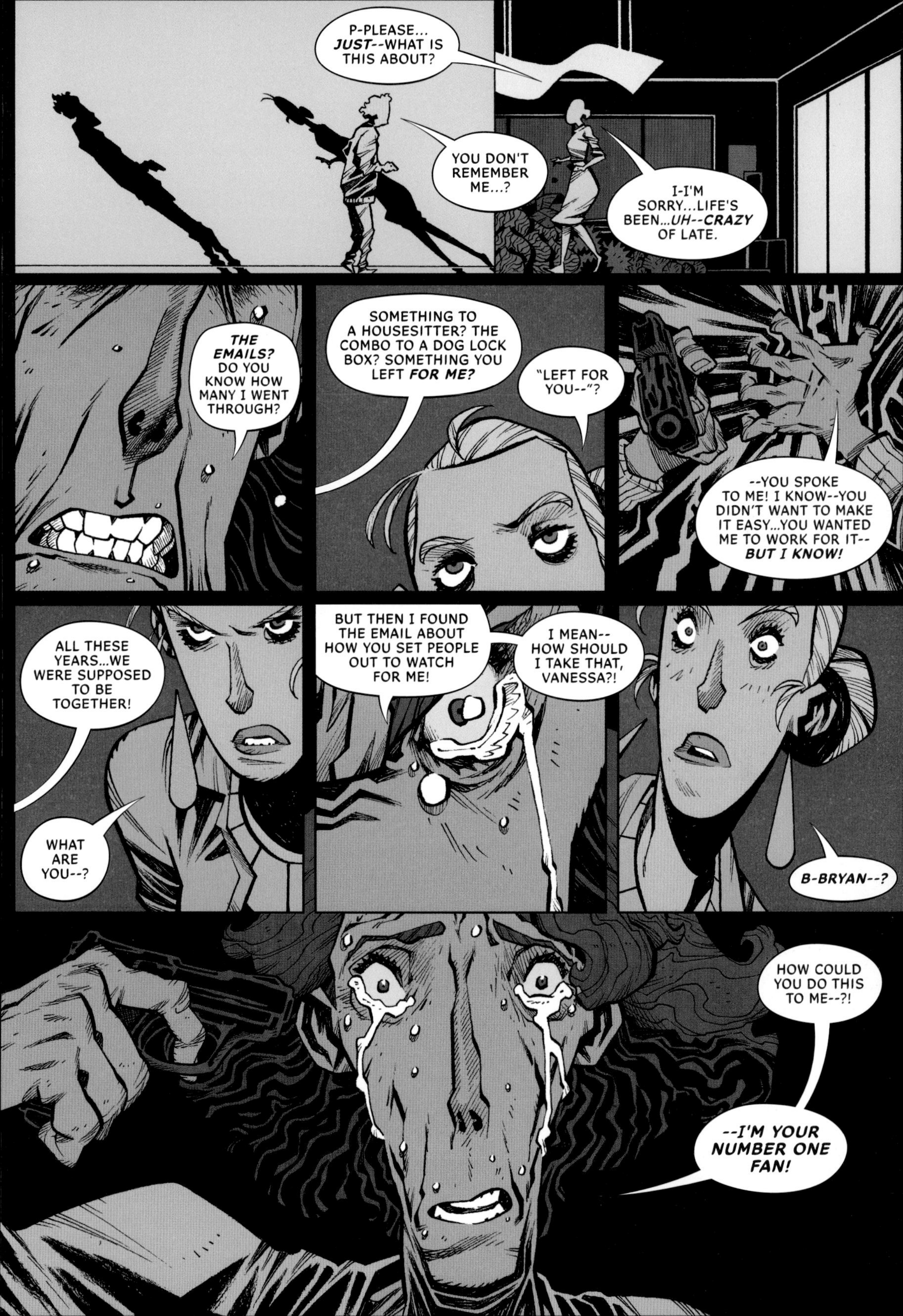
P-PLEASE... JUST--WHAT IS THIS ABOUT?
YOU DON'T REMEMBER ME...?
I-I'M SORRY...LIFE'S BEEN...UH--CRAZY OF LATE.
THE EMAILS? DO YOU KNOW HOW MANY I WENT THROUGH?
SOMETHING TO A HOUSESITTER? THE COMBO TO A DOG LOCK BOX? SOMETHING YOU LEFT FOR ME?
"LEFT FOR YOU--"?
--YOU SPOKE TO ME! I KNOW--YOU DIDN'T WANT TO MAKE IT EASY...YOU WANTED ME TO WORK FOR IT-- BUT I KNOW!
ALL THESE YEARS...WE WERE SUPPOSED TO BE TOGETHER!
WHAT ARE YOU--?
BUT THEN I FOUND THE EMAIL ABOUT HOW YOU SET PEOPLE OUT TO WATCH FOR ME!
I MEAN-- HOW SHOULD I TAKE THAT, VANESSA?!
B-BRYAN--?
HOW COULD YOU DO THIS TO ME--?!
--I'M YOUR NUMBER ONE FAN!

JACOB SEMAHN
creator/writer

JORGE CORONA
creator/artist

JEN HICKMAN
colorist

STEVE WANDS
letterer/designs

ERIN LEVY
editor

HERE FOR THE COMMENTS

SARA CHARLES & CASEY GILLY
moderators

FOR IMAGE COMICS, INC.

ROBERT KIRKMAN
chief operating officer

ERIK LARSEN
chief financial officer

TODD MCFARLANE
president

MARC SILVESTRI
chief executive officer

JIM VALENTINO
vice-president

ERIC STEPHENSON
publisher/chief creative officer

COREY HART / director of sales
JEFF BOISON / director of publishing planning & book trade sales
CHRIS ROSS / director of digital sales
JEFF STANG / director of specialty sales
KAT SALAZAR / director of pr & marketing
DREW GILL / art director
HEATHER DOORNINK / production director
NICOLE LAPALME / controller

DEANNA PHELPS & TRICIA RAMOS & VINCENT KUKUA
production artists for NO. 1 WITH A BULLET
MELISSA GIFFORD
content manager for NO. 1 WITH A BULLET

IMAGECOMICS.COM

IMAGE COMICS Presents

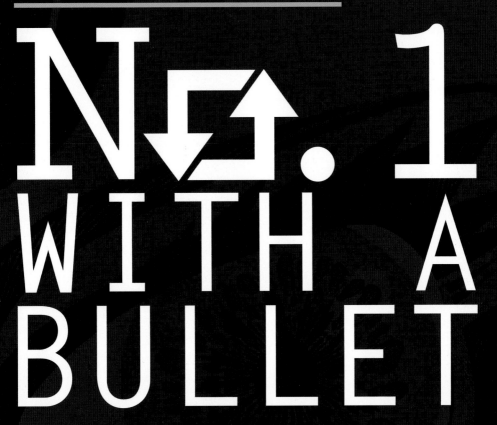

N⤵⤴. 1 WITH A BULLET

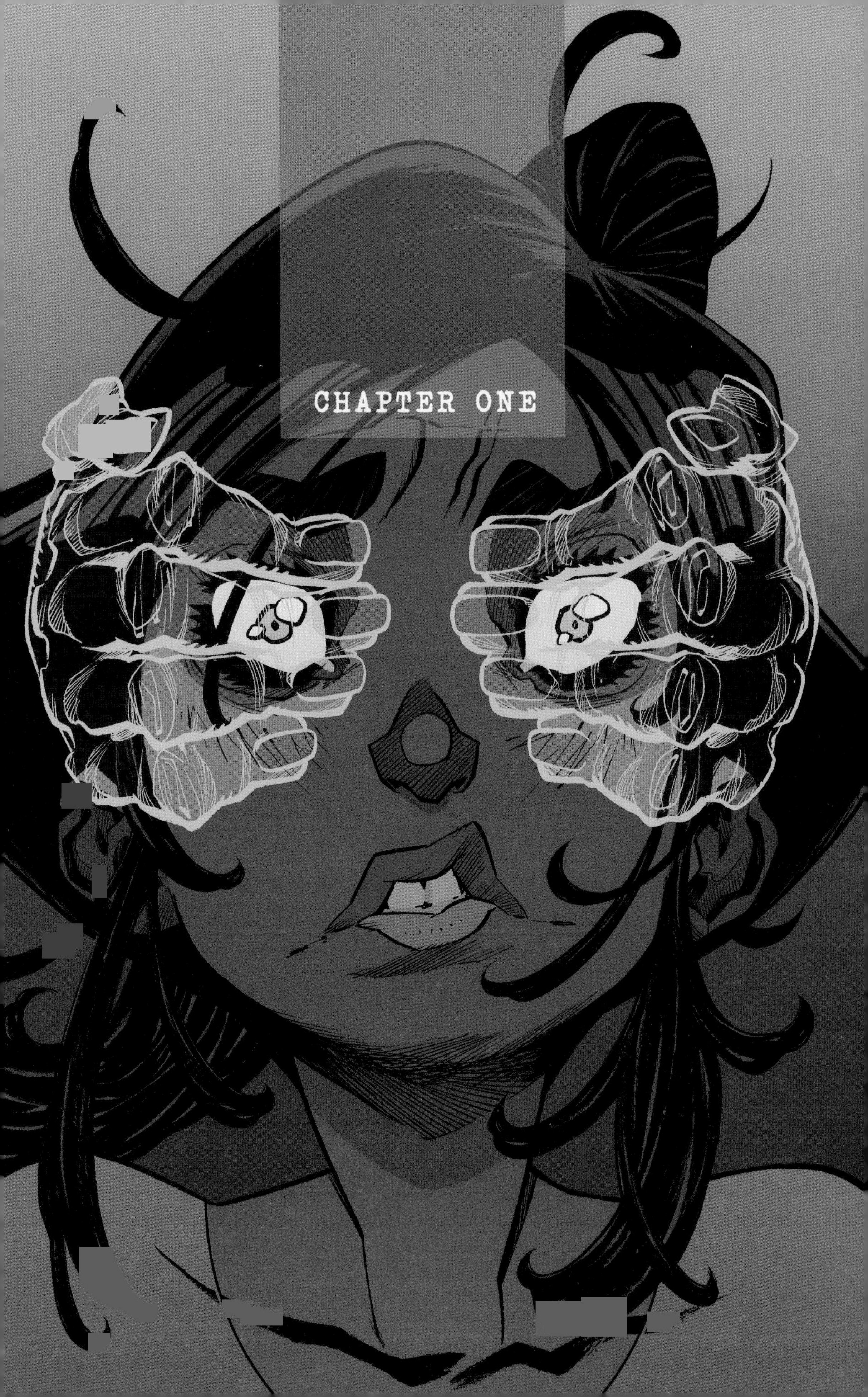
CHAPTER ONE

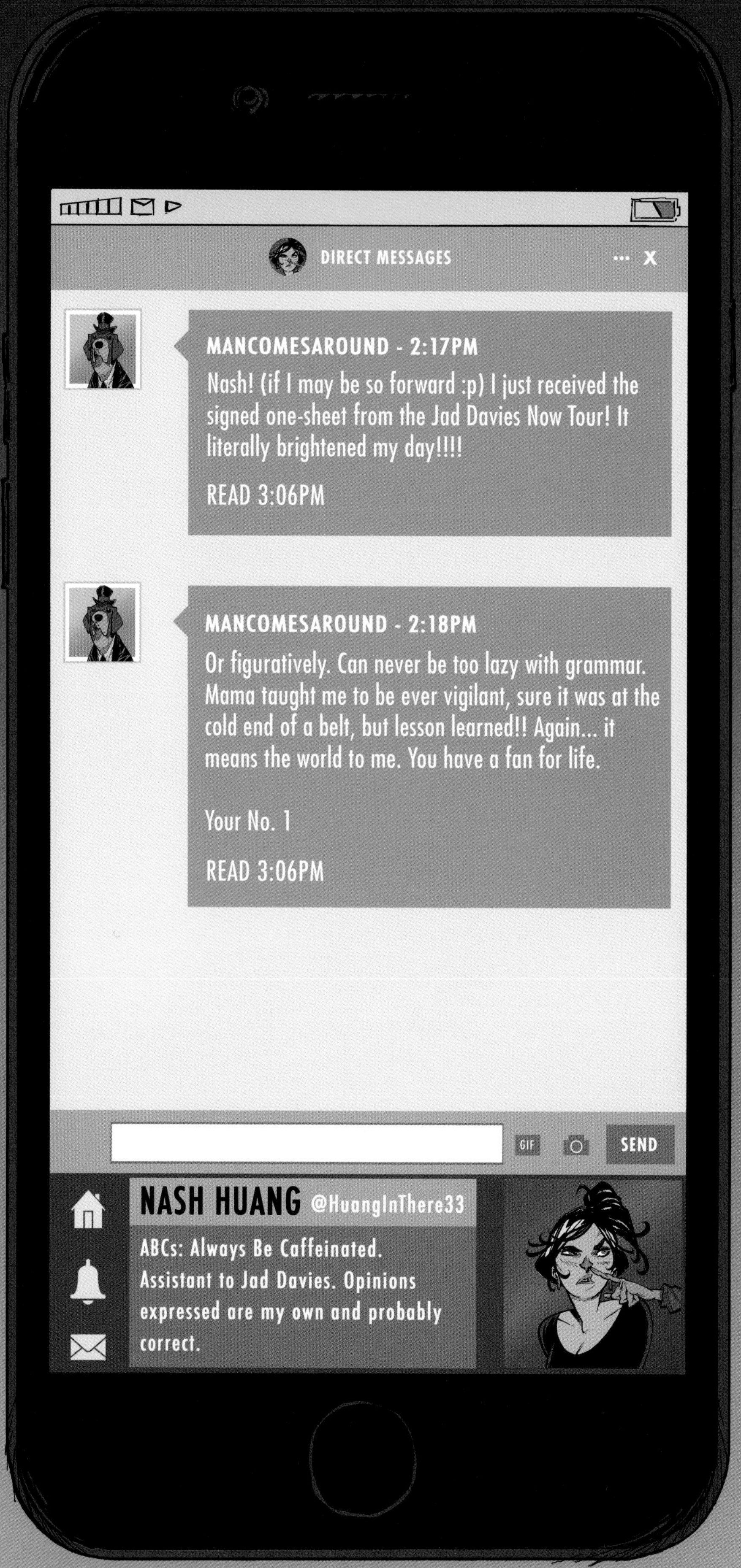

MANCOMESAROUND - 2:17PM

Nash! (if I may be so forward :p) I just received the signed one-sheet from the Jad Davies Now Tour! It literally brightened my day!!!!

READ 3:06PM

MANCOMESAROUND - 2:18PM

Or figuratively. Can never be too lazy with grammar. Mama taught me to be ever vigilant, sure it was at the cold end of a belt, but lesson learned!! Again... it means the world to me. You have a fan for life.

Your No. 1

READ 3:06PM

GIF 📷 SEND

NASH HUANG @HuangInThere33

ABCs: Always Be Caffeinated. Assistant to Jad Davies. Opinions expressed are my own and probably correct.

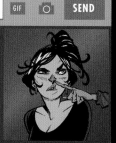

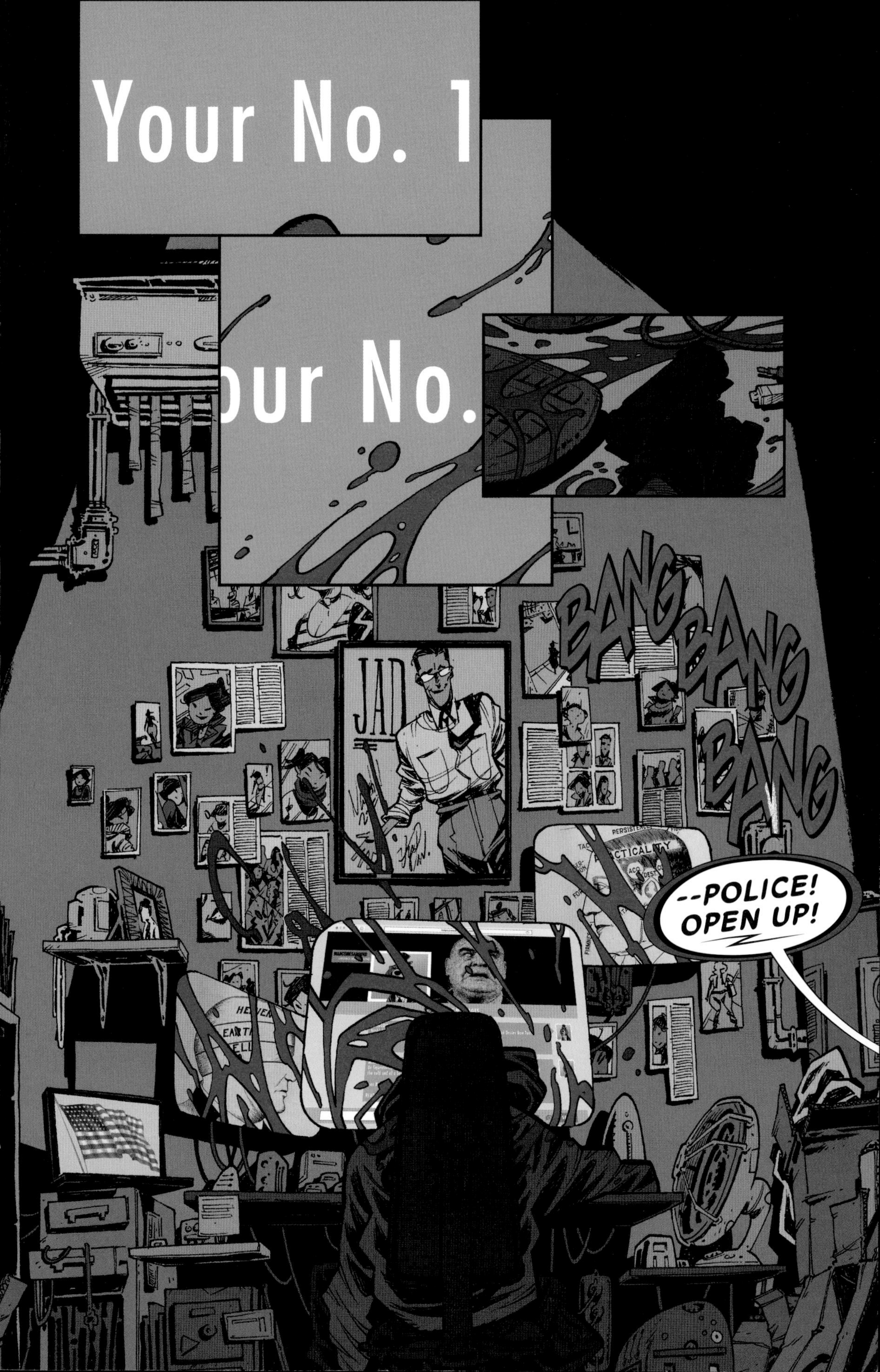

Your No. 1
our No.
BANG
BANG
BANG
--POLICE! OPEN UP!

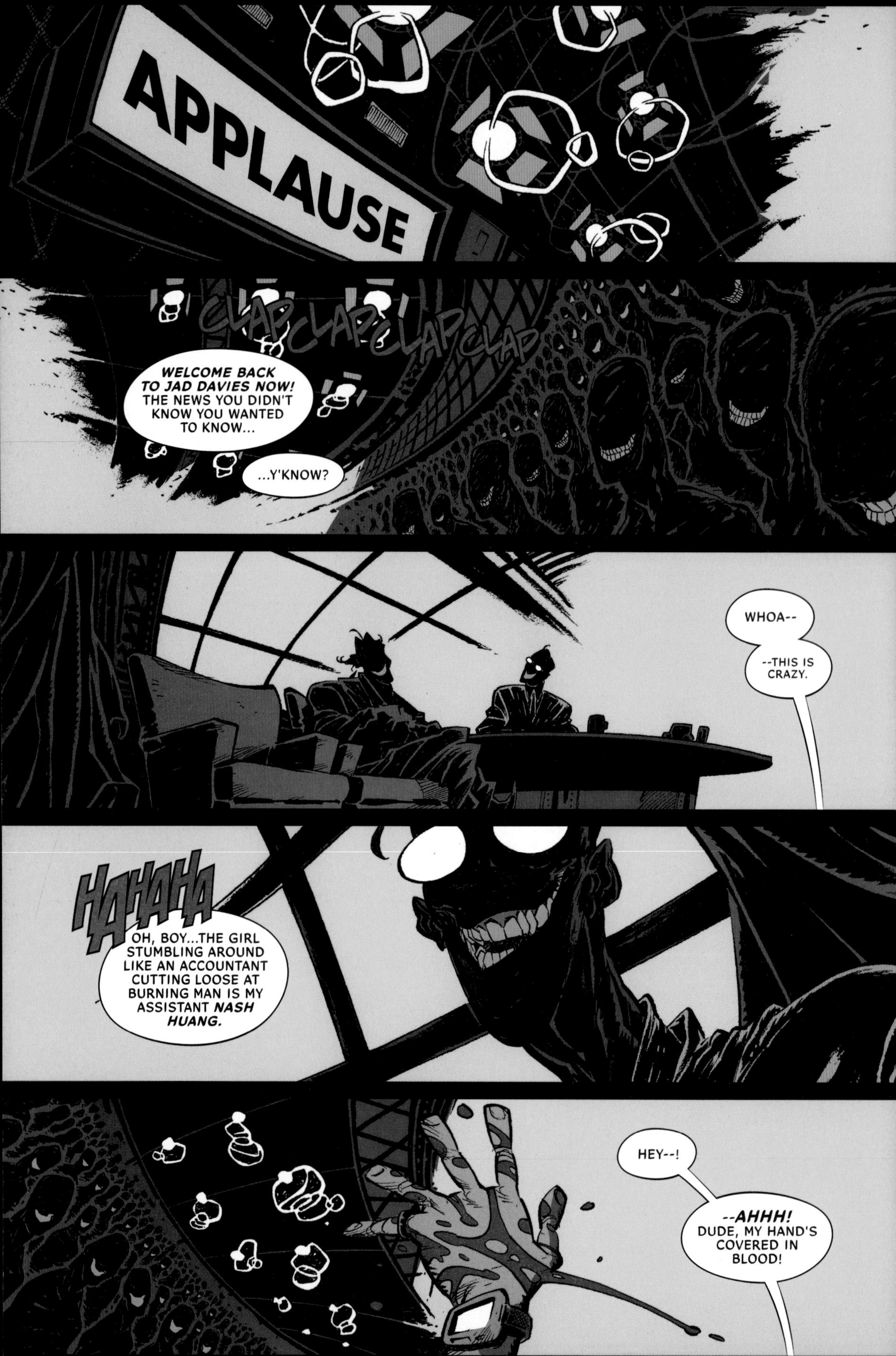

APPLAUSE
CLAP CLAP CLAP CLAP CLAP
WELCOME BACK TO JAD DAVIES NOW! THE NEWS YOU DIDN'T KNOW YOU WANTED TO KNOW...
...Y'KNOW?
WHOA--
--THIS IS CRAZY.
HAHAHA
OH, BOY...THE GIRL STUMBLING AROUND LIKE AN ACCOUNTANT CUTTING LOOSE AT BURNING MAN IS MY ASSISTANT NASH HUANG.
HEY--!
--AHHH! DUDE, MY HAND'S COVERED IN BLOOD!

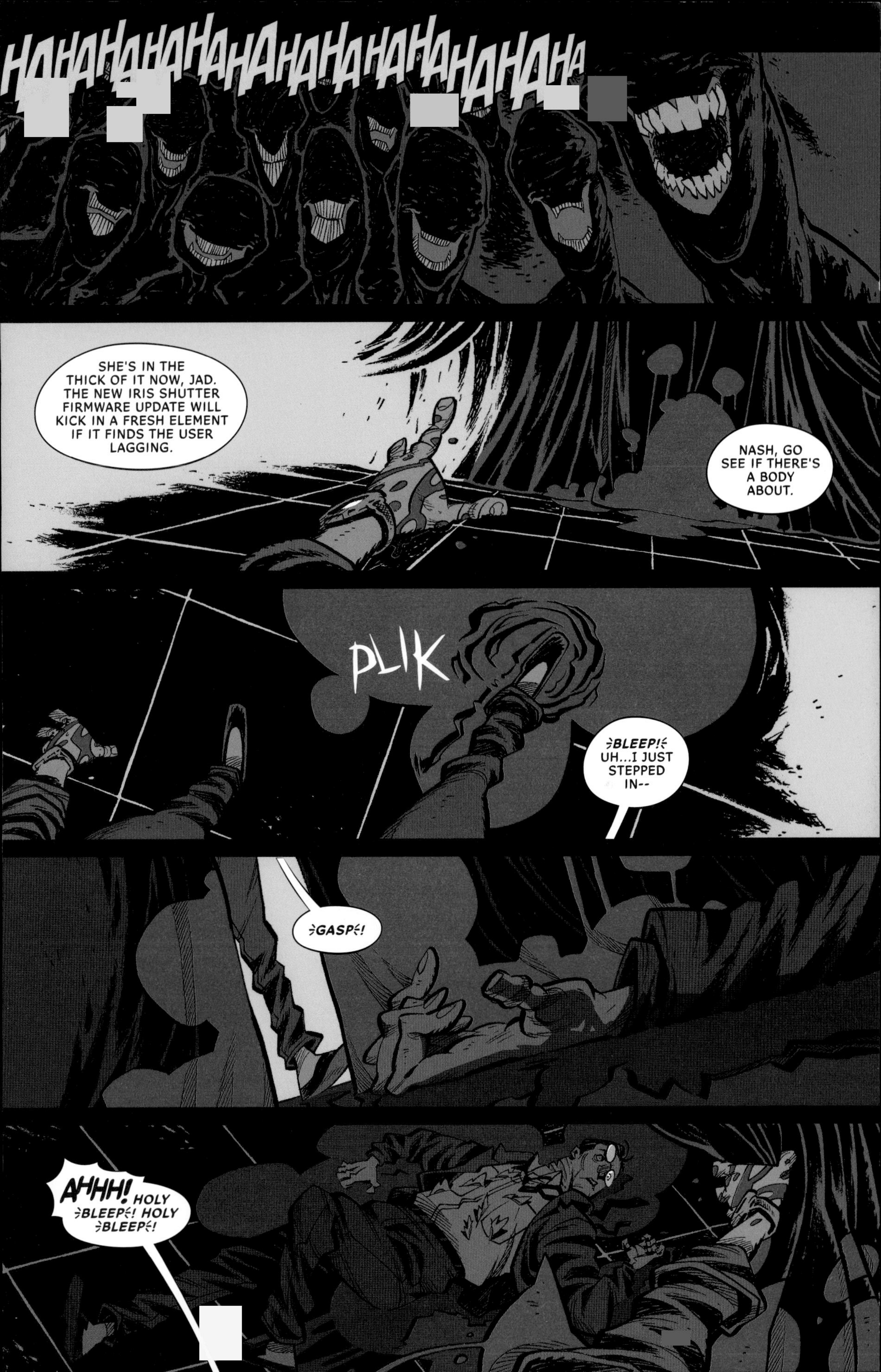

HAHAHAHAHAHAHAHAHAHAHAHAHAHAHAHA
SHE'S IN THE THICK OF IT NOW, JAD. THE NEW IRIS SHUTTER FIRMWARE UPDATE WILL KICK IN A FRESH ELEMENT IF IT FINDS THE USER LAGGING.
NASH, GO SEE IF THERE'S A BODY ABOUT.
PLIK
BLEEP! UH...I JUST STEPPED IN--
GASP!
AHHH! HOLY BLEEP! HOLY BLEEP!

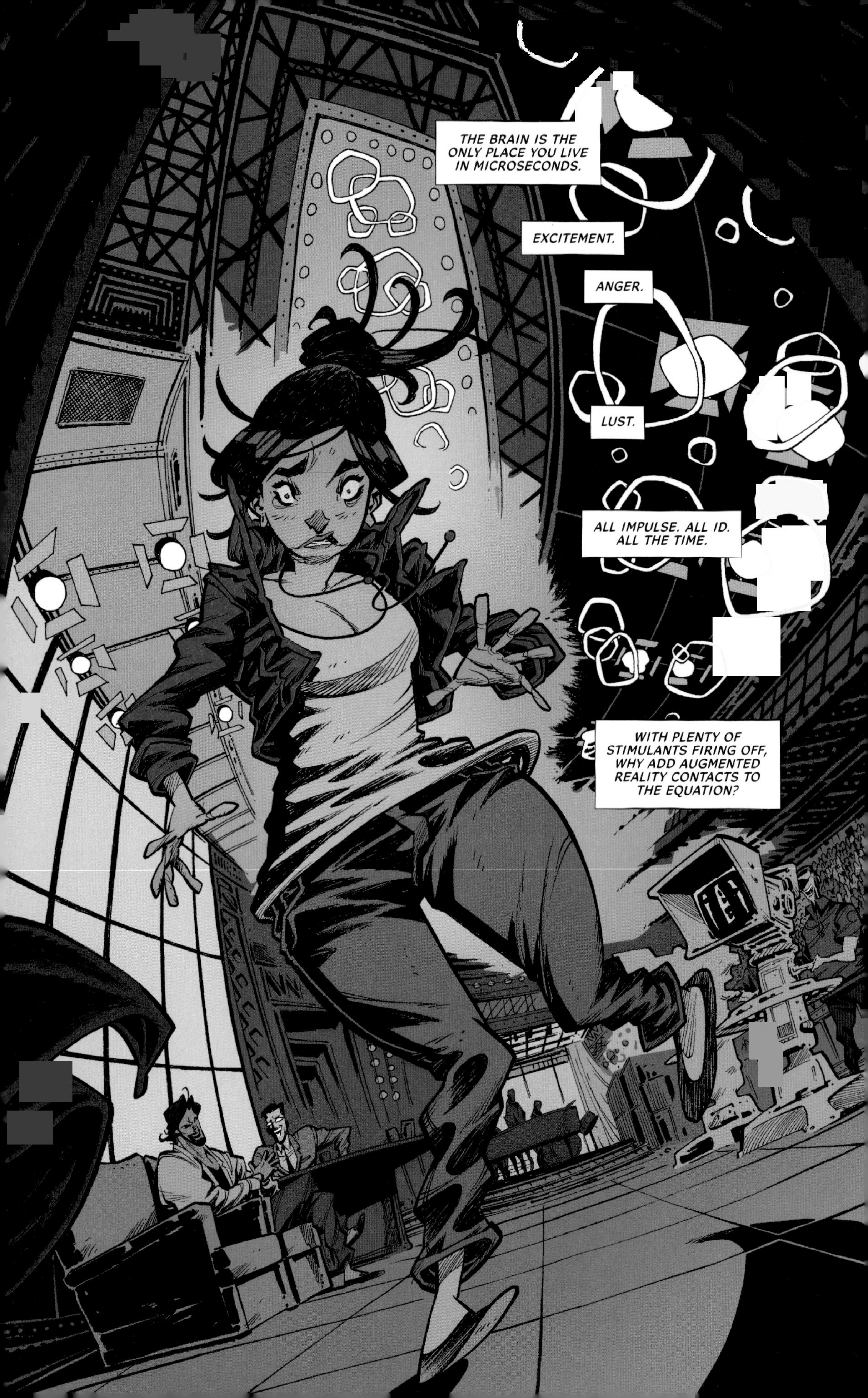
THE BRAIN IS THE ONLY PLACE YOU LIVE IN MICROSECONDS.
EXCITEMENT.
ANGER.
LUST.
ALL IMPULSE. ALL ID. ALL THE TIME.
WITH PLENTY OF STIMULANTS FIRING OFF, WHY ADD AUGMENTED REALITY CONTACTS TO THE EQUATION?

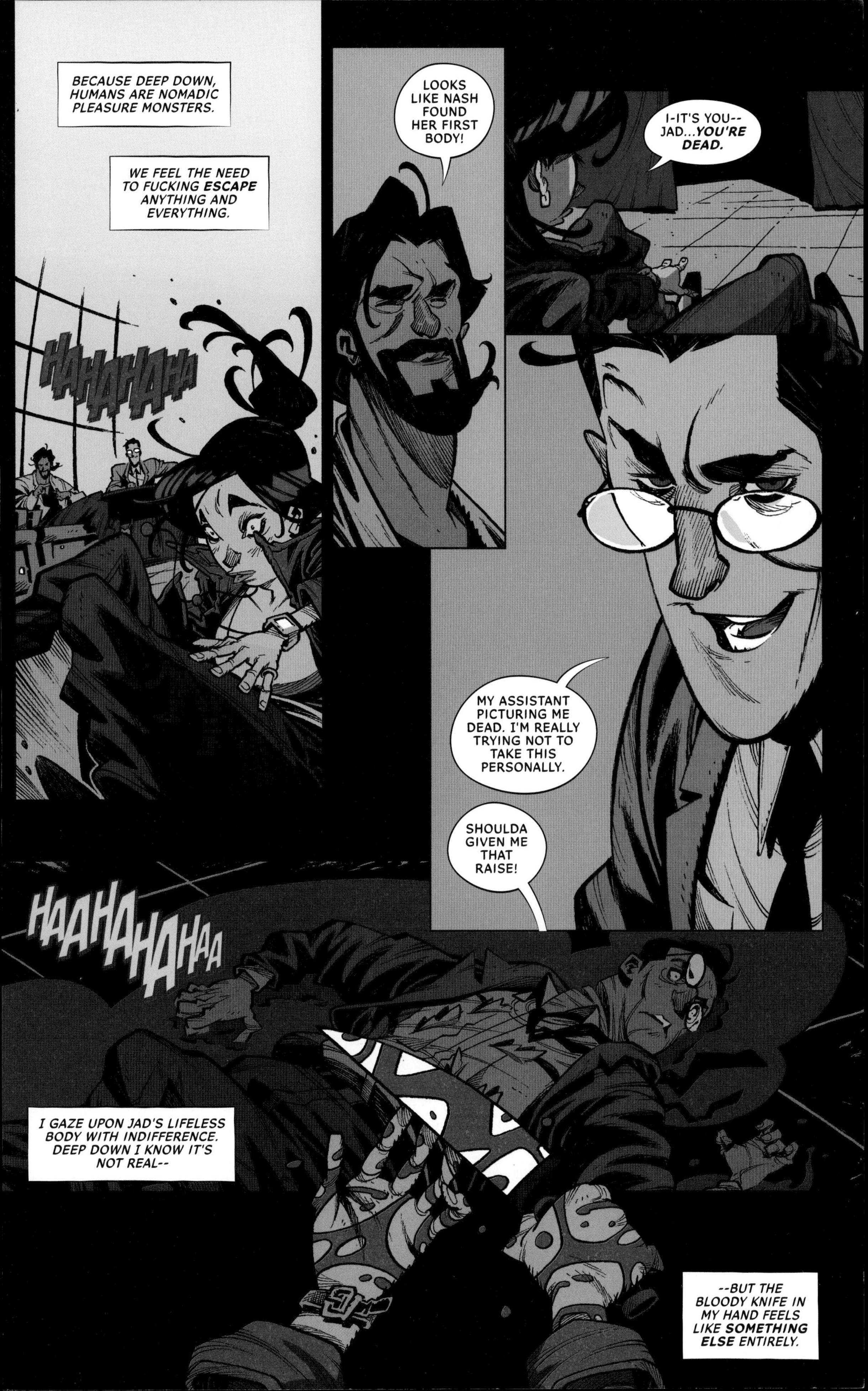
BECAUSE DEEP DOWN, HUMANS ARE NOMADIC PLEASURE MONSTERS.
WE FEEL THE NEED TO FUCKING **ESCAPE** ANYTHING AND EVERYTHING.
HAHAHAHAHA
LOOKS LIKE NASH FOUND HER FIRST BODY!
I-IT'S YOU-- JAD... **YOU'RE DEAD.**
MY ASSISTANT PICTURING ME DEAD. I'M REALLY TRYING NOT TO TAKE THIS PERSONALLY.
SHOULDA GIVEN ME THAT RAISE!
HAAHAHAHAHAA
I GAZE UPON JAD'S LIFELESS BODY WITH INDIFFERENCE. DEEP DOWN I KNOW IT'S NOT REAL--
--BUT THE BLOODY KNIFE IN MY HAND FEELS LIKE **SOMETHING ELSE** ENTIRELY.

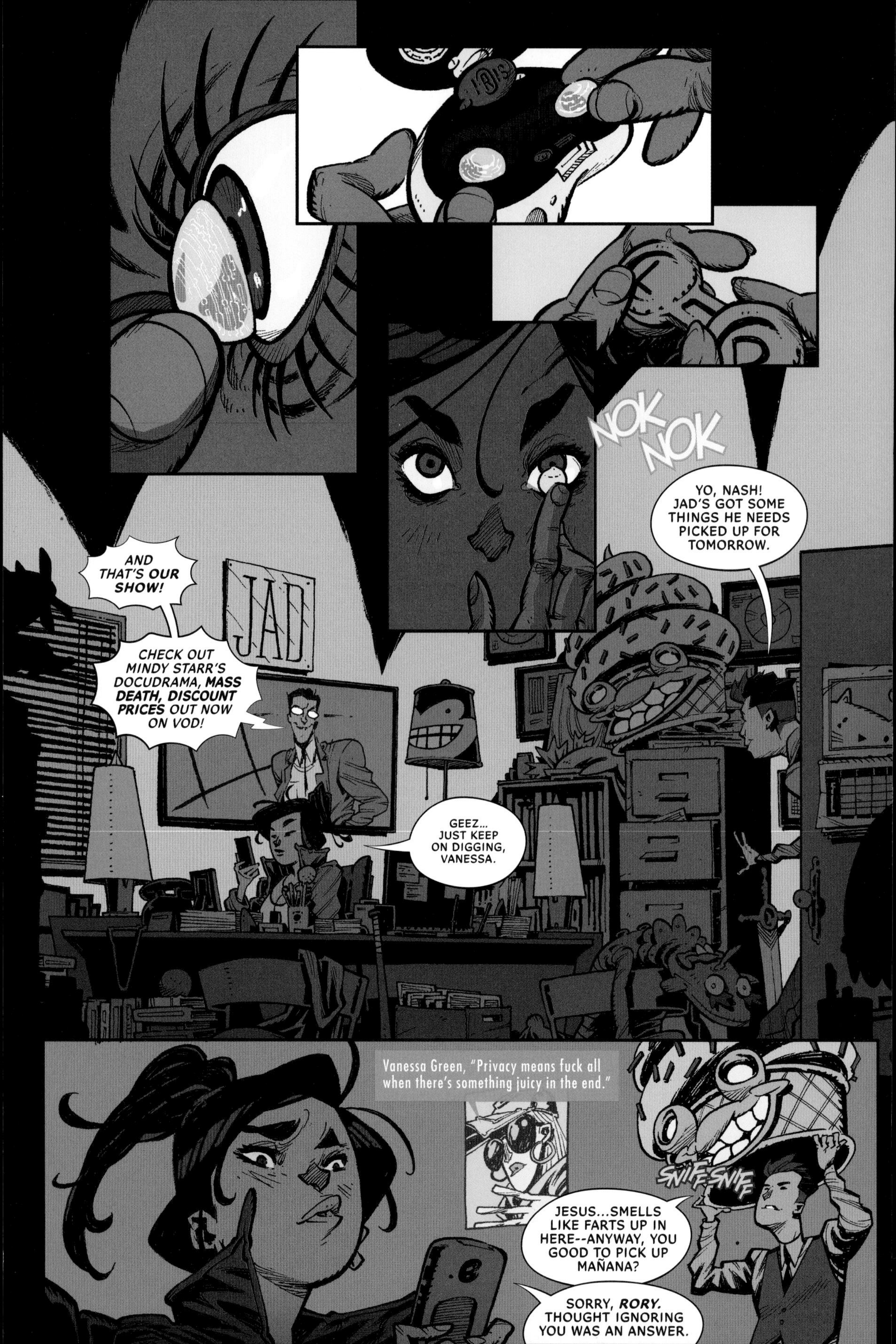
NOK NOK
YO, NASH! JAD'S GOT SOME THINGS HE NEEDS PICKED UP FOR TOMORROW.
JAD
AND THAT'S OUR SHOW!
CHECK OUT MINDY STARR'S DOCUDRAMA, MASS DEATH, DISCOUNT PRICES OUT NOW ON VOD!
GEEZ... JUST KEEP ON DIGGING, VANESSA.
Vanessa Green, "Privacy means fuck all when there's something juicy in the end."
SNIFF SNIFF
JESUS...SMELLS LIKE FARTS UP IN HERE--ANYWAY, YOU GOOD TO PICK UP MAÑANA?
SORRY, RORY. THOUGHT IGNORING YOU WAS AN ANSWER.

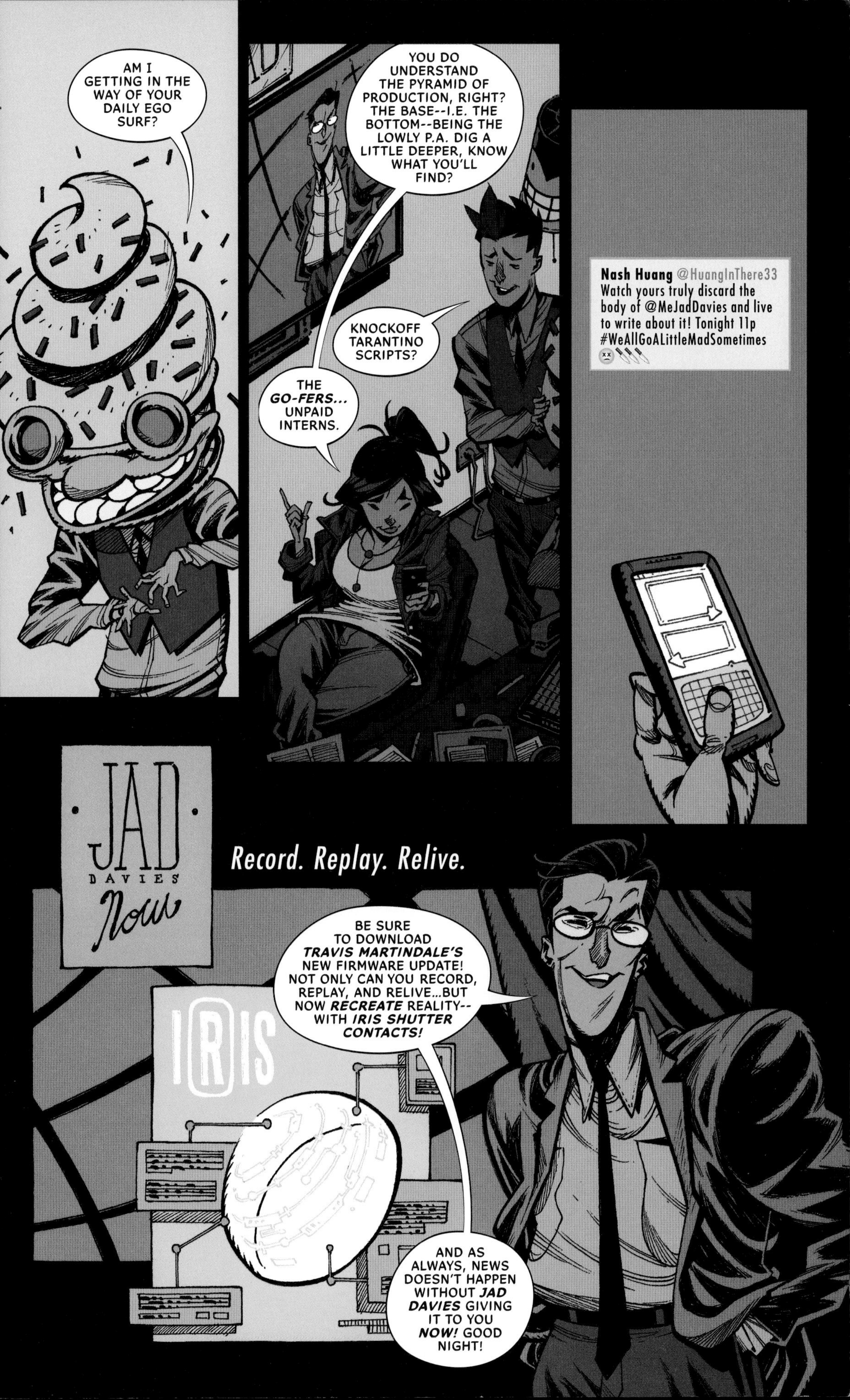

AM I GETTING IN THE WAY OF YOUR DAILY EGO SURF?
YOU DO UNDERSTAND THE PYRAMID OF PRODUCTION, RIGHT? THE BASE--I.E. THE BOTTOM--BEING THE LOWLY P.A. DIG A LITTLE DEEPER, KNOW WHAT YOU'LL FIND?
KNOCKOFF TARANTINO SCRIPTS?
THE GO-FERS... UNPAID INTERNS.
Nash Huang @HuangInThere33
Watch yours truly discard the body of @MeJadDavies and live to write about it! Tonight 11p #WeAllGoALittleMadSometimes
JAD DAVIES Now
Record. Replay. Relive.
IRIS
BE SURE TO DOWNLOAD TRAVIS MARTINDALE'S NEW FIRMWARE UPDATE! NOT ONLY CAN YOU RECORD, REPLAY, AND RELIVE...BUT NOW RECREATE REALITY--WITH IRIS SHUTTER CONTACTS!
AND AS ALWAYS, NEWS DOESN'T HAPPEN WITHOUT JAD DAVIES GIVING IT TO YOU NOW! GOOD NIGHT!

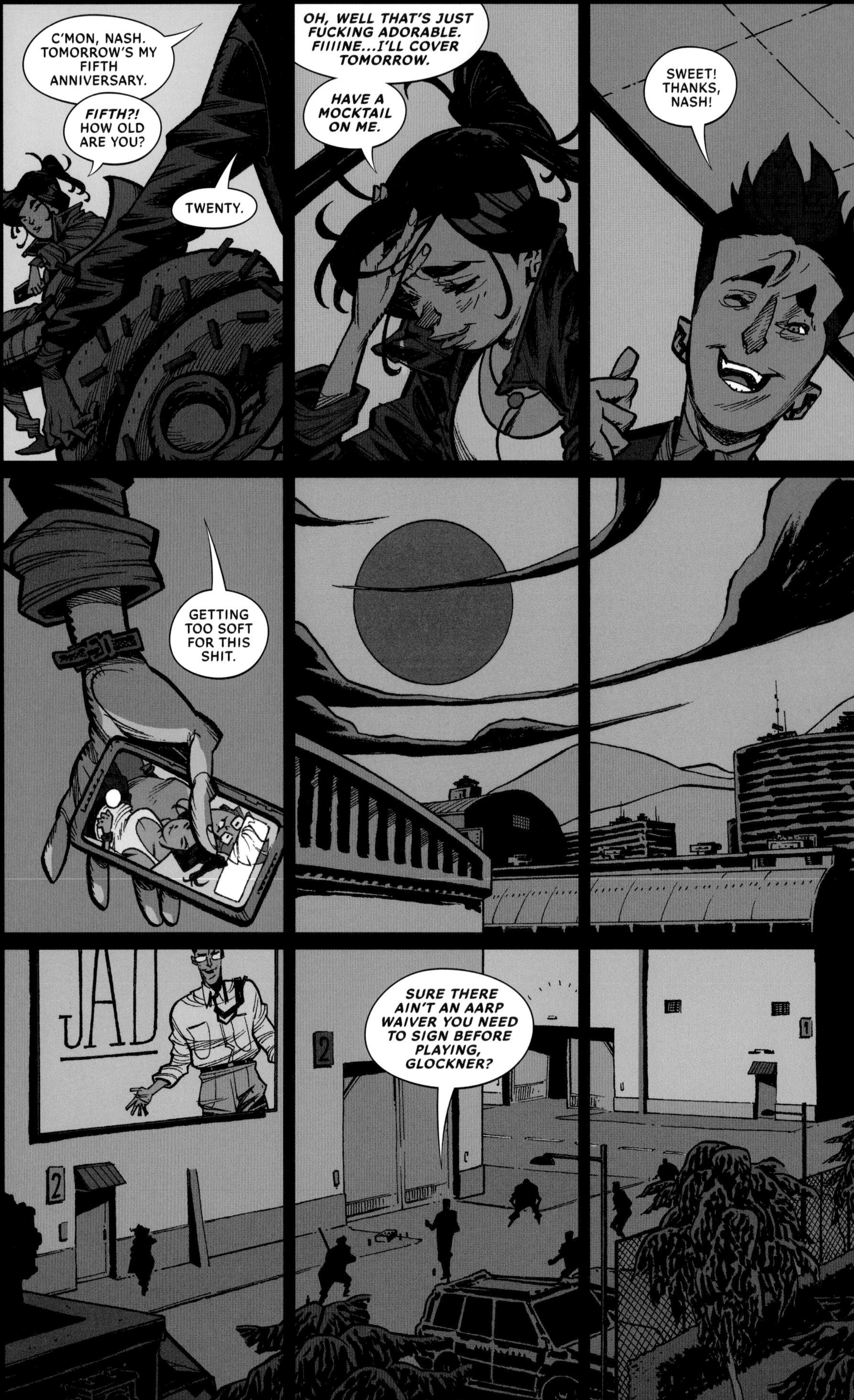
C'MON, NASH. TOMORROW'S MY FIFTH ANNIVERSARY.
FIFTH?! HOW OLD ARE YOU?
TWENTY.
OH, WELL THAT'S JUST FUCKING ADORABLE. FIIIINE...I'LL COVER TOMORROW.
HAVE A MOCKTAIL ON ME.
SWEET! THANKS, NASH!
GETTING TOO SOFT FOR THIS SHIT.
JAD
2
SURE THERE AIN'T AN AARP WAIVER YOU NEED TO SIGN BEFORE PLAYING, GLOCKNER?

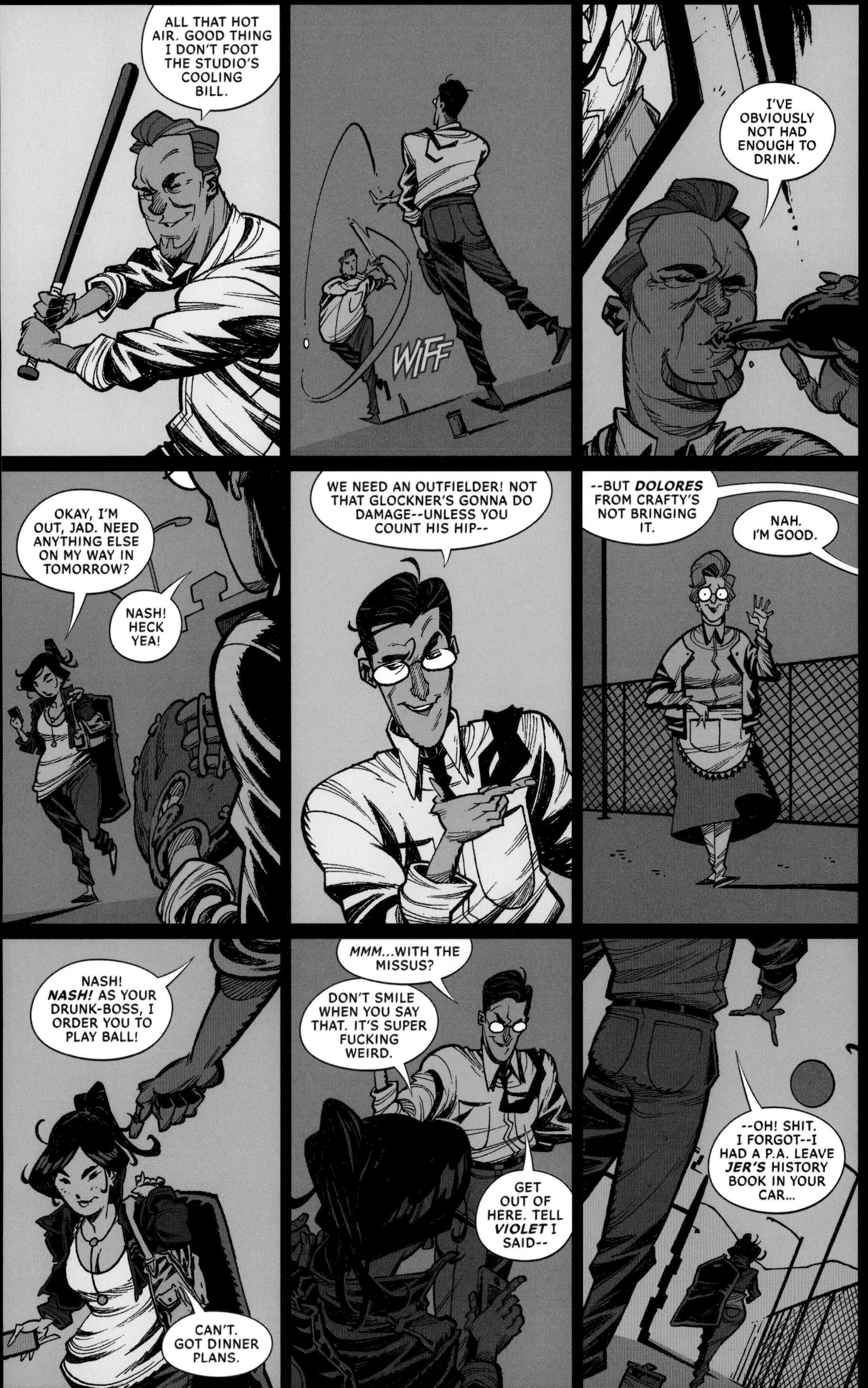
ALL THAT HOT AIR. GOOD THING I DON'T FOOT THE STUDIO'S COOLING BILL.
WIFF
I'VE OBVIOUSLY NOT HAD ENOUGH TO DRINK.
OKAY, I'M OUT, JAD. NEED ANYTHING ELSE ON MY WAY IN TOMORROW?
NASH! HECK YEA!
WE NEED AN OUTFIELDER! NOT THAT GLOCKNER'S GONNA DO DAMAGE--UNLESS YOU COUNT HIS HIP--
--BUT *DOLORES* FROM CRAFTY'S NOT BRINGING IT.
NAH. I'M GOOD.
NASH! *NASH!* AS YOUR DRUNK-BOSS, I ORDER YOU TO PLAY BALL!
CAN'T. GOT DINNER PLANS.
*MMM...*WITH THE MISSUS?
DON'T SMILE WHEN YOU SAY THAT. IT'S SUPER FUCKING WEIRD.
GET OUT OF HERE. TELL *VIOLET* I SAID--
--OH! SHIT. I FORGOT--I HAD A P.A. LEAVE *JER'S* HISTORY BOOK IN YOUR CAR...

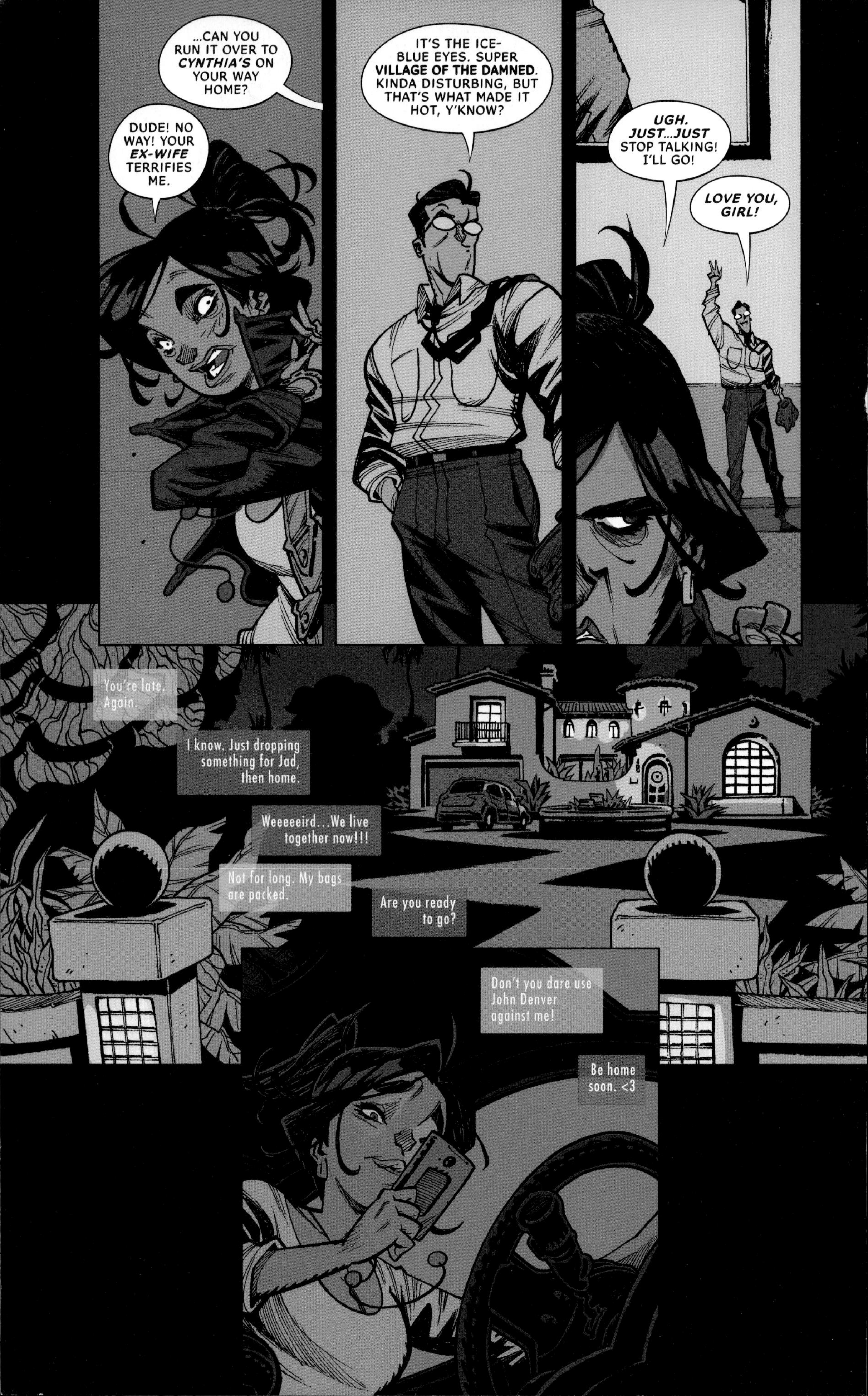
...CAN YOU RUN IT OVER TO *CYNTHIA'S* ON YOUR WAY HOME?
DUDE! NO WAY! YOUR *EX-WIFE* TERRIFIES ME.
IT'S THE ICE-BLUE EYES. SUPER **VILLAGE OF THE DAMNED**. KINDA DISTURBING, BUT THAT'S WHAT MADE IT HOT, Y'KNOW?
UGH. JUST...JUST STOP TALKING! I'LL GO!
LOVE YOU, GIRL!
You're late. Again.
I know. Just dropping something for Jad, then home.
Weeeeeird...We live together now!!!
Not for long. My bags are packed.
Are you ready to go?
Don't you dare use John Denver against me!
Be home soon. <3

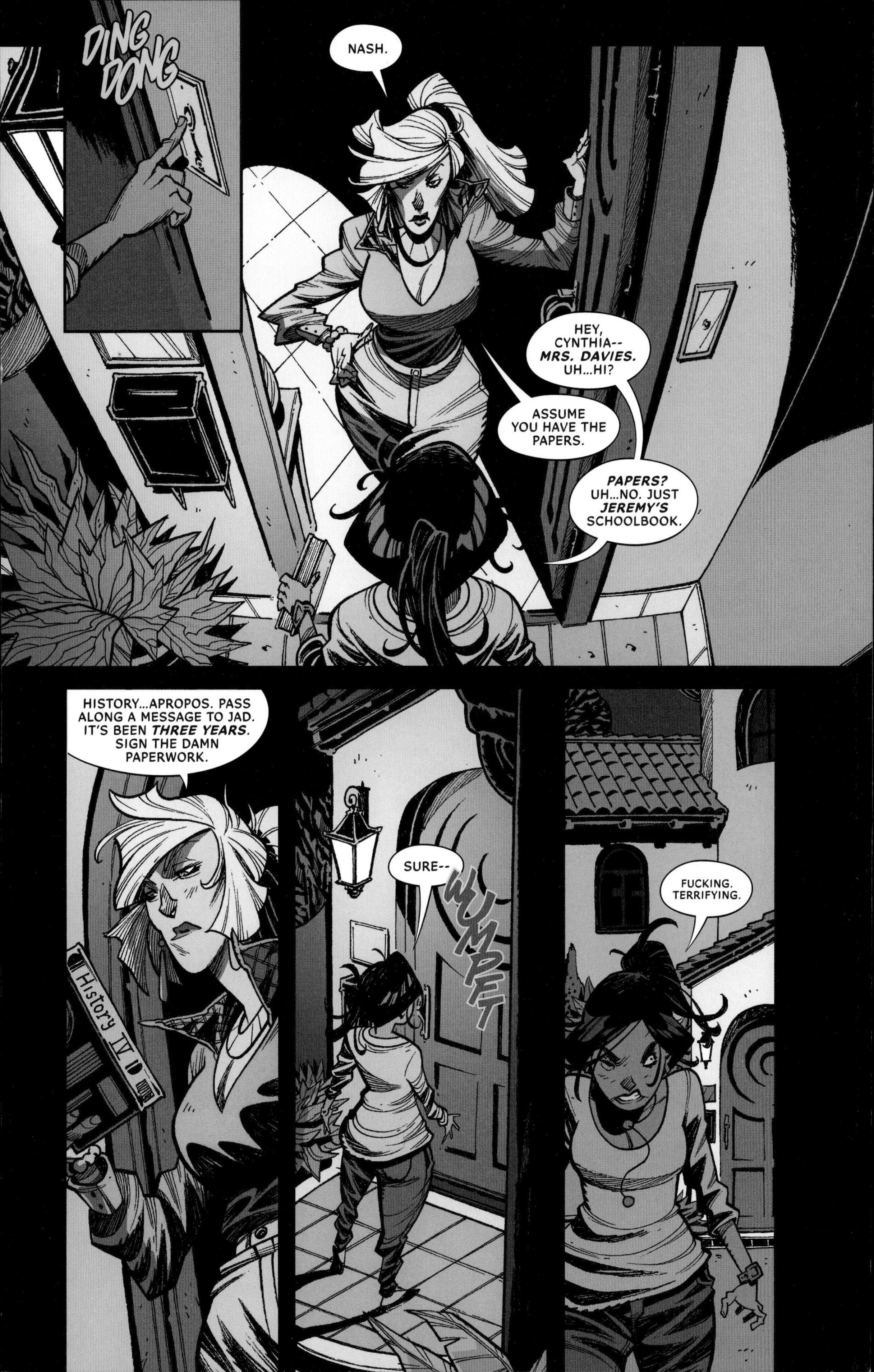
DING DONG
NASH.
HEY, CYNTHIA-- MRS. DAVIES. UH...HI?
ASSUME YOU HAVE THE PAPERS.
PAPERS? UH...NO. JUST JEREMY'S SCHOOLBOOK.
HISTORY...APROPOS. PASS ALONG A MESSAGE TO JAD. IT'S BEEN THREE YEARS. SIGN THE DAMN PAPERWORK.
History IV
SURE--
WUMPFF
FUCKING. TERRIFYING.

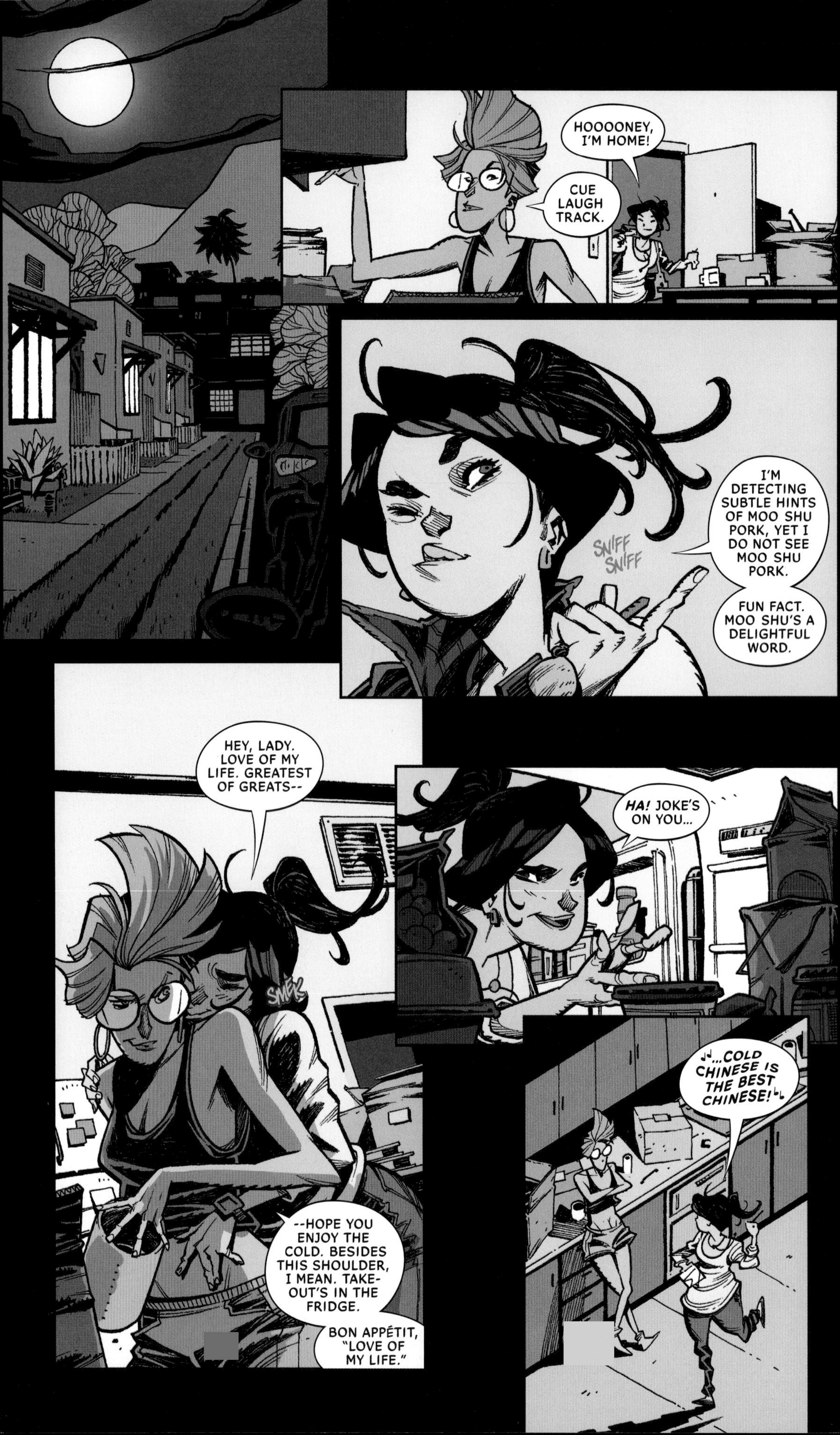
HOOOONEY, I'M HOME!
CUE LAUGH TRACK.
I'M DETECTING SUBTLE HINTS OF MOO SHU PORK, YET I DO NOT SEE MOO SHU PORK.
SNIFF SNIFF
FUN FACT. MOO SHU'S A DELIGHTFUL WORD.
HEY, LADY. LOVE OF MY LIFE. GREATEST OF GREATS--
SMEK
--HOPE YOU ENJOY THE COLD. BESIDES THIS SHOULDER, I MEAN. TAKE-OUT'S IN THE FRIDGE.
BON APPÉTIT, "LOVE OF MY LIFE."
HA! JOKE'S ON YOU...
♪...COLD CHINESE IS THE BEST CHINESE!♪

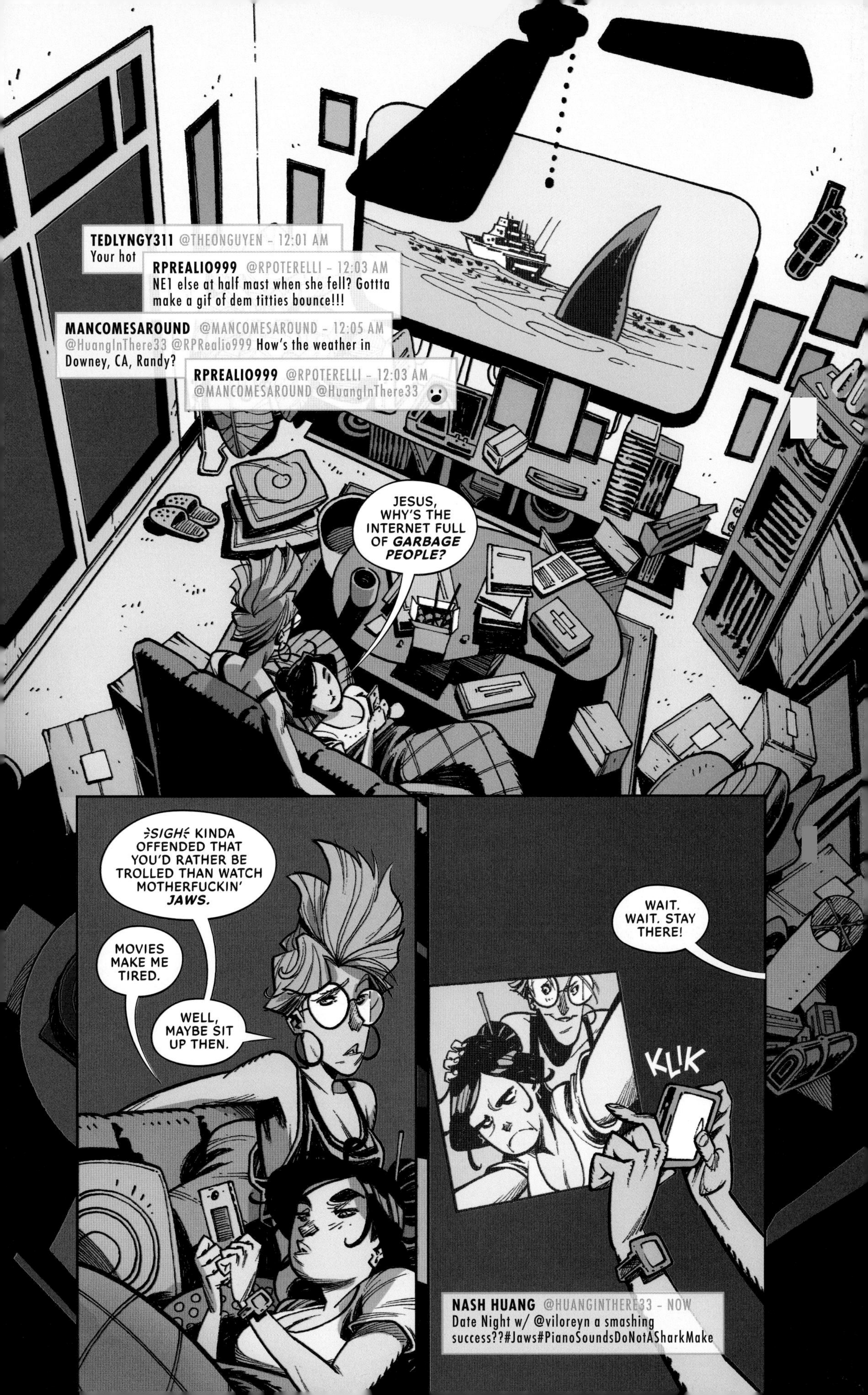
TEDLYNGY311 @THEONGUYEN – 12:01 AM
Your hot
RPREALIO999 @RPOTERELLI – 12:03 AM
NE1 else at half mast when she fell? Gotta make a gif of dem titties bounce!!!
MANCOMESAROUND @MANCOMESAROUND – 12:05 AM
@HuangInThere33 @RPRealio999 How's the weather in Downey, CA, Randy?
RPREALIO999 @RPOTERELLI – 12:03 AM
@MANCOMESAROUND @HuangInThere33
JESUS, WHY'S THE INTERNET FULL OF *GARBAGE PEOPLE?*
SIGH KINDA OFFENDED THAT YOU'D RATHER BE TROLLED THAN WATCH MOTHERFUCKIN' *JAWS.*
MOVIES MAKE ME TIRED.
WELL, MAYBE SIT UP THEN.
WAIT. WAIT. STAY THERE!
KLIK
NASH HUANG @HUANGINTHERE33 – NOW
Date Night w/ @viloreyn a smashing success??#Jaws#PianoSoundsDoNotASharkMake

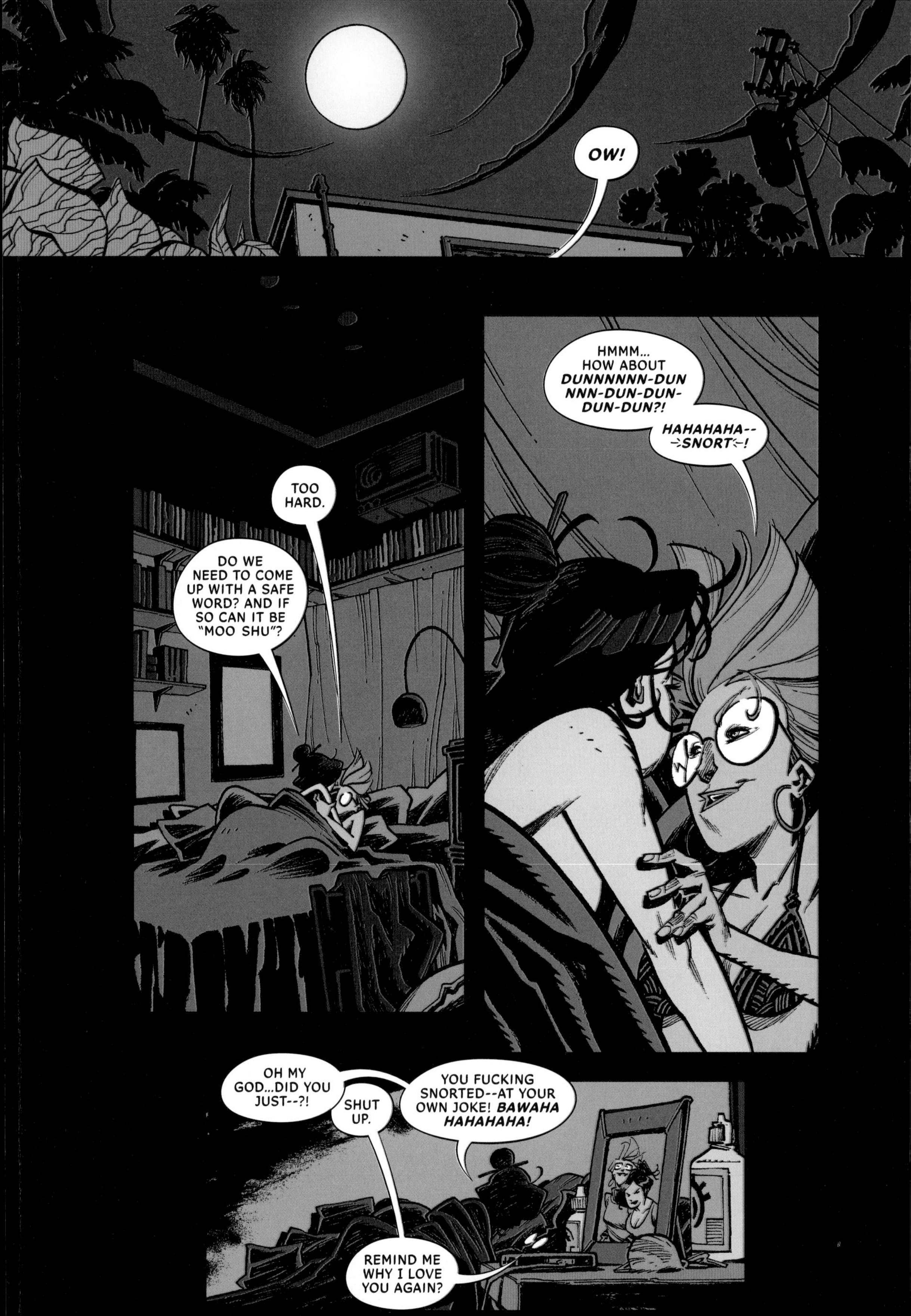
OW!
TOO HARD.
DO WE NEED TO COME UP WITH A SAFE WORD? AND IF SO CAN IT BE "MOO SHU"?
HMMM... HOW ABOUT DUNNNNNN-DUN NNN-DUN-DUN-DUN-DUN?!
HAHAHAHA-- →SNORT←!
OH MY GOD...DID YOU JUST--?!
SHUT UP.
YOU FUCKING SNORTED--AT YOUR OWN JOKE! BAWAHA HAHAHAHA!
REMIND ME WHY I LOVE YOU AGAIN?

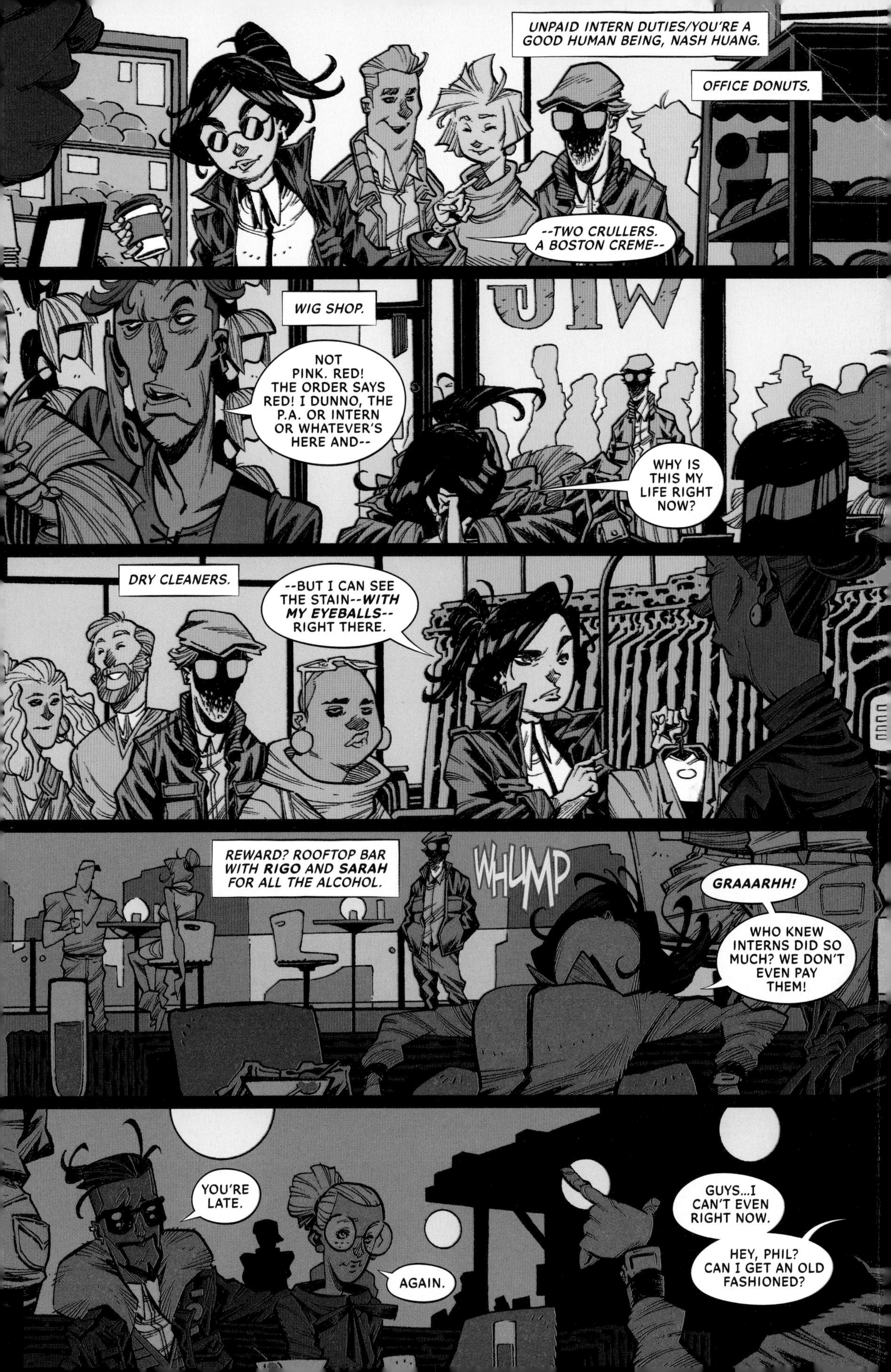
UNPAID INTERN DUTIES/YOU'RE A GOOD HUMAN BEING, NASH HUANG.
OFFICE DONUTS.
--TWO CRULLERS. A BOSTON CREME--
WIG SHOP.
NOT PINK. RED! THE ORDER SAYS RED! I DUNNO, THE P.A. OR INTERN OR WHATEVER'S HERE AND--
WHY IS THIS MY LIFE RIGHT NOW?
DRY CLEANERS.
--BUT I CAN SEE THE STAIN--WITH MY EYEBALLS-- RIGHT THERE.
REWARD? ROOFTOP BAR WITH RIGO AND SARAH FOR ALL THE ALCOHOL.
WHUMP
GRAAARHH!
WHO KNEW INTERNS DID SO MUCH? WE DON'T EVEN PAY THEM!
YOU'RE LATE.
AGAIN.
GUYS...I CAN'T EVEN RIGHT NOW.
HEY, PHIL? CAN I GET AN OLD FASHIONED?

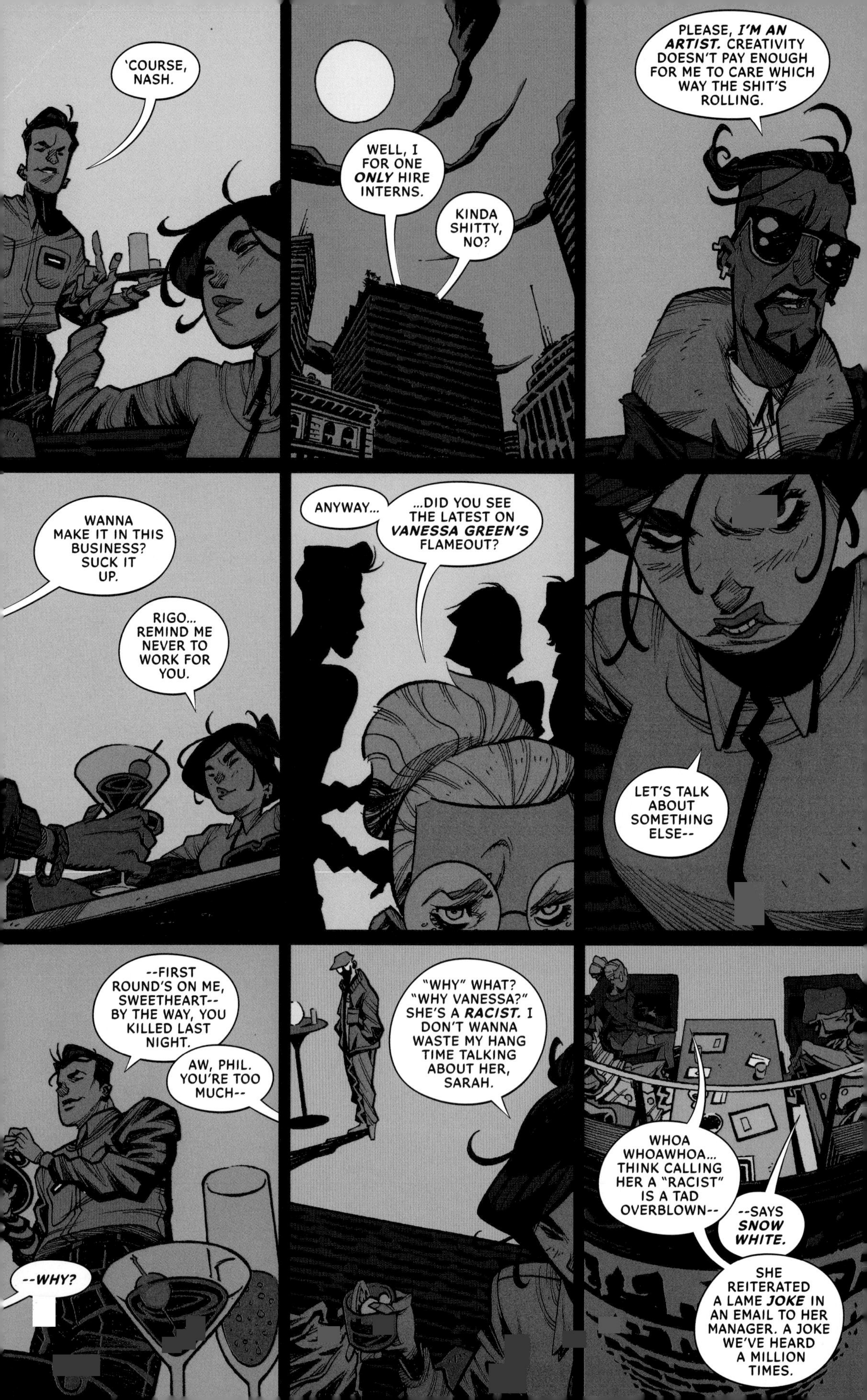
'COURSE, NASH.
WELL, I FOR ONE *ONLY* HIRE INTERNS.
KINDA SHITTY, NO?
PLEASE, *I'M AN ARTIST.* CREATIVITY DOESN'T PAY ENOUGH FOR ME TO CARE WHICH WAY THE SHIT'S ROLLING.
WANNA MAKE IT IN THIS BUSINESS? SUCK IT UP.
RIGO... REMIND ME NEVER TO WORK FOR YOU.
ANYWAY...
...DID YOU SEE THE LATEST ON *VANESSA GREEN'S* FLAMEOUT?
LET'S TALK ABOUT SOMETHING ELSE--
--FIRST ROUND'S ON ME, SWEETHEART-- BY THE WAY, YOU KILLED LAST NIGHT.
AW, PHIL. YOU'RE TOO MUCH--
--WHY?
"WHY" WHAT? "WHY VANESSA?" SHE'S A *RACIST.* I DON'T WANNA WASTE MY HANG TIME TALKING ABOUT HER, SARAH.
WHOA WHOAWHOA... THINK CALLING HER A "RACIST" IS A TAD OVERBLOWN--
--SAYS *SNOW WHITE.*
SHE REITERATED A LAME *JOKE* IN AN EMAIL TO HER MANAGER. A JOKE WE'VE HEARD A MILLION TIMES.

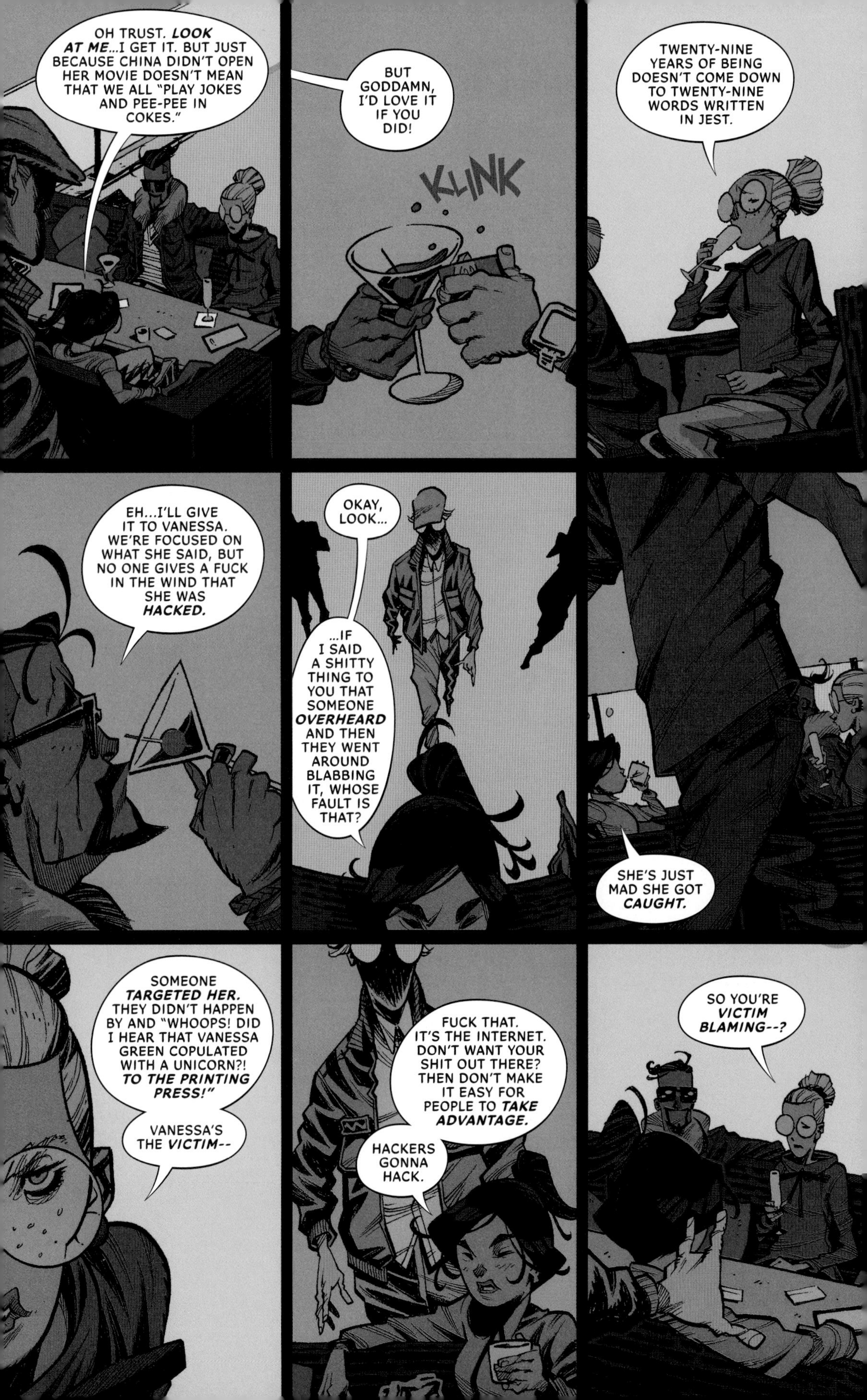
OH TRUST. LOOK AT ME...I GET IT. BUT JUST BECAUSE CHINA DIDN'T OPEN HER MOVIE DOESN'T MEAN THAT WE ALL "PLAY JOKES AND PEE-PEE IN COKES."
BUT GODDAMN, I'D LOVE IT IF YOU DID!
KLINK
TWENTY-NINE YEARS OF BEING DOESN'T COME DOWN TO TWENTY-NINE WORDS WRITTEN IN JEST.
EH...I'LL GIVE IT TO VANESSA. WE'RE FOCUSED ON WHAT SHE SAID, BUT NO ONE GIVES A FUCK IN THE WIND THAT SHE WAS HACKED.
OKAY, LOOK...
...IF I SAID A SHITTY THING TO YOU THAT SOMEONE OVERHEARD AND THEN THEY WENT AROUND BLABBING IT, WHOSE FAULT IS THAT?
SHE'S JUST MAD SHE GOT CAUGHT.
SOMEONE TARGETED HER. THEY DIDN'T HAPPEN BY AND "WHOOPS! DID I HEAR THAT VANESSA GREEN COPULATED WITH A UNICORN?! TO THE PRINTING PRESS!"
VANESSA'S THE VICTIM--
FUCK THAT. IT'S THE INTERNET. DON'T WANT YOUR SHIT OUT THERE? THEN DON'T MAKE IT EASY FOR PEOPLE TO TAKE ADVANTAGE.
HACKERS GONNA HACK.
SO YOU'RE VICTIM BLAMING--?

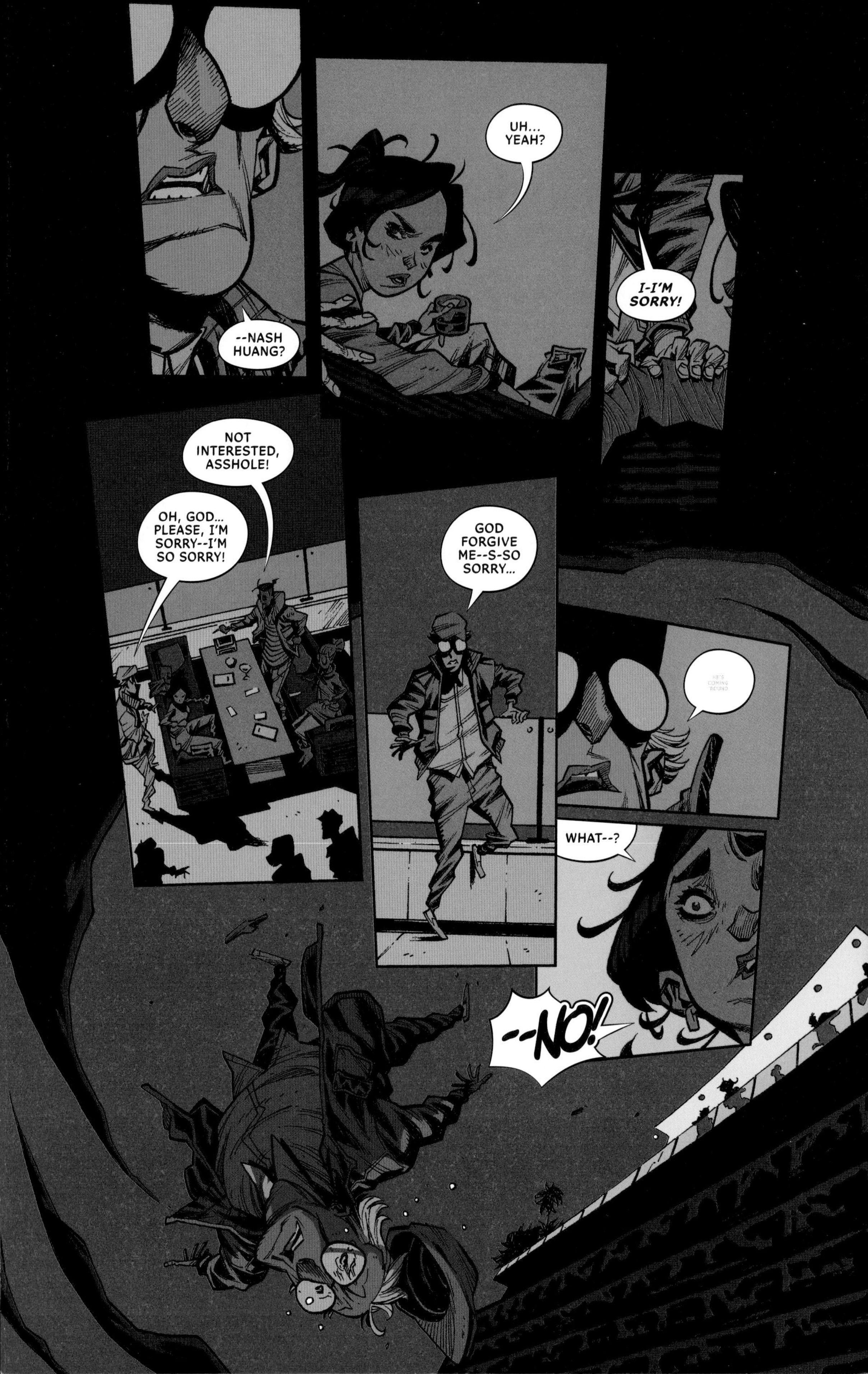
--NASH HUANG?
UH... YEAH?
I-I'M SORRY!
NOT INTERESTED, ASSHOLE!
OH, GOD... PLEASE, I'M SORRY--I'M SO SORRY!
GOD FORGIVE ME--S-SO SORRY...
WHAT--?
--NO!

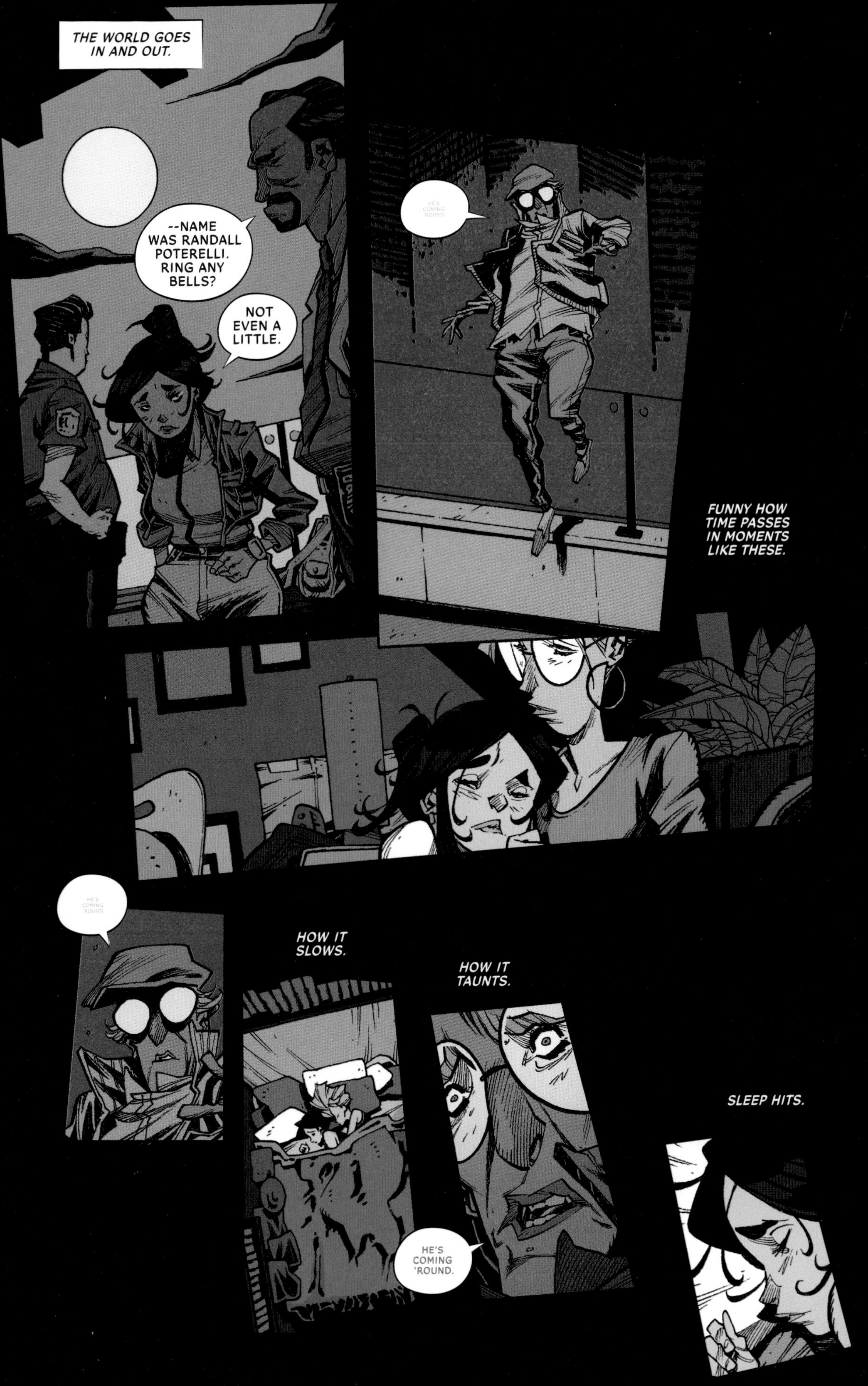
THE WORLD GOES IN AND OUT.
--NAME WAS RANDALL POTERELLI. RING ANY BELLS?
NOT EVEN A LITTLE.
FUNNY HOW TIME PASSES IN MOMENTS LIKE THESE.
HOW IT SLOWS.
HOW IT TAUNTS.
HE'S COMING 'ROUND.
SLEEP HITS.

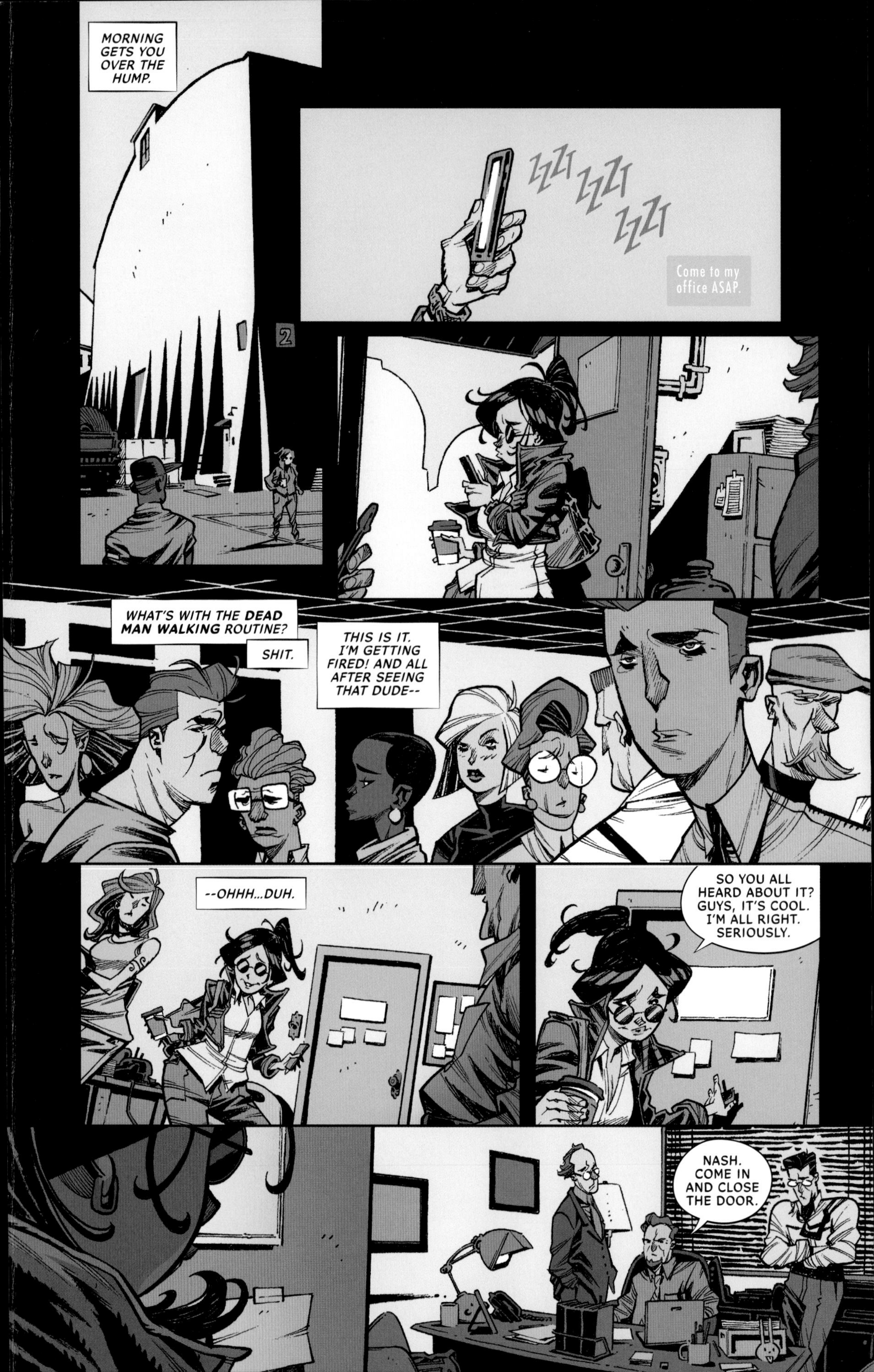

MORNING GETS YOU OVER THE HUMP.
ZZZT ZZZT ZZZT
Come to my office ASAP.
WHAT'S WITH THE DEAD MAN WALKING ROUTINE?
SHIT.
THIS IS IT. I'M GETTING FIRED! AND ALL AFTER SEEING THAT DUDE--
--OHHH...DUH.
SO YOU ALL HEARD ABOUT IT? GUYS, IT'S COOL. I'M ALL RIGHT. SERIOUSLY.
NASH. COME IN AND CLOSE THE DOOR.

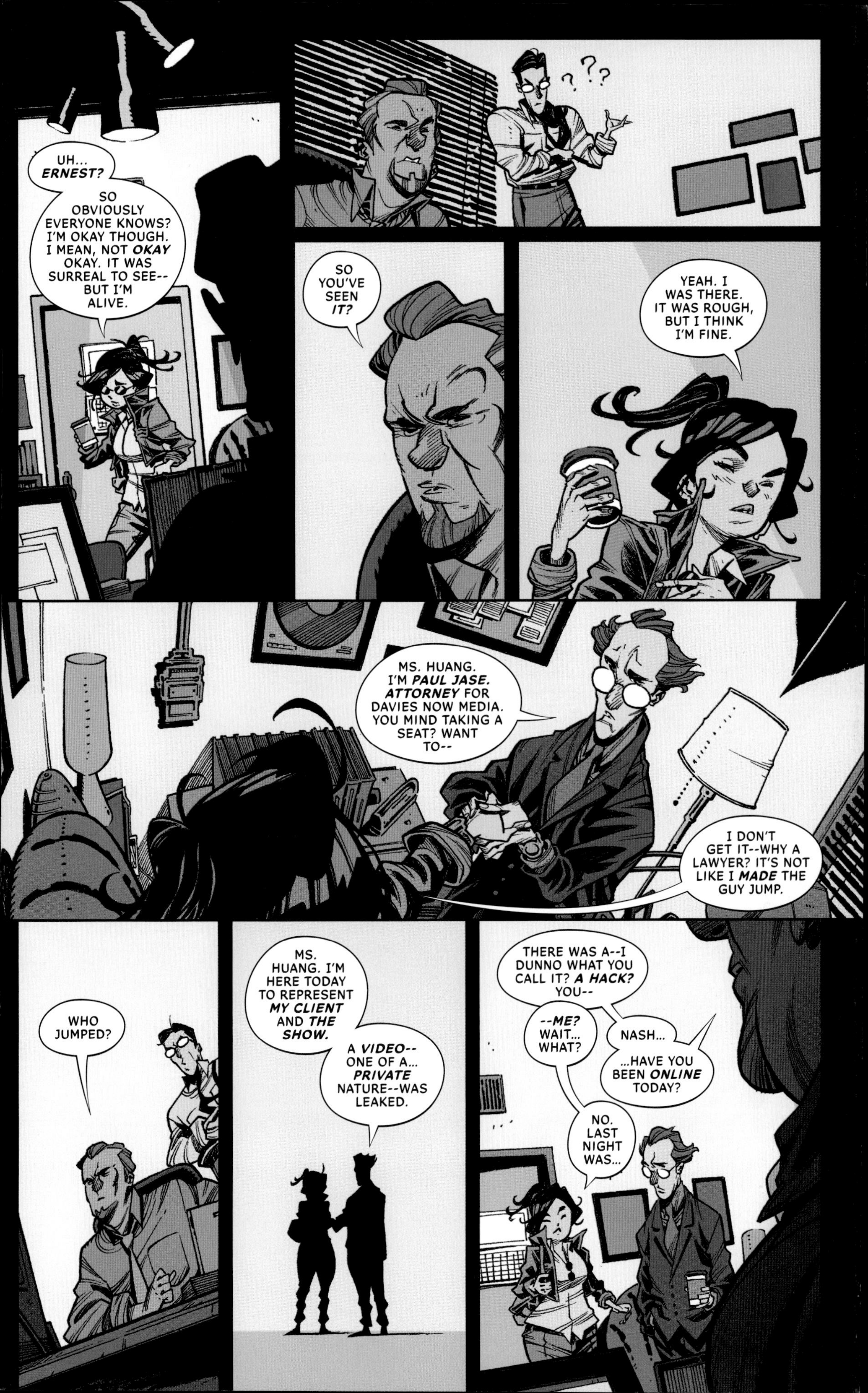
UH... ERNEST?
SO OBVIOUSLY EVERYONE KNOWS? I'M OKAY THOUGH. I MEAN, NOT OKAY OKAY. IT WAS SURREAL TO SEE--BUT I'M ALIVE.
? ? ?
SO YOU'VE SEEN IT?
YEAH. I WAS THERE. IT WAS ROUGH, BUT I THINK I'M FINE.
MS. HUANG. I'M PAUL JASE. ATTORNEY FOR DAVIES NOW MEDIA. YOU MIND TAKING A SEAT? WANT TO--
I DON'T GET IT--WHY A LAWYER? IT'S NOT LIKE I MADE THE GUY JUMP.
WHO JUMPED?
MS. HUANG. I'M HERE TODAY TO REPRESENT MY CLIENT AND THE SHOW.
A VIDEO--ONE OF A... PRIVATE NATURE--WAS LEAKED.
THERE WAS A--I DUNNO WHAT YOU CALL IT? A HACK? YOU--
--ME? WAIT... WHAT?
NASH...
...HAVE YOU BEEN ONLINE TODAY?
NO. LAST NIGHT WAS...

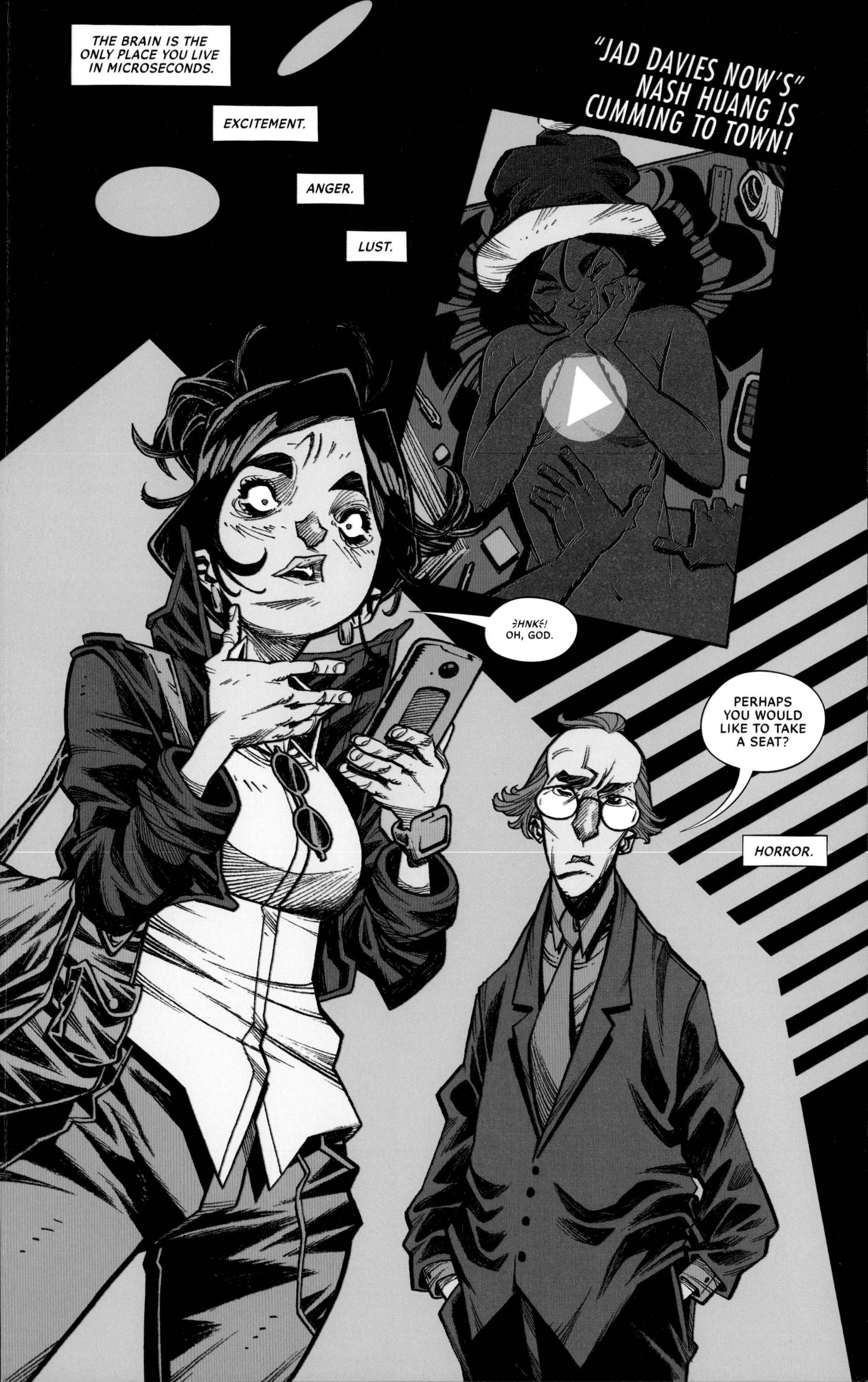

THE BRAIN IS THE ONLY PLACE YOU LIVE IN MICROSECONDS.
"JAD DAVIES NOW'S" NASH HUANG IS CUMMING TO TOWN!
EXCITEMENT.
ANGER.
LUST.
HNK! OH, GOD.
PERHAPS YOU WOULD LIKE TO TAKE A SEAT?
HORROR.

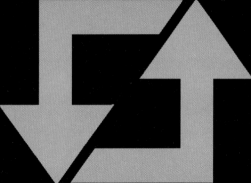

CHAPTER TWO

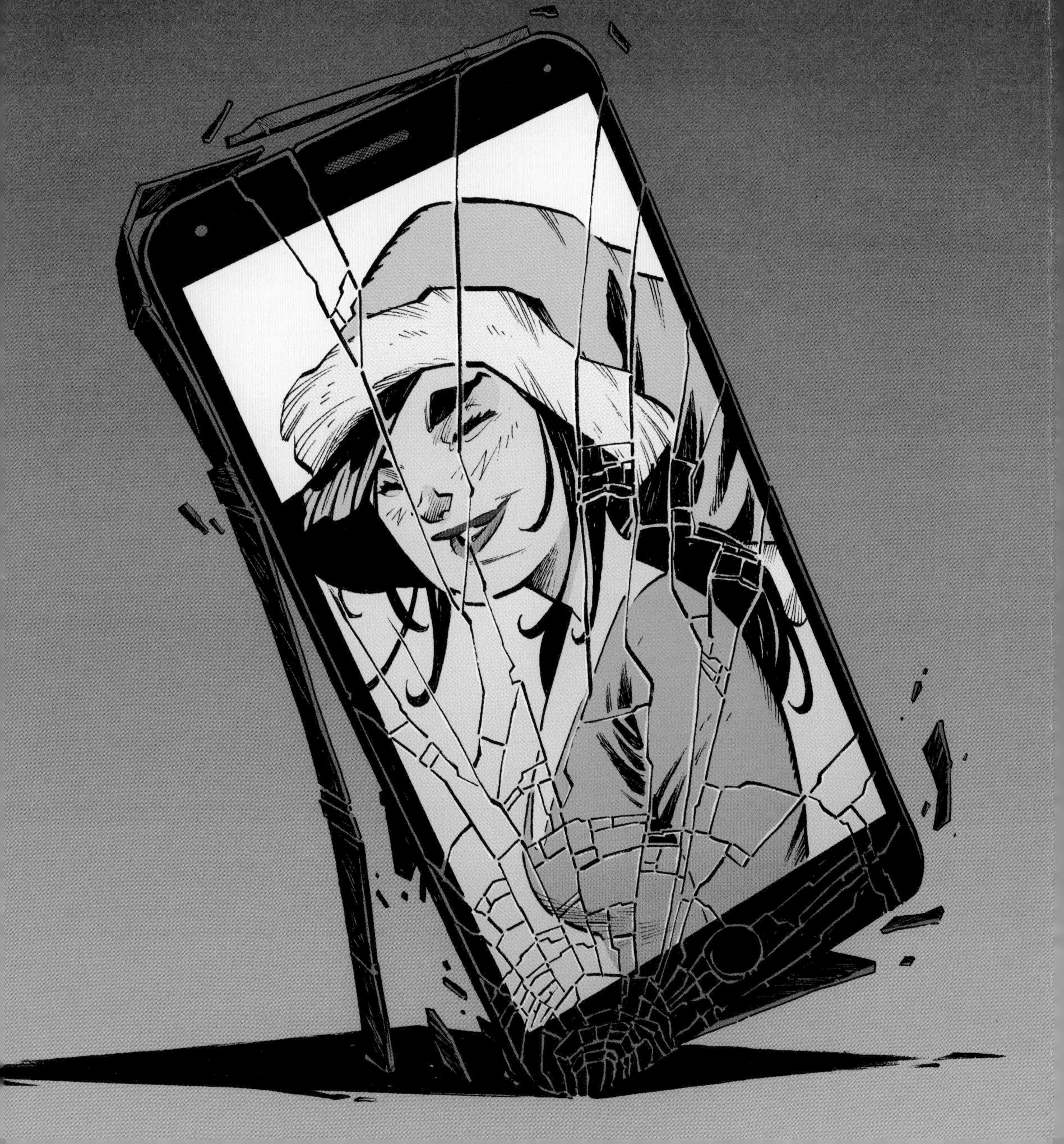

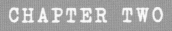

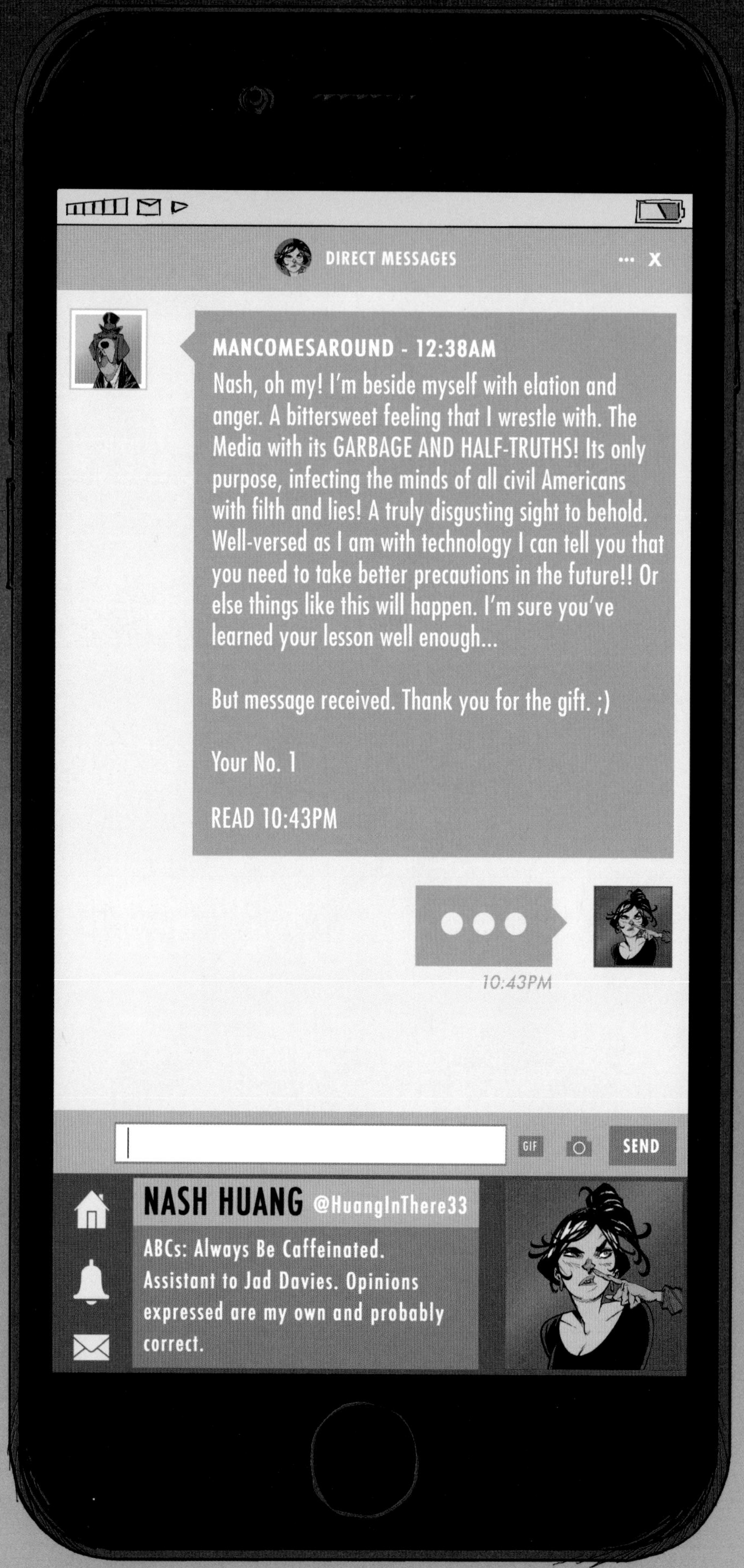
DIRECT MESSAGES
MANCOMESAROUND - 12:38AM
Nash, oh my! I'm beside myself with elation and anger. A bittersweet feeling that I wrestle with. The Media with its GARBAGE AND HALF-TRUTHS! Its only purpose, infecting the minds of all civil Americans with filth and lies! A truly disgusting sight to behold. Well-versed as I am with technology I can tell you that you need to take better precautions in the future!! Or else things like this will happen. I'm sure you've learned your lesson well enough...
But message received. Thank you for the gift. ;)
Your No. 1
READ 10:43PM
10:43PM
GIF
SEND
NASH HUANG @HuangInThere33
ABCs: Always Be Caffeinated. Assistant to Jad Davies. Opinions expressed are my own and probably correct.

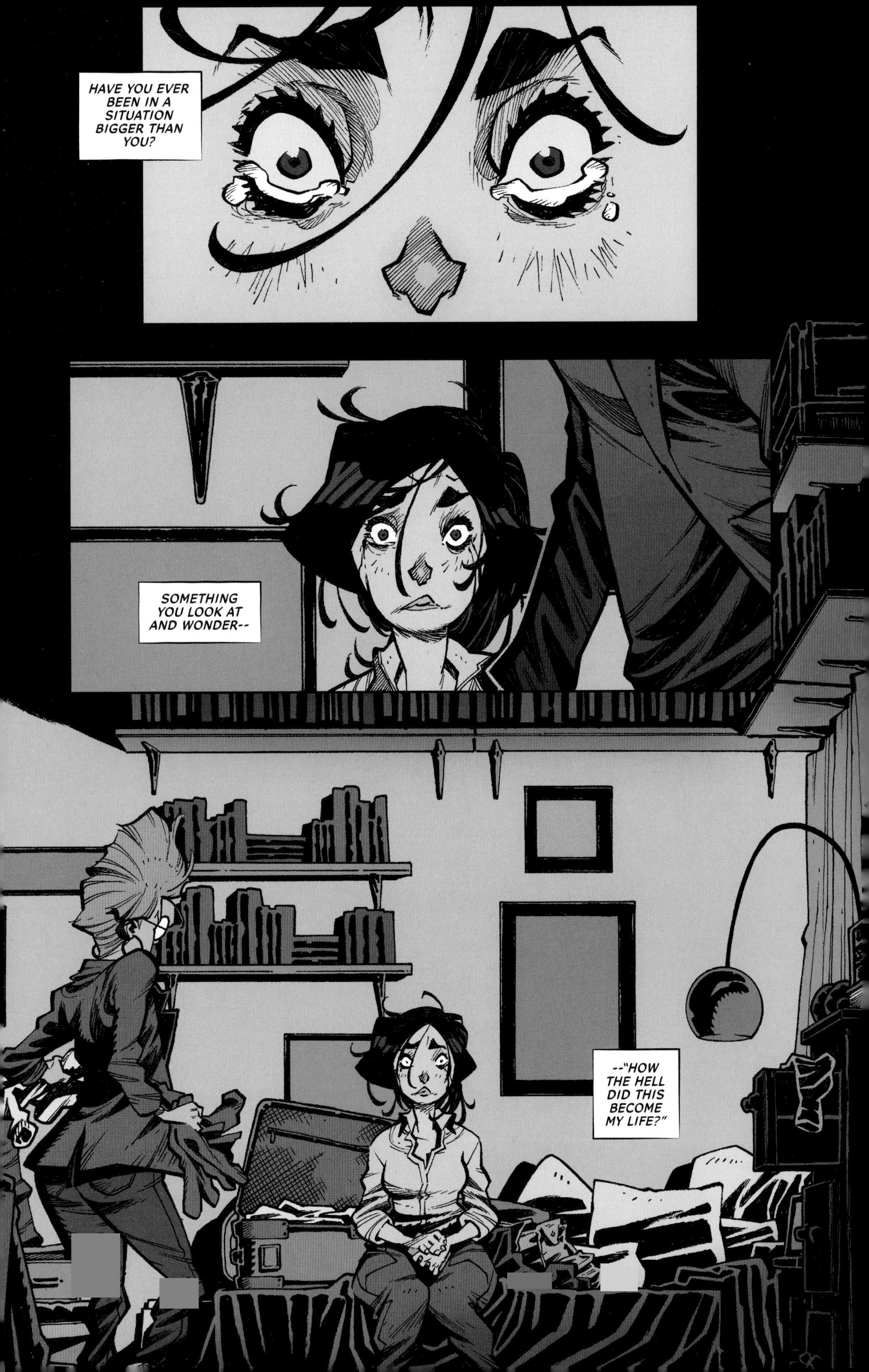
HAVE YOU EVER BEEN IN A SITUATION BIGGER THAN YOU?
SOMETHING YOU LOOK AT AND WONDER--
--"HOW THE HELL DID THIS BECOME MY LIFE?"

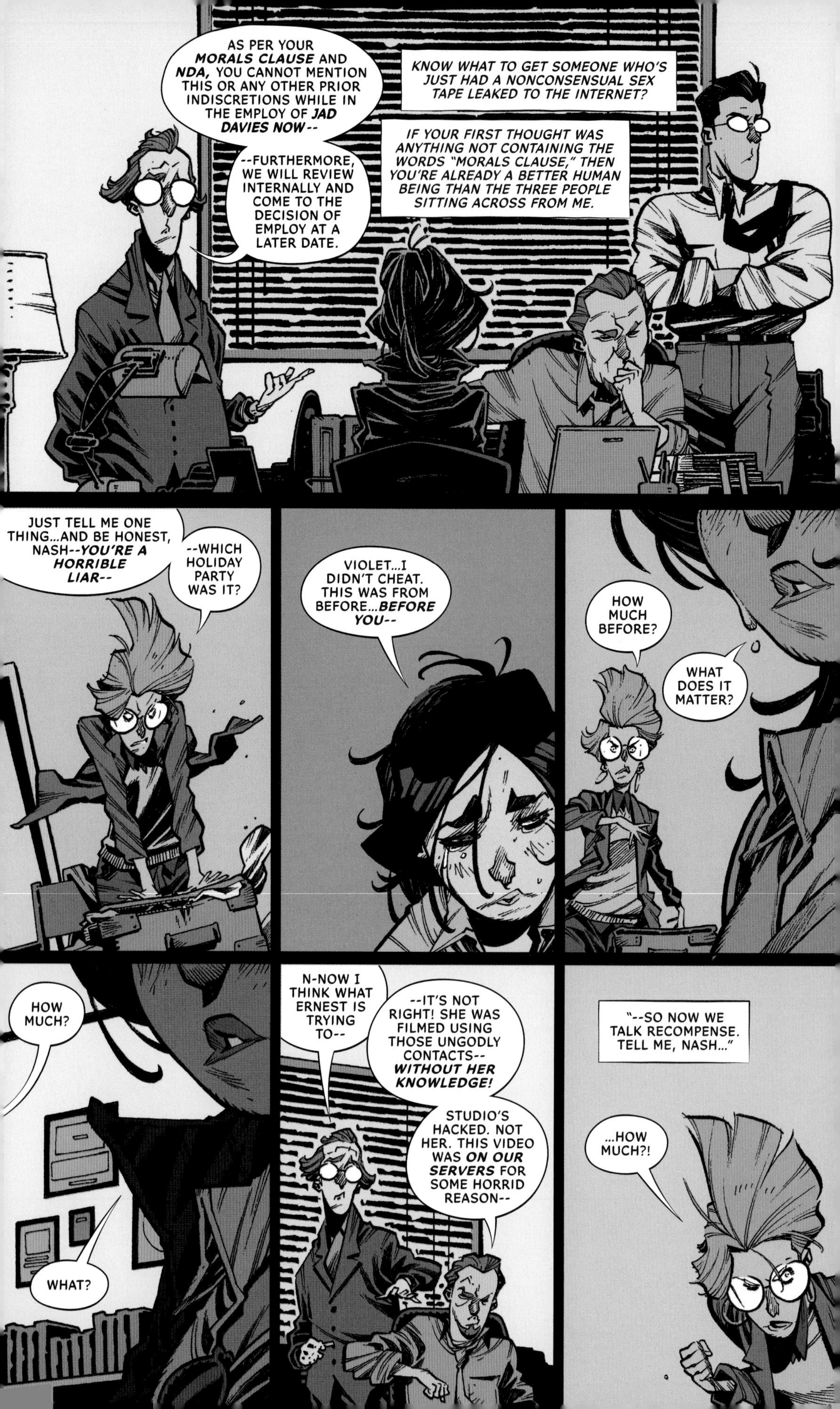
AS PER YOUR MORALS CLAUSE AND NDA, YOU CANNOT MENTION THIS OR ANY OTHER PRIOR INDISCRETIONS WHILE IN THE EMPLOY OF JAD DAVIES NOW--
--FURTHERMORE, WE WILL REVIEW INTERNALLY AND COME TO THE DECISION OF EMPLOY AT A LATER DATE.
KNOW WHAT TO GET SOMEONE WHO'S JUST HAD A NONCONSENSUAL SEX TAPE LEAKED TO THE INTERNET?
IF YOUR FIRST THOUGHT WAS ANYTHING NOT CONTAINING THE WORDS "MORALS CLAUSE," THEN YOU'RE ALREADY A BETTER HUMAN BEING THAN THE THREE PEOPLE SITTING ACROSS FROM ME.
JUST TELL ME ONE THING...AND BE HONEST, NASH--YOU'RE A HORRIBLE LIAR--
--WHICH HOLIDAY PARTY WAS IT?
VIOLET...I DIDN'T CHEAT. THIS WAS FROM BEFORE...BEFORE YOU--
HOW MUCH BEFORE?
WHAT DOES IT MATTER?
HOW MUCH?
WHAT?
N-NOW I THINK WHAT ERNEST IS TRYING TO--
--IT'S NOT RIGHT! SHE WAS FILMED USING THOSE UNGODLY CONTACTS--WITHOUT HER KNOWLEDGE!
STUDIO'S HACKED. NOT HER. THIS VIDEO WAS ON OUR SERVERS FOR SOME HORRID REASON--
"--SO NOW WE TALK RECOMPENSE. TELL ME, NASH..."
...HOW MUCH?!

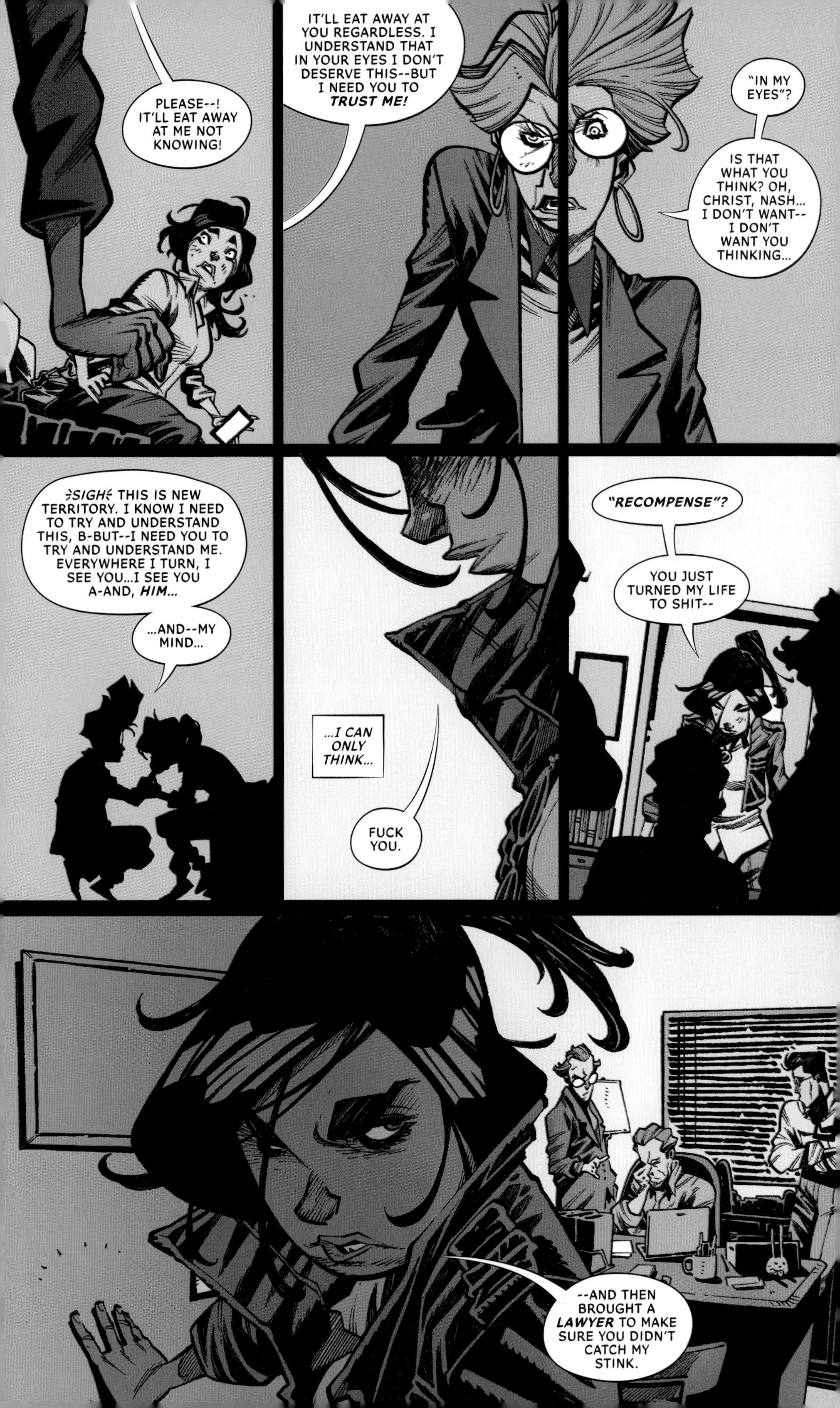
PLEASE--! IT'LL EAT AWAY AT ME NOT KNOWING!
IT'LL EAT AWAY AT YOU REGARDLESS. I UNDERSTAND THAT IN YOUR EYES I DON'T DESERVE THIS--BUT I NEED YOU TO TRUST ME!
"IN MY EYES"?
IS THAT WHAT YOU THINK? OH, CHRIST, NASH... I DON'T WANT-- I DON'T WANT YOU THINKING...
SIGH THIS IS NEW TERRITORY. I KNOW I NEED TO TRY AND UNDERSTAND THIS, B-BUT--I NEED YOU TO TRY AND UNDERSTAND ME. EVERYWHERE I TURN, I SEE YOU...I SEE YOU A-AND, HIM...
...AND--MY MIND...
...I CAN ONLY THINK...
FUCK YOU.
"RECOMPENSE"?
YOU JUST TURNED MY LIFE TO SHIT--
--AND THEN BROUGHT A LAWYER TO MAKE SURE YOU DIDN'T CATCH MY STINK.

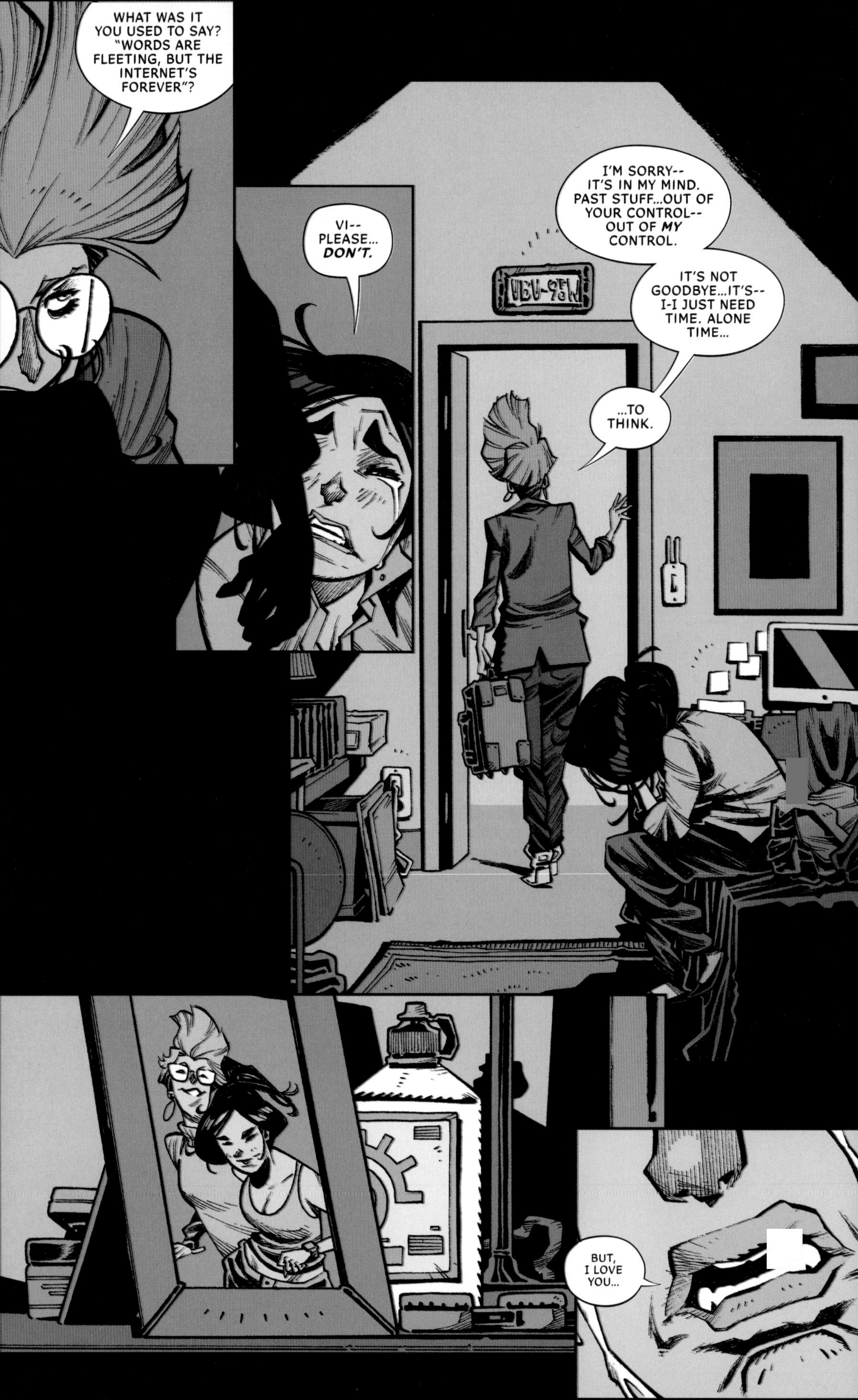
WHAT WAS IT YOU USED TO SAY? "WORDS ARE FLEETING, BUT THE INTERNET'S FOREVER"?
VI-- PLEASE... *DON'T.*
I'M SORRY-- IT'S IN MY MIND. PAST STUFF...OUT OF YOUR CONTROL-- OUT OF *MY* CONTROL.
VBU-95W
IT'S NOT GOODBYE...IT'S-- I-I JUST NEED TIME. ALONE TIME...
...TO THINK.
BUT, I LOVE YOU...

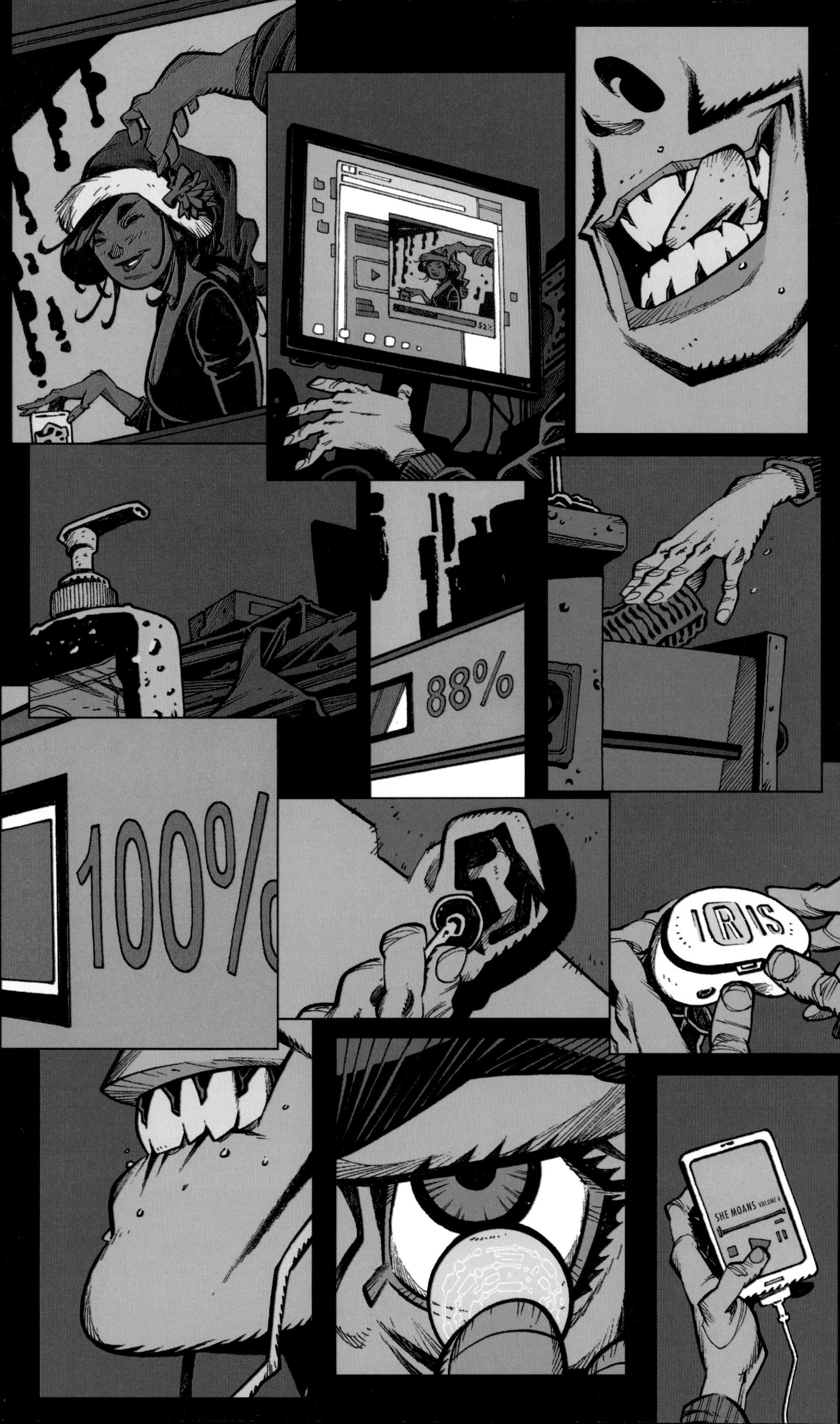
52%
88%
100%
IRIS
SHE MOANS VOLUME 6

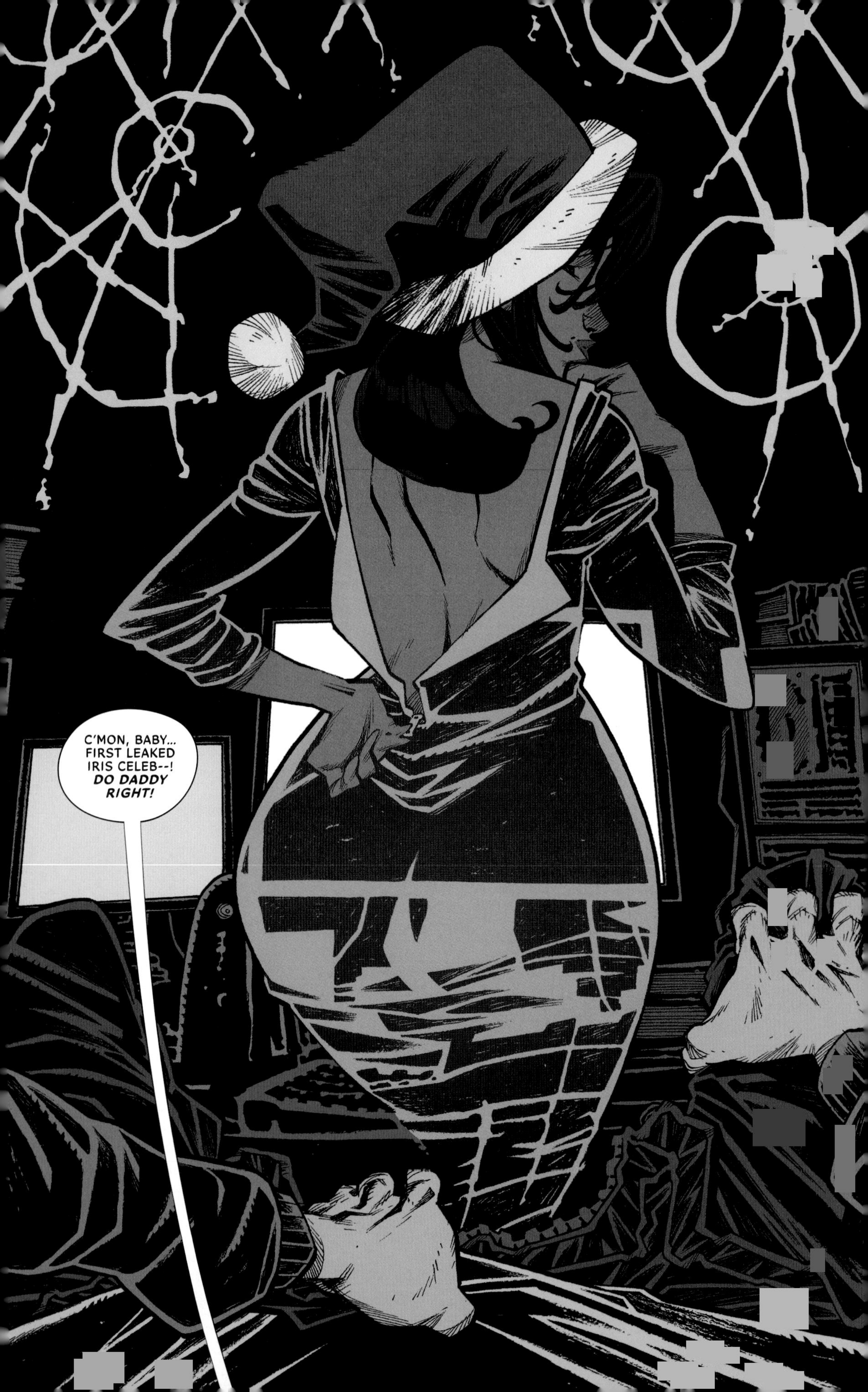
C'MON, BABY... FIRST LEAKED IRIS CELEB--! *DO DADDY RIGHT!*

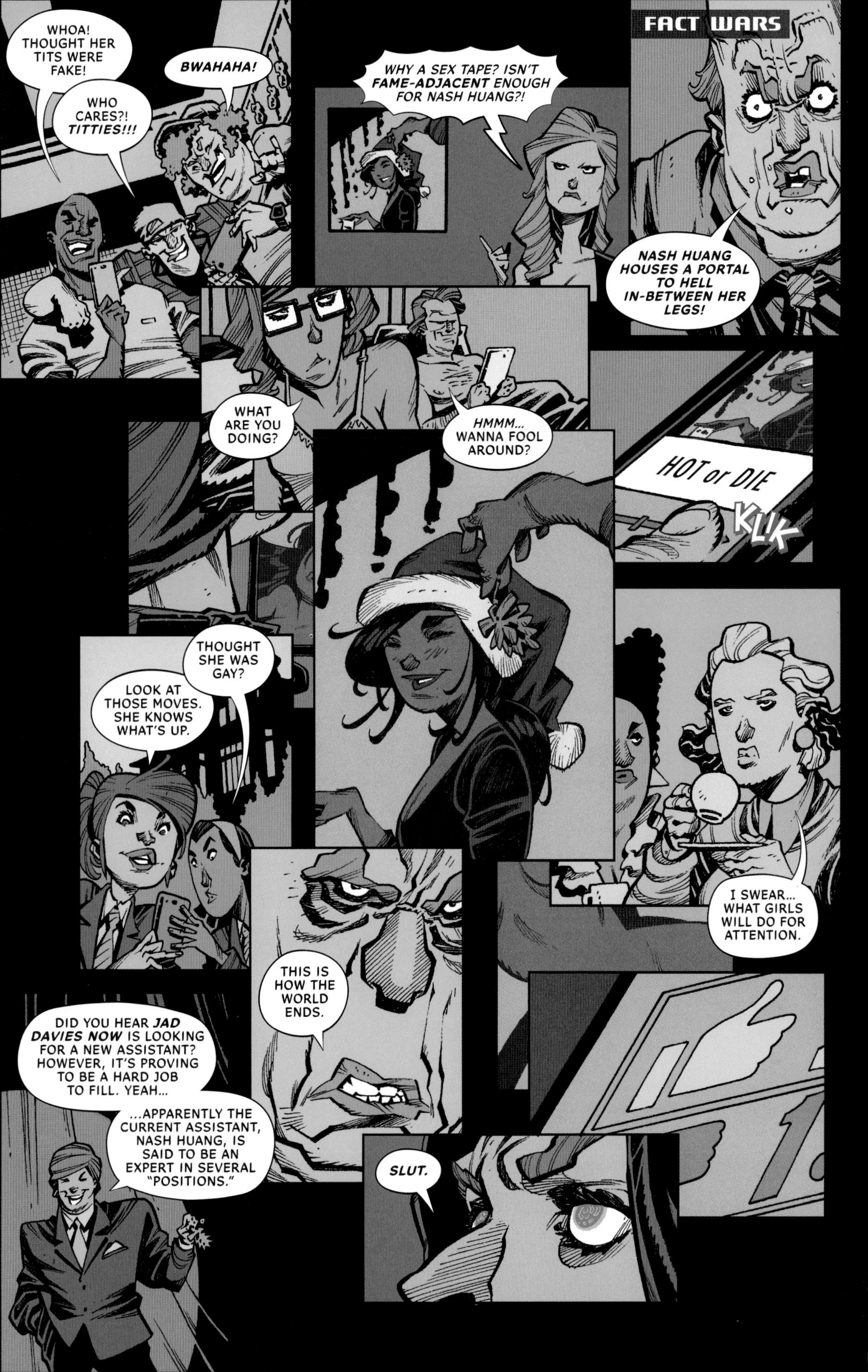
WHOA! THOUGHT HER TITS WERE FAKE!
BWAHAHA!
WHO CARES?! TITTIES!!!
WHY A SEX TAPE? ISN'T FAME-ADJACENT ENOUGH FOR NASH HUANG?!
FACT WARS
NASH HUANG HOUSES A PORTAL TO HELL IN-BETWEEN HER LEGS!
WHAT ARE YOU DOING?
HMMM... WANNA FOOL AROUND?
HOT or DIE
KLIK
THOUGHT SHE WAS GAY?
LOOK AT THOSE MOVES. SHE KNOWS WHAT'S UP.
I SWEAR... WHAT GIRLS WILL DO FOR ATTENTION.
THIS IS HOW THE WORLD ENDS.
DID YOU HEAR JAD DAVIES NOW IS LOOKING FOR A NEW ASSISTANT? HOWEVER, IT'S PROVING TO BE A HARD JOB TO FILL. YEAH...
...APPARENTLY THE CURRENT ASSISTANT, NASH HUANG, IS SAID TO BE AN EXPERT IN SEVERAL "POSITIONS."
SLUT.

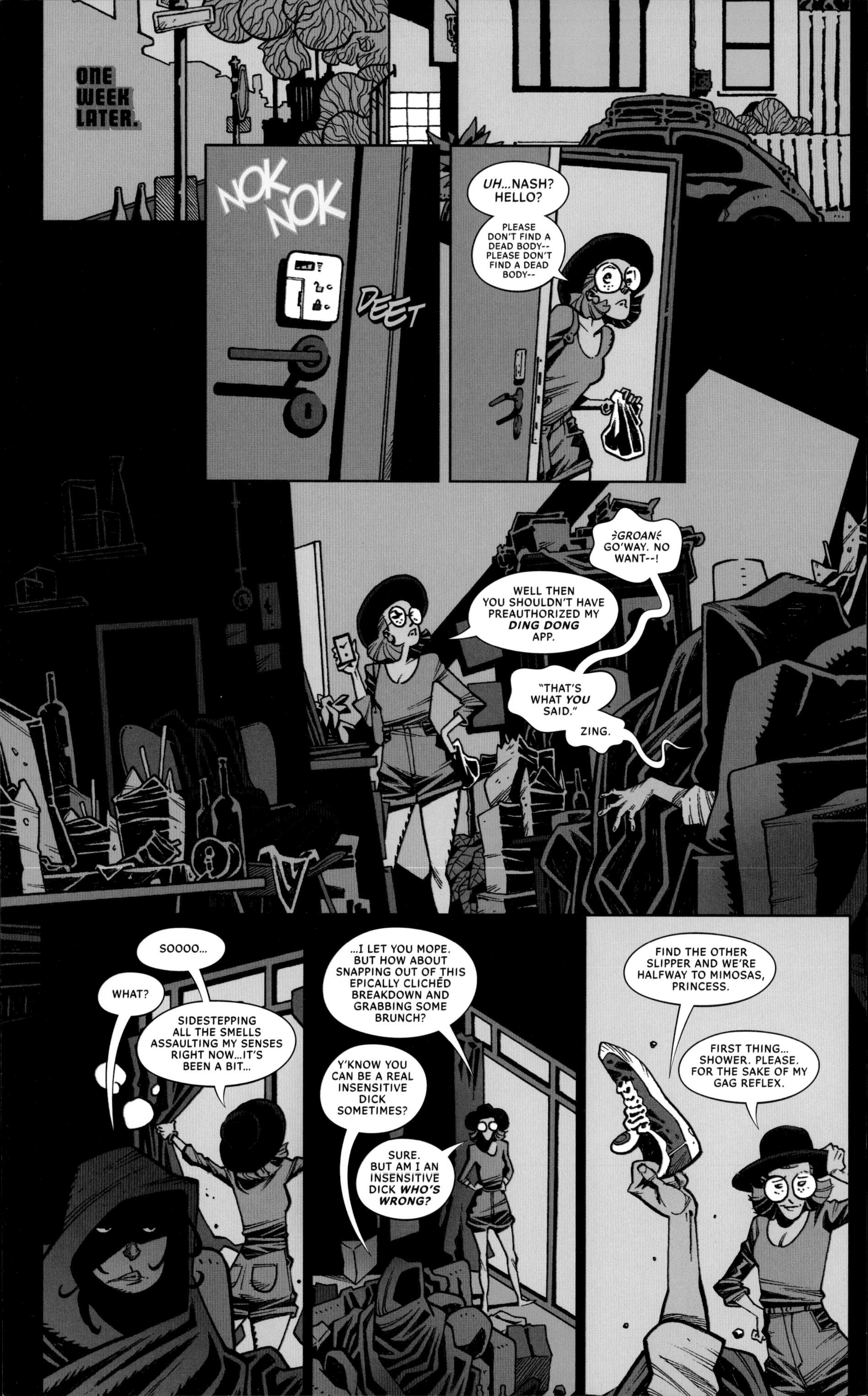
ONE WEEK LATER.
NOK NOK
DEET
UH...NASH? HELLO?
PLEASE DON'T FIND A DEAD BODY-- PLEASE DON'T FIND A DEAD BODY--
GROAN GO'WAY. NO WANT--!
WELL THEN YOU SHOULDN'T HAVE PREAUTHORIZED MY *DING DONG* APP.
"THAT'S WHAT *YOU* SAID."
ZING.
SOOOO...
WHAT?
SIDESTEPPING ALL THE SMELLS ASSAULTING MY SENSES RIGHT NOW...IT'S BEEN A BIT...
...I LET YOU MOPE. BUT HOW ABOUT SNAPPING OUT OF THIS EPICALLY CLICHÉD BREAKDOWN AND GRABBING SOME BRUNCH?
Y'KNOW YOU CAN BE A REAL INSENSITIVE DICK SOMETIMES?
SURE. BUT AM I AN INSENSITIVE DICK *WHO'S WRONG?*
FIND THE OTHER SLIPPER AND WE'RE HALFWAY TO MIMOSAS, PRINCESS.
FIRST THING... SHOWER. PLEASE. FOR THE SAKE OF MY GAG REFLEX.

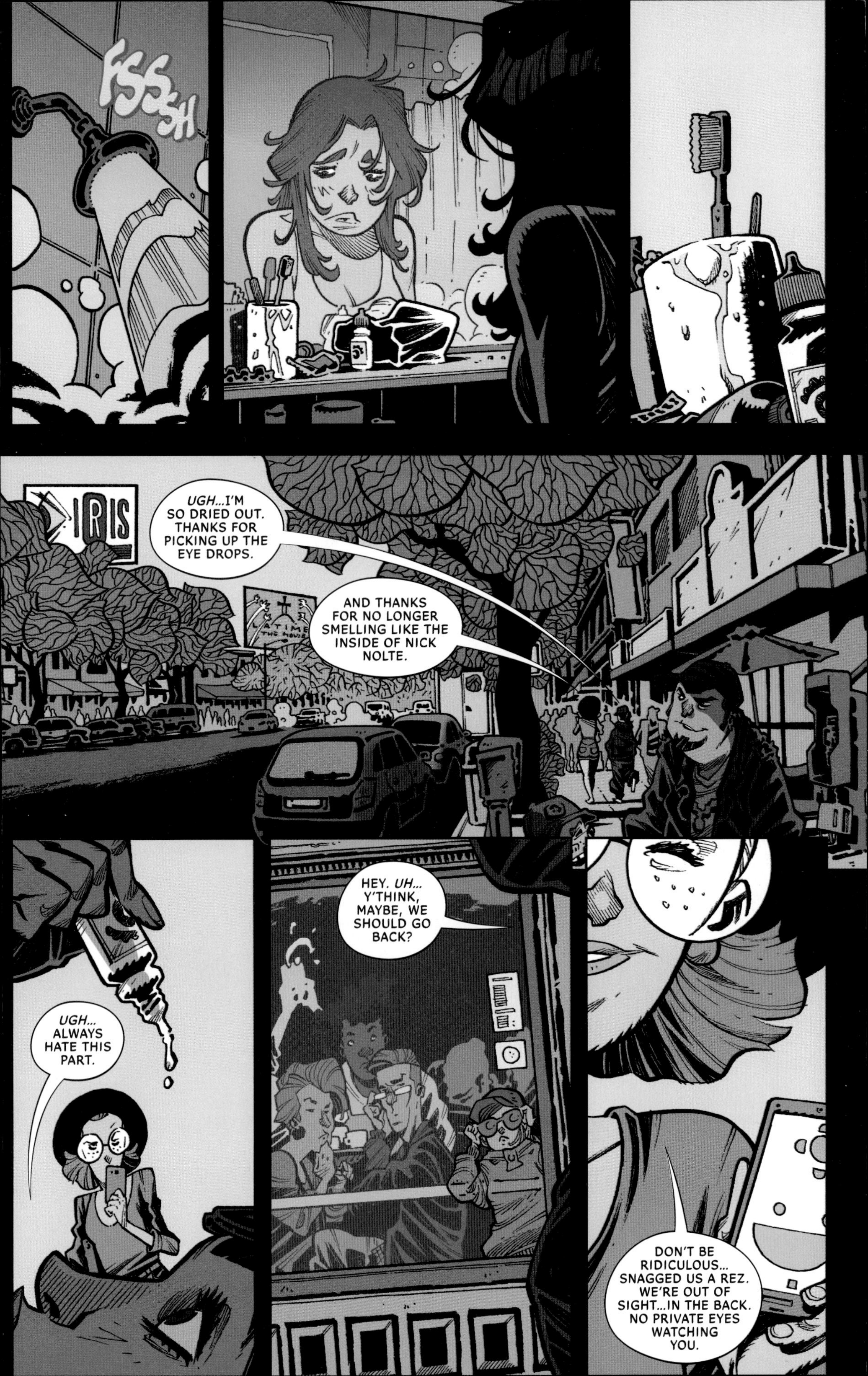
FSSSH
IRIS
UGH...I'M SO DRIED OUT. THANKS FOR PICKING UP THE EYE DROPS.
AND THANKS FOR NO LONGER SMELLING LIKE THE INSIDE OF NICK NOLTE.
UGH... ALWAYS HATE THIS PART.
HEY. UH... Y'THINK, MAYBE, WE SHOULD GO BACK?
DON'T BE RIDICULOUS... SNAGGED US A REZ. WE'RE OUT OF SIGHT...IN THE BACK. NO PRIVATE EYES WATCHING YOU.

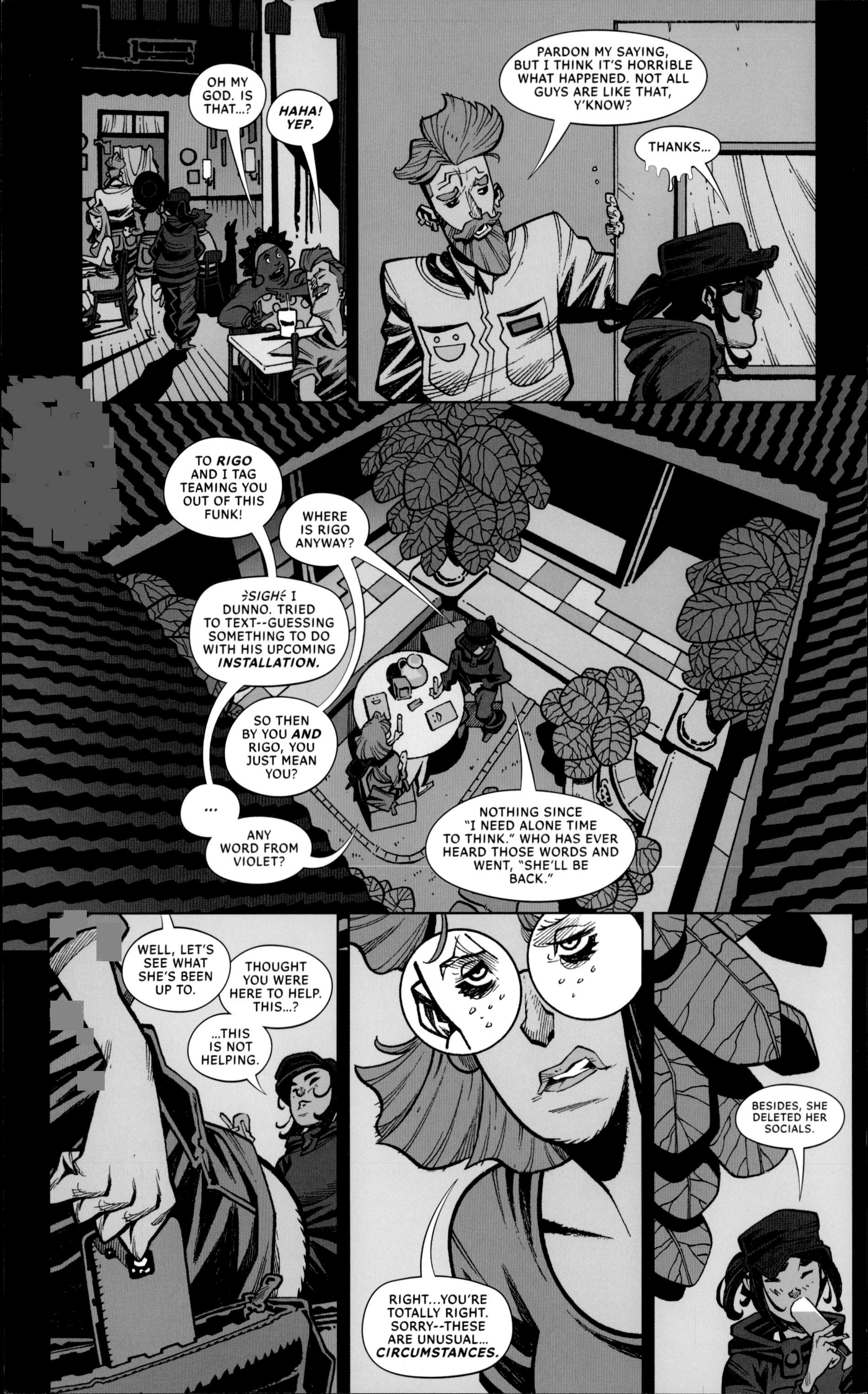
OH MY GOD. IS THAT...?
HAHA! YEP.
PARDON MY SAYING, BUT I THINK IT'S HORRIBLE WHAT HAPPENED. NOT ALL GUYS ARE LIKE THAT, Y'KNOW?
THANKS...
TO RIGO AND I TAG TEAMING YOU OUT OF THIS FUNK!
WHERE IS RIGO ANYWAY?
SIGH I DUNNO. TRIED TO TEXT--GUESSING SOMETHING TO DO WITH HIS UPCOMING INSTALLATION.
SO THEN BY YOU AND RIGO, YOU JUST MEAN YOU?
...
ANY WORD FROM VIOLET?
NOTHING SINCE "I NEED ALONE TIME TO THINK." WHO HAS EVER HEARD THOSE WORDS AND WENT, "SHE'LL BE BACK."
WELL, LET'S SEE WHAT SHE'S BEEN UP TO.
THOUGHT YOU WERE HERE TO HELP. THIS...?
...THIS IS NOT HELPING.
RIGHT...YOU'RE TOTALLY RIGHT. SORRY--THESE ARE UNUSUAL... CIRCUMSTANCES.
BESIDES, SHE DELETED HER SOCIALS.

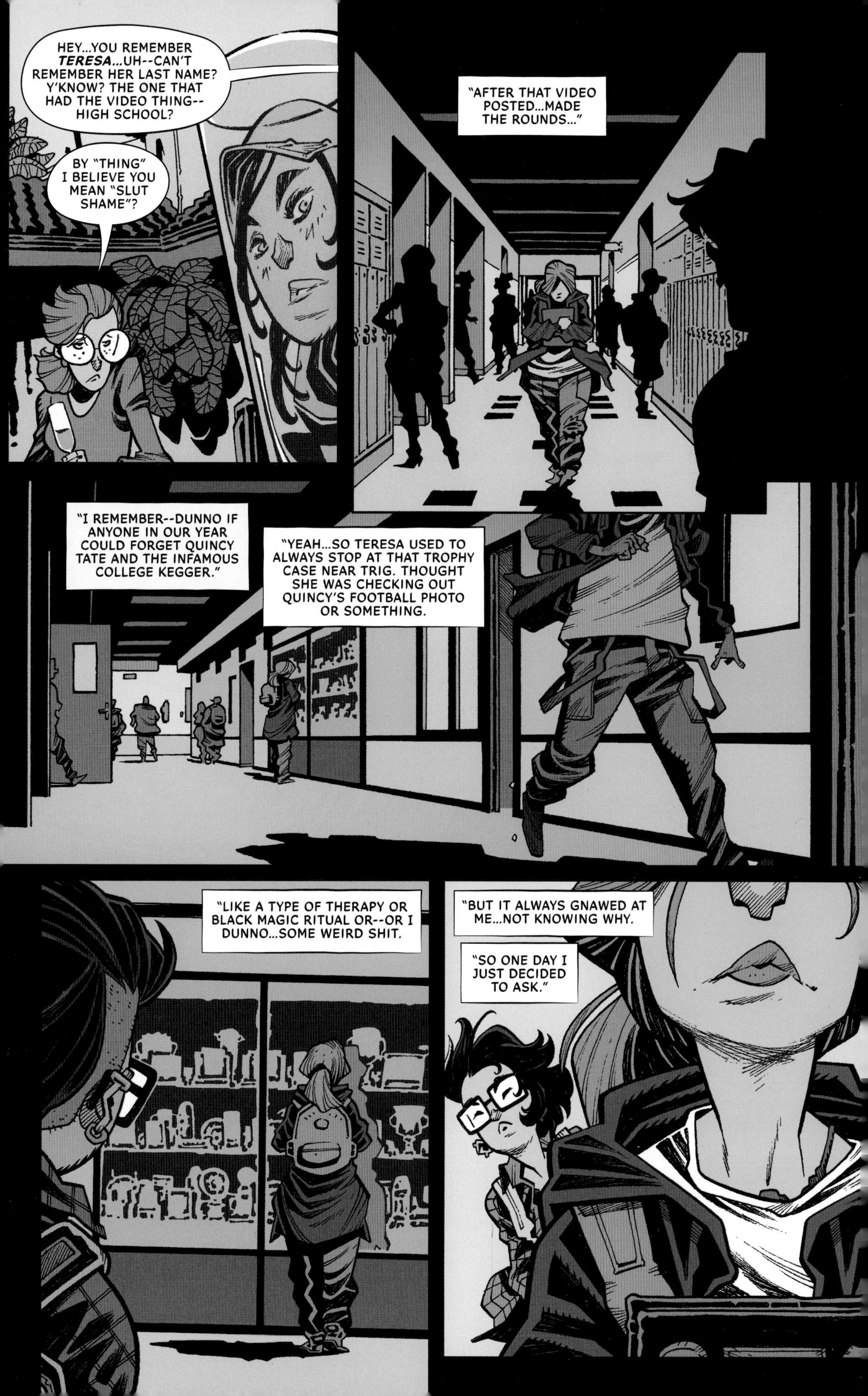
HEY...YOU REMEMBER *TERESA*...UH--CAN'T REMEMBER HER LAST NAME? Y'KNOW? THE ONE THAT HAD THE VIDEO THING--HIGH SCHOOL?
BY "THING" I BELIEVE YOU MEAN "SLUT SHAME"?
"AFTER THAT VIDEO POSTED...MADE THE ROUNDS..."
"I REMEMBER--DUNNO IF ANYONE IN OUR YEAR COULD FORGET QUINCY TATE AND THE INFAMOUS COLLEGE KEGGER."
"YEAH...SO TERESA USED TO ALWAYS STOP AT THAT TROPHY CASE NEAR TRIG. THOUGHT SHE WAS CHECKING OUT QUINCY'S FOOTBALL PHOTO OR SOMETHING.
"LIKE A TYPE OF THERAPY OR BLACK MAGIC RITUAL OR--OR I DUNNO...SOME WEIRD SHIT.
"BUT IT ALWAYS GNAWED AT ME...NOT KNOWING WHY.
"SO ONE DAY I JUST DECIDED TO ASK."

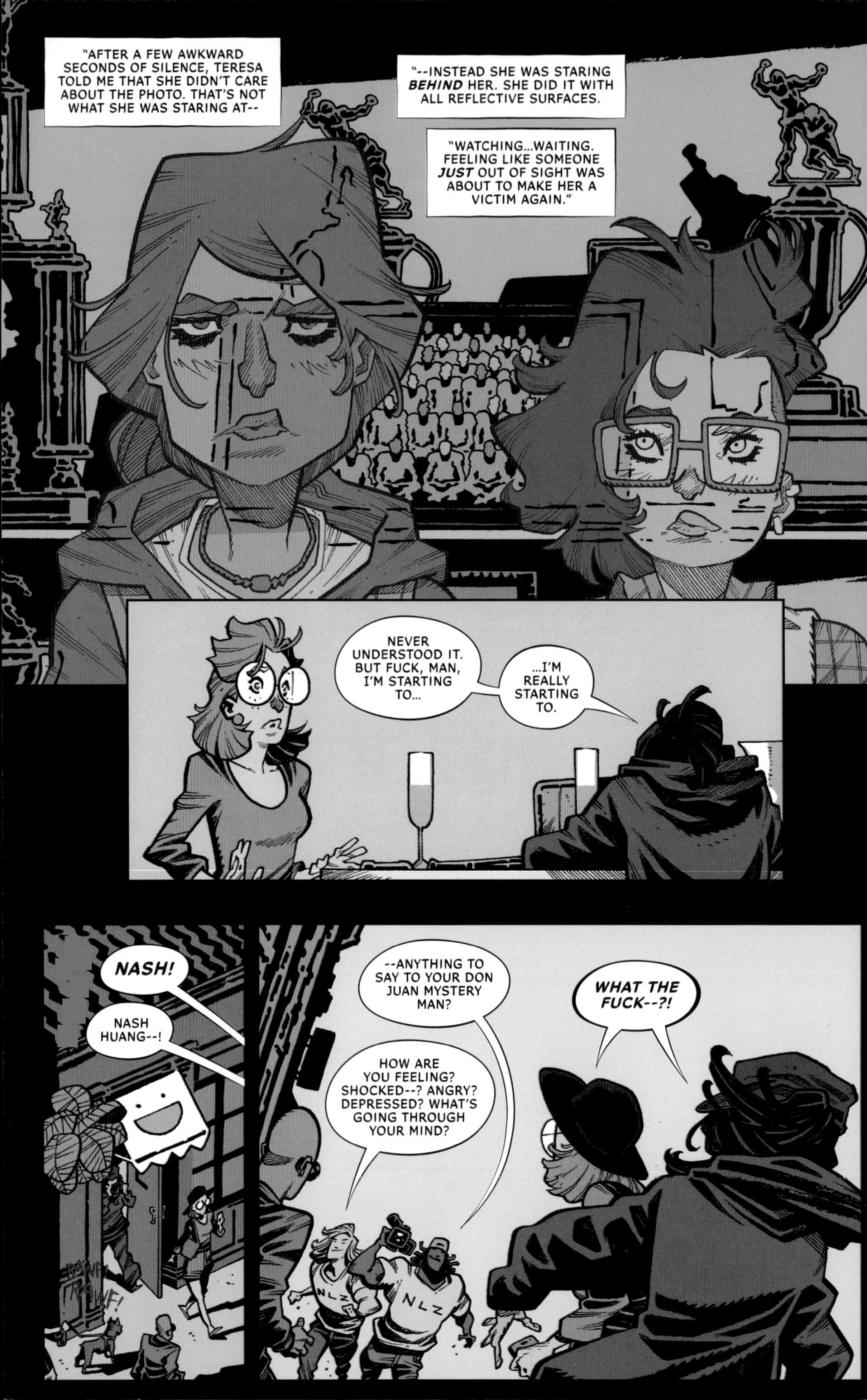

"AFTER A FEW AWKWARD SECONDS OF SILENCE, TERESA TOLD ME THAT SHE DIDN'T CARE ABOUT THE PHOTO. THAT'S NOT WHAT SHE WAS STARING AT--
"--INSTEAD SHE WAS STARING *BEHIND* HER. SHE DID IT WITH ALL REFLECTIVE SURFACES.
"WATCHING...WAITING. FEELING LIKE SOMEONE *JUST* OUT OF SIGHT WAS ABOUT TO MAKE HER A VICTIM AGAIN."
NEVER UNDERSTOOD IT. BUT FUCK, MAN, I'M STARTING TO...
...I'M REALLY STARTING TO.
NASH!
NASH HUANG--!
RAWF RAWF!
--ANYTHING TO SAY TO YOUR DON JUAN MYSTERY MAN?
HOW ARE YOU FEELING? SHOCKED--? ANGRY? DEPRESSED? WHAT'S GOING THROUGH YOUR MIND?
WHAT THE FUCK--?!
NLZ
NLZ

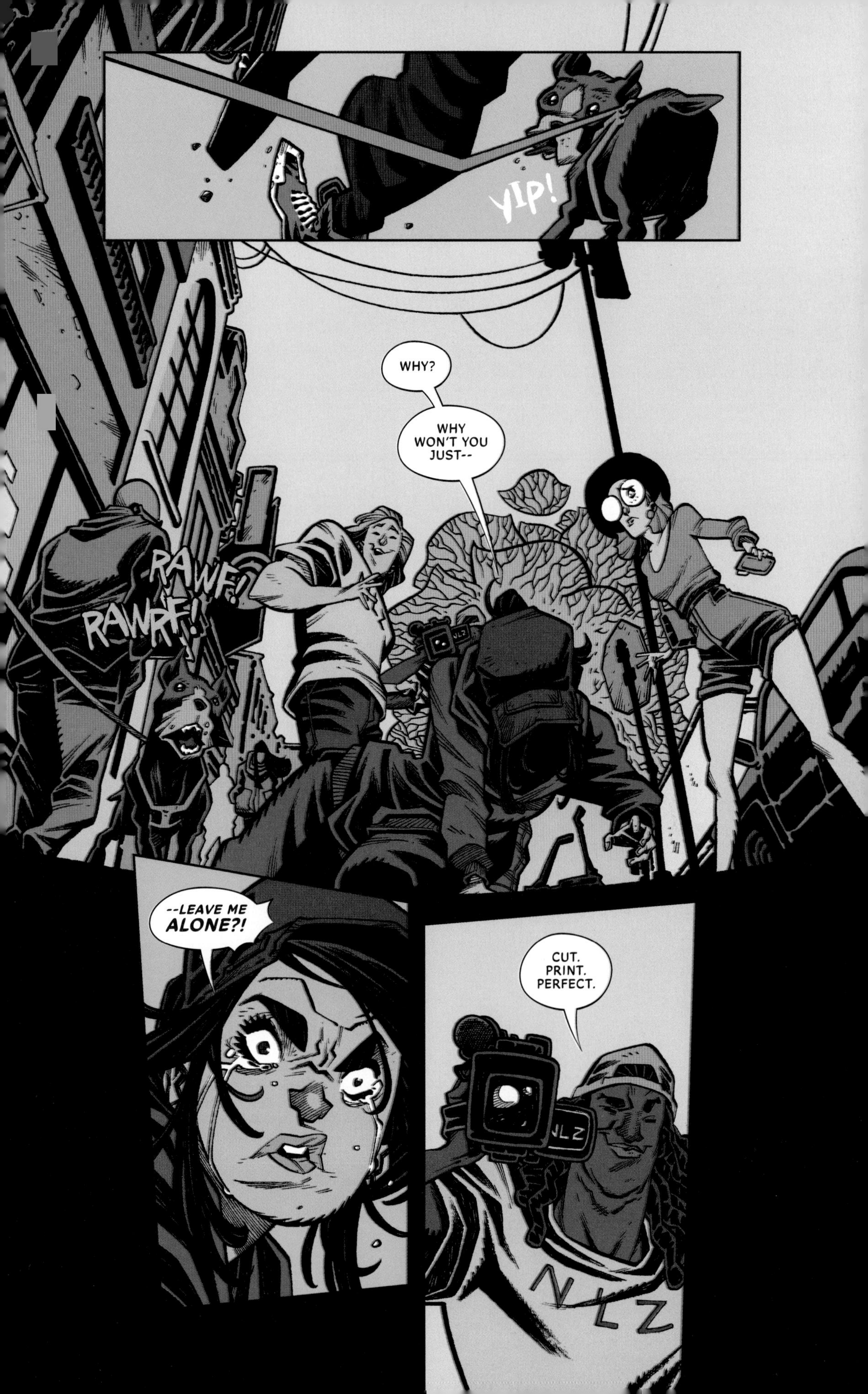
YIP!
WHY?
WHY WON'T YOU JUST--
RAWF!
RAWRF!
--LEAVE ME **ALONE?!**
CUT. PRINT. PERFECT.
NLZ

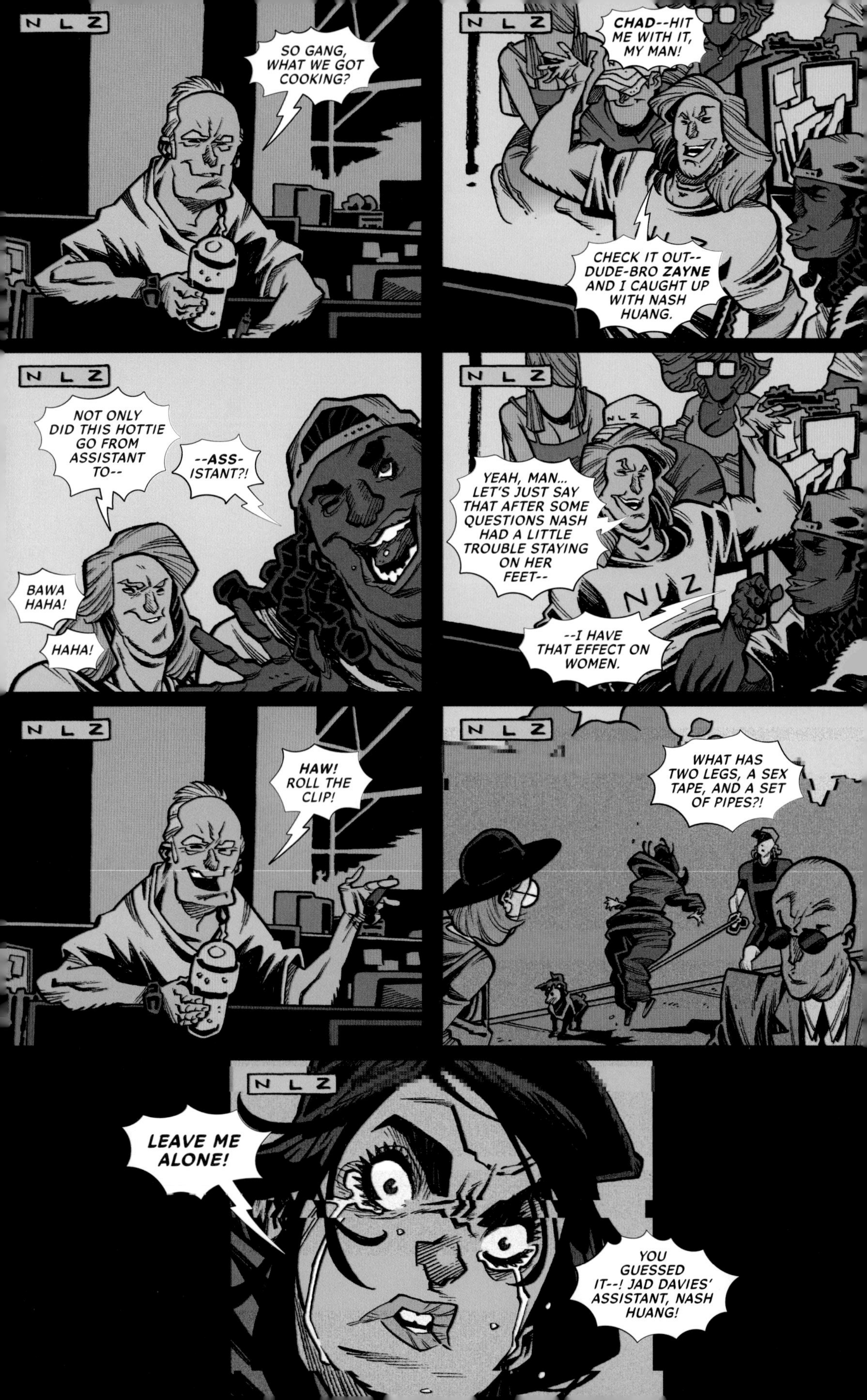
NLZ
SO GANG, WHAT WE GOT COOKING?
NLZ
CHAD--HIT ME WITH IT, MY MAN!
CHECK IT OUT-- DUDE-BRO ZAYNE AND I CAUGHT UP WITH NASH HUANG.
NLZ
NOT ONLY DID THIS HOTTIE GO FROM ASSISTANT TO--
--ASS-ISTANT?!
BAWA HAHA!
HAHA!
NLZ
YEAH, MAN... LET'S JUST SAY THAT AFTER SOME QUESTIONS NASH HAD A LITTLE TROUBLE STAYING ON HER FEET--
NLZ
--I HAVE THAT EFFECT ON WOMEN.
NLZ
HAW! ROLL THE CLIP!
NLZ
WHAT HAS TWO LEGS, A SEX TAPE, AND A SET OF PIPES?!
NLZ
LEAVE ME ALONE!
YOU GUESSED IT--! JAD DAVIES' ASSISTANT, NASH HUANG!

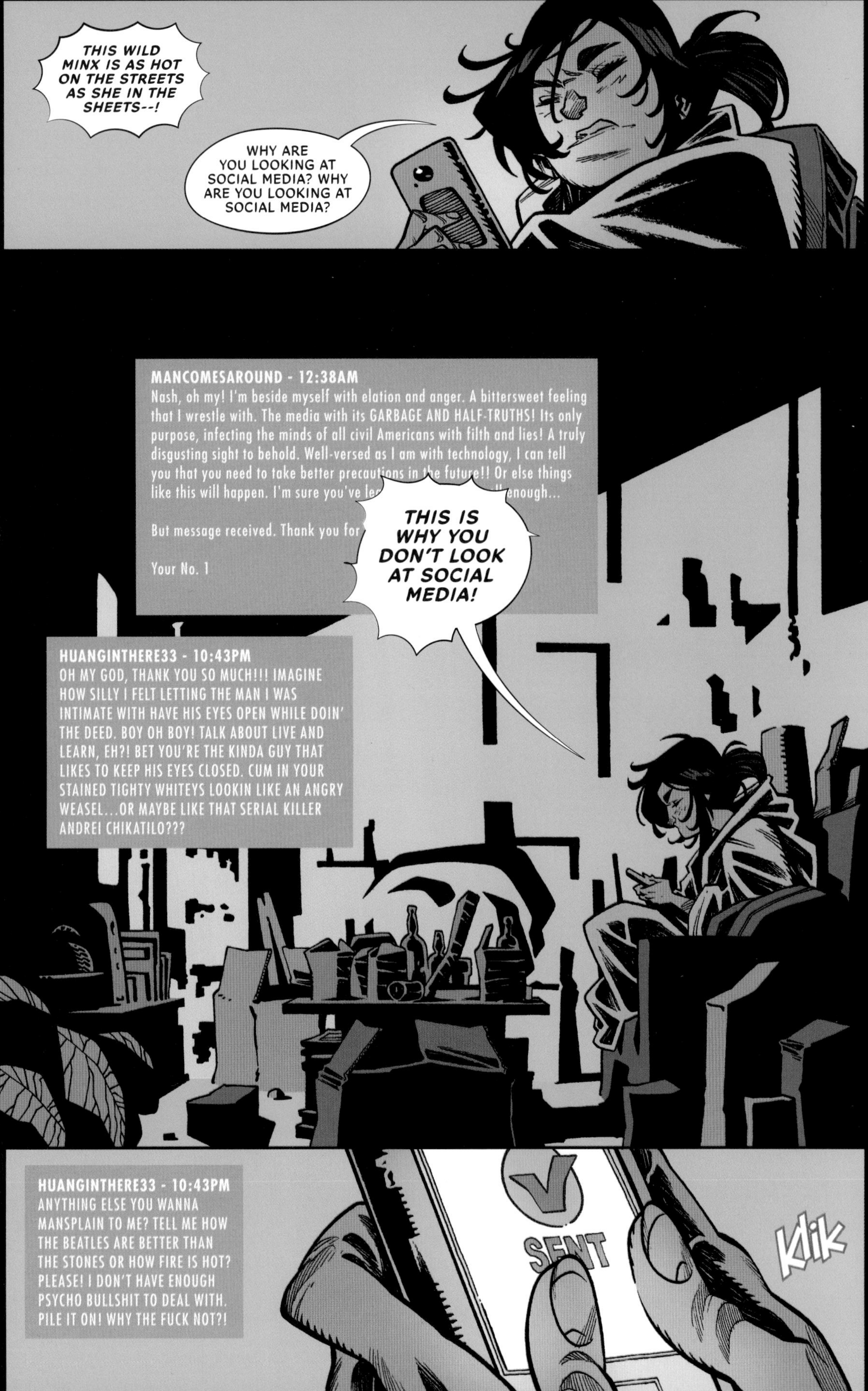
THIS WILD MINX IS AS HOT ON THE STREETS AS SHE IN THE SHEETS--!
WHY ARE YOU LOOKING AT SOCIAL MEDIA? WHY ARE YOU LOOKING AT SOCIAL MEDIA?
MANCOMESAROUND - 12:38AM
Nash, oh my! I'm beside myself with elation and anger. A bittersweet feeling that I wrestle with. The media with its GARBAGE AND HALF-TRUTHS! Its only purpose, infecting the minds of all civil Americans with filth and lies! A truly disgusting sight to behold. Well-versed as I am with technology, I can tell you that you need to take better precautions in the future!! Or else things like this will happen. I'm sure you've le enough...
But message received. Thank you for
Your No. 1
THIS IS WHY YOU DON'T LOOK AT SOCIAL MEDIA!
HUANGINTHERE33 - 10:43PM
OH MY GOD, THANK YOU SO MUCH!!! IMAGINE HOW SILLY I FELT LETTING THE MAN I WAS INTIMATE WITH HAVE HIS EYES OPEN WHILE DOIN' THE DEED. BOY OH BOY! TALK ABOUT LIVE AND LEARN, EH?! BET YOU'RE THE KINDA GUY THAT LIKES TO KEEP HIS EYES CLOSED. CUM IN YOUR STAINED TIGHTY WHITEYS LOOKIN LIKE AN ANGRY WEASEL...OR MAYBE LIKE THAT SERIAL KILLER ANDREI CHIKATILO???
HUANGINTHERE33 - 10:43PM
ANYTHING ELSE YOU WANNA MANSPLAIN TO ME? TELL ME HOW THE BEATLES ARE BETTER THAN THE STONES OR HOW FIRE IS HOT? PLEASE! I DON'T HAVE ENOUGH PSYCHO BULLSHIT TO DEAL WITH. PILE IT ON! WHY THE FUCK NOT?!
SENT
Klik

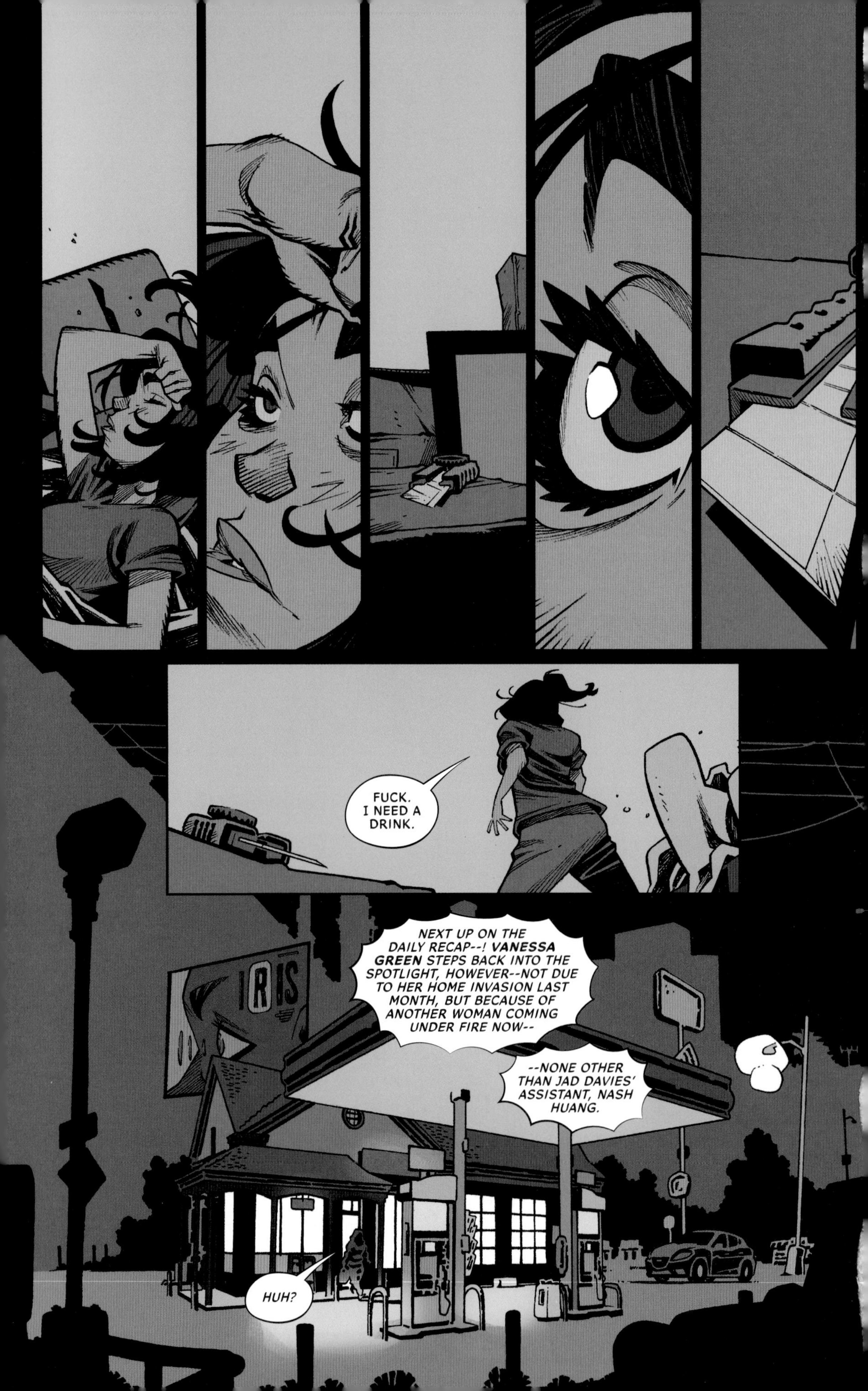
FUCK. I NEED A DRINK.
IRIS
NEXT UP ON THE DAILY RECAP--! VANESSA GREEN STEPS BACK INTO THE SPOTLIGHT, HOWEVER--NOT DUE TO HER HOME INVASION LAST MONTH, BUT BECAUSE OF ANOTHER WOMAN COMING UNDER FIRE NOW--
--NONE OTHER THAN JAD DAVIES' ASSISTANT, NASH HUANG.
HUH?

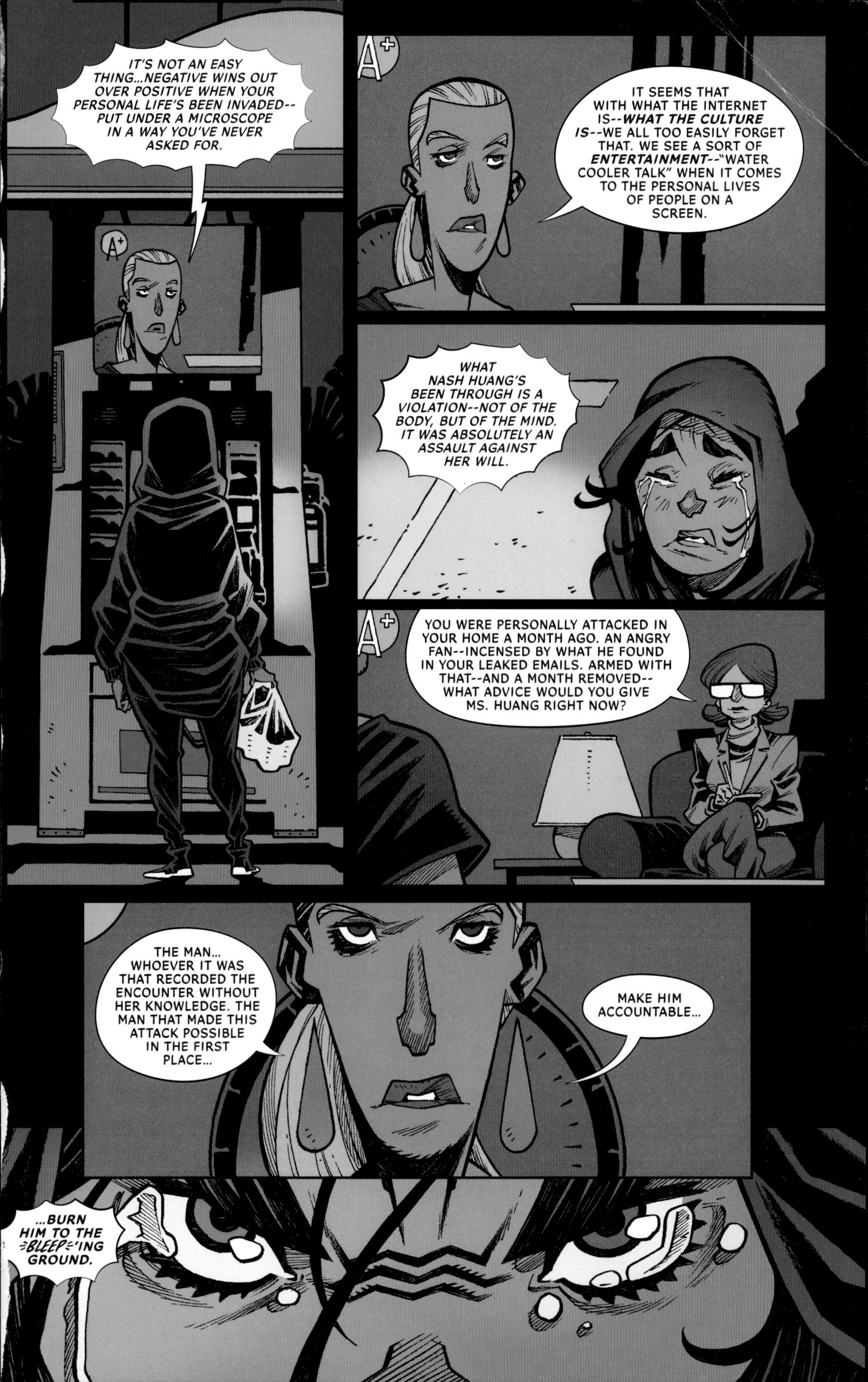
IT'S NOT AN EASY THING...NEGATIVE WINS OUT OVER POSITIVE WHEN YOUR PERSONAL LIFE'S BEEN INVADED--PUT UNDER A MICROSCOPE IN A WAY YOU'VE NEVER ASKED FOR.
A+
IT SEEMS THAT WITH WHAT THE INTERNET IS--WHAT THE CULTURE IS--WE ALL TOO EASILY FORGET THAT. WE SEE A SORT OF ENTERTAINMENT--"WATER COOLER TALK" WHEN IT COMES TO THE PERSONAL LIVES OF PEOPLE ON A SCREEN.
WHAT NASH HUANG'S BEEN THROUGH IS A VIOLATION--NOT OF THE BODY, BUT OF THE MIND. IT WAS ABSOLUTELY AN ASSAULT AGAINST HER WILL.
YOU WERE PERSONALLY ATTACKED IN YOUR HOME A MONTH AGO. AN ANGRY FAN--INCENSED BY WHAT HE FOUND IN YOUR LEAKED EMAILS. ARMED WITH THAT--AND A MONTH REMOVED--WHAT ADVICE WOULD YOU GIVE MS. HUANG RIGHT NOW?
THE MAN... WHOEVER IT WAS THAT RECORDED THE ENCOUNTER WITHOUT HER KNOWLEDGE. THE MAN THAT MADE THIS ATTACK POSSIBLE IN THE FIRST PLACE...
MAKE HIM ACCOUNTABLE...
...BURN HIM TO THE BLEEP'ING GROUND.

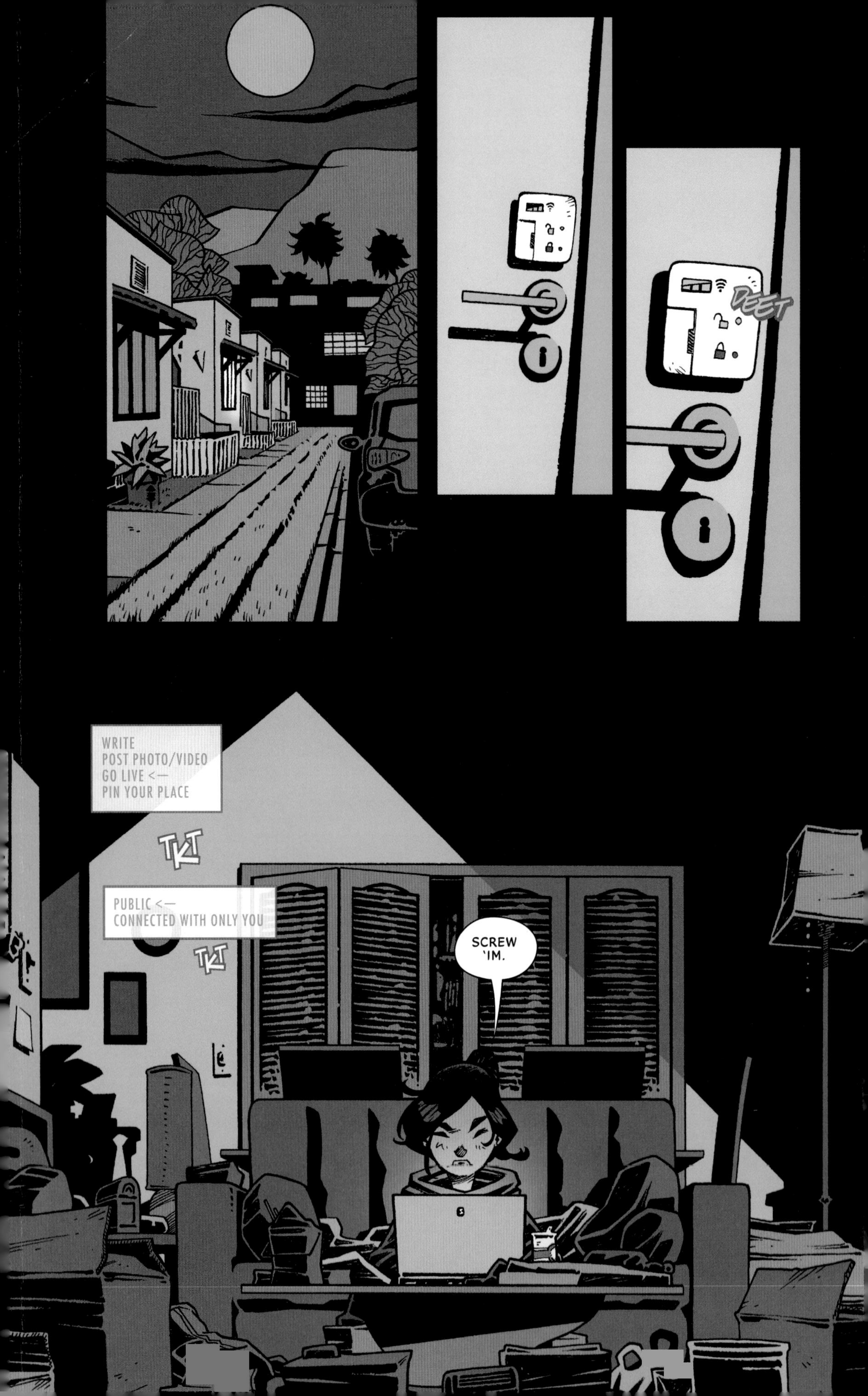
DEET
WRITE
POST PHOTO/VIDEO
GO LIVE <—
PIN YOUR PLACE
TKT
PUBLIC <—
CONNECTED WITH ONLY YOU
TKT
SCREW 'IM.

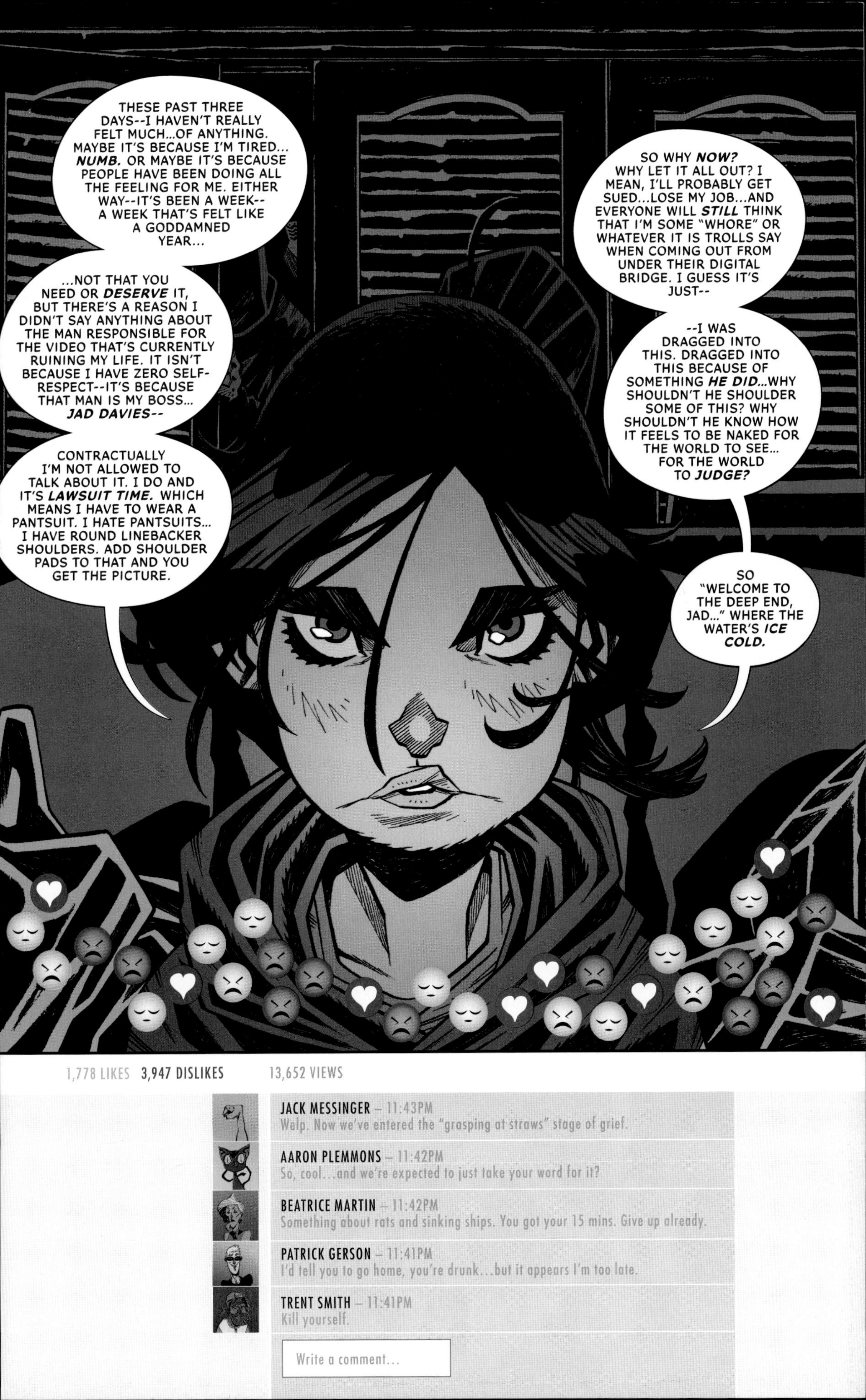
THESE PAST THREE DAYS--I HAVEN'T REALLY FELT MUCH...OF ANYTHING. MAYBE IT'S BECAUSE I'M TIRED... NUMB. OR MAYBE IT'S BECAUSE PEOPLE HAVE BEEN DOING ALL THE FEELING FOR ME. EITHER WAY--IT'S BEEN A WEEK-- A WEEK THAT'S FELT LIKE A GODDAMNED YEAR...
...NOT THAT YOU NEED OR DESERVE IT, BUT THERE'S A REASON I DIDN'T SAY ANYTHING ABOUT THE MAN RESPONSIBLE FOR THE VIDEO THAT'S CURRENTLY RUINING MY LIFE. IT ISN'T BECAUSE I HAVE ZERO SELF-RESPECT--IT'S BECAUSE THAT MAN IS MY BOSS... JAD DAVIES--
CONTRACTUALLY I'M NOT ALLOWED TO TALK ABOUT IT. I DO AND IT'S LAWSUIT TIME. WHICH MEANS I HAVE TO WEAR A PANTSUIT. I HATE PANTSUITS... I HAVE ROUND LINEBACKER SHOULDERS. ADD SHOULDER PADS TO THAT AND YOU GET THE PICTURE.
SO WHY NOW? WHY LET IT ALL OUT? I MEAN, I'LL PROBABLY GET SUED...LOSE MY JOB...AND EVERYONE WILL STILL THINK THAT I'M SOME "WHORE" OR WHATEVER IT IS TROLLS SAY WHEN COMING OUT FROM UNDER THEIR DIGITAL BRIDGE. I GUESS IT'S JUST--
--I WAS DRAGGED INTO THIS. DRAGGED INTO THIS BECAUSE OF SOMETHING HE DID...WHY SHOULDN'T HE SHOULDER SOME OF THIS? WHY SHOULDN'T HE KNOW HOW IT FEELS TO BE NAKED FOR THE WORLD TO SEE... FOR THE WORLD TO JUDGE?
SO "WELCOME TO THE DEEP END, JAD..." WHERE THE WATER'S ICE COLD.
1,778 LIKES 3,947 DISLIKES 13,652 VIEWS
JACK MESSINGER – 11:43PM
Welp. Now we've entered the "grasping at straws" stage of grief.
AARON PLEMMONS – 11:42PM
So, cool...and we're expected to just take your word for it?
BEATRICE MARTIN – 11:42PM
Something about rats and sinking ships. You got your 15 mins. Give up already.
PATRICK GERSON – 11:41PM
I'd tell you to go home, you're drunk...but it appears I'm too late.
TRENT SMITH – 11:41PM
Kill yourself.
Write a comment...

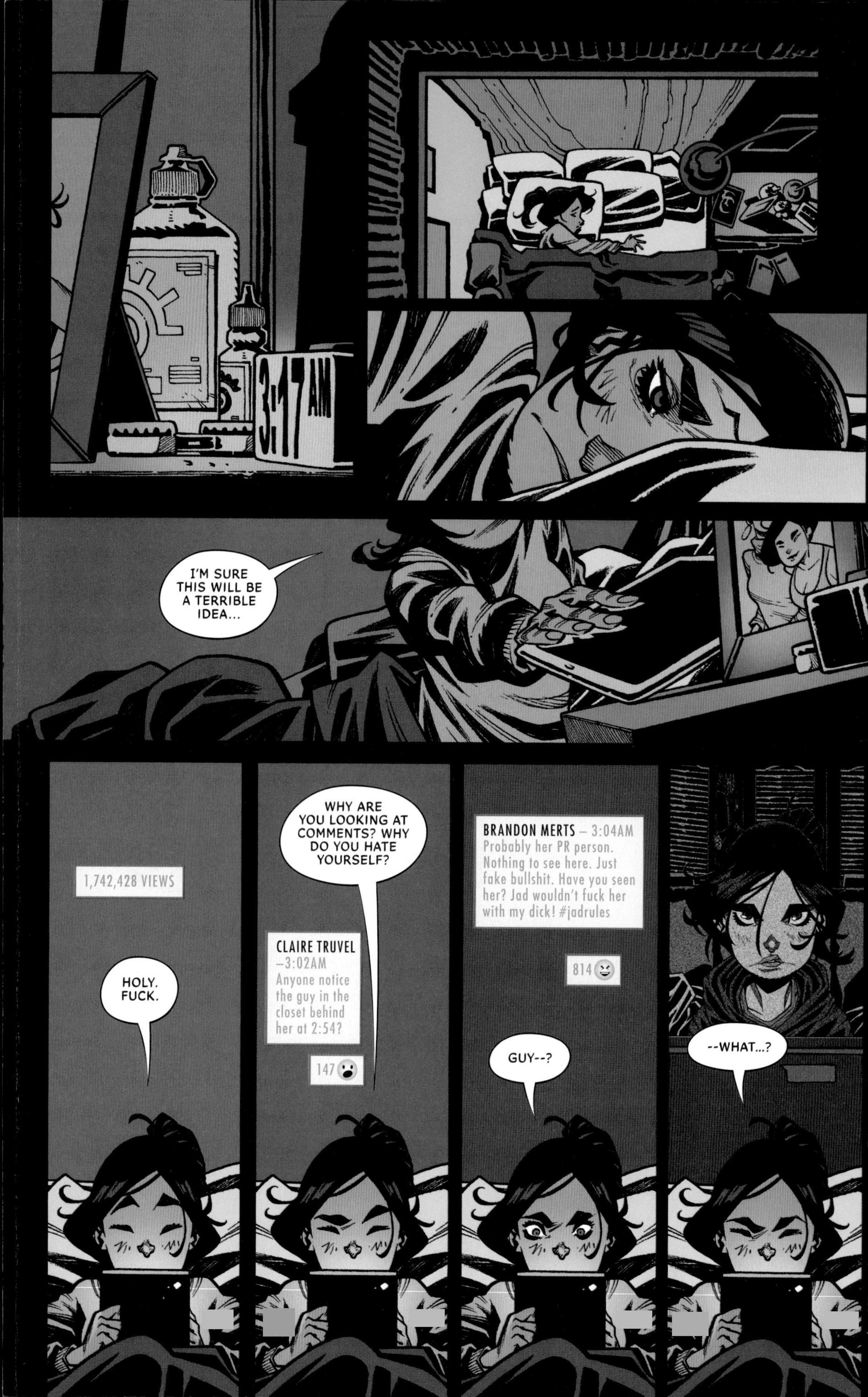
3:17 AM
I'M SURE THIS WILL BE A TERRIBLE IDEA...
1,742,428 VIEWS
HOLY. FUCK.
WHY ARE YOU LOOKING AT COMMENTS? WHY DO YOU HATE YOURSELF?
CLAIRE TRUVEL —3:02AM Anyone notice the guy in the closet behind her at 2:54?
147
BRANDON MERTS — 3:04AM Probably her PR person. Nothing to see here. Just fake bullshit. Have you seen her? Jad wouldn't fuck her with my dick! #jadrules
814
GUY--?
--WHAT...?

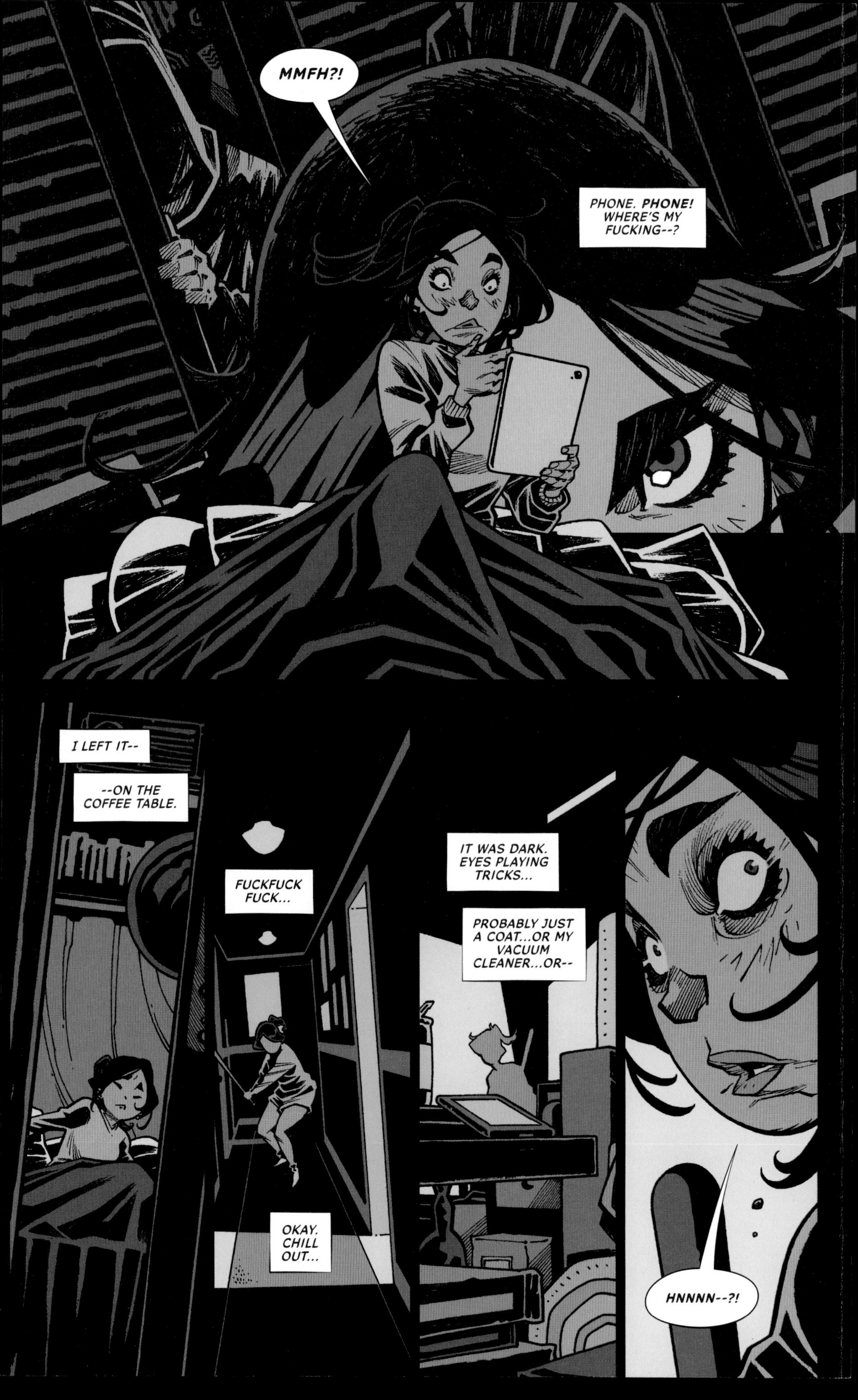
MMFH?!
PHONE. **PHONE!** WHERE'S MY FUCKING--?
I LEFT IT--
--ON THE COFFEE TABLE.
FUCKFUCK FUCK...
OKAY. CHILL OUT...
IT WAS DARK. EYES PLAYING TRICKS...
PROBABLY JUST A COAT...OR MY VACUUM CLEANER...OR--
HNNNN--?!

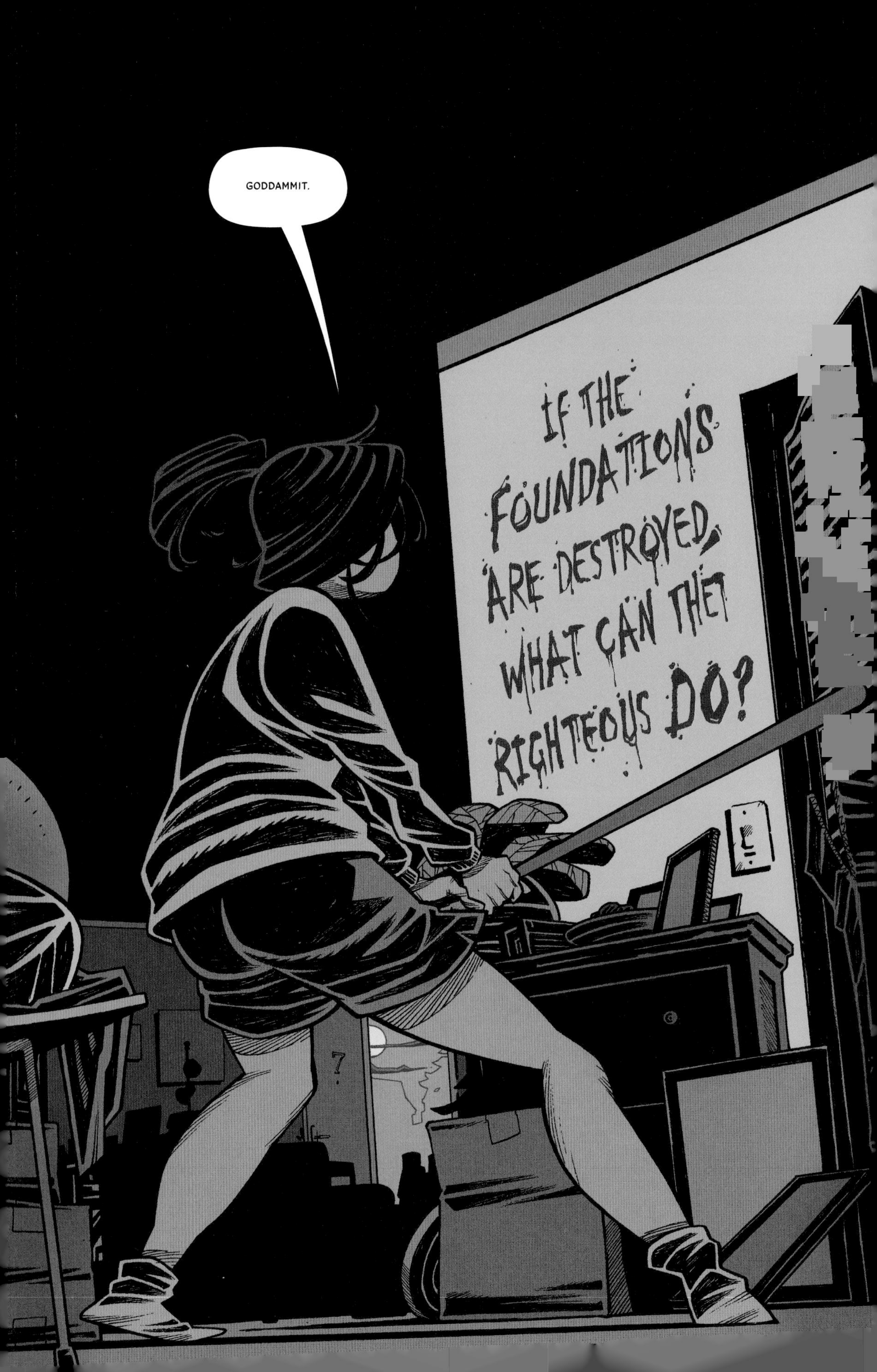
GODDAMMIT.
IF THE FOUNDATIONS ARE DESTROYED, WHAT CAN THE RIGHTEOUS DO?

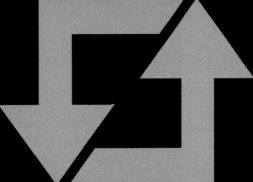

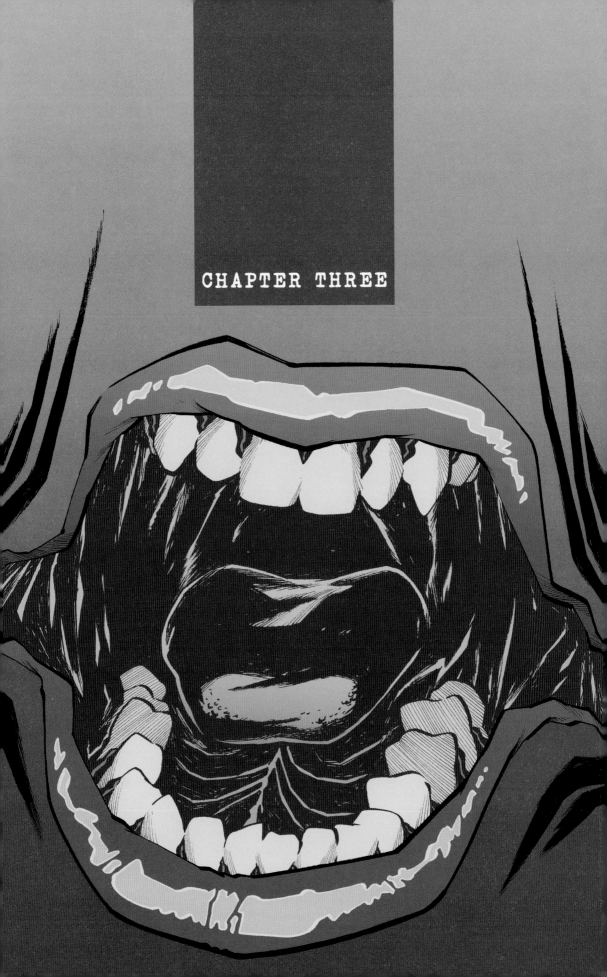

CHAPTER THREE

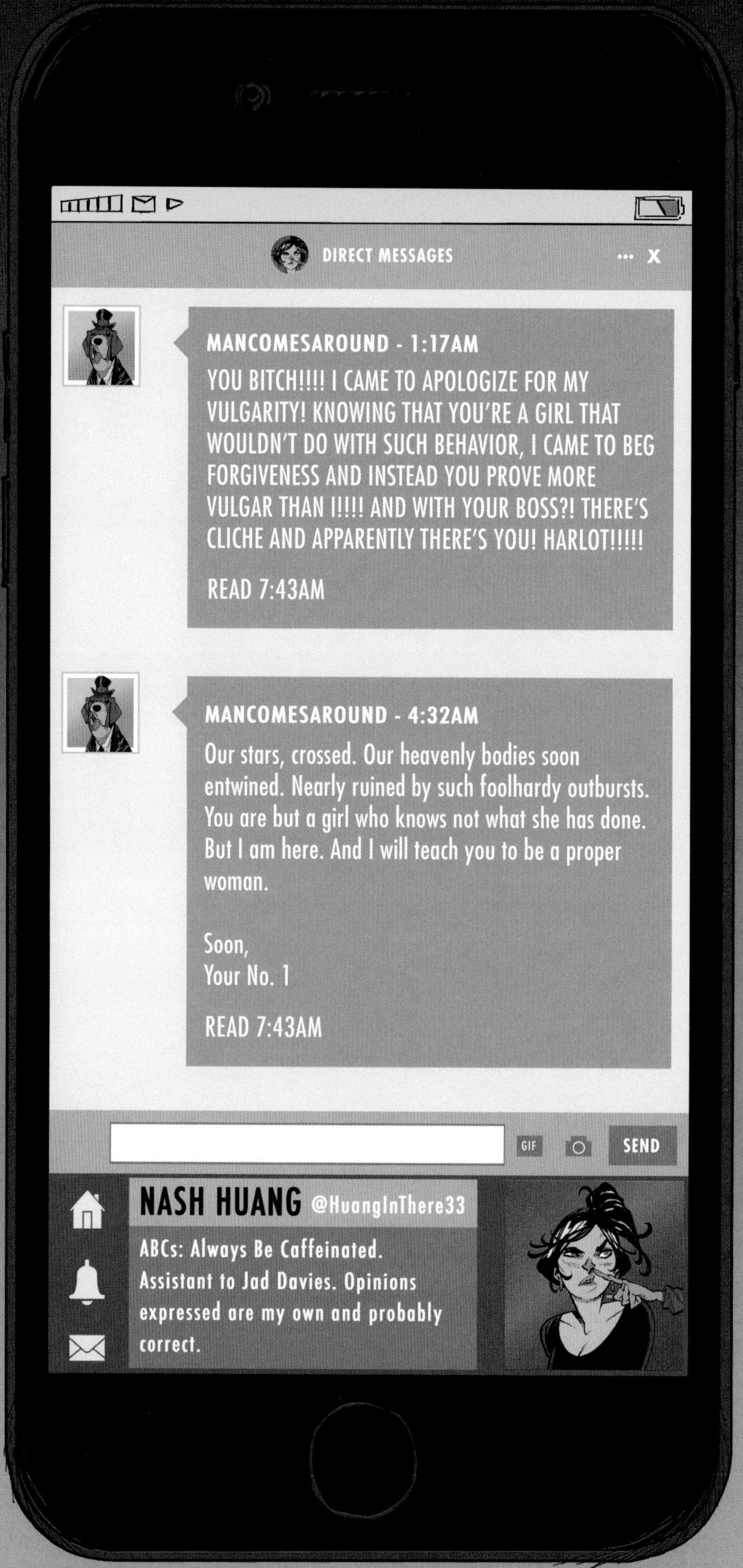
DIRECT MESSAGES
MANCOMESAROUND - 1:17AM
YOU BITCH!!!! I CAME TO APOLOGIZE FOR MY VULGARITY! KNOWING THAT YOU'RE A GIRL THAT WOULDN'T DO WITH SUCH BEHAVIOR, I CAME TO BEG FORGIVENESS AND INSTEAD YOU PROVE MORE VULGAR THAN I!!!!! AND WITH YOUR BOSS?! THERE'S CLICHE AND APPARENTLY THERE'S YOU! HARLOT!!!!!
READ 7:43AM
MANCOMESAROUND - 4:32AM
Our stars, crossed. Our heavenly bodies soon entwined. Nearly ruined by such foolhardy outbursts. You are but a girl who knows not what she has done. But I am here. And I will teach you to be a proper woman.
Soon,
Your No. 1
READ 7:43AM
GIF
SEND
NASH HUANG @HuangInThere33
ABCs: Always Be Caffeinated. Assistant to Jad Davies. Opinions expressed are my own and probably correct.

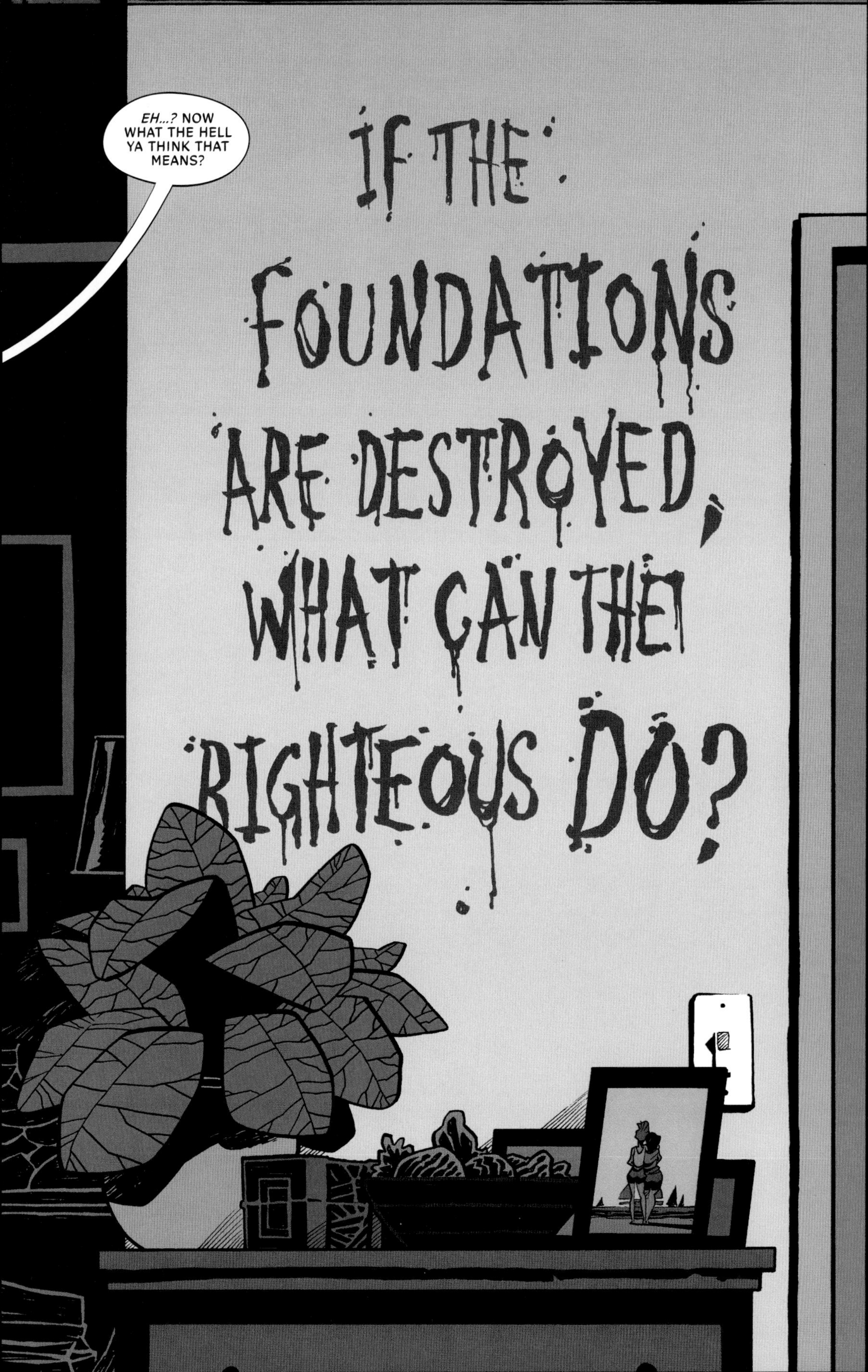
EH...? NOW WHAT THE HELL YA THINK THAT MEANS?
IF THE FOUNDATIONS ARE DESTROYED, WHAT CAN THE RIGHTEOUS DO?

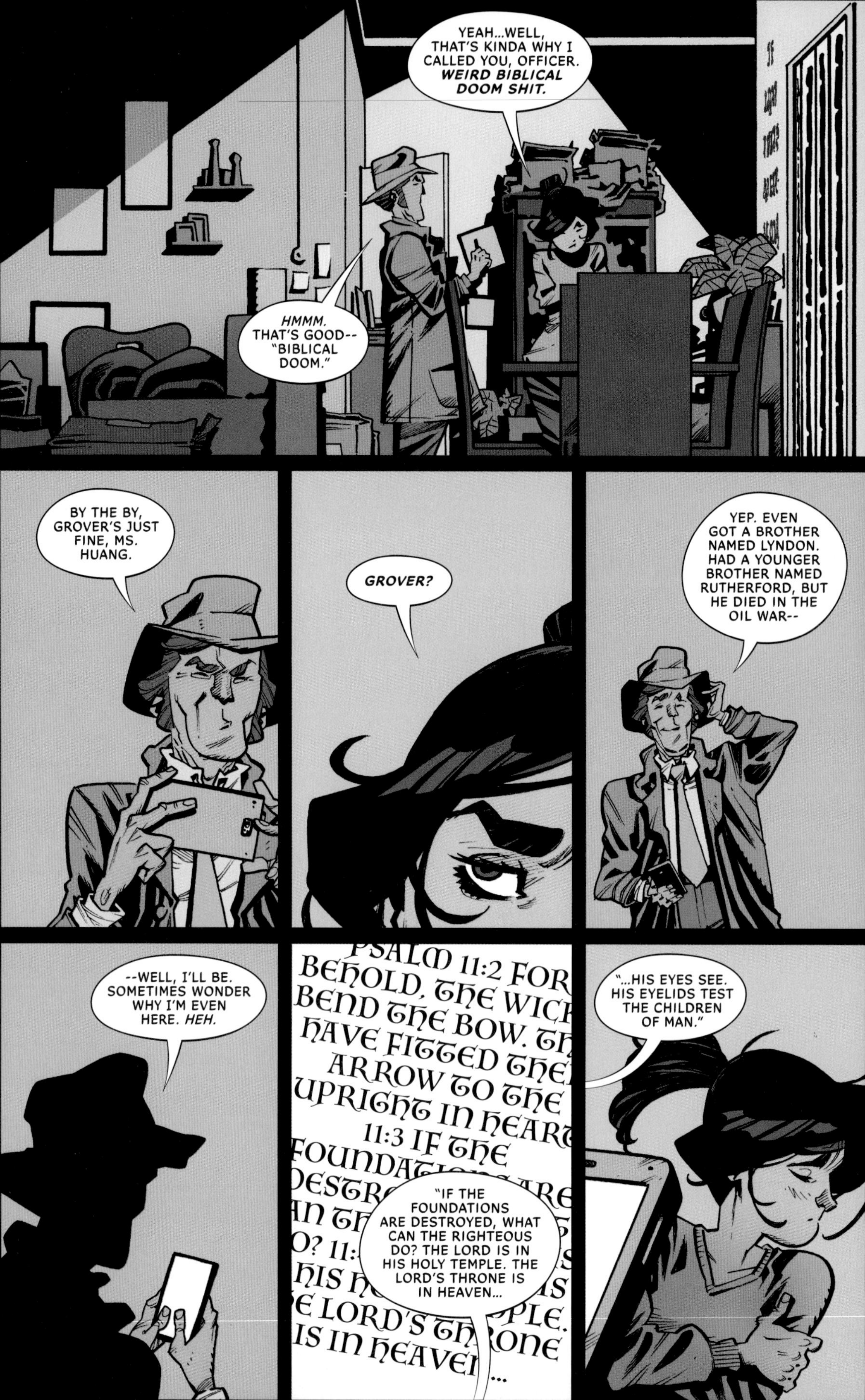
YEAH...WELL, THAT'S KINDA WHY I CALLED YOU, OFFICER. ***WEIRD BIBLICAL DOOM SHIT.***
HMMM. THAT'S GOOD-- "BIBLICAL DOOM."
BY THE BY, GROVER'S JUST FINE, MS. HUANG.
GROVER?
YEP. EVEN GOT A BROTHER NAMED LYNDON. HAD A YOUNGER BROTHER NAMED RUTHERFORD, BUT HE DIED IN THE OIL WAR--
--WELL, I'LL BE. SOMETIMES WONDER WHY I'M EVEN HERE. *HEH.*
"IF THE FOUNDATIONS ARE DESTROYED, WHAT CAN THE RIGHTEOUS DO? THE LORD IS IN HIS HOLY TEMPLE. THE LORD'S THRONE IS IN HEAVEN...
"...HIS EYES SEE. HIS EYELIDS TEST THE CHILDREN OF MAN."

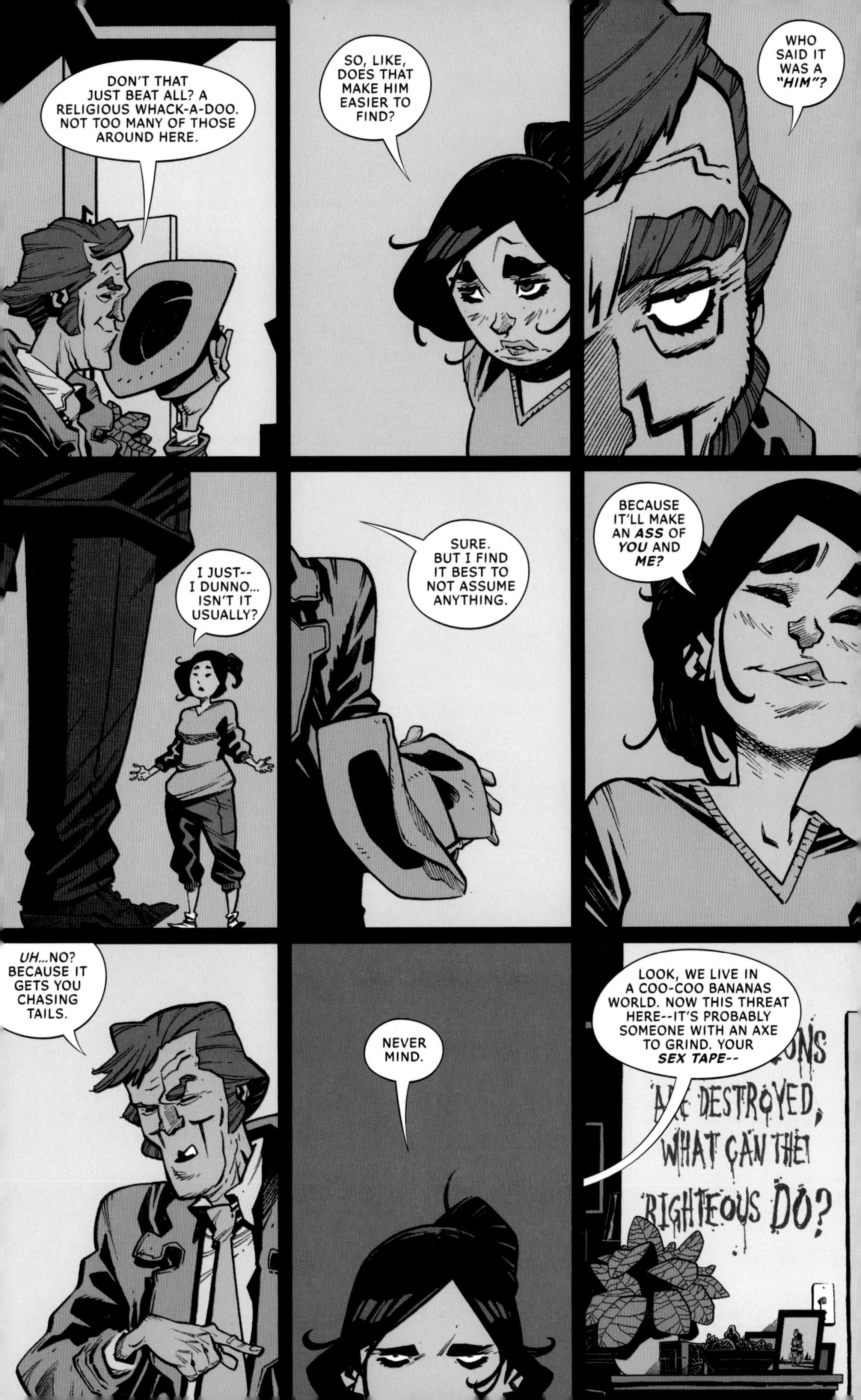
DON'T THAT JUST BEAT ALL? A RELIGIOUS WHACK-A-DOO. NOT TOO MANY OF THOSE AROUND HERE.
SO, LIKE, DOES THAT MAKE HIM EASIER TO FIND?
WHO SAID IT WAS A "HIM"?
I JUST-- I DUNNO... ISN'T IT USUALLY?
SURE. BUT I FIND IT BEST TO NOT ASSUME ANYTHING.
BECAUSE IT'LL MAKE AN ASS OF YOU AND ME?
UH...NO? BECAUSE IT GETS YOU CHASING TAILS.
NEVER MIND.
LOOK, WE LIVE IN A COO-COO BANANAS WORLD. NOW THIS THREAT HERE--IT'S PROBABLY SOMEONE WITH AN AXE TO GRIND. YOUR SEX TAPE--
ARE DESTROYED, WHAT CAN THE RIGHTEOUS DO?

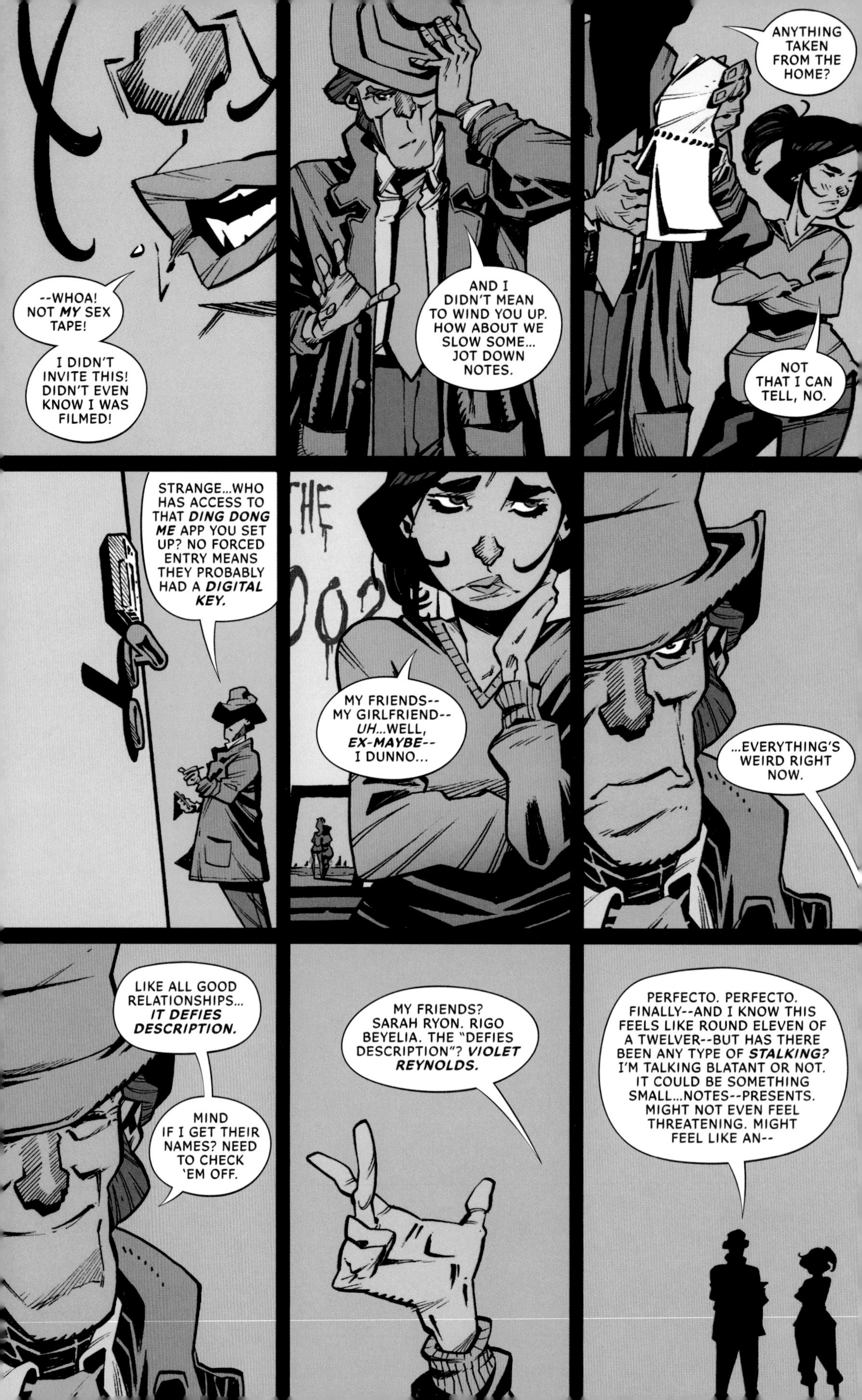
--WHOA! NOT MY SEX TAPE!
I DIDN'T INVITE THIS! DIDN'T EVEN KNOW I WAS FILMED!
AND I DIDN'T MEAN TO WIND YOU UP. HOW ABOUT WE SLOW SOME... JOT DOWN NOTES.
ANYTHING TAKEN FROM THE HOME?
NOT THAT I CAN TELL, NO.
STRANGE...WHO HAS ACCESS TO THAT DING DONG ME APP YOU SET UP? NO FORCED ENTRY MEANS THEY PROBABLY HAD A DIGITAL KEY.
MY FRIENDS-- MY GIRLFRIEND-- UH...WELL, EX-MAYBE-- I DUNNO...
...EVERYTHING'S WEIRD RIGHT NOW.
LIKE ALL GOOD RELATIONSHIPS... IT DEFIES DESCRIPTION.
MIND IF I GET THEIR NAMES? NEED TO CHECK 'EM OFF.
MY FRIENDS? SARAH RYON. RIGO BEYELIA. THE "DEFIES DESCRIPTION"? VIOLET REYNOLDS.
PERFECTO. PERFECTO. FINALLY--AND I KNOW THIS FEELS LIKE ROUND ELEVEN OF A TWELVER--BUT HAS THERE BEEN ANY TYPE OF STALKING? I'M TALKING BLATANT OR NOT. IT COULD BE SOMETHING SMALL...NOTES--PRESENTS. MIGHT NOT EVEN FEEL THREATENING. MIGHT FEEL LIKE AN--

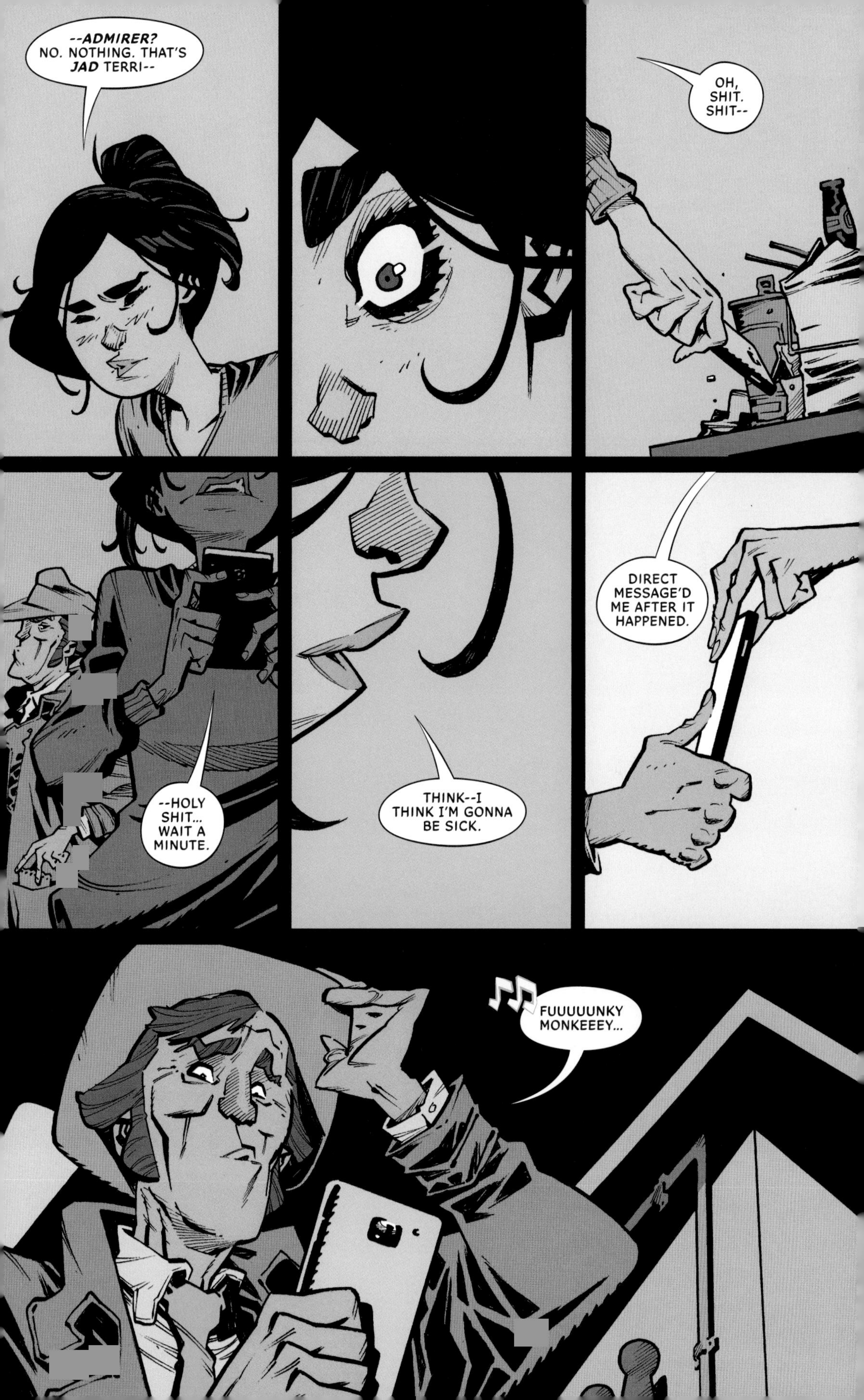
--ADMIRER? NO. NOTHING. THAT'S JAD TERRI--
OH, SHIT. SHIT--
--HOLY SHIT... WAIT A MINUTE.
THINK--I THINK I'M GONNA BE SICK.
DIRECT MESSAGE'D ME AFTER IT HAPPENED.
FUUUUUNKY MONKEEEY...

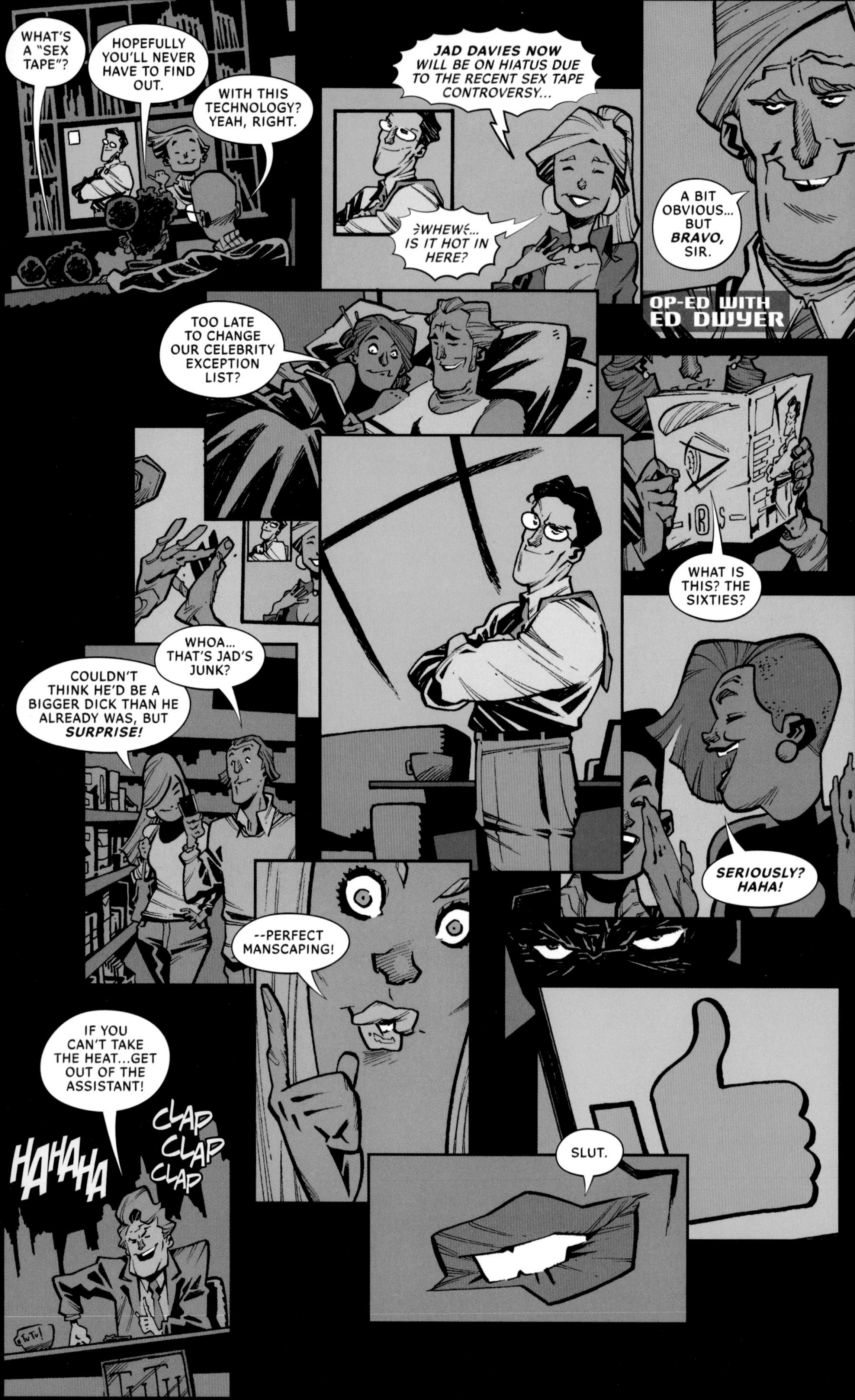

WHAT'S A "SEX TAPE"?
HOPEFULLY YOU'LL NEVER HAVE TO FIND OUT.
WITH THIS TECHNOLOGY? YEAH, RIGHT.
JAD DAVIES NOW WILL BE ON HIATUS DUE TO THE RECENT SEX TAPE CONTROVERSY...
WHEW... IS IT HOT IN HERE?
A BIT OBVIOUS... BUT BRAVO, SIR.
OP-ED WITH ED DWYER
TOO LATE TO CHANGE OUR CELEBRITY EXCEPTION LIST?
WHAT IS THIS? THE SIXTIES?
WHOA... THAT'S JAD'S JUNK?
COULDN'T THINK HE'D BE A BIGGER DICK THAN HE ALREADY WAS, BUT SURPRISE!
SERIOUSLY? HAHA!
--PERFECT MANSCAPING!
IF YOU CAN'T TAKE THE HEAT...GET OUT OF THE ASSISTANT!
HAHAHA
CLAP CLAP CLAP
SLUT.

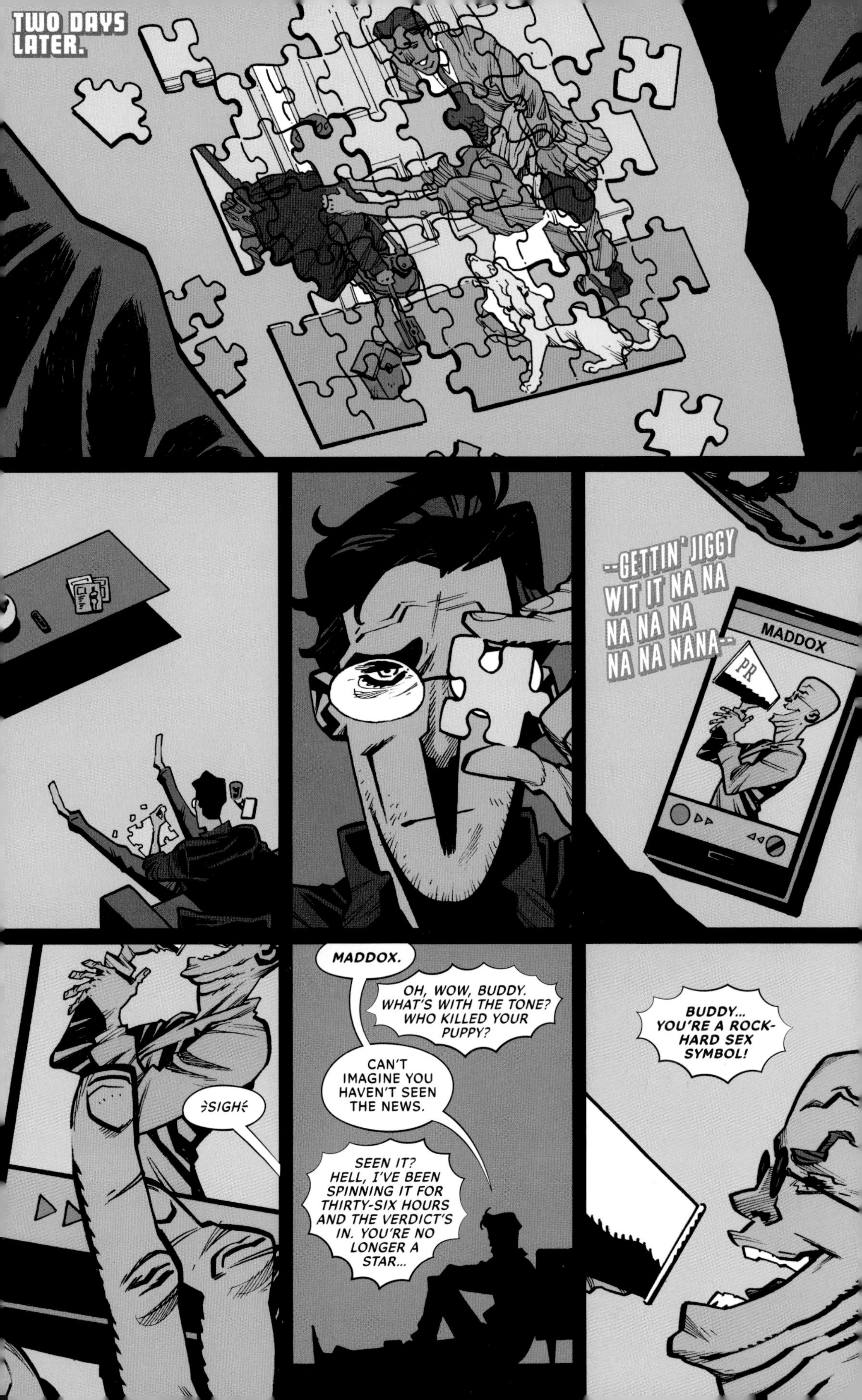
TWO DAYS LATER.
--GETTIN' JIGGY WIT IT NA NA NA NA NA NA NA NANA--
MADDOX
PR
SIGH
MADDOX.
OH, WOW, BUDDY. WHAT'S WITH THE TONE? WHO KILLED YOUR PUPPY?
CAN'T IMAGINE YOU HAVEN'T SEEN THE NEWS.
SEEN IT? HELL, I'VE BEEN SPINNING IT FOR THIRTY-SIX HOURS AND THE VERDICT'S IN. YOU'RE NO LONGER A STAR...
BUDDY... YOU'RE A ROCK-HARD SEX SYMBOL!

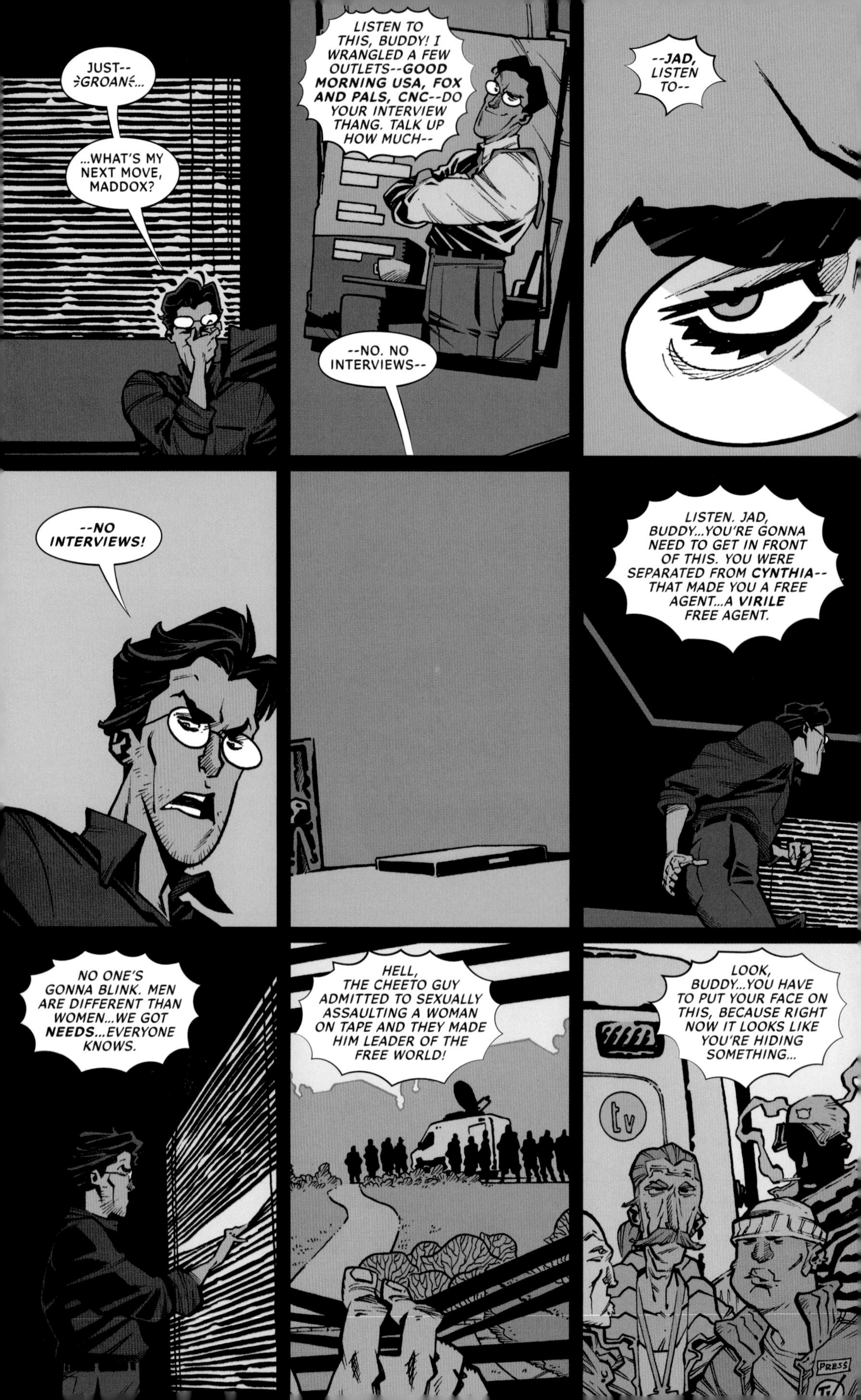

JUST--
GROAN...
...WHAT'S MY NEXT MOVE, MADDOX?
LISTEN TO THIS, BUDDY! I WRANGLED A FEW OUTLETS--GOOD MORNING USA, FOX AND PALS, CNC--DO YOUR INTERVIEW THANG. TALK UP HOW MUCH--
--NO. NO INTERVIEWS--
--JAD, LISTEN TO--
--NO INTERVIEWS!
LISTEN. JAD, BUDDY...YOU'RE GONNA NEED TO GET IN FRONT OF THIS. YOU WERE SEPARATED FROM CYNTHIA--THAT MADE YOU A FREE AGENT...A VIRILE FREE AGENT.
NO ONE'S GONNA BLINK. MEN ARE DIFFERENT THAN WOMEN...WE GOT NEEDS...EVERYONE KNOWS.
HELL, THE CHEETO GUY ADMITTED TO SEXUALLY ASSAULTING A WOMAN ON TAPE AND THEY MADE HIM LEADER OF THE FREE WORLD!
LOOK, BUDDY...YOU HAVE TO PUT YOUR FACE ON THIS, BECAUSE RIGHT NOW IT LOOKS LIKE YOU'RE HIDING SOMETHING...
TV
PRESS

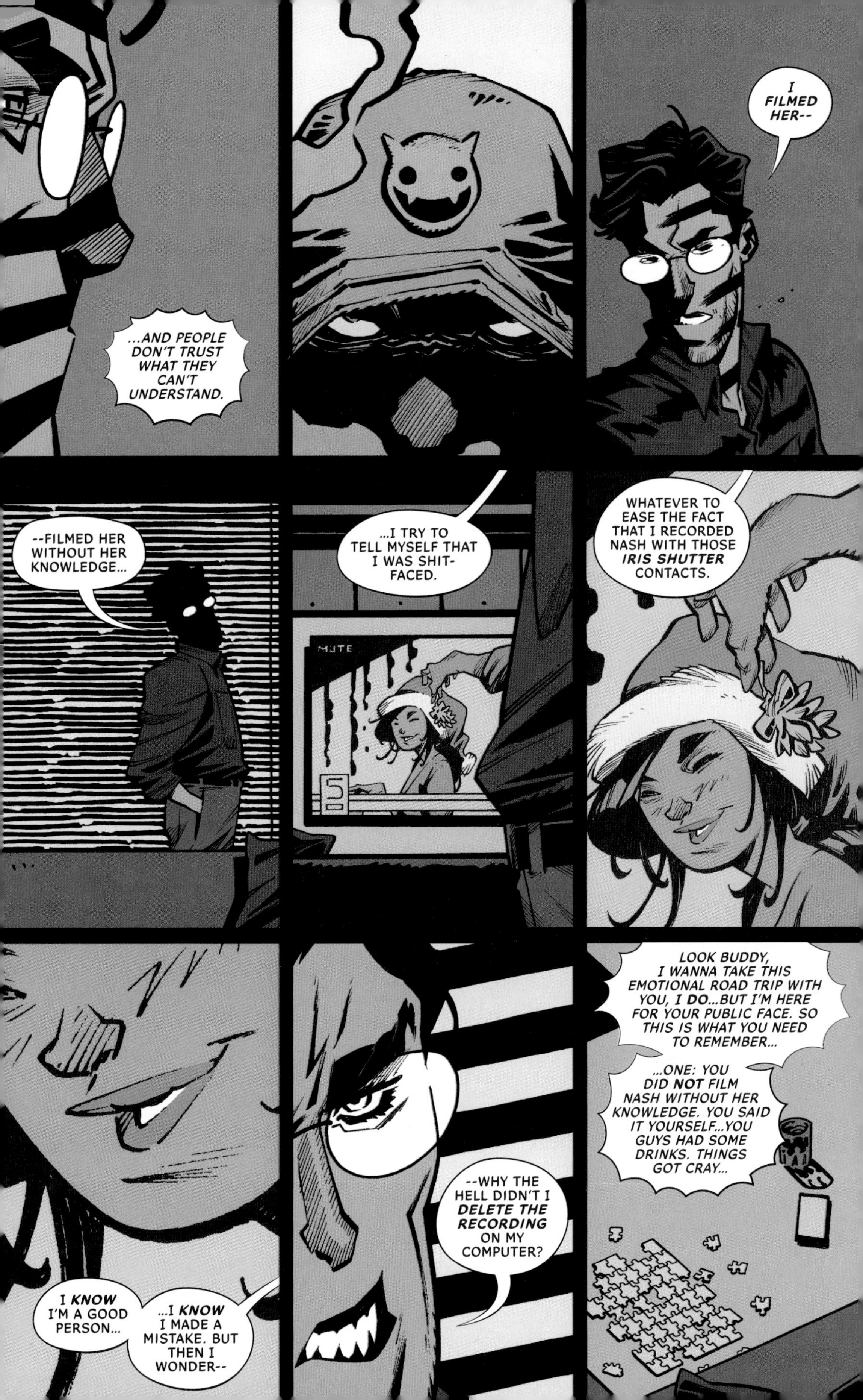
...AND PEOPLE DON'T TRUST WHAT THEY CAN'T UNDERSTAND.
I FILMED HER--
--FILMED HER WITHOUT HER KNOWLEDGE...
...I TRY TO TELL MYSELF THAT I WAS SHIT-FACED.
MUTE
WHATEVER TO EASE THE FACT THAT I RECORDED NASH WITH THOSE IRIS SHUTTER CONTACTS.
I KNOW I'M A GOOD PERSON...
...I KNOW I MADE A MISTAKE. BUT THEN I WONDER--
--WHY THE HELL DIDN'T I DELETE THE RECORDING ON MY COMPUTER?
LOOK BUDDY, I WANNA TAKE THIS EMOTIONAL ROAD TRIP WITH YOU, I DO...BUT I'M HERE FOR YOUR PUBLIC FACE. SO THIS IS WHAT YOU NEED TO REMEMBER...
...ONE: YOU DID NOT FILM NASH WITHOUT HER KNOWLEDGE. YOU SAID IT YOURSELF...YOU GUYS HAD SOME DRINKS. THINGS GOT CRAY...

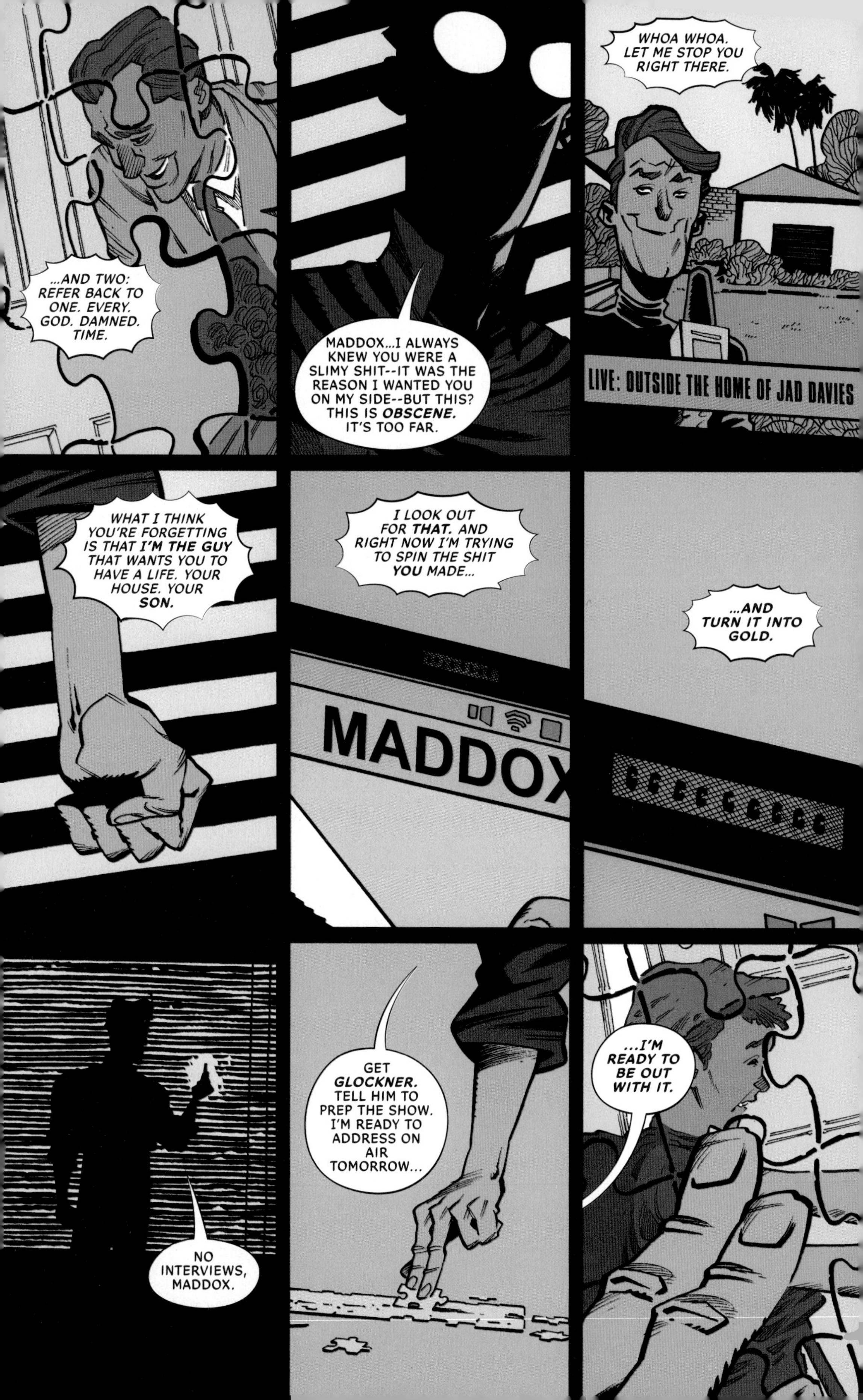
...AND TWO: REFER BACK TO ONE. EVERY. GOD. DAMNED. TIME.
MADDOX...I ALWAYS KNEW YOU WERE A SLIMY SHIT--IT WAS THE REASON I WANTED YOU ON MY SIDE--BUT THIS? THIS IS OBSCENE. IT'S TOO FAR.
WHOA WHOA. LET ME STOP YOU RIGHT THERE.
LIVE: OUTSIDE THE HOME OF JAD DAVIES
WHAT I THINK YOU'RE FORGETTING IS THAT I'M THE GUY THAT WANTS YOU TO HAVE A LIFE. YOUR HOUSE. YOUR SON.
I LOOK OUT FOR THAT. AND RIGHT NOW I'M TRYING TO SPIN THE SHIT YOU MADE...
MADDOX
...AND TURN IT INTO GOLD.
NO INTERVIEWS, MADDOX.
GET GLOCKNER. TELL HIM TO PREP THE SHOW. I'M READY TO ADDRESS ON AIR TOMORROW...
...I'M READY TO BE OUT WITH IT.

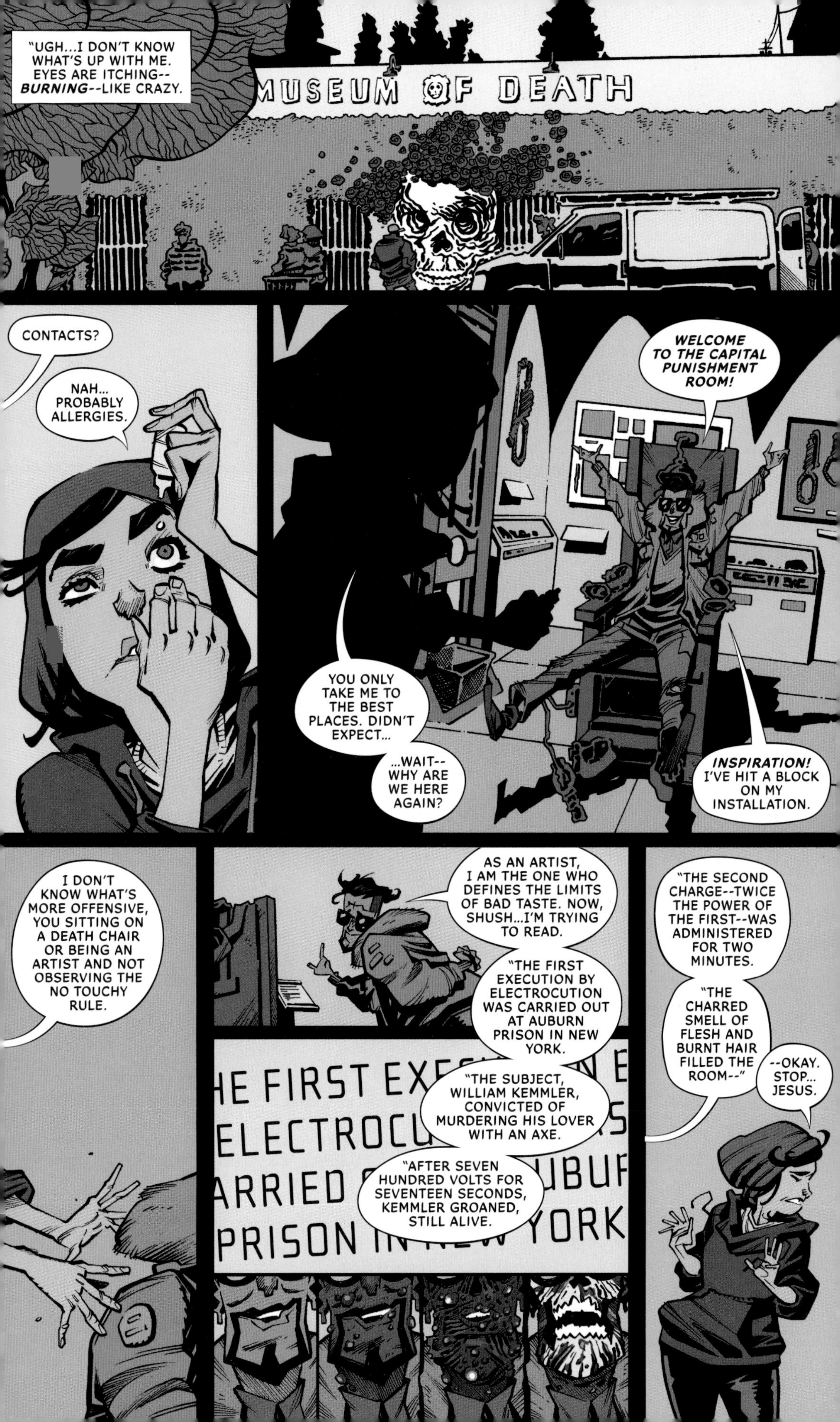
"UGH...I DON'T KNOW WHAT'S UP WITH ME. EYES ARE ITCHING--*BURNING*--LIKE CRAZY.
MUSEUM OF DEATH
CONTACTS?
NAH... PROBABLY ALLERGIES.
WELCOME TO THE CAPITAL PUNISHMENT ROOM!
YOU ONLY TAKE ME TO THE BEST PLACES. DIDN'T EXPECT...
...WAIT-- WHY ARE WE HERE AGAIN?
INSPIRATION! I'VE HIT A BLOCK ON MY INSTALLATION.
I DON'T KNOW WHAT'S MORE OFFENSIVE, YOU SITTING ON A DEATH CHAIR OR BEING AN ARTIST AND NOT OBSERVING THE NO TOUCHY RULE.
AS AN ARTIST, I AM THE ONE WHO DEFINES THE LIMITS OF BAD TASTE. NOW, SHUSH...I'M TRYING TO READ.
"THE FIRST EXECUTION BY ELECTROCUTION WAS CARRIED OUT AT AUBURN PRISON IN NEW YORK.
"THE SUBJECT, WILLIAM KEMMLER, CONVICTED OF MURDERING HIS LOVER WITH AN AXE.
"AFTER SEVEN HUNDRED VOLTS FOR SEVENTEEN SECONDS, KEMMLER GROANED, STILL ALIVE.
"THE SECOND CHARGE--TWICE THE POWER OF THE FIRST--WAS ADMINISTERED FOR TWO MINUTES.
"THE CHARRED SMELL OF FLESH AND BURNT HAIR FILLED THE ROOM--"
--OKAY. STOP... JESUS.

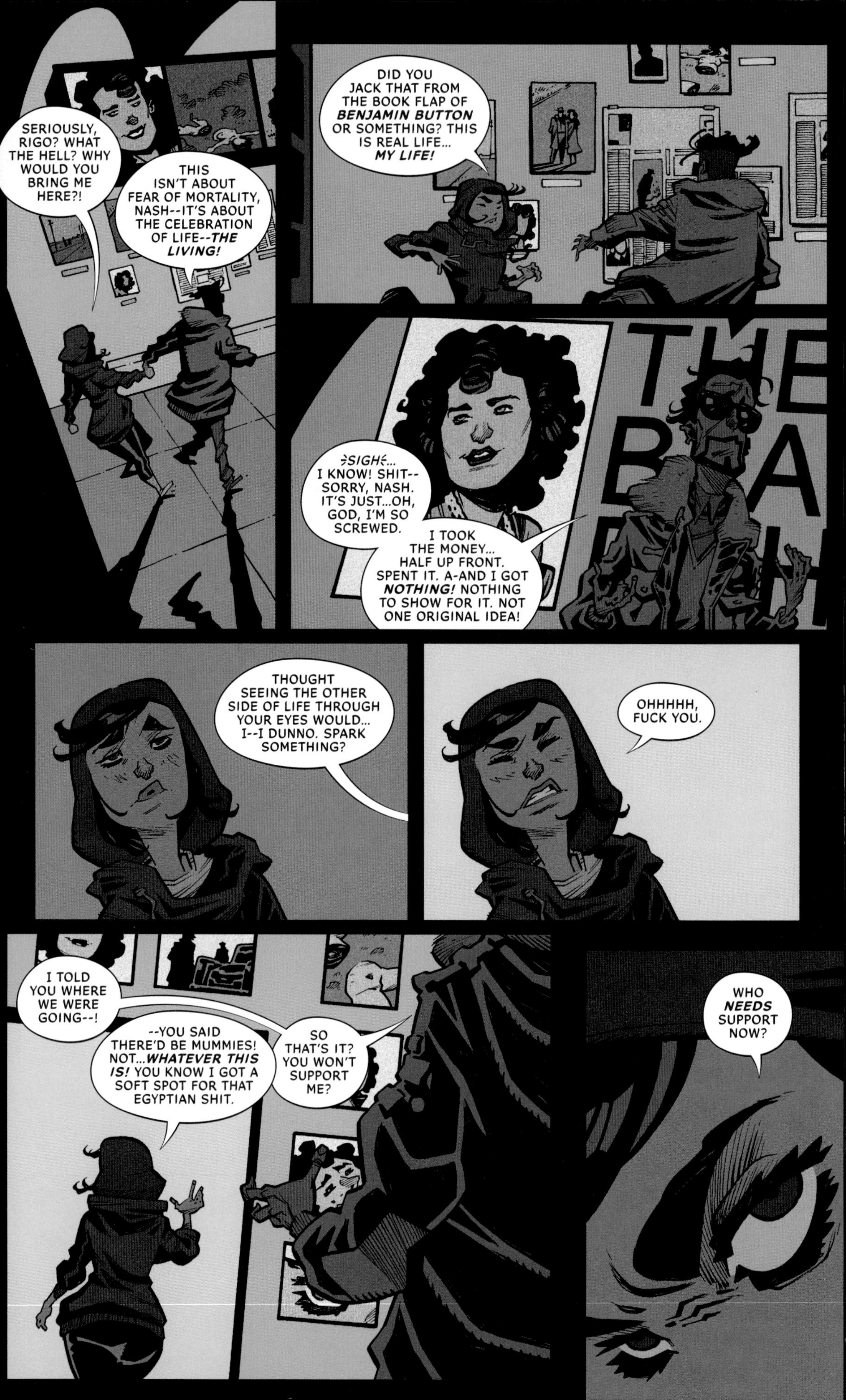
SERIOUSLY, RIGO? WHAT THE HELL? WHY WOULD YOU BRING ME HERE?!
THIS ISN'T ABOUT FEAR OF MORTALITY, NASH--IT'S ABOUT THE CELEBRATION OF LIFE--*THE LIVING!*
DID YOU JACK THAT FROM THE BOOK FLAP OF *BENJAMIN BUTTON* OR SOMETHING? THIS IS REAL LIFE... *MY LIFE!*
THE
SIGH... I KNOW! SHIT--SORRY, NASH. IT'S JUST...OH, GOD, I'M SO SCREWED.
I TOOK THE MONEY... HALF UP FRONT. SPENT IT. A-AND I GOT *NOTHING!* NOTHING TO SHOW FOR IT. NOT ONE ORIGINAL IDEA!
THOUGHT SEEING THE OTHER SIDE OF LIFE THROUGH YOUR EYES WOULD... I--I DUNNO. SPARK SOMETHING?
OHHHHH, FUCK YOU.
I TOLD YOU WHERE WE WERE GOING--!
--YOU SAID THERE'D BE MUMMIES! NOT...*WHATEVER THIS IS!* YOU KNOW I GOT A SOFT SPOT FOR THAT EGYPTIAN SHIT.
SO THAT'S IT? YOU WON'T SUPPORT ME?
WHO *NEEDS* SUPPORT NOW?

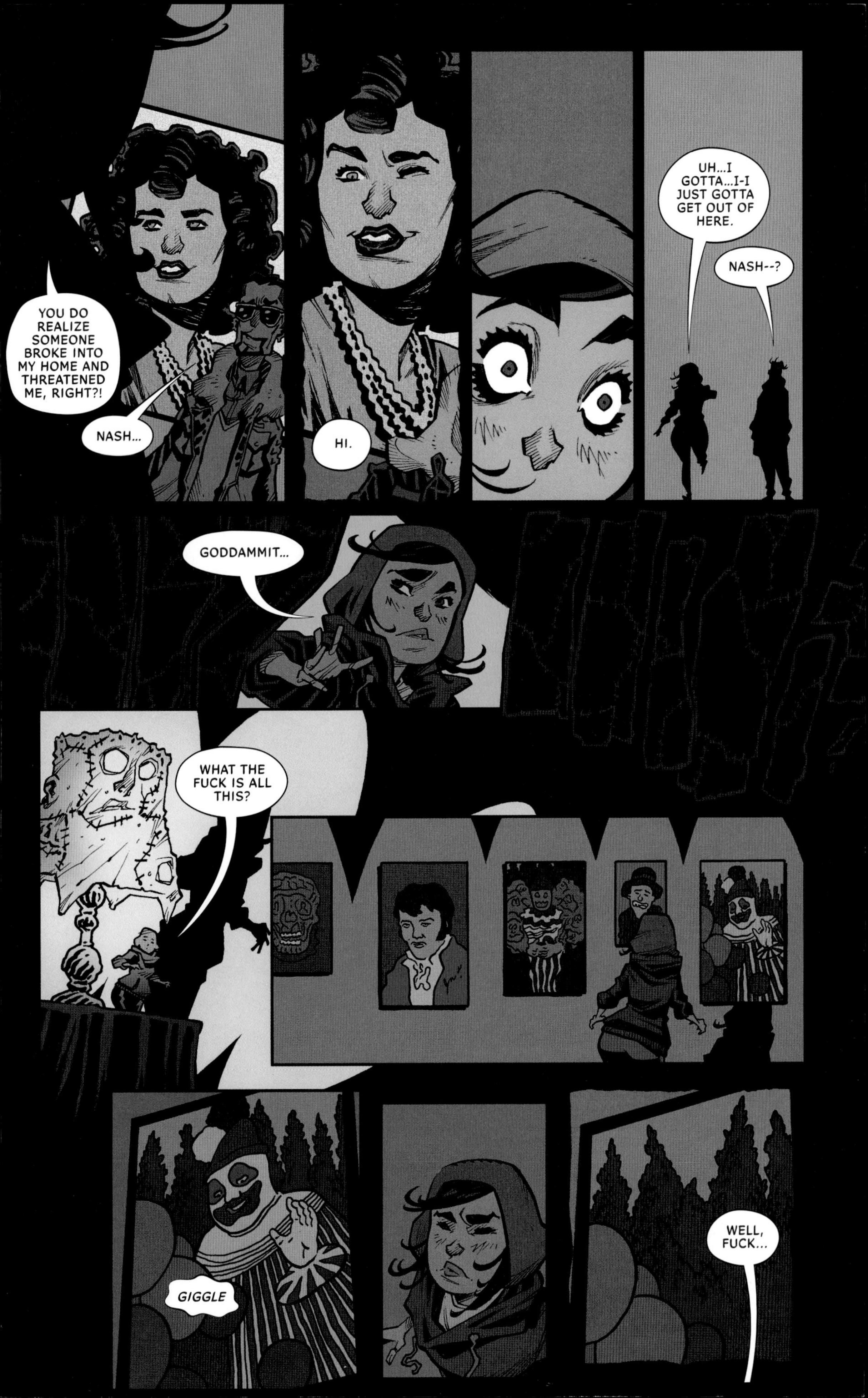
YOU DO REALIZE SOMEONE BROKE INTO MY HOME AND THREATENED ME, RIGHT?!
NASH...
HI.
UH...I GOTTA...I-I JUST GOTTA GET OUT OF HERE.
NASH--?
GODDAMMIT...
WHAT THE FUCK IS ALL THIS?
GIGGLE
WELL, FUCK...

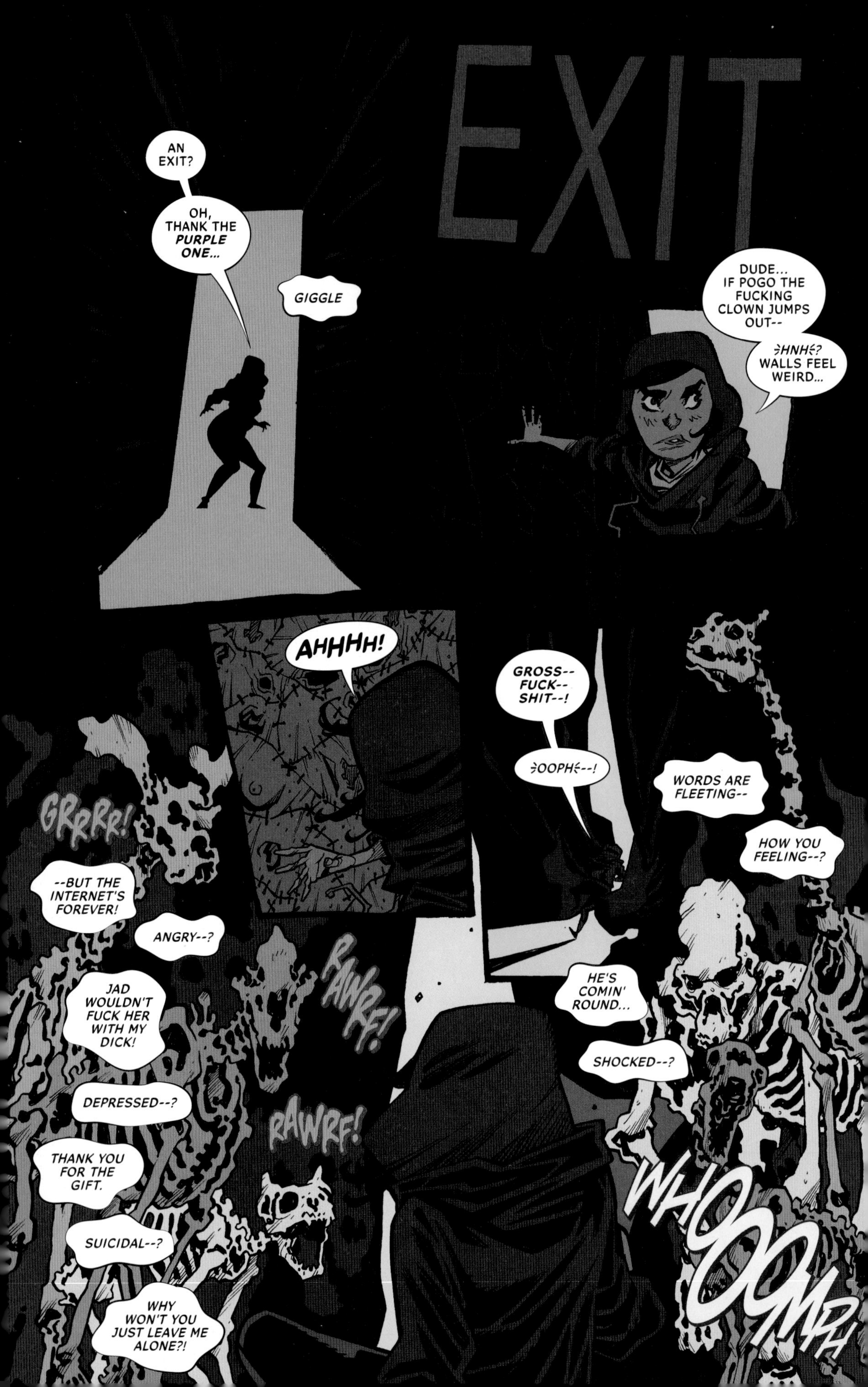
EXIT
AN EXIT?
OH, THANK THE PURPLE ONE...
GIGGLE
DUDE... IF POGO THE FUCKING CLOWN JUMPS OUT--
HNH? WALLS FEEL WEIRD...
AHHHH!
GROSS-- FUCK-- SHIT--!
OOPH--!
WORDS ARE FLEETING--
HOW YOU FEELING--?
GRRRR!
--BUT THE INTERNET'S FOREVER!
ANGRY--?
RAWRF!
JAD WOULDN'T FUCK HER WITH MY DICK!
DEPRESSED--?
RAWRF!
THANK YOU FOR THE GIFT.
SUICIDAL--?
WHY WON'T YOU JUST LEAVE ME ALONE?!
HE'S COMIN' ROUND...
SHOCKED--?
WHOOOMPH

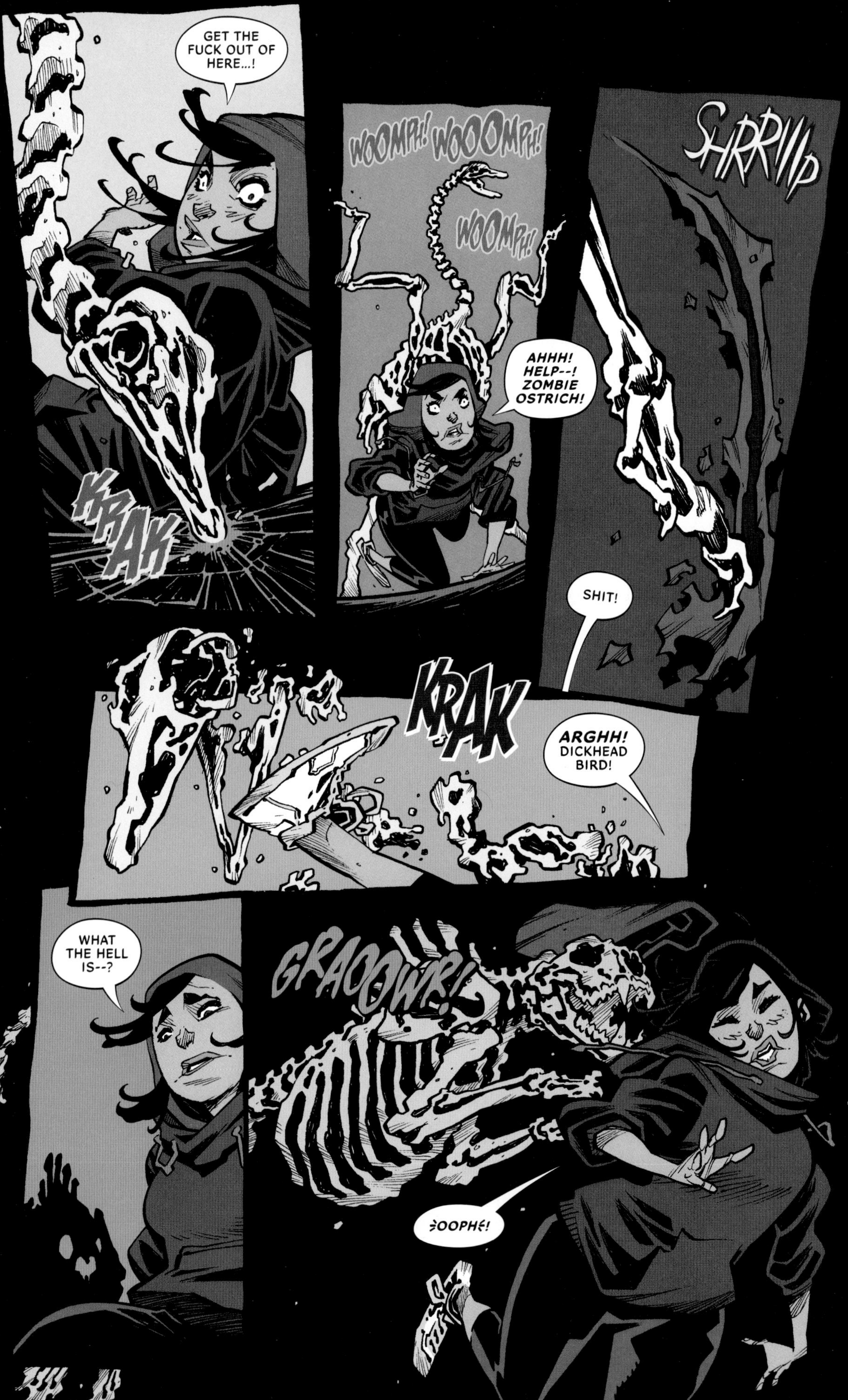
GET THE FUCK OUT OF HERE...!
KRAK
WOOMPH! WOOOMPH!
WOOMPH!
AHHH! HELP--! ZOMBIE OSTRICH!
SHRRIIP
SHIT!
KRAK
ARGHH! DICKHEAD BIRD!
WHAT THE HELL IS--?
GRAOOWR!
OOPH!

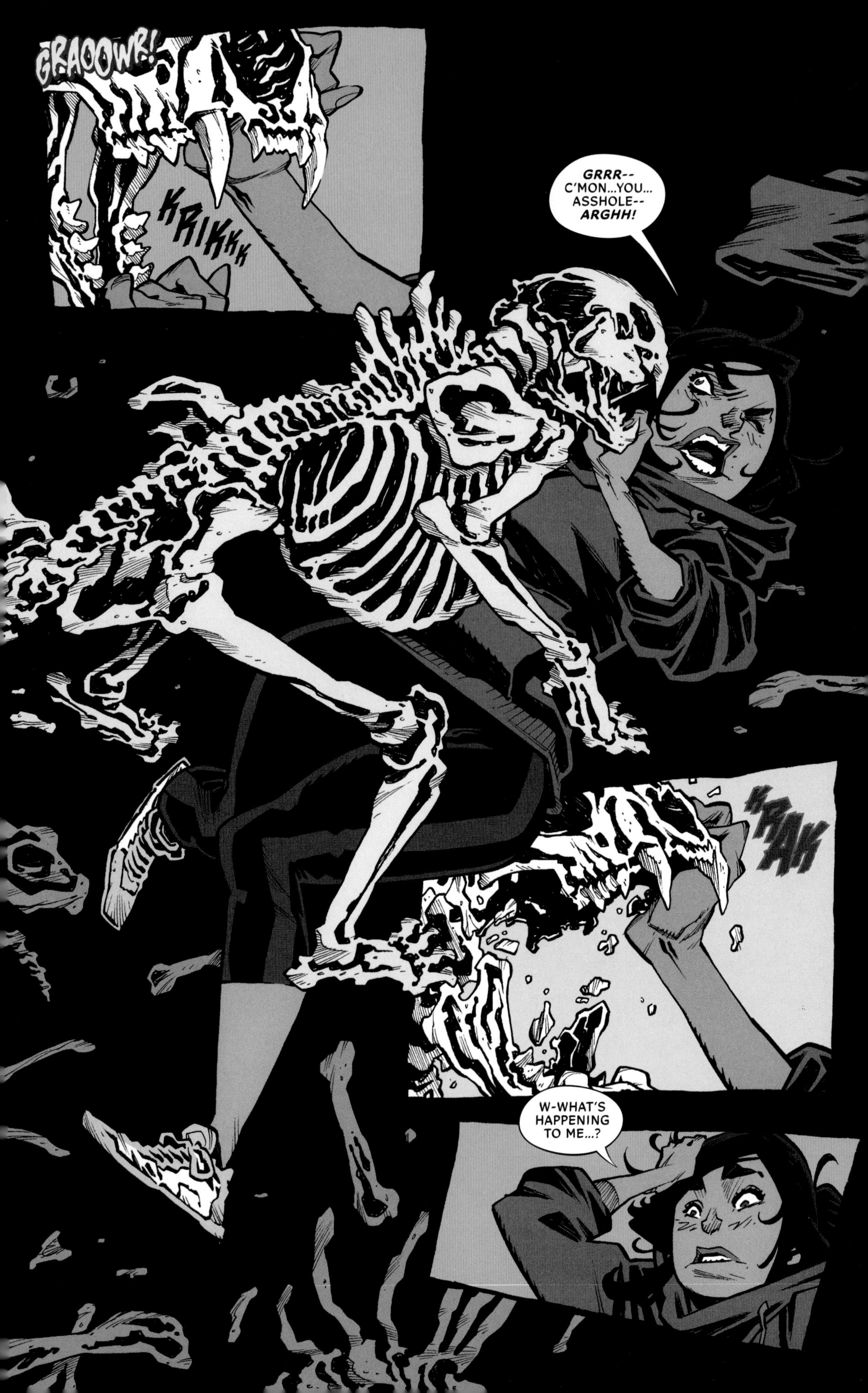
GRAOOWR!
KRIKKK
GRRR-- C'MON...YOU... ASSHOLE-- ARGHH!
KRAK
W-WHAT'S HAPPENING TO ME...?

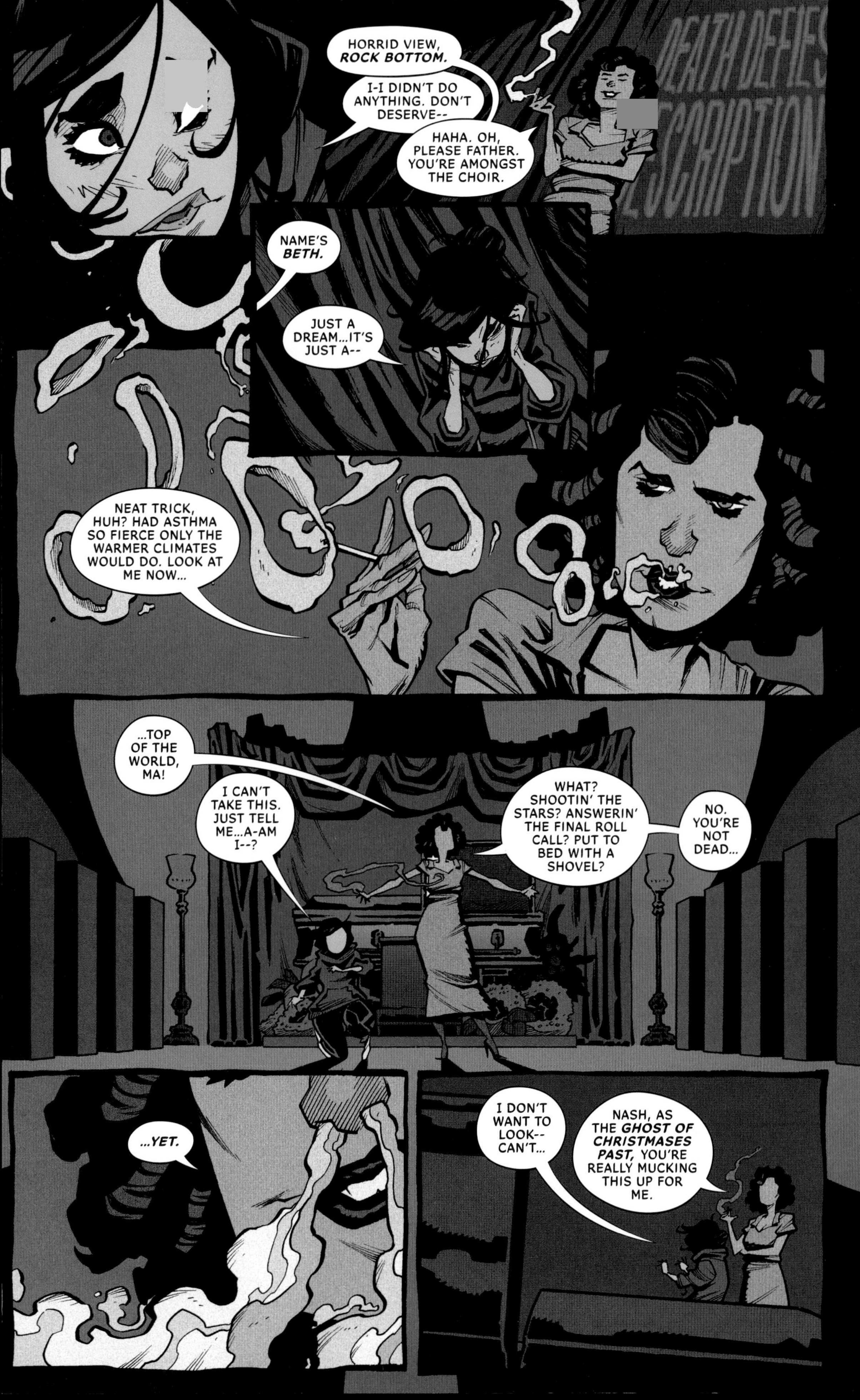
HORRID VIEW, **ROCK BOTTOM.**
I-I DIDN'T DO ANYTHING. DON'T DESERVE--
HAHA. OH, PLEASE FATHER. YOU'RE AMONGST THE CHOIR.
DEATH DEFIES
NAME'S **BETH.**
JUST A DREAM...IT'S JUST A--
NEAT TRICK, HUH? HAD ASTHMA SO FIERCE ONLY THE WARMER CLIMATES WOULD DO. LOOK AT ME NOW...
...TOP OF THE WORLD, MA!
I CAN'T TAKE THIS. JUST TELL ME...A-AM I--?
WHAT? SHOOTIN' THE STARS? ANSWERIN' THE FINAL ROLL CALL? PUT TO BED WITH A SHOVEL?
NO. YOU'RE NOT DEAD...
...YET.
I DON'T WANT TO LOOK-- CAN'T...
NASH, AS THE ***GHOST OF CHRISTMASES PAST,*** YOU'RE REALLY MUCKING THIS UP FOR ME.

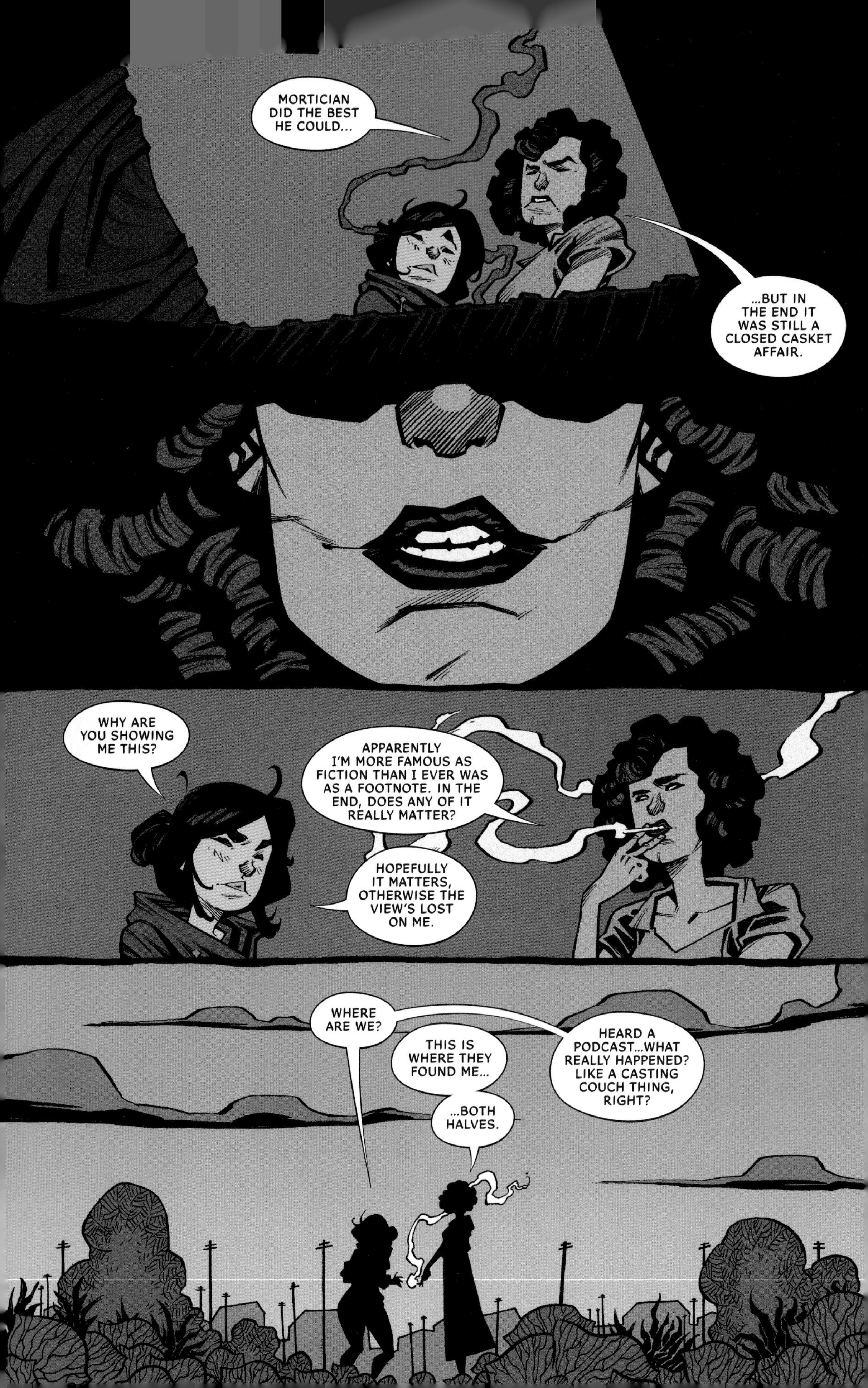
MORTICIAN DID THE BEST HE COULD...
...BUT IN THE END IT WAS STILL A CLOSED CASKET AFFAIR.
WHY ARE YOU SHOWING ME THIS?
APPARENTLY I'M MORE FAMOUS AS FICTION THAN I EVER WAS AS A FOOTNOTE. IN THE END, DOES ANY OF IT REALLY MATTER?
HOPEFULLY IT MATTERS, OTHERWISE THE VIEW'S LOST ON ME.
WHERE ARE WE?
THIS IS WHERE THEY FOUND ME...
...BOTH HALVES.
HEARD A PODCAST...WHAT REALLY HAPPENED? LIKE A CASTING COUCH THING, RIGHT?

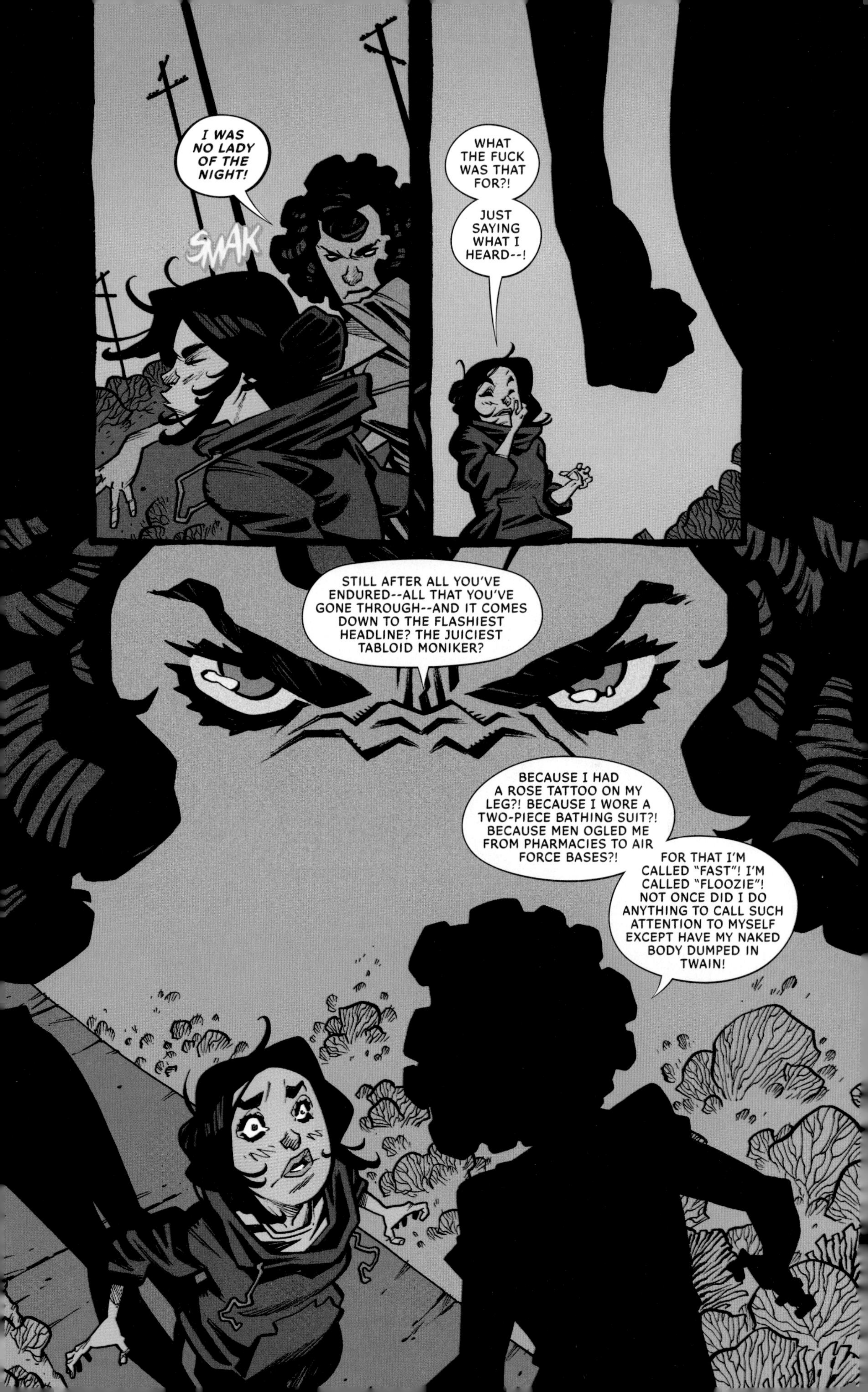
I WAS NO LADY OF THE NIGHT!
SMAK
WHAT THE FUCK WAS THAT FOR?!
JUST SAYING WHAT I HEARD--!
STILL AFTER ALL YOU'VE ENDURED--ALL THAT YOU'VE GONE THROUGH--AND IT COMES DOWN TO THE FLASHIEST HEADLINE? THE JUICIEST TABLOID MONIKER?
BECAUSE I HAD A ROSE TATTOO ON MY LEG?! BECAUSE I WORE A TWO-PIECE BATHING SUIT?! BECAUSE MEN OGLED ME FROM PHARMACIES TO AIR FORCE BASES?!
FOR THAT I'M CALLED "FAST"! I'M CALLED "FLOOZIE"! NOT ONCE DID I DO ANYTHING TO CALL SUCH ATTENTION TO MYSELF EXCEPT HAVE MY NAKED BODY DUMPED IN TWAIN!

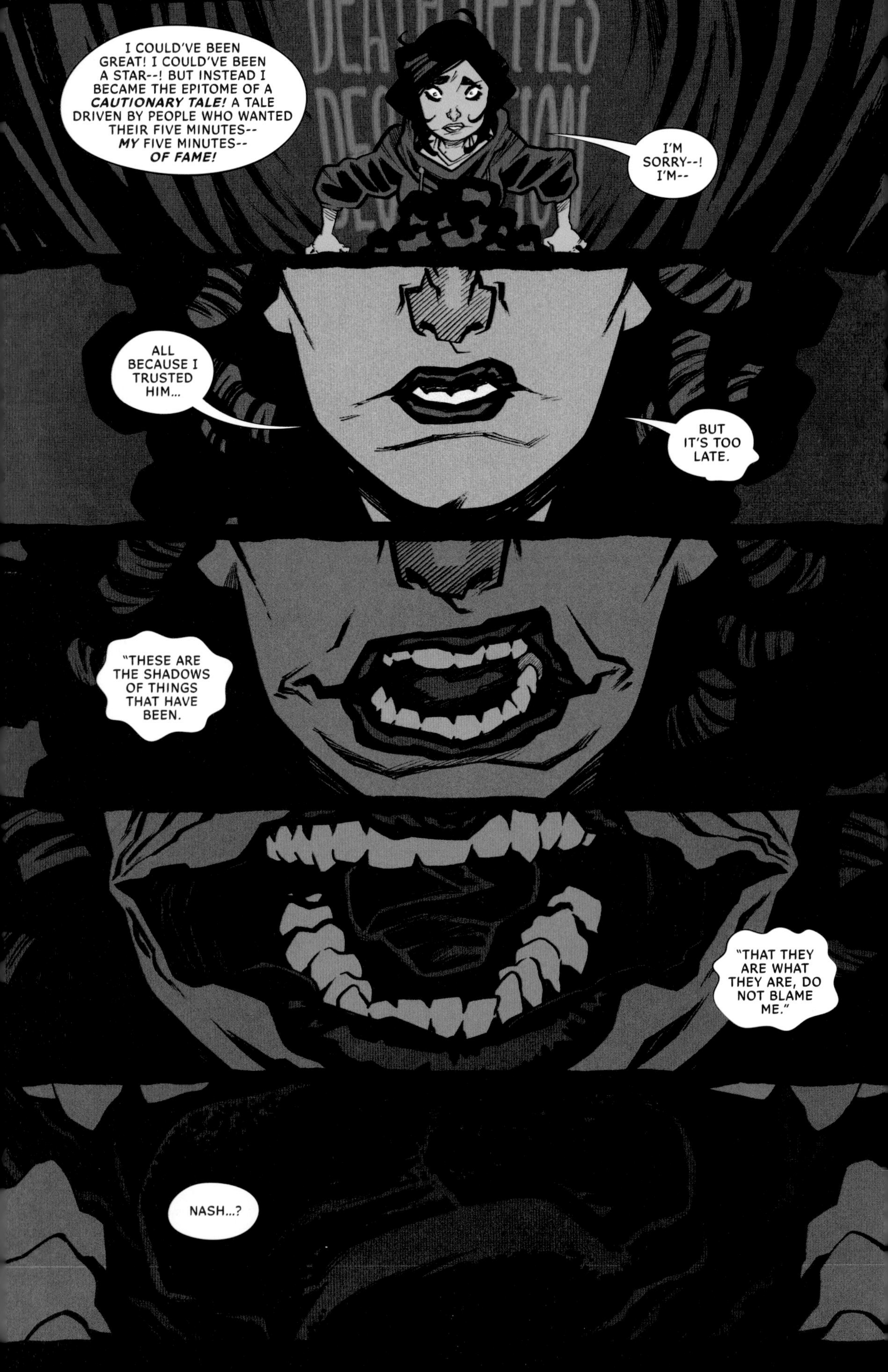
I COULD'VE BEEN GREAT! I COULD'VE BEEN A STAR--! BUT INSTEAD I BECAME THE EPITOME OF A ***CAUTIONARY TALE!*** A TALE DRIVEN BY PEOPLE WHO WANTED THEIR FIVE MINUTES-- ***MY*** FIVE MINUTES-- ***OF FAME!***
I'M SORRY--! I'M--
ALL BECAUSE I TRUSTED HIM...
BUT IT'S TOO LATE.
"THESE ARE THE SHADOWS OF THINGS THAT HAVE BEEN.
"THAT THEY ARE WHAT THEY ARE, DO NOT BLAME ME."
NASH...?

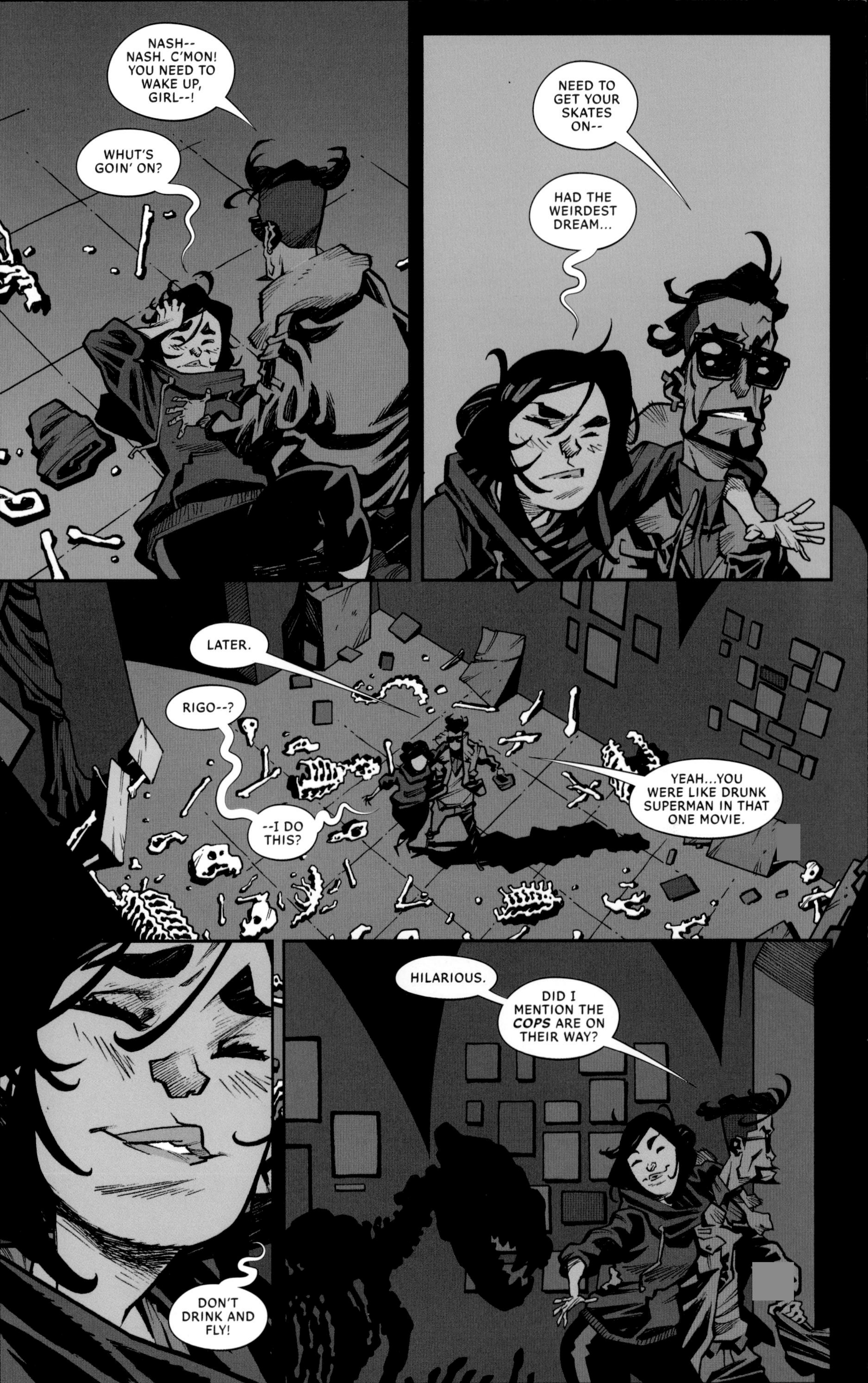
NASH-- NASH. C'MON! YOU NEED TO WAKE UP, GIRL--!
WHUT'S GOIN' ON?
NEED TO GET YOUR SKATES ON--
HAD THE WEIRDEST DREAM...
LATER.
RIGO--?
--I DO THIS?
YEAH...YOU WERE LIKE DRUNK SUPERMAN IN THAT ONE MOVIE.
DON'T DRINK AND FLY!
HILARIOUS.
DID I MENTION THE *COPS* ARE ON THEIR WAY?

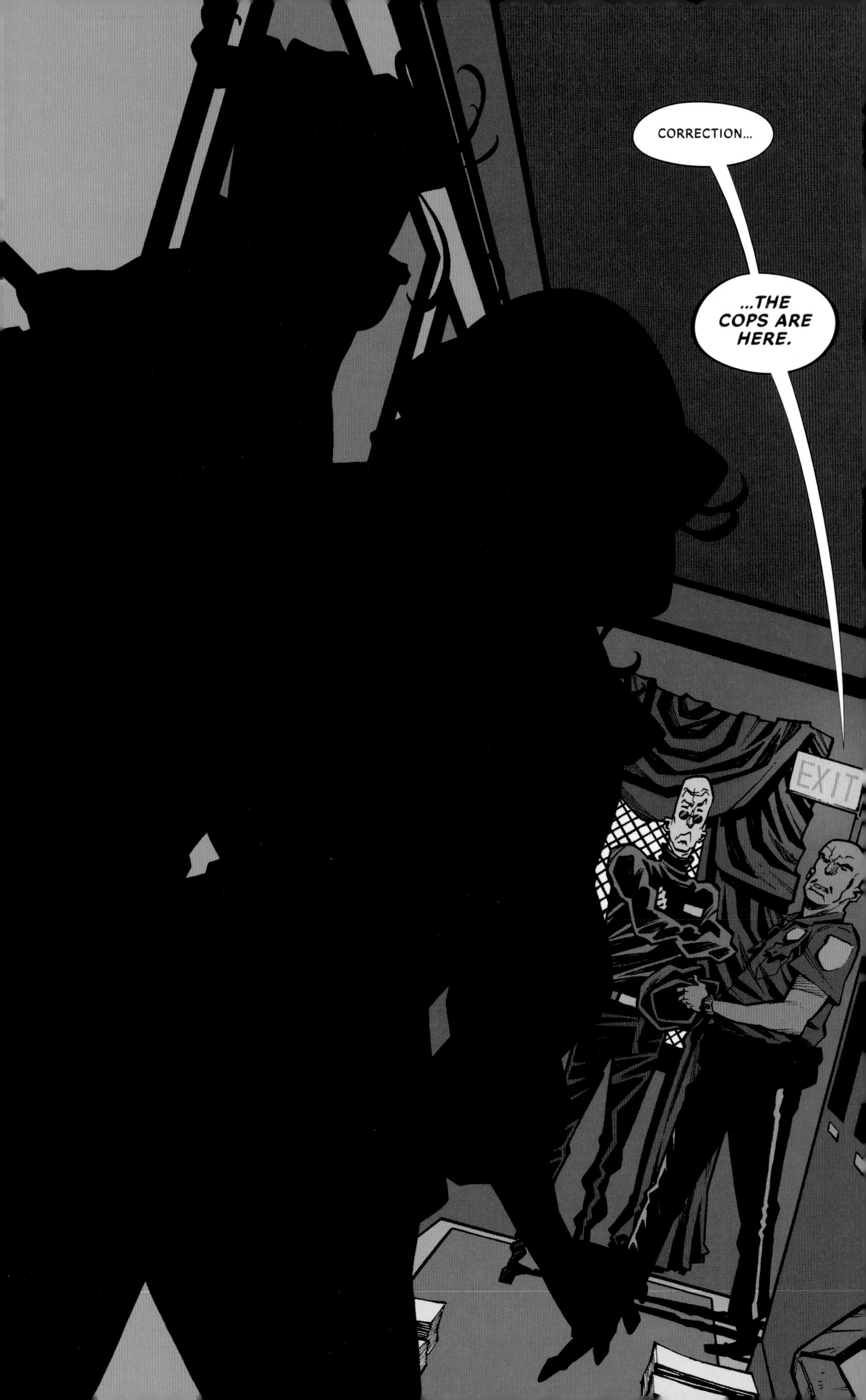
CORRECTION...
...THE COPS ARE HERE.
EXIT

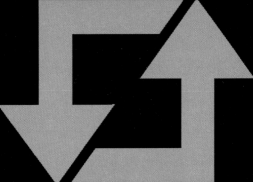

CHAPTER FOUR

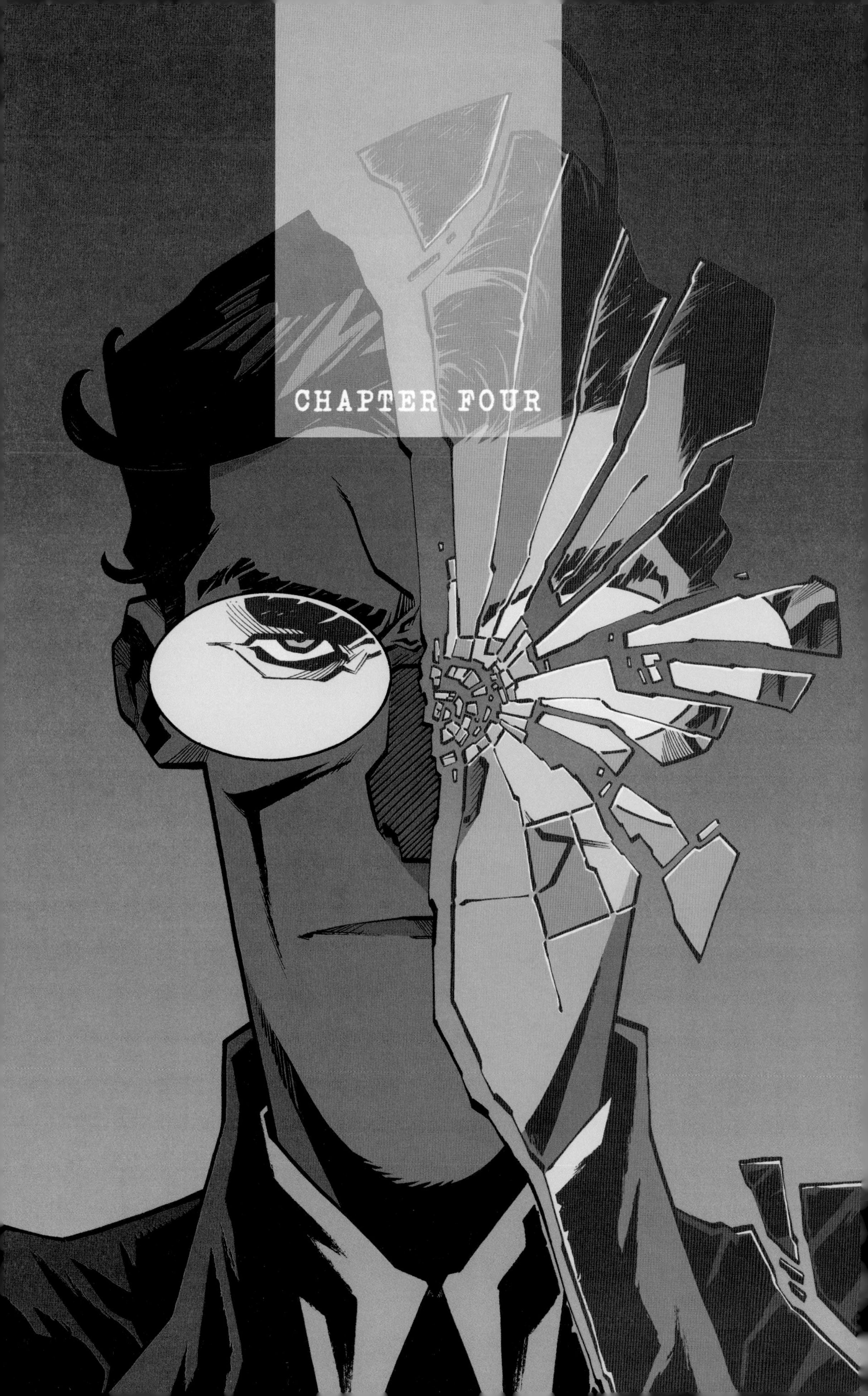

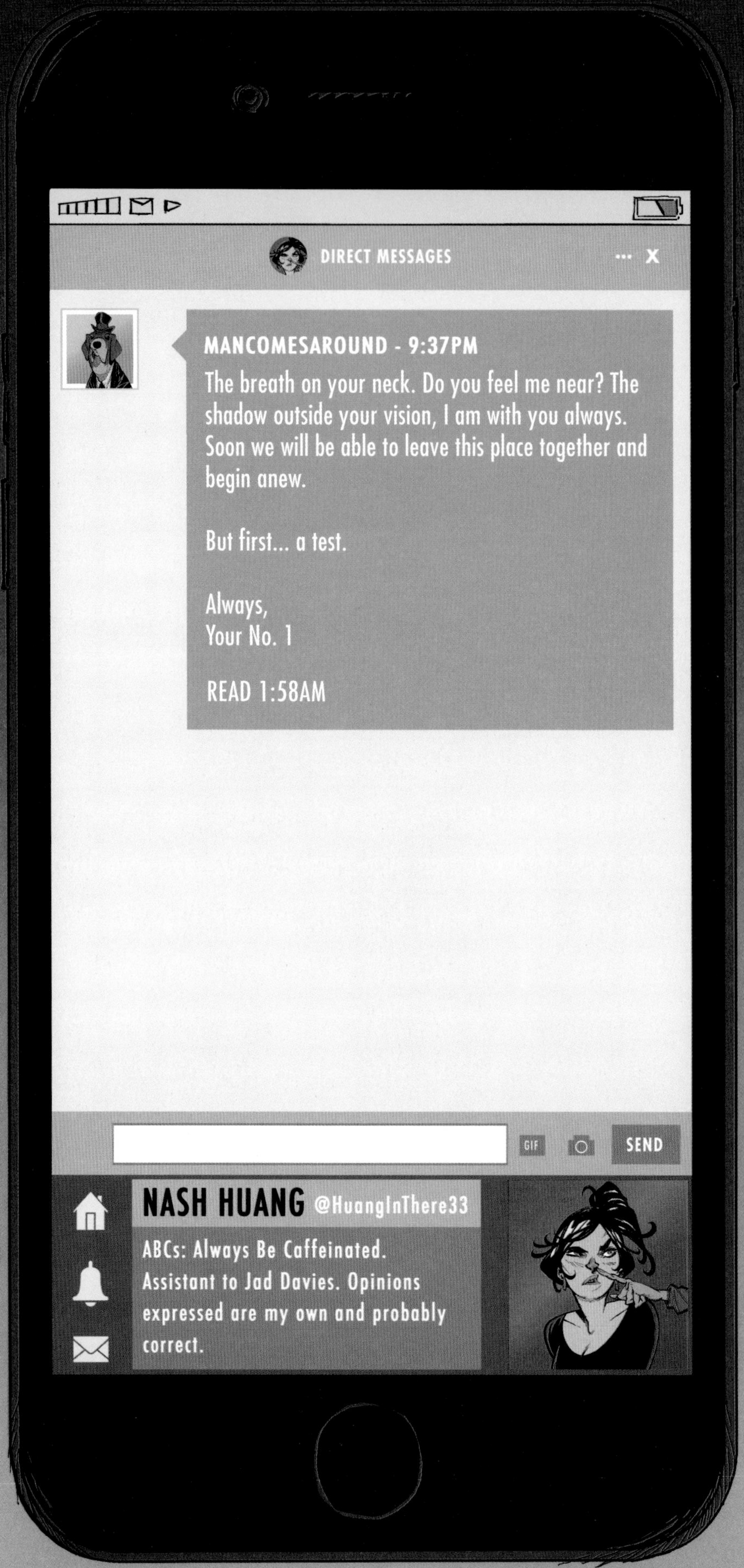
DIRECT MESSAGES
MANCOMESAROUND - 9:37PM
The breath on your neck. Do you feel me near? The shadow outside your vision, I am with you always. Soon we will be able to leave this place together and begin anew.
But first... a test.
Always,
Your No. 1
READ 1:58AM
GIF
SEND
NASH HUANG @HuangInThere33
ABCs: Always Be Caffeinated. Assistant to Jad Davies. Opinions expressed are my own and probably correct.

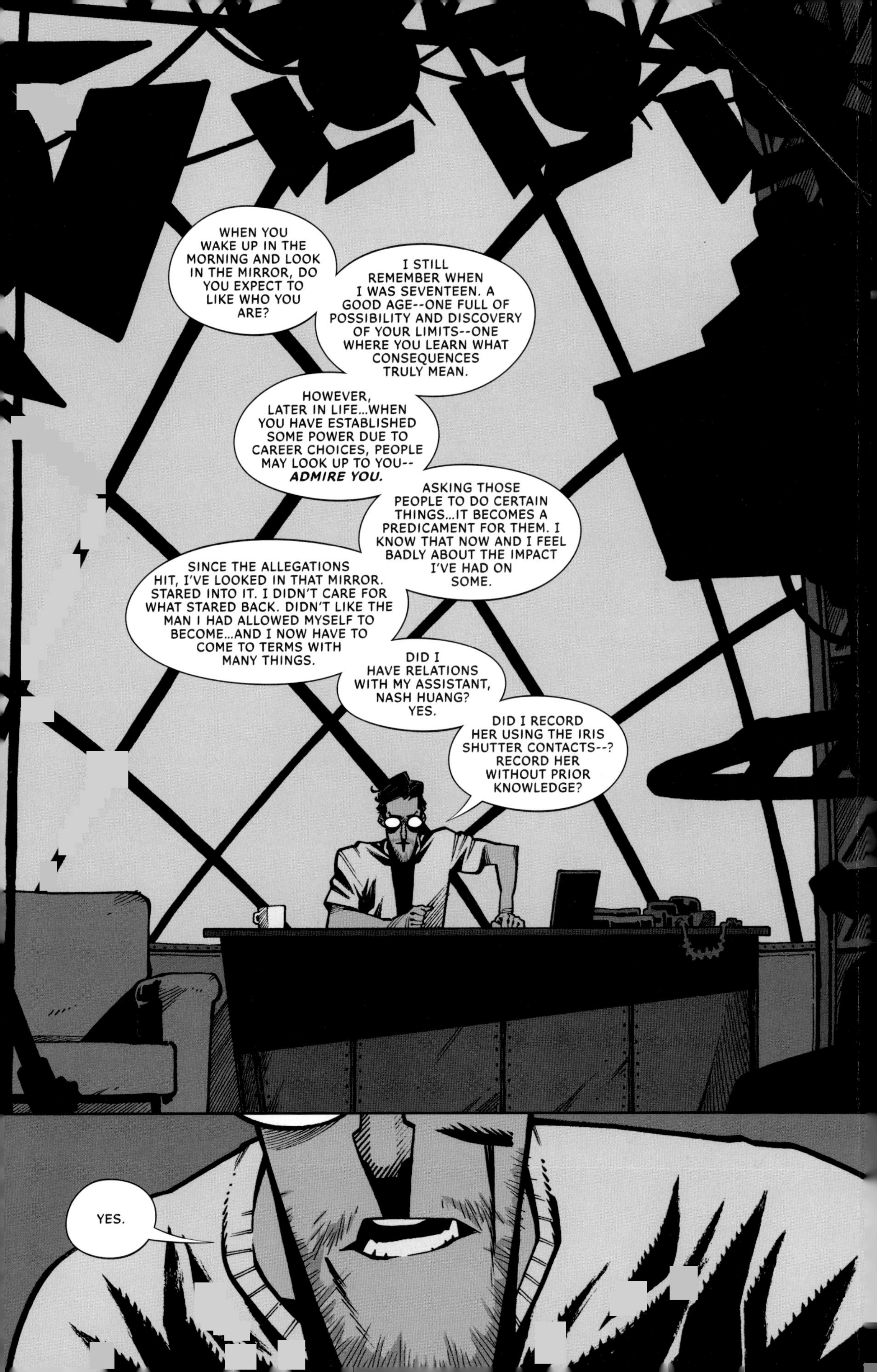
WHEN YOU WAKE UP IN THE MORNING AND LOOK IN THE MIRROR, DO YOU EXPECT TO LIKE WHO YOU ARE?
I STILL REMEMBER WHEN I WAS SEVENTEEN. A GOOD AGE--ONE FULL OF POSSIBILITY AND DISCOVERY OF YOUR LIMITS--ONE WHERE YOU LEARN WHAT CONSEQUENCES TRULY MEAN.
HOWEVER, LATER IN LIFE...WHEN YOU HAVE ESTABLISHED SOME POWER DUE TO CAREER CHOICES, PEOPLE MAY LOOK UP TO YOU-- *ADMIRE YOU.*
ASKING THOSE PEOPLE TO DO CERTAIN THINGS...IT BECOMES A PREDICAMENT FOR THEM. I KNOW THAT NOW AND I FEEL BADLY ABOUT THE IMPACT I'VE HAD ON SOME.
SINCE THE ALLEGATIONS HIT, I'VE LOOKED IN THAT MIRROR. STARED INTO IT. I DIDN'T CARE FOR WHAT STARED BACK. DIDN'T LIKE THE MAN I HAD ALLOWED MYSELF TO BECOME...AND I NOW HAVE TO COME TO TERMS WITH MANY THINGS.
DID I HAVE RELATIONS WITH MY ASSISTANT, NASH HUANG? YES.
DID I RECORD HER USING THE IRIS SHUTTER CONTACTS--? RECORD HER WITHOUT PRIOR KNOWLEDGE?
YES.

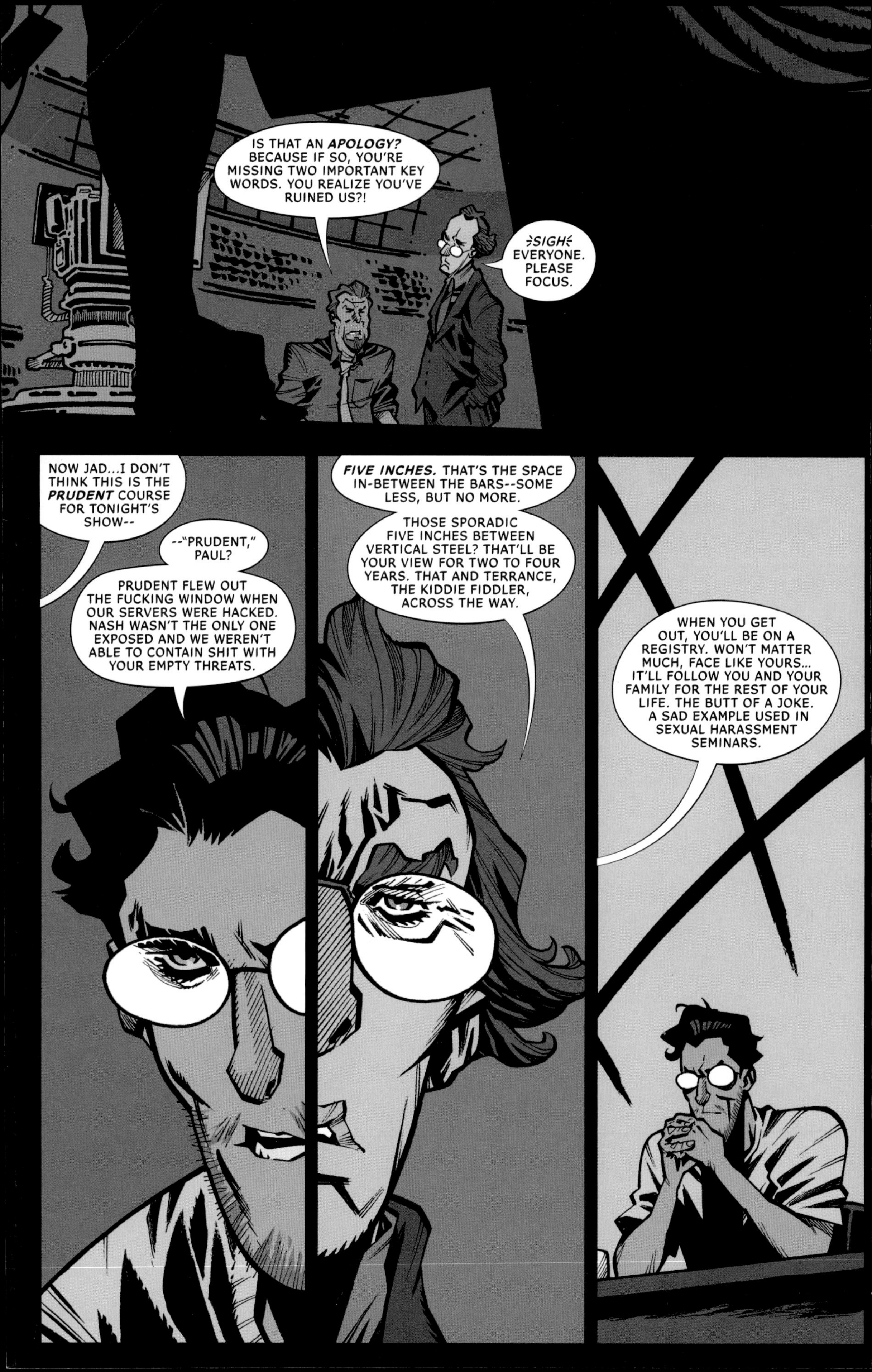
IS THAT AN *APOLOGY?* BECAUSE IF SO, YOU'RE MISSING TWO IMPORTANT KEY WORDS. YOU REALIZE YOU'VE RUINED US?!
SIGH EVERYONE. PLEASE FOCUS.
NOW JAD...I DON'T THINK THIS IS THE *PRUDENT* COURSE FOR TONIGHT'S SHOW--
--"PRUDENT," PAUL?
PRUDENT FLEW OUT THE FUCKING WINDOW WHEN OUR SERVERS WERE HACKED. NASH WASN'T THE ONLY ONE EXPOSED AND WE WEREN'T ABLE TO CONTAIN SHIT WITH YOUR EMPTY THREATS.
FIVE INCHES. THAT'S THE SPACE IN-BETWEEN THE BARS--SOME LESS, BUT NO MORE.
THOSE SPORADIC FIVE INCHES BETWEEN VERTICAL STEEL? THAT'LL BE YOUR VIEW FOR TWO TO FOUR YEARS. THAT AND TERRANCE, THE KIDDIE FIDDLER, ACROSS THE WAY.
WHEN YOU GET OUT, YOU'LL BE ON A REGISTRY. WON'T MATTER MUCH, FACE LIKE YOURS... IT'LL FOLLOW YOU AND YOUR FAMILY FOR THE REST OF YOUR LIFE. THE BUTT OF A JOKE. A SAD EXAMPLE USED IN SEXUAL HARASSMENT SEMINARS.

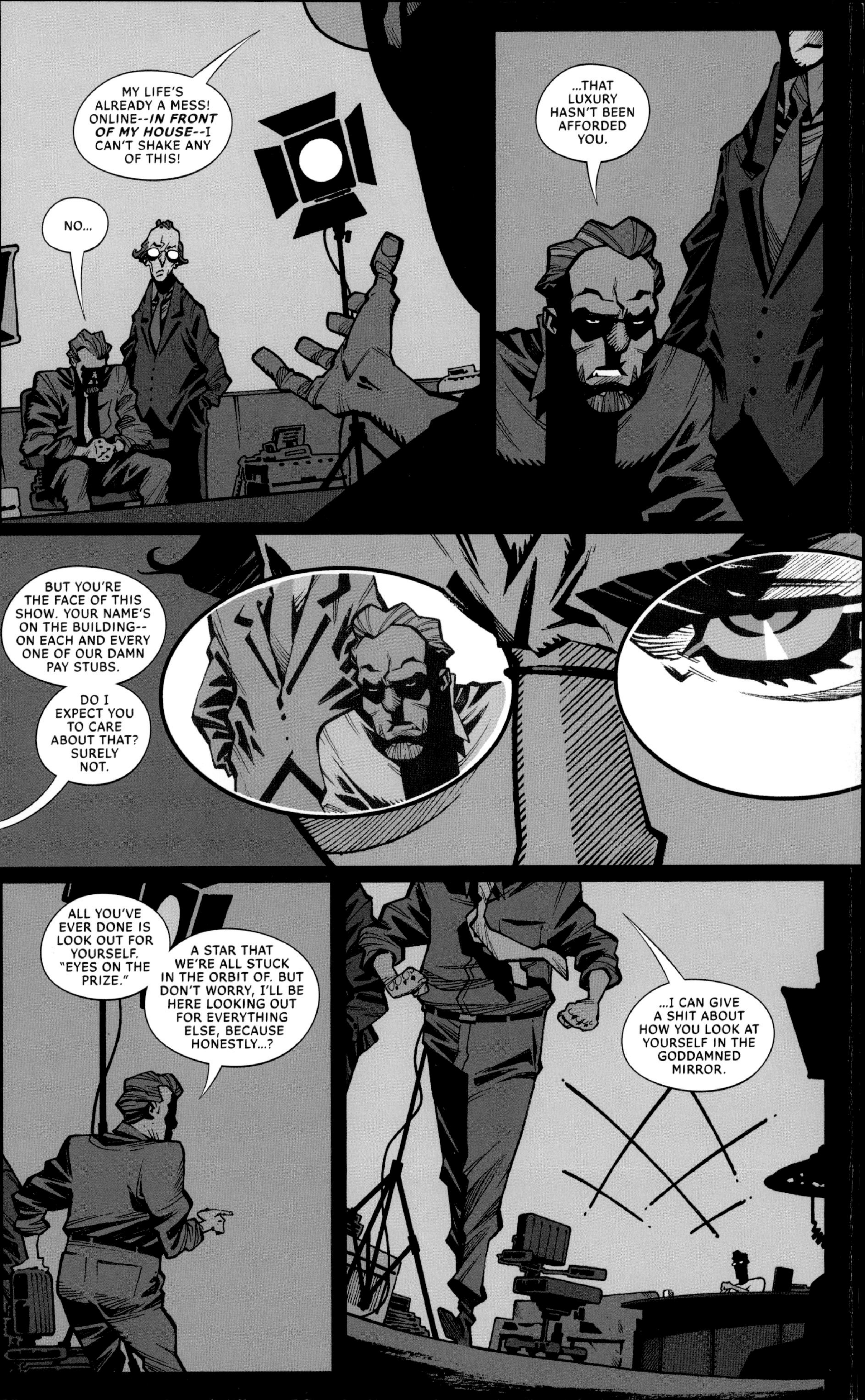
MY LIFE'S ALREADY A MESS! ONLINE--*IN FRONT OF MY HOUSE*--I CAN'T SHAKE ANY OF THIS!
NO...
...THAT LUXURY HASN'T BEEN AFFORDED YOU.
BUT YOU'RE THE FACE OF THIS SHOW. YOUR NAME'S ON THE BUILDING--ON EACH AND EVERY ONE OF OUR DAMN PAY STUBS.
DO I EXPECT YOU TO CARE ABOUT THAT? SURELY NOT.
ALL YOU'VE EVER DONE IS LOOK OUT FOR YOURSELF. "EYES ON THE PRIZE."
A STAR THAT WE'RE ALL STUCK IN THE ORBIT OF. BUT DON'T WORRY, I'LL BE HERE LOOKING OUT FOR EVERYTHING ELSE, BECAUSE HONESTLY...?
...I CAN GIVE A SHIT ABOUT HOW YOU LOOK AT YOURSELF IN THE GODDAMNED MIRROR.

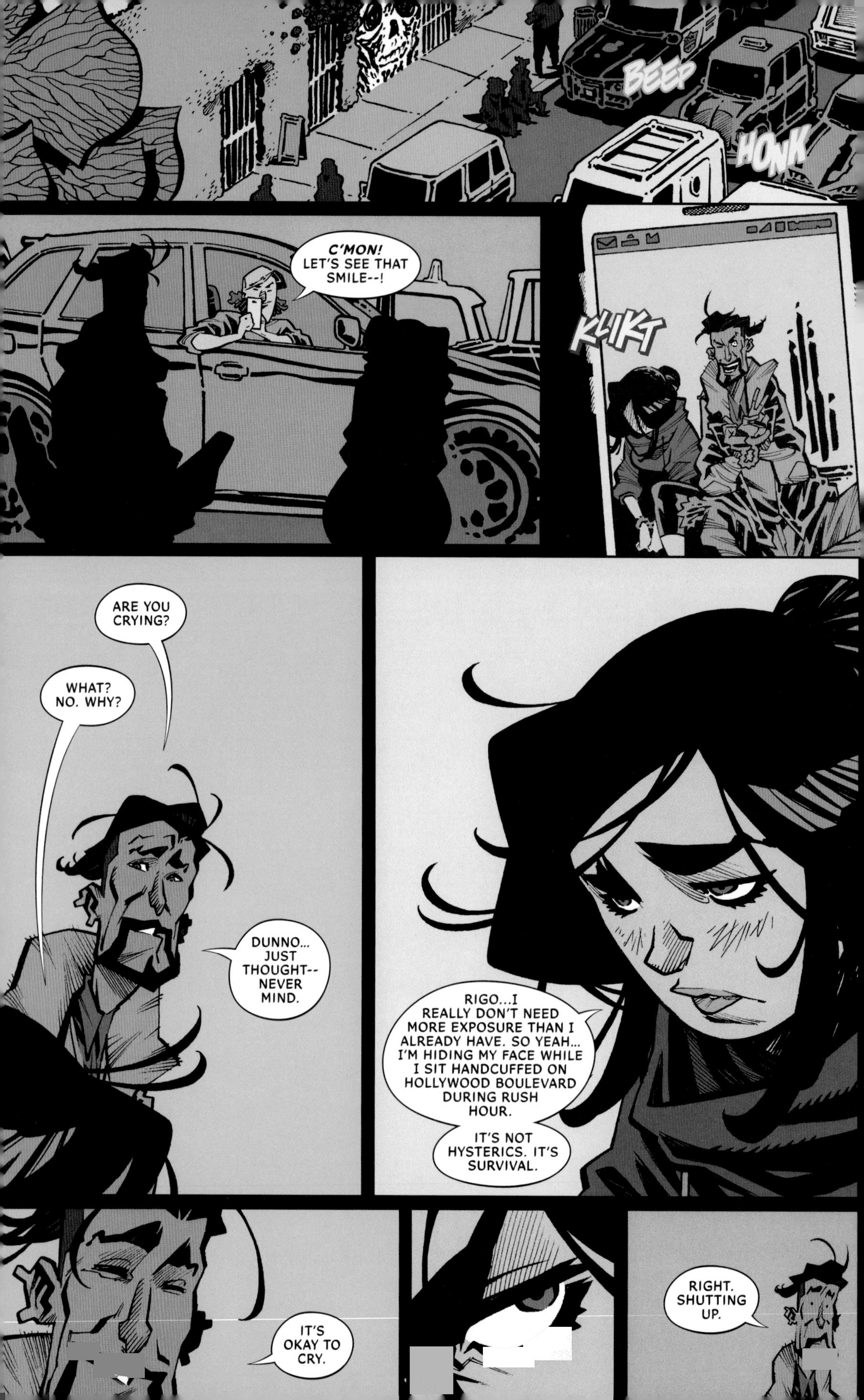
BEEP
HONK
C'MON! LET'S SEE THAT SMILE--!
KLIKT
ARE YOU CRYING?
WHAT? NO. WHY?
DUNNO... JUST THOUGHT-- NEVER MIND.
RIGO...I REALLY DON'T NEED MORE EXPOSURE THAN I ALREADY HAVE. SO YEAH... I'M HIDING MY FACE WHILE I SIT HANDCUFFED ON HOLLYWOOD BOULEVARD DURING RUSH HOUR.
IT'S NOT HYSTERICS. IT'S SURVIVAL.
IT'S OKAY TO CRY.
RIGHT. SHUTTING UP.

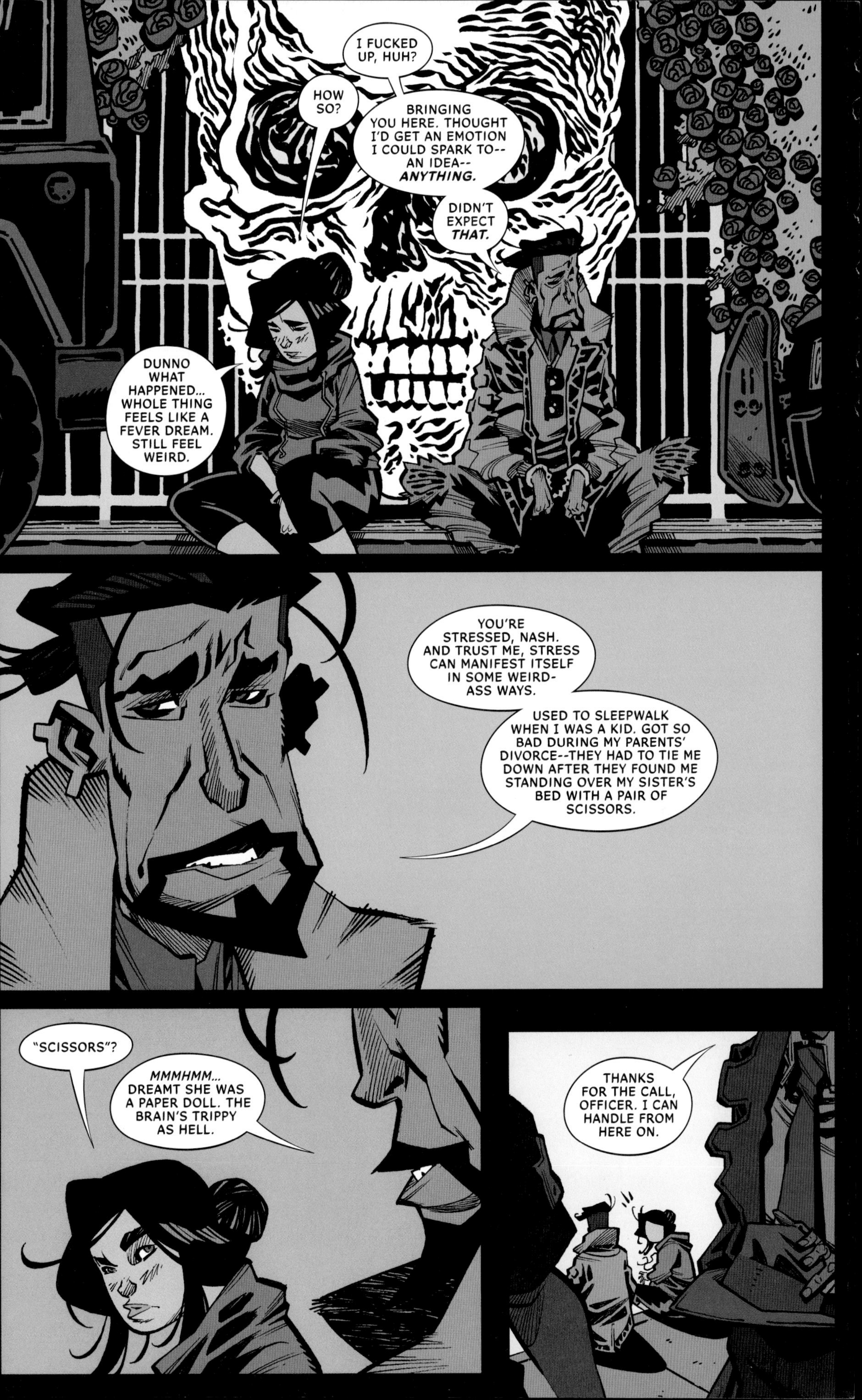
I FUCKED UP, HUH?
HOW SO?
BRINGING YOU HERE. THOUGHT I'D GET AN EMOTION I COULD SPARK TO-- AN IDEA-- *ANYTHING.*
DIDN'T EXPECT *THAT.*
DUNNO WHAT HAPPENED... WHOLE THING FEELS LIKE A FEVER DREAM. STILL FEEL WEIRD.
YOU'RE STRESSED, NASH. AND TRUST ME, STRESS CAN MANIFEST ITSELF IN SOME WEIRD-ASS WAYS.
USED TO SLEEPWALK WHEN I WAS A KID. GOT SO BAD DURING MY PARENTS' DIVORCE--THEY HAD TO TIE ME DOWN AFTER THEY FOUND ME STANDING OVER MY SISTER'S BED WITH A PAIR OF SCISSORS.
"SCISSORS"?
MMMHMM... DREAMT SHE WAS A PAPER DOLL. THE BRAIN'S TRIPPY AS HELL.
THANKS FOR THE CALL, OFFICER. I CAN HANDLE FROM HERE ON.

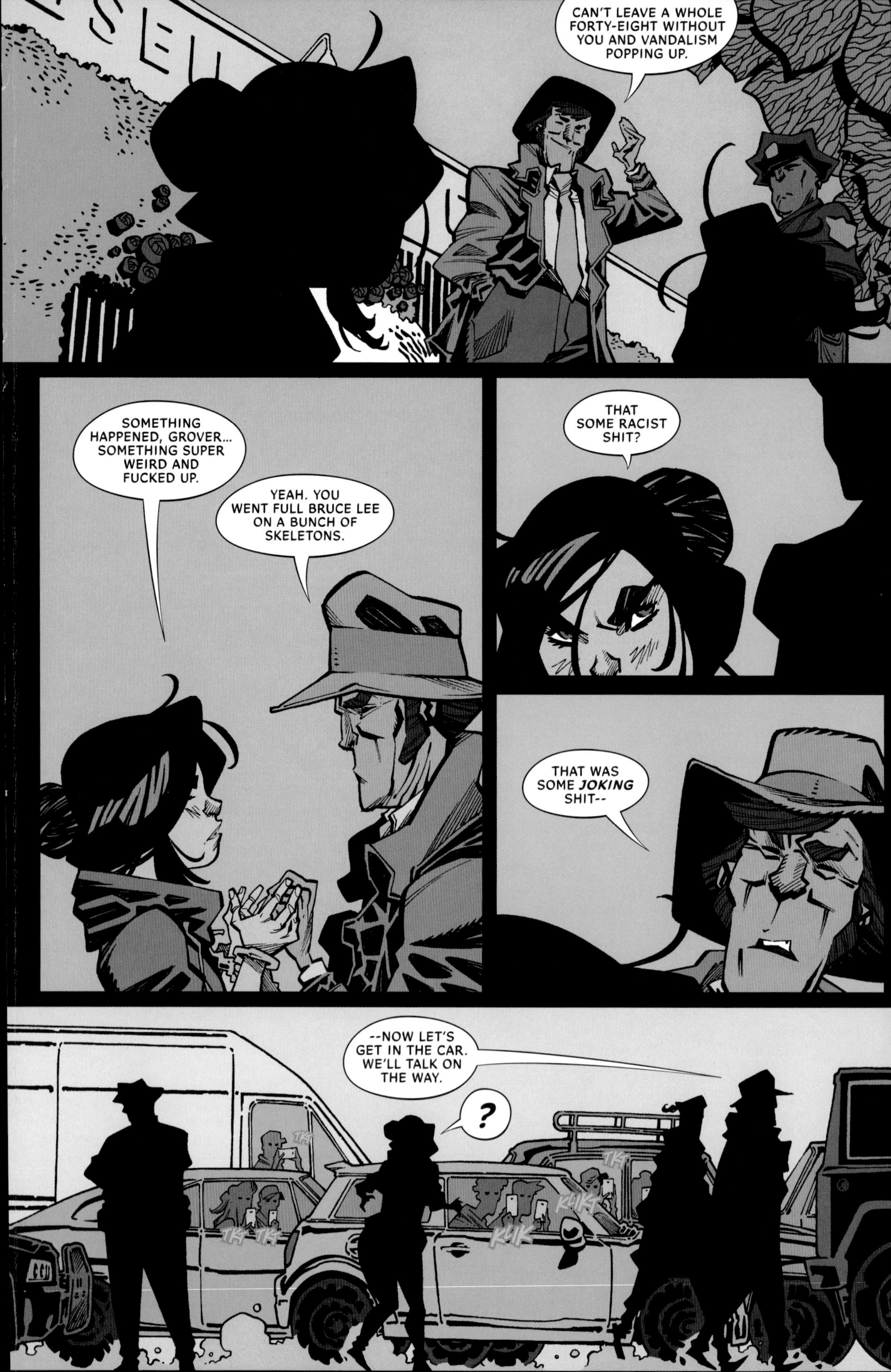
CAN'T LEAVE A WHOLE FORTY-EIGHT WITHOUT YOU AND VANDALISM POPPING UP.
SOMETHING HAPPENED, GROVER... SOMETHING SUPER WEIRD AND FUCKED UP.
YEAH. YOU WENT FULL BRUCE LEE ON A BUNCH OF SKELETONS.
THAT SOME RACIST SHIT?
THAT WAS SOME *JOKING* SHIT--
--NOW LET'S GET IN THE CAR. WE'LL TALK ON THE WAY.
?

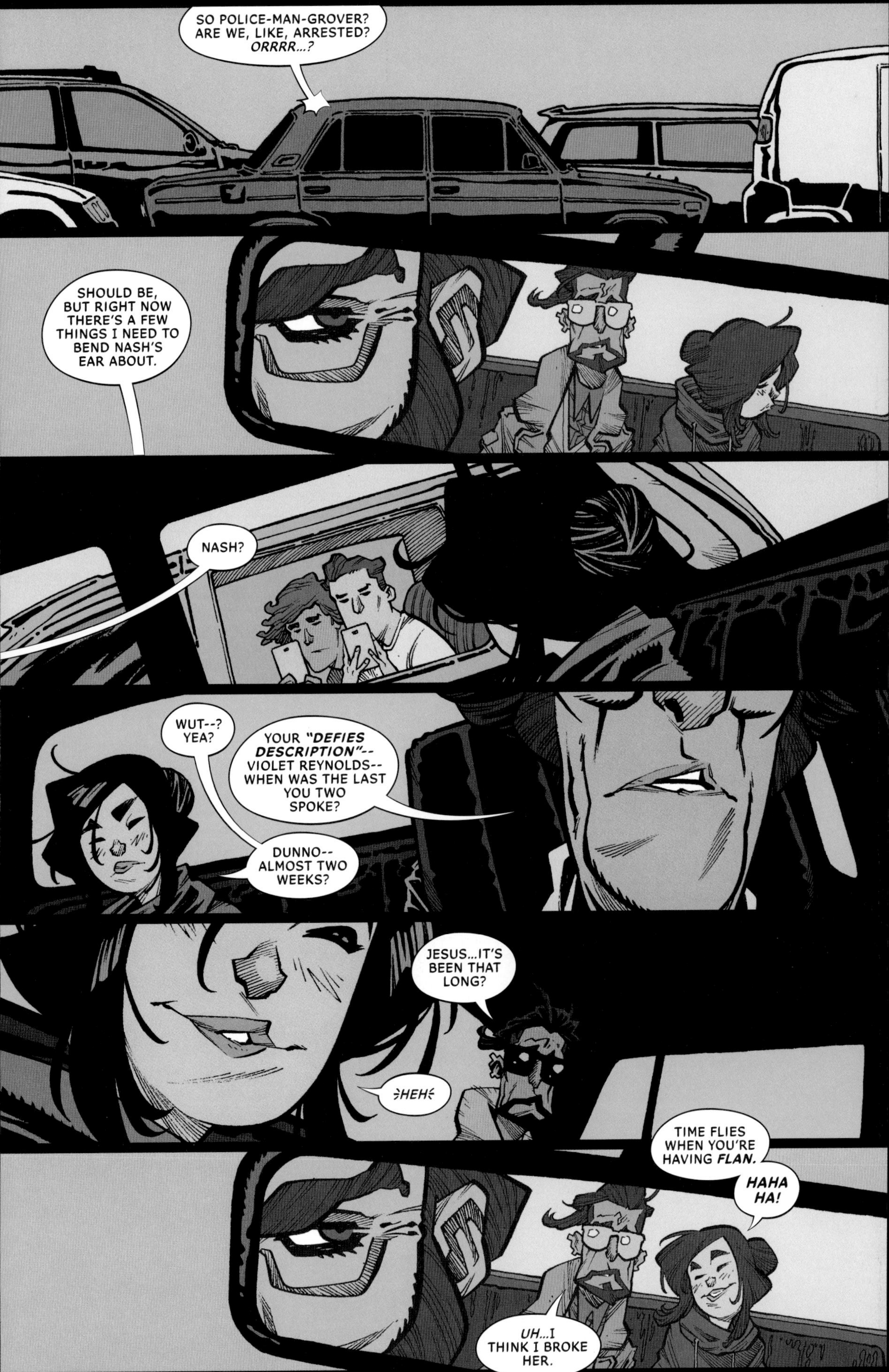
SO POLICE-MAN-GROVER? ARE WE, LIKE, ARRESTED? *ORRRR...?*
SHOULD BE, BUT RIGHT NOW THERE'S A FEW THINGS I NEED TO BEND NASH'S EAR ABOUT.
NASH?
WUT--? YEA?
YOUR ***"DEFIES DESCRIPTION"***-- VIOLET REYNOLDS-- WHEN WAS THE LAST YOU TWO SPOKE?
DUNNO-- ALMOST TWO WEEKS?
JESUS...IT'S BEEN THAT LONG?
HEH
TIME FLIES WHEN YOU'RE HAVING ***FLAN.***
HAHA HA!
UH...I THINK I BROKE HER.

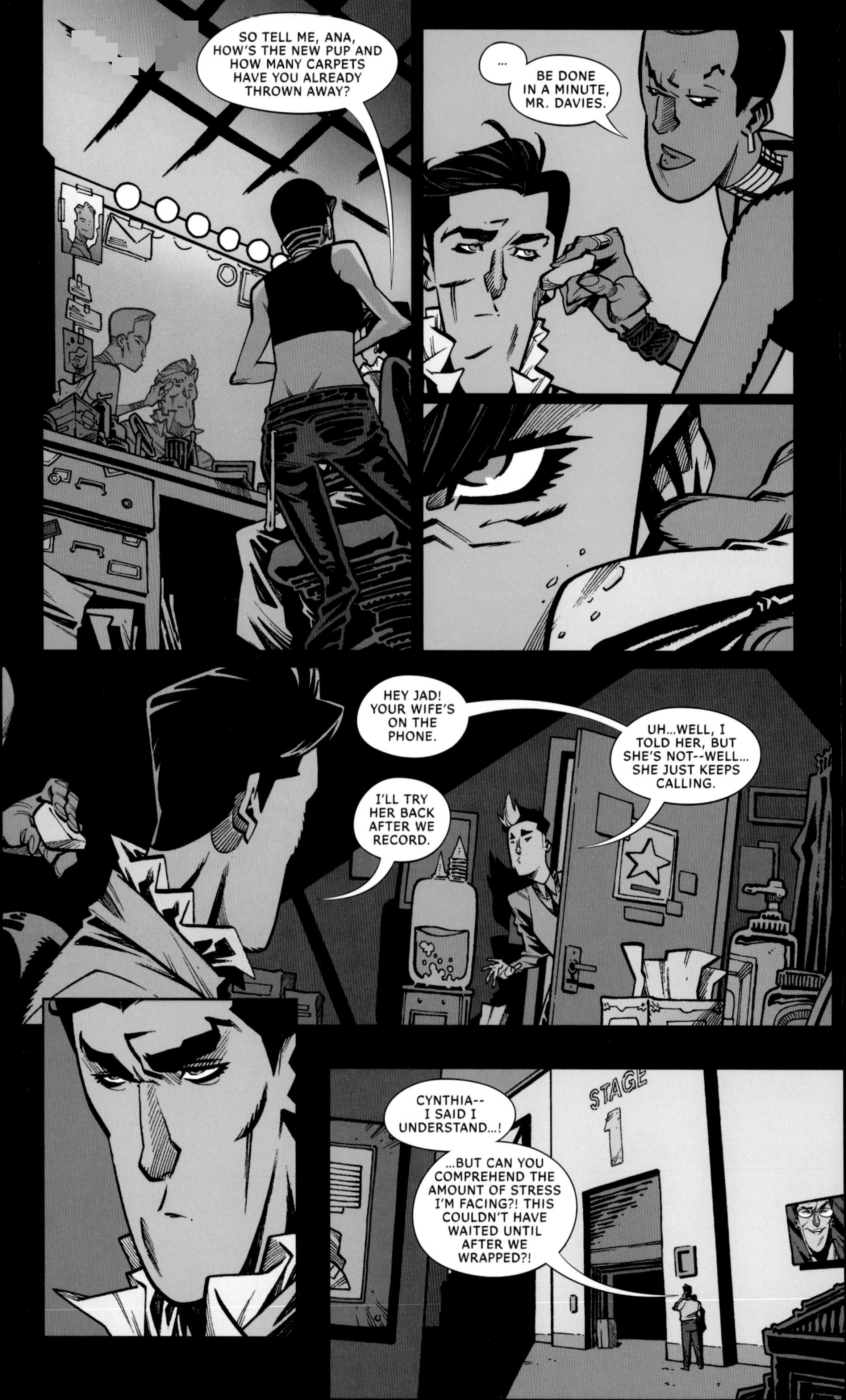
SO TELL ME, ANA, HOW'S THE NEW PUP AND HOW MANY CARPETS HAVE YOU ALREADY THROWN AWAY?
...
BE DONE IN A MINUTE, MR. DAVIES.
HEY JAD! YOUR WIFE'S ON THE PHONE.
UH...WELL, I TOLD HER, BUT SHE'S NOT--WELL... SHE JUST KEEPS CALLING.
I'LL TRY HER BACK AFTER WE RECORD.
STAGE 1
CYNTHIA-- I SAID I UNDERSTAND...!
...BUT CAN YOU COMPREHEND THE AMOUNT OF STRESS I'M FACING?! THIS COULDN'T HAVE WAITED UNTIL AFTER WE WRAPPED?!

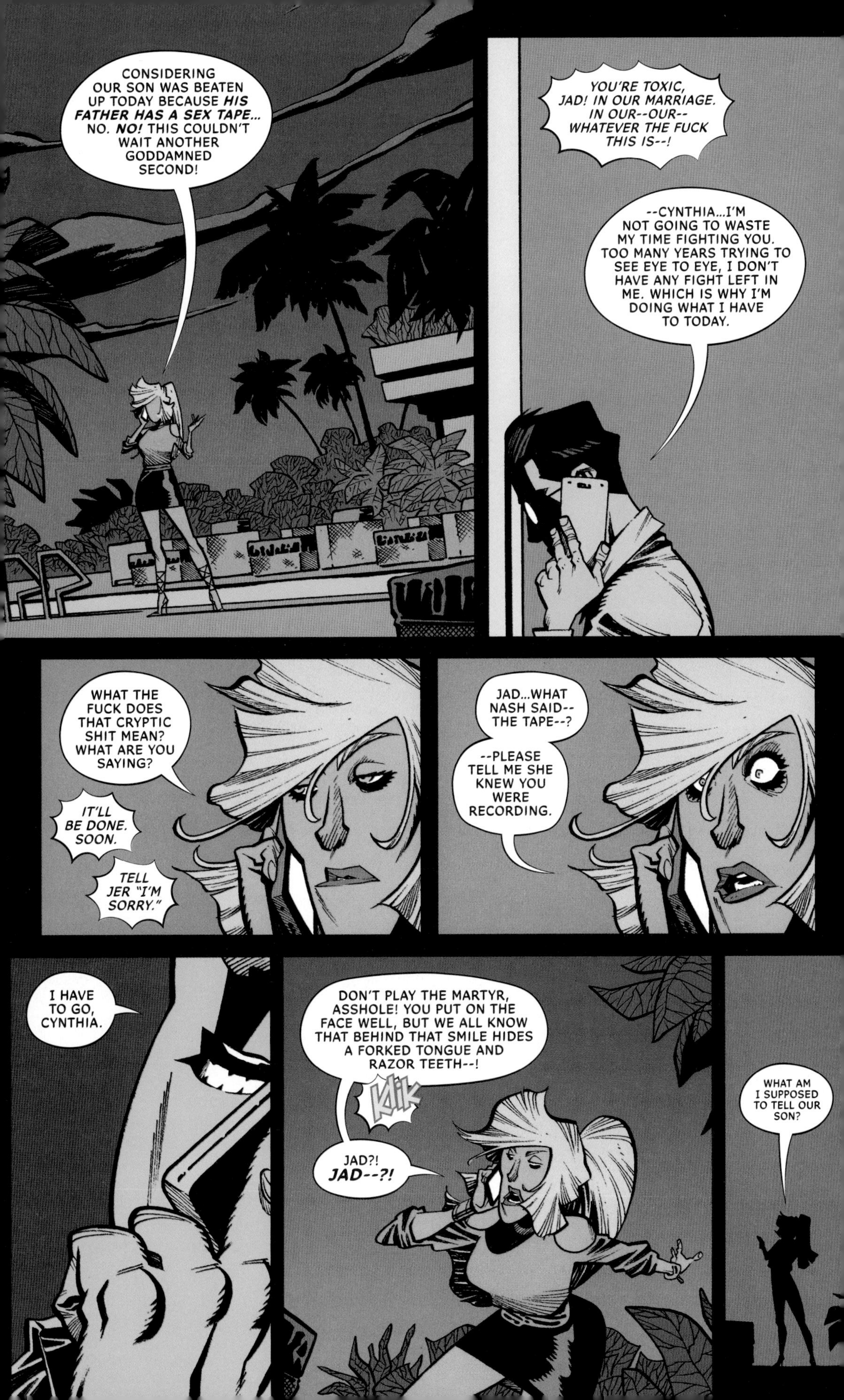
CONSIDERING OUR SON WAS BEATEN UP TODAY BECAUSE ***HIS FATHER HAS A SEX TAPE...*** NO. ***NO!*** THIS COULDN'T WAIT ANOTHER GODDAMNED SECOND!
YOU'RE TOXIC, JAD! IN OUR MARRIAGE. IN OUR--OUR-- WHATEVER THE FUCK THIS IS--!
--CYNTHIA...I'M NOT GOING TO WASTE MY TIME FIGHTING YOU. TOO MANY YEARS TRYING TO SEE EYE TO EYE, I DON'T HAVE ANY FIGHT LEFT IN ME. WHICH IS WHY I'M DOING WHAT I HAVE TO TODAY.
WHAT THE FUCK DOES THAT CRYPTIC SHIT MEAN? WHAT ARE YOU SAYING?
IT'LL BE DONE. SOON.
TELL JER "I'M SORRY."
JAD...WHAT NASH SAID-- THE TAPE--?
--PLEASE TELL ME SHE KNEW YOU WERE RECORDING.
I HAVE TO GO, CYNTHIA.
DON'T PLAY THE MARTYR, ASSHOLE! YOU PUT ON THE FACE WELL, BUT WE ALL KNOW THAT BEHIND THAT SMILE HIDES A FORKED TONGUE AND RAZOR TEETH--!
KLIK
JAD?! ***JAD--?!***
WHAT AM I SUPPOSED TO TELL OUR SON?

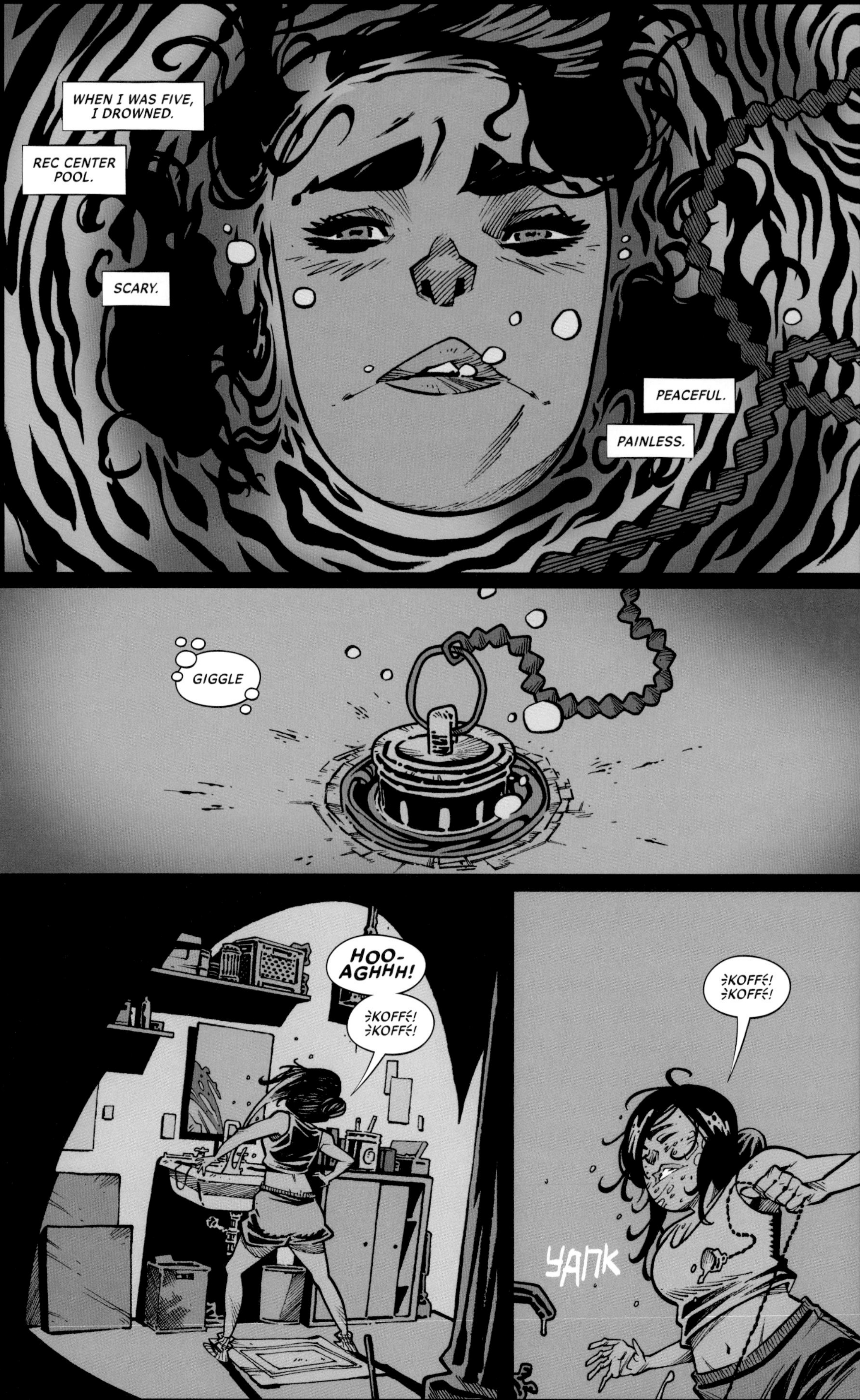
WHEN I WAS FIVE, I DROWNED.
REC CENTER POOL.
SCARY.
PEACEFUL.
PAINLESS.
GIGGLE
HOO-AGHHH!
KOFF! KOFF!
KOFF! KOFF!
YANK

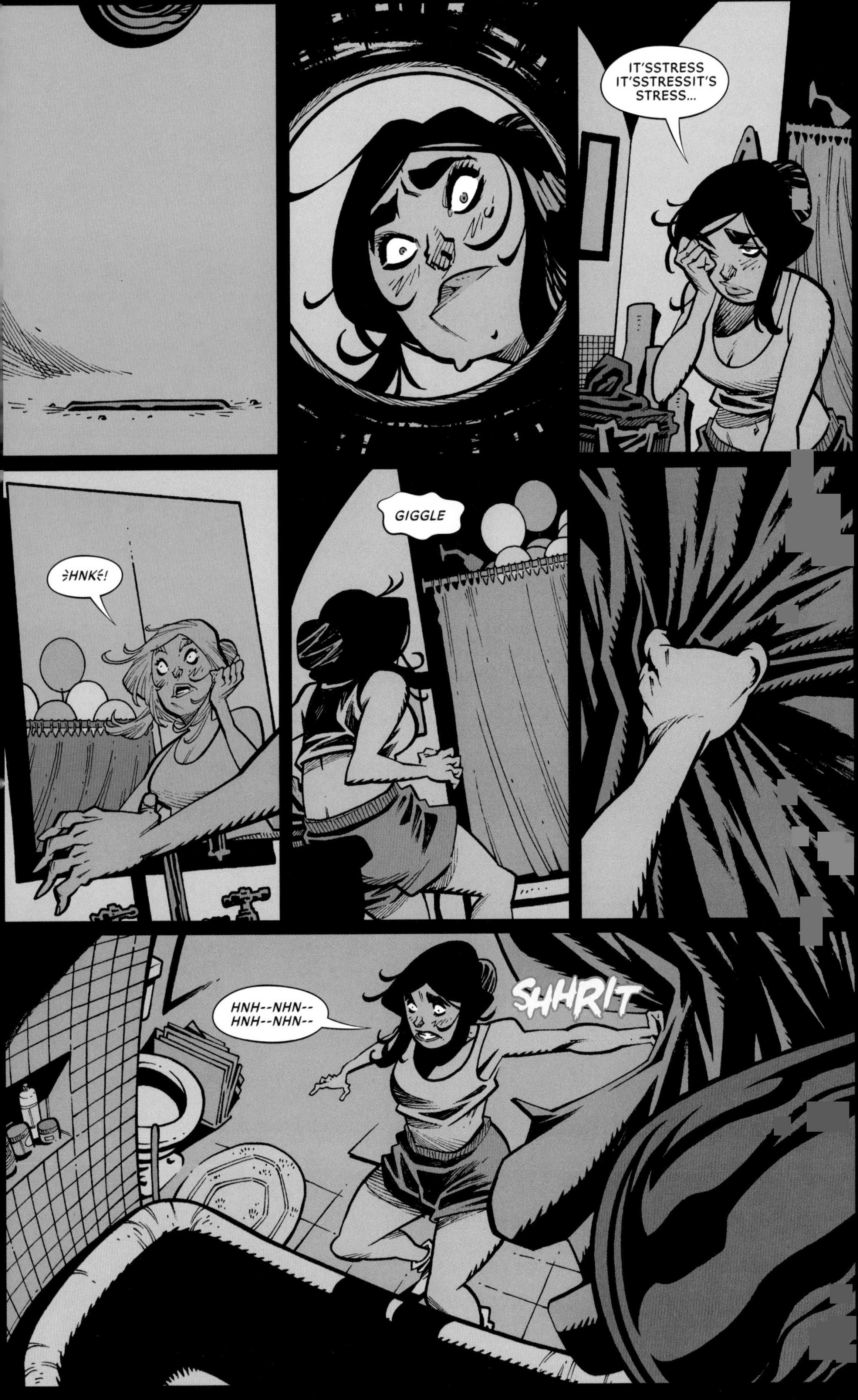
IT'SSTRESS IT'SSTRESSIT'S STRESS...
HNK!
GIGGLE
HNH--NHN-- HNH--NHN--
SHHRIT

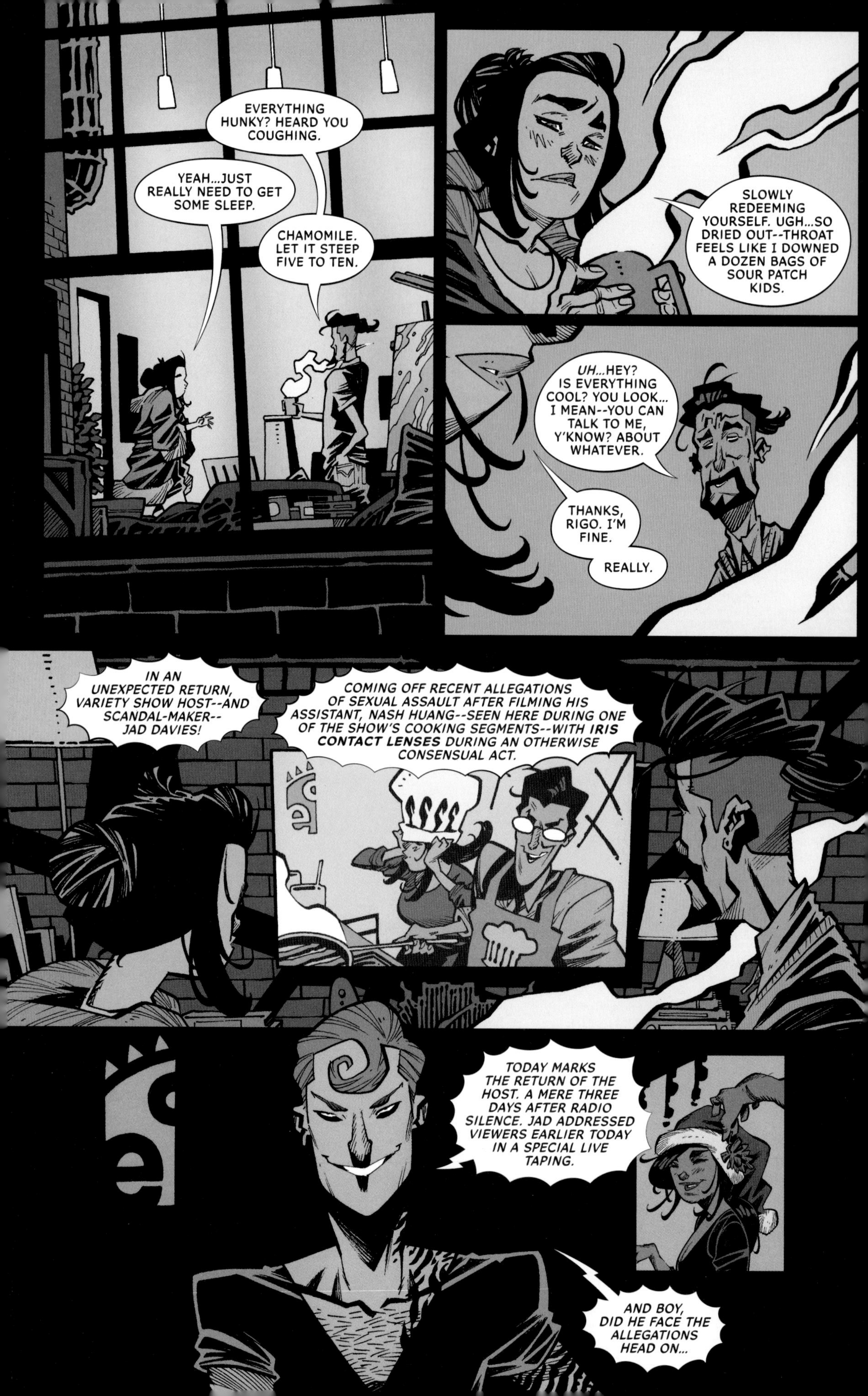
EVERYTHING HUNKY? HEARD YOU COUGHING.
YEAH...JUST REALLY NEED TO GET SOME SLEEP.
CHAMOMILE. LET IT STEEP FIVE TO TEN.
SLOWLY REDEEMING YOURSELF. UGH...SO DRIED OUT--THROAT FEELS LIKE I DOWNED A DOZEN BAGS OF SOUR PATCH KIDS.
UH...HEY? IS EVERYTHING COOL? YOU LOOK... I MEAN--YOU CAN TALK TO ME, Y'KNOW? ABOUT WHATEVER.
THANKS, RIGO. I'M FINE.
REALLY.
IN AN UNEXPECTED RETURN, VARIETY SHOW HOST--AND SCANDAL-MAKER--JAD DAVIES!
COMING OFF RECENT ALLEGATIONS OF SEXUAL ASSAULT AFTER FILMING HIS ASSISTANT, NASH HUANG--SEEN HERE DURING ONE OF THE SHOW'S COOKING SEGMENTS--WITH IRIS CONTACT LENSES DURING AN OTHERWISE CONSENSUAL ACT.
TODAY MARKS THE RETURN OF THE HOST. A MERE THREE DAYS AFTER RADIO SILENCE. JAD ADDRESSED VIEWERS EARLIER TODAY IN A SPECIAL LIVE TAPING.
AND BOY, DID HE FACE THE ALLEGATIONS HEAD ON...

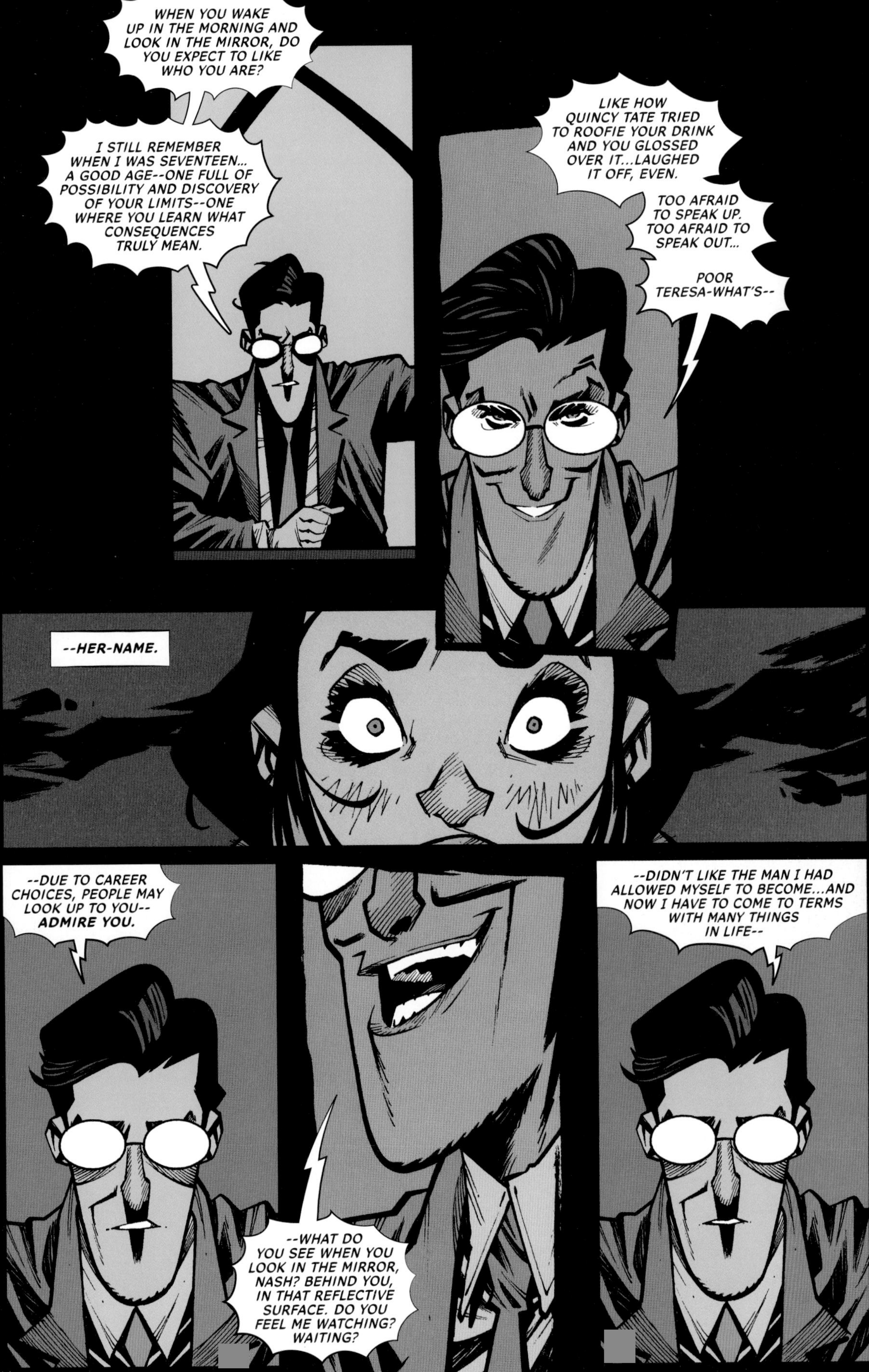
WHEN YOU WAKE UP IN THE MORNING AND LOOK IN THE MIRROR, DO YOU EXPECT TO LIKE WHO YOU ARE?
I STILL REMEMBER WHEN I WAS SEVENTEEN... A GOOD AGE--ONE FULL OF POSSIBILITY AND DISCOVERY OF YOUR LIMITS--ONE WHERE YOU LEARN WHAT CONSEQUENCES TRULY MEAN.
LIKE HOW QUINCY TATE TRIED TO ROOFIE YOUR DRINK AND YOU GLOSSED OVER IT...LAUGHED IT OFF, EVEN.
TOO AFRAID TO SPEAK UP. TOO AFRAID TO SPEAK OUT...
POOR TERESA-WHAT'S--
--HER-NAME.
--DUE TO CAREER CHOICES, PEOPLE MAY LOOK UP TO YOU-- ADMIRE YOU.
--WHAT DO YOU SEE WHEN YOU LOOK IN THE MIRROR, NASH? BEHIND YOU, IN THAT REFLECTIVE SURFACE. DO YOU FEEL ME WATCHING? WAITING?
--DIDN'T LIKE THE MAN I HAD ALLOWED MYSELF TO BECOME...AND NOW I HAVE TO COME TO TERMS WITH MANY THINGS IN LIFE--

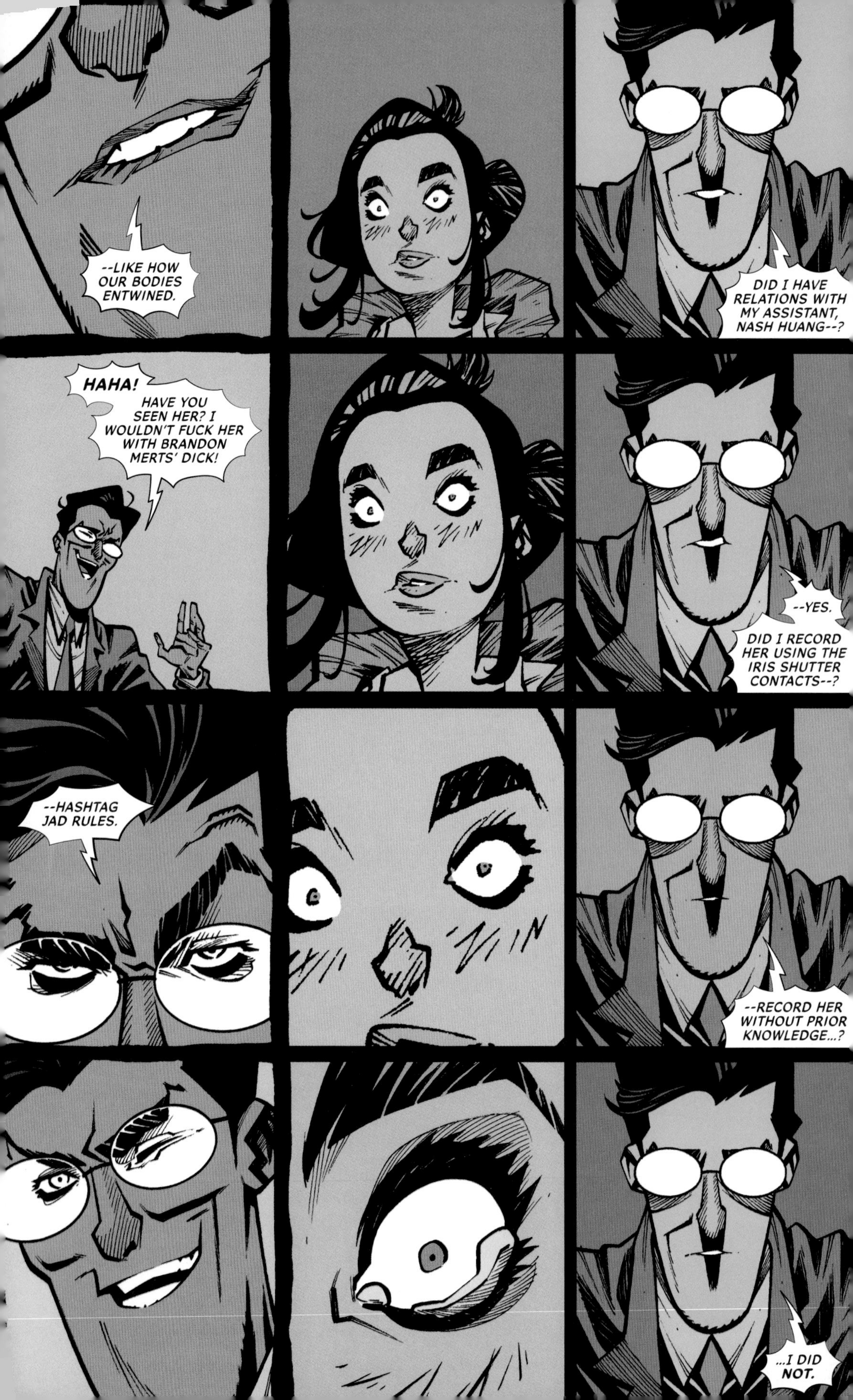
--LIKE HOW OUR BODIES ENTWINED.
DID I HAVE RELATIONS WITH MY ASSISTANT, NASH HUANG--?
HAHA!
HAVE YOU SEEN HER? I WOULDN'T FUCK HER WITH BRANDON MERTS' DICK!
--YES.
DID I RECORD HER USING THE IRIS SHUTTER CONTACTS--?
--HASHTAG JAD RULES.
--RECORD HER WITHOUT PRIOR KNOWLEDGE...?
...I DID NOT.

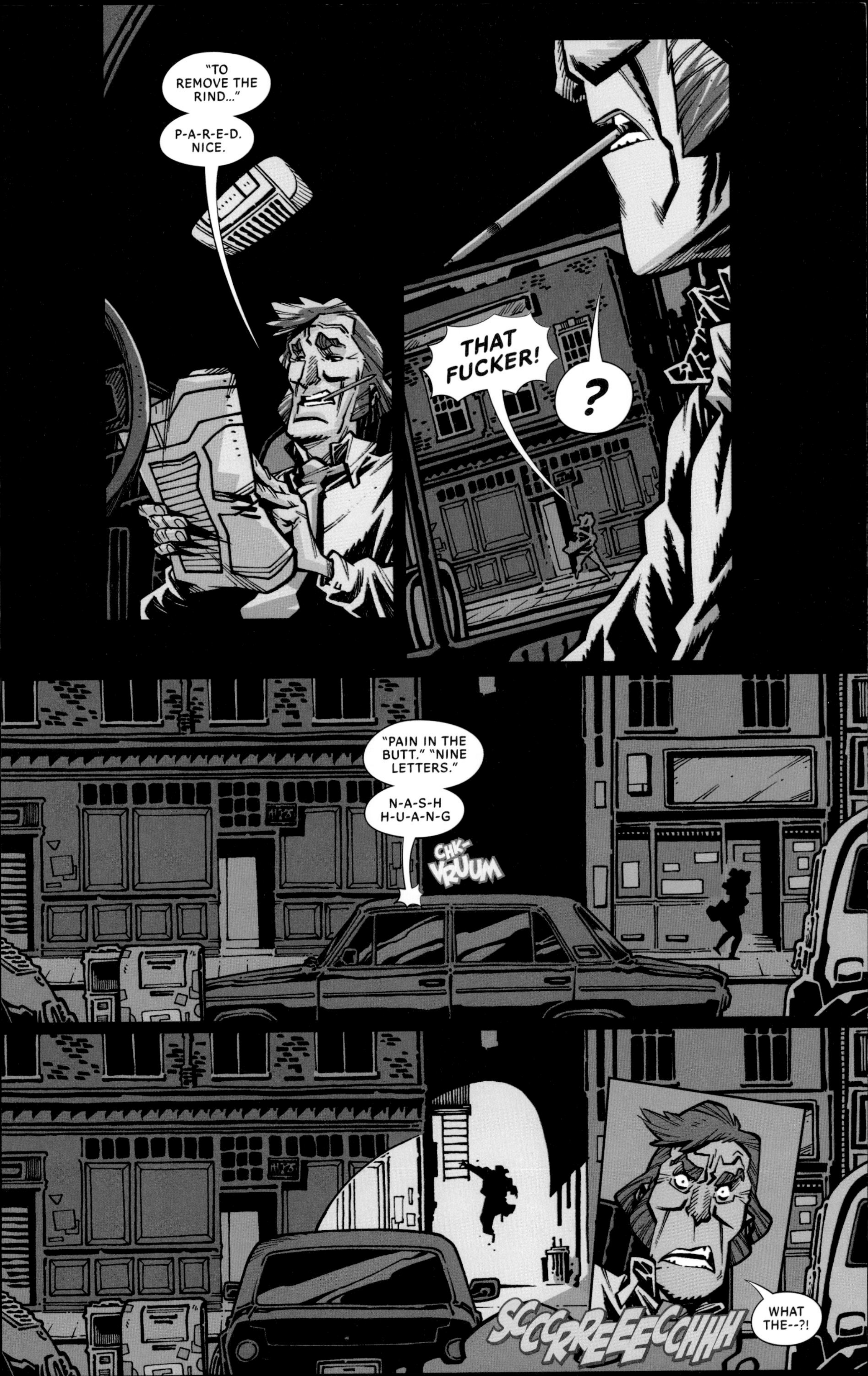
"TO REMOVE THE RIND..."
P-A-R-E-D. NICE.
THAT FUCKER!
?
"PAIN IN THE BUTT." "NINE LETTERS."
N-A-S-H H-U-A-N-G
CHK-VRUUM
SCCCREEEECHHH
WHAT THE--?!

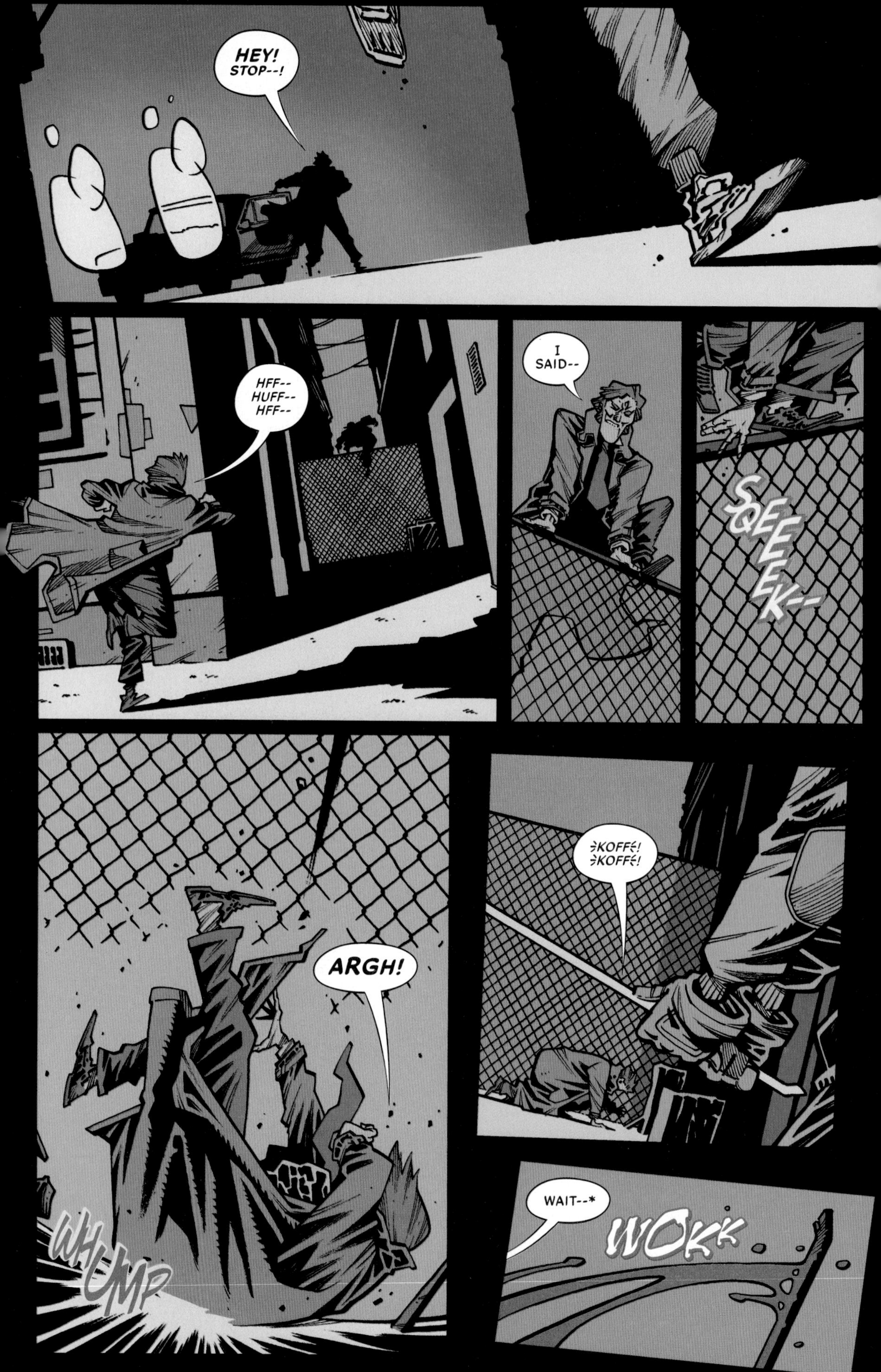
HEY! STOP--!
HFF-- HUFF-- HFF--
I SAID--
SQEEEK--
ARGH!
WHUMP
KOFF! *KOFF*!
WAIT--*
WOKK

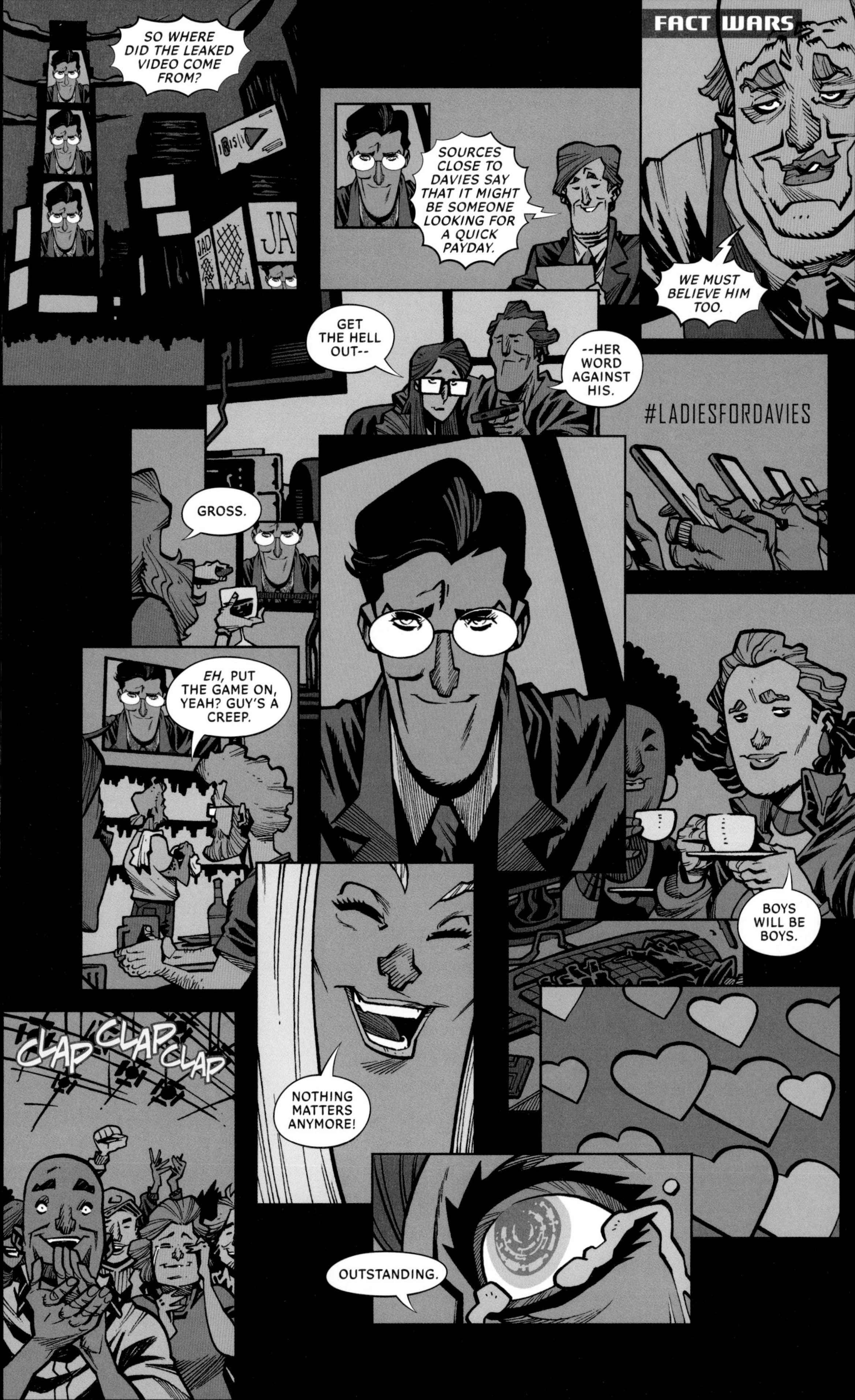
FACT WARS
SO WHERE DID THE LEAKED VIDEO COME FROM?
SOURCES CLOSE TO DAVIES SAY THAT IT MIGHT BE SOMEONE LOOKING FOR A QUICK PAYDAY.
WE MUST BELIEVE HIM TOO.
GET THE HELL OUT--
--HER WORD AGAINST HIS.
#LADIESFORDAVIES
GROSS.
EH, PUT THE GAME ON, YEAH? GUY'S A CREEP.
BOYS WILL BE BOYS.
CLAP CLAP CLAP
NOTHING MATTERS ANYMORE!
OUTSTANDING.

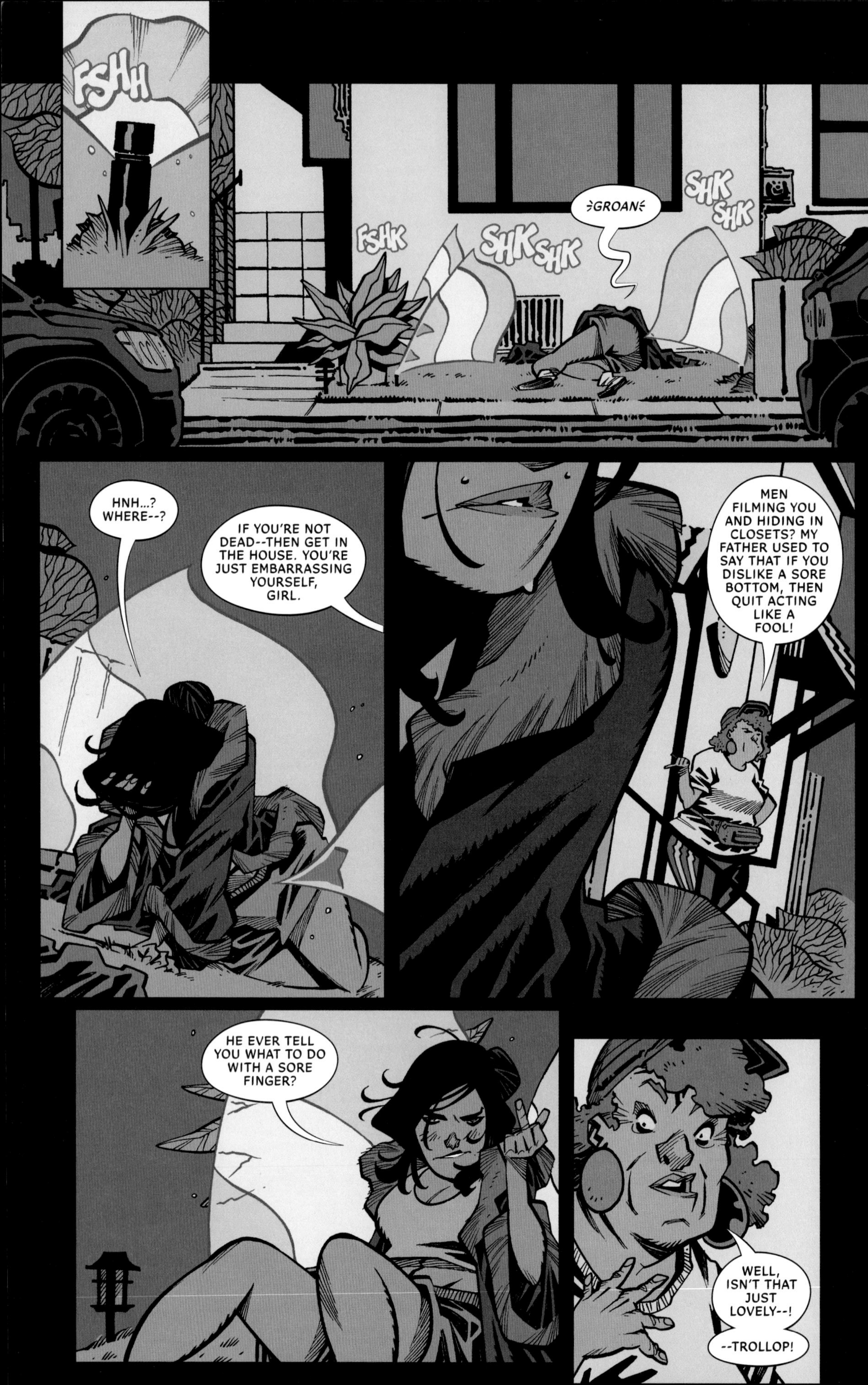
FSHH
FSHK
SHK SHK
GROAN
SHK SHK
HNH...? WHERE--?
IF YOU'RE NOT DEAD--THEN GET IN THE HOUSE. YOU'RE JUST EMBARRASSING YOURSELF, GIRL.
MEN FILMING YOU AND HIDING IN CLOSETS? MY FATHER USED TO SAY THAT IF YOU DISLIKE A SORE BOTTOM, THEN QUIT ACTING LIKE A FOOL!
HE EVER TELL YOU WHAT TO DO WITH A SORE FINGER?
WELL, ISN'T THAT JUST LOVELY--!
--TROLLOP!

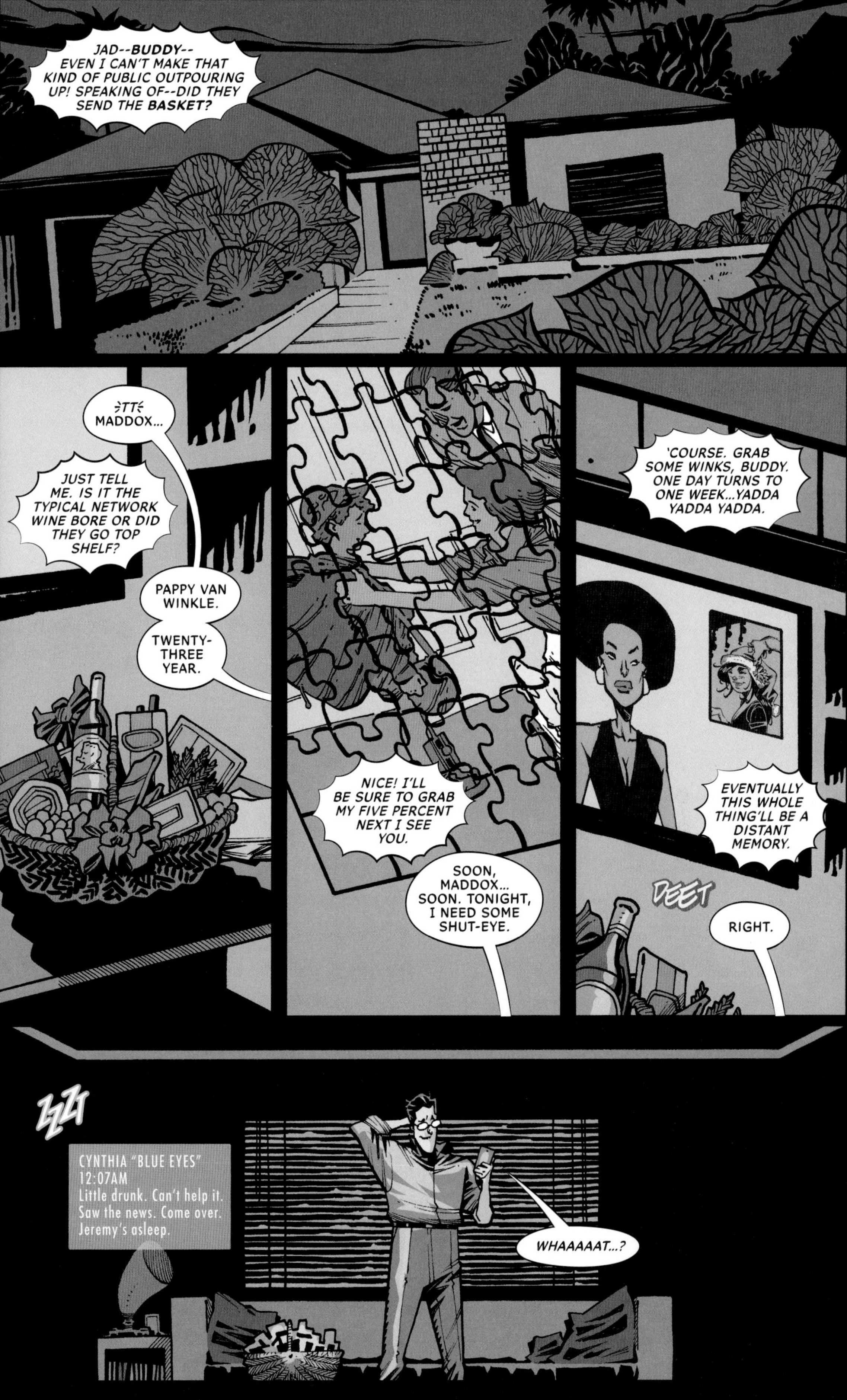
JAD--BUDDY--
EVEN I CAN'T MAKE THAT KIND OF PUBLIC OUTPOURING UP! SPEAKING OF--DID THEY SEND THE BASKET?
TT
MADDOX...
JUST TELL ME. IS IT THE TYPICAL NETWORK WINE BORE OR DID THEY GO TOP SHELF?
PAPPY VAN WINKLE.
TWENTY-THREE YEAR.
NICE! I'LL BE SURE TO GRAB MY FIVE PERCENT NEXT I SEE YOU.
SOON, MADDOX... SOON. TONIGHT, I NEED SOME SHUT-EYE.
'COURSE. GRAB SOME WINKS, BUDDY. ONE DAY TURNS TO ONE WEEK...YADDA YADDA YADDA.
EVENTUALLY THIS WHOLE THING'LL BE A DISTANT MEMORY.
DEET
RIGHT.
ZZZT
CYNTHIA "BLUE EYES"
12:07AM
Little drunk. Can't help it.
Saw the news. Come over.
Jeremy's asleep.
WHAAAAAT...?

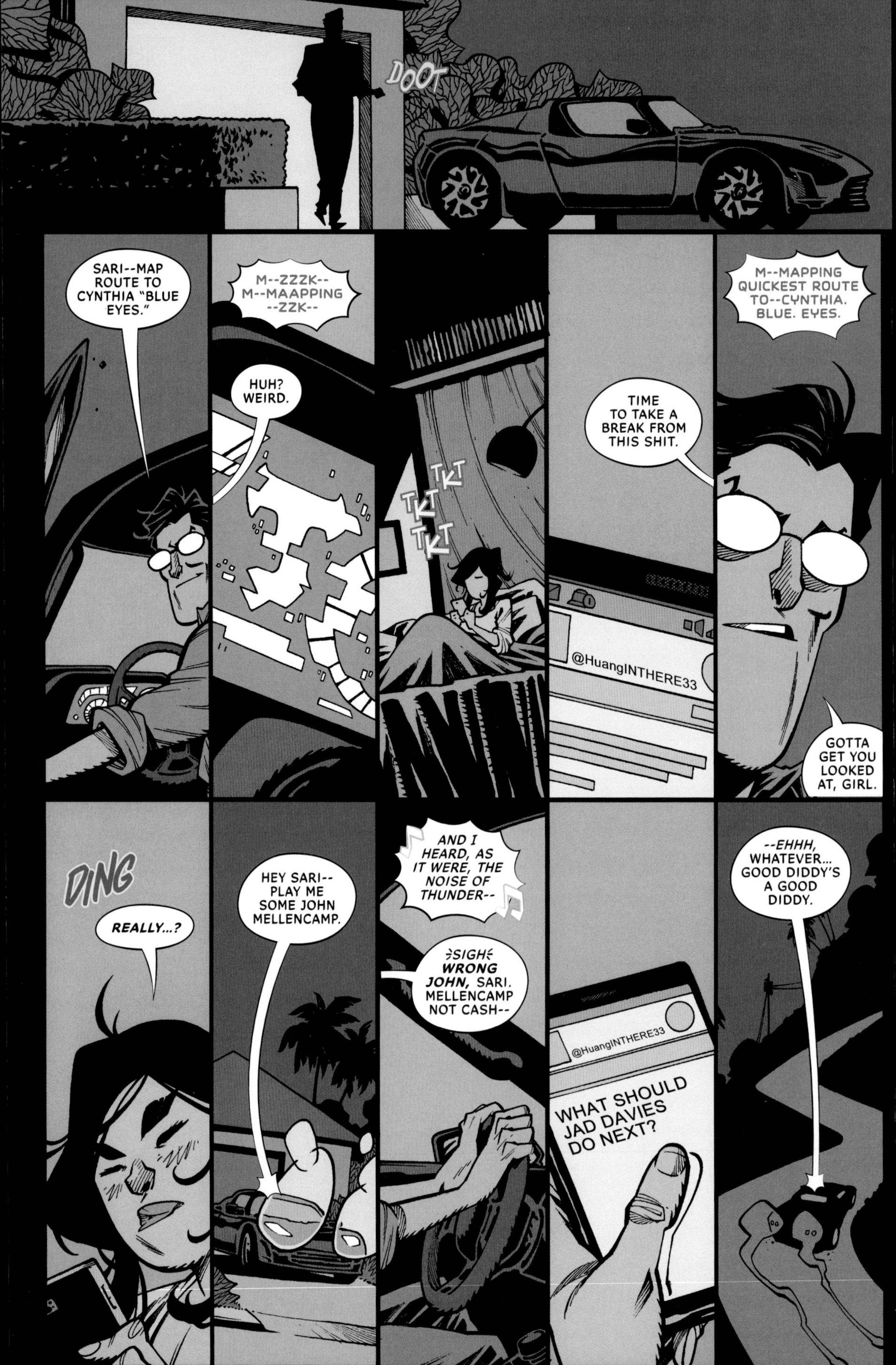
DOOT
SARI--MAP ROUTE TO CYNTHIA "BLUE EYES."
M--ZZZK-- M--MAAPPING --ZZK--
HUH? WEIRD.
TKT TKT TKT
TIME TO TAKE A BREAK FROM THIS SHIT.
@HuangINTHERE33
M--MAPPING QUICKEST ROUTE TO--CYNTHIA. BLUE. EYES.
GOTTA GET YOU LOOKED AT, GIRL.
DING
REALLY...?
HEY SARI-- PLAY ME SOME JOHN MELLENCAMP.
AND I HEARD, AS IT WERE, THE NOISE OF THUNDER--
SIGH WRONG JOHN, SARI. MELLENCAMP NOT CASH--
@HuangINTHERE33
WHAT SHOULD JAD DAVIES DO NEXT?
--EHHH, WHATEVER... GOOD DIDDY'S A GOOD DIDDY.

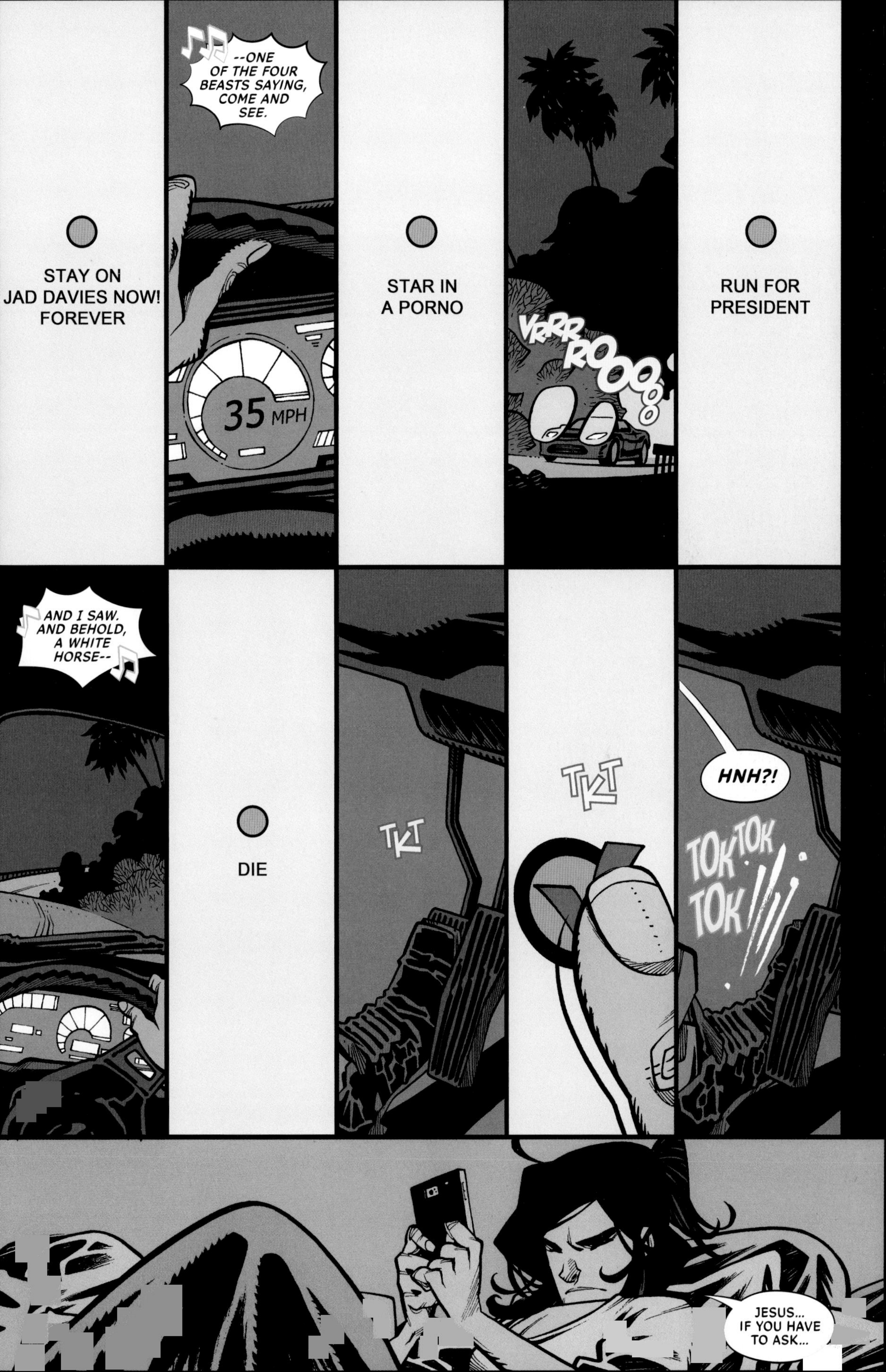
STAY ON JAD DAVIES NOW! FOREVER
--ONE OF THE FOUR BEASTS SAYING, COME AND SEE.
35 MPH
STAR IN A PORNO
VRRRROOOOo
RUN FOR PRESIDENT
AND I SAW. AND BEHOLD, A WHITE HORSE--
DIE
TKT
TKT
HNH?!
TOK TOK TOK
JESUS... IF YOU HAVE TO ASK...

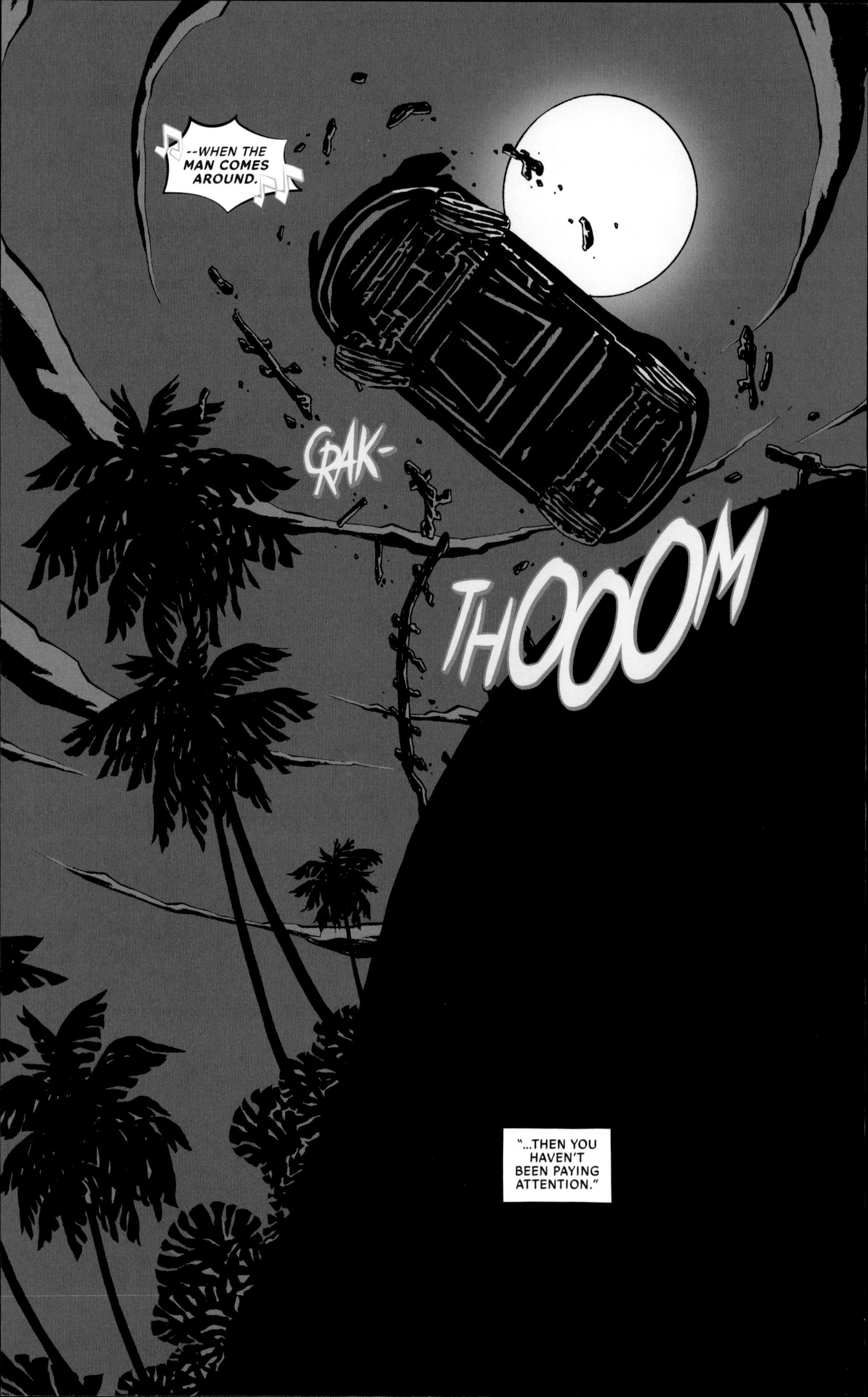
--WHEN THE MAN COMES AROUND.
CRAK-
THOOOM
"...THEN YOU HAVEN'T BEEN PAYING ATTENTION."

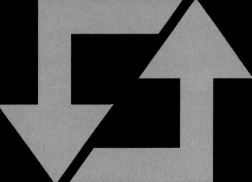

CHAPTER FIVE

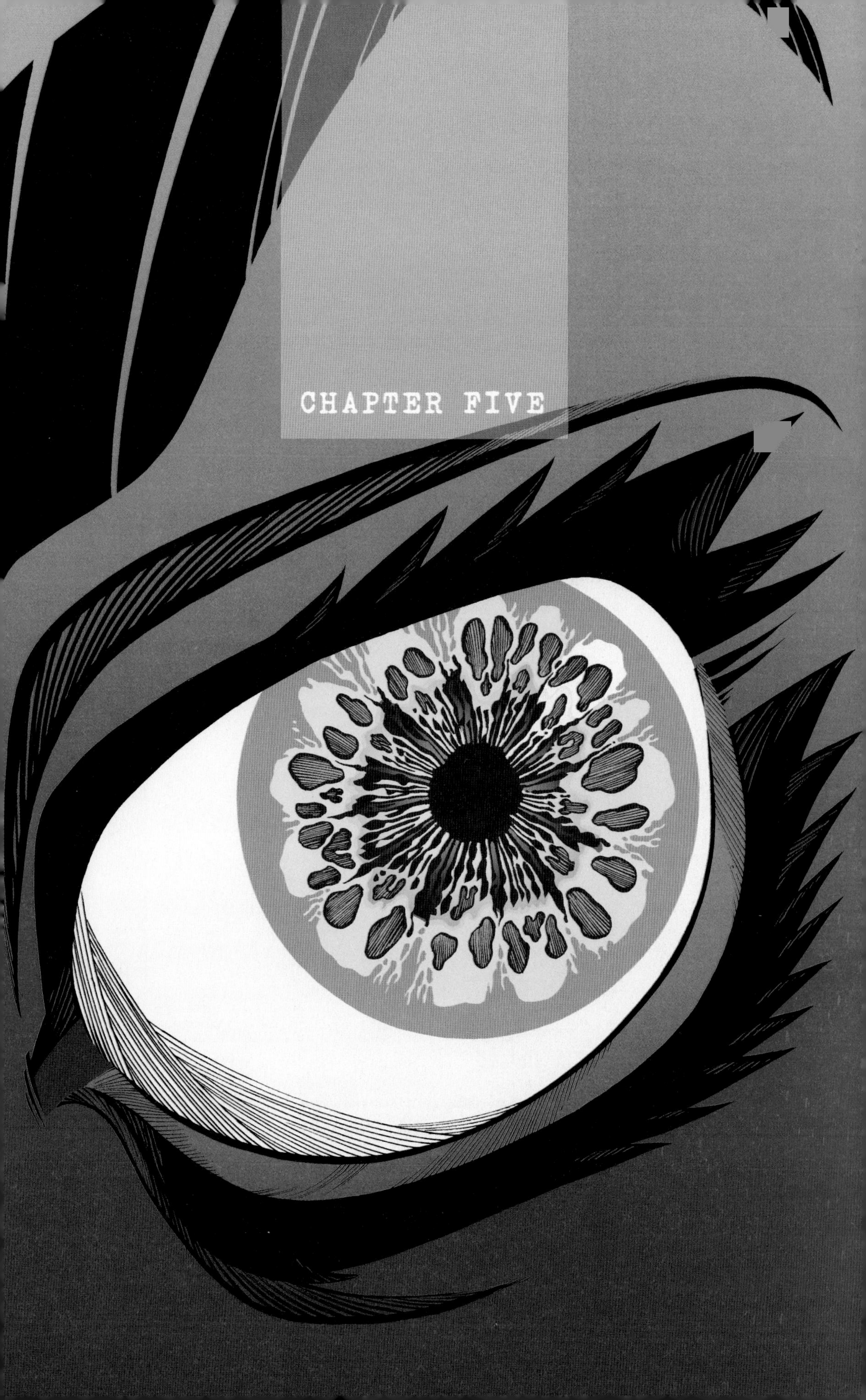

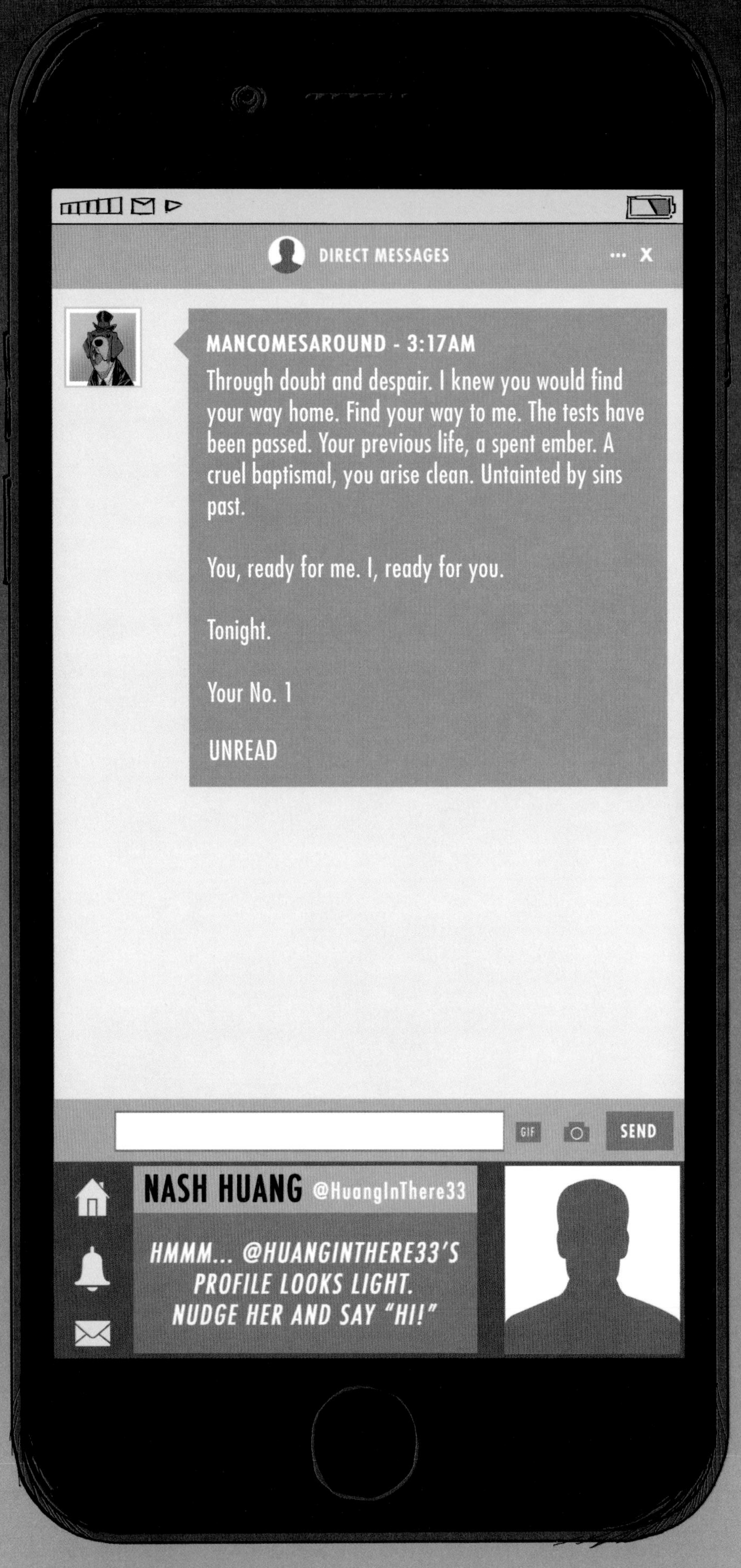
DIRECT MESSAGES
MANCOMESAROUND - 3:17AM
Through doubt and despair. I knew you would find your way home. Find your way to me. The tests have been passed. Your previous life, a spent ember. A cruel baptismal, you arise clean. Untainted by sins past.
You, ready for me. I, ready for you.
Tonight.
Your No. 1
UNREAD
GIF
SEND
NASH HUANG @HuangInThere33
HMMM... @HUANGINTHERE33'S PROFILE LOOKS LIGHT. NUDGE HER AND SAY "HI!"

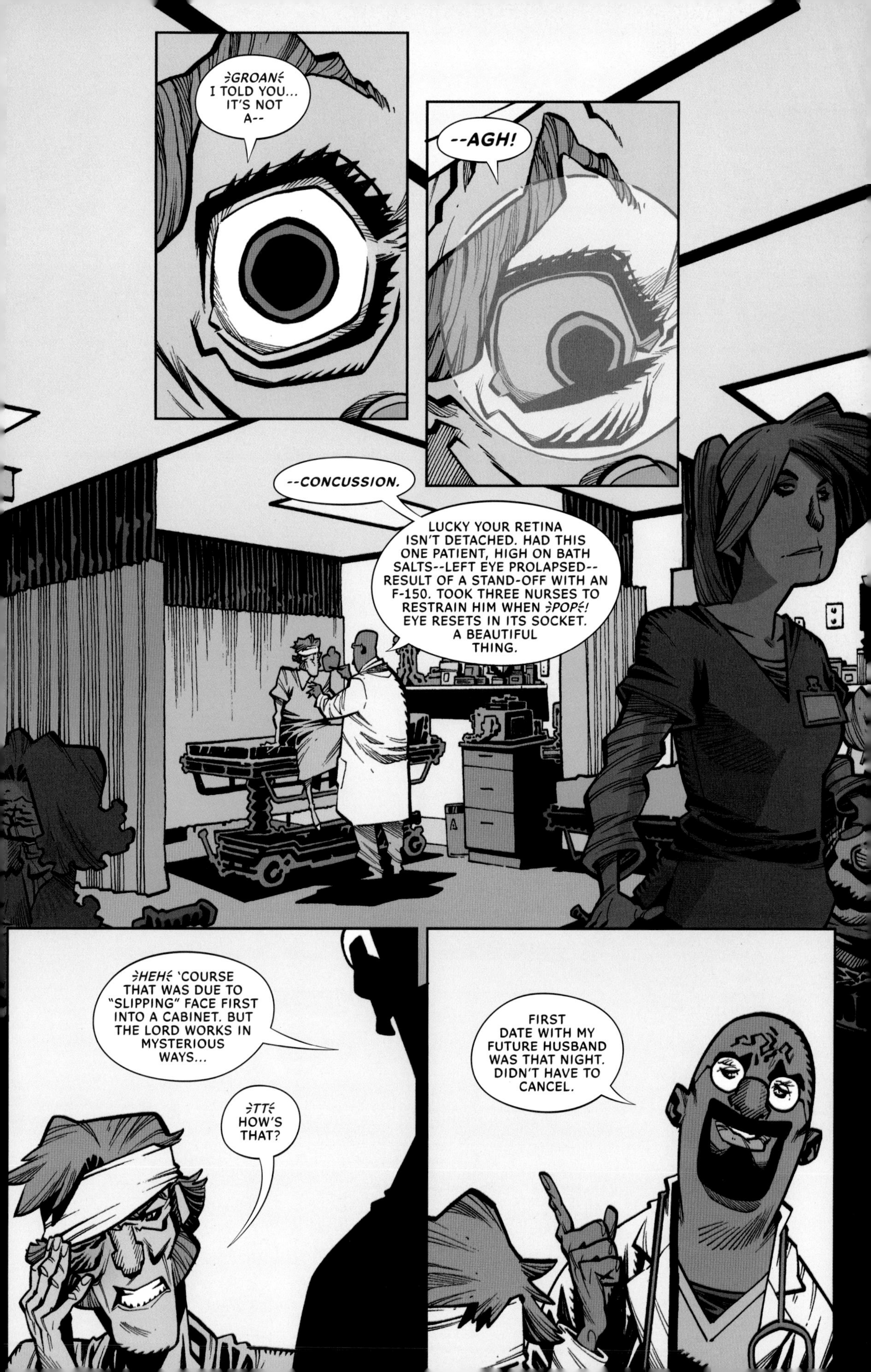

GROAN I TOLD YOU... IT'S NOT A--
--AGH!
--CONCUSSION.
LUCKY YOUR RETINA ISN'T DETACHED. HAD THIS ONE PATIENT, HIGH ON BATH SALTS--LEFT EYE PROLAPSED--RESULT OF A STAND-OFF WITH AN F-150. TOOK THREE NURSES TO RESTRAIN HIM WHEN POP! EYE RESETS IN ITS SOCKET. A BEAUTIFUL THING.
HEH 'COURSE THAT WAS DUE TO "SLIPPING" FACE FIRST INTO A CABINET. BUT THE LORD WORKS IN MYSTERIOUS WAYS...
TT HOW'S THAT?
FIRST DATE WITH MY FUTURE HUSBAND WAS THAT NIGHT. DIDN'T HAVE TO CANCEL.

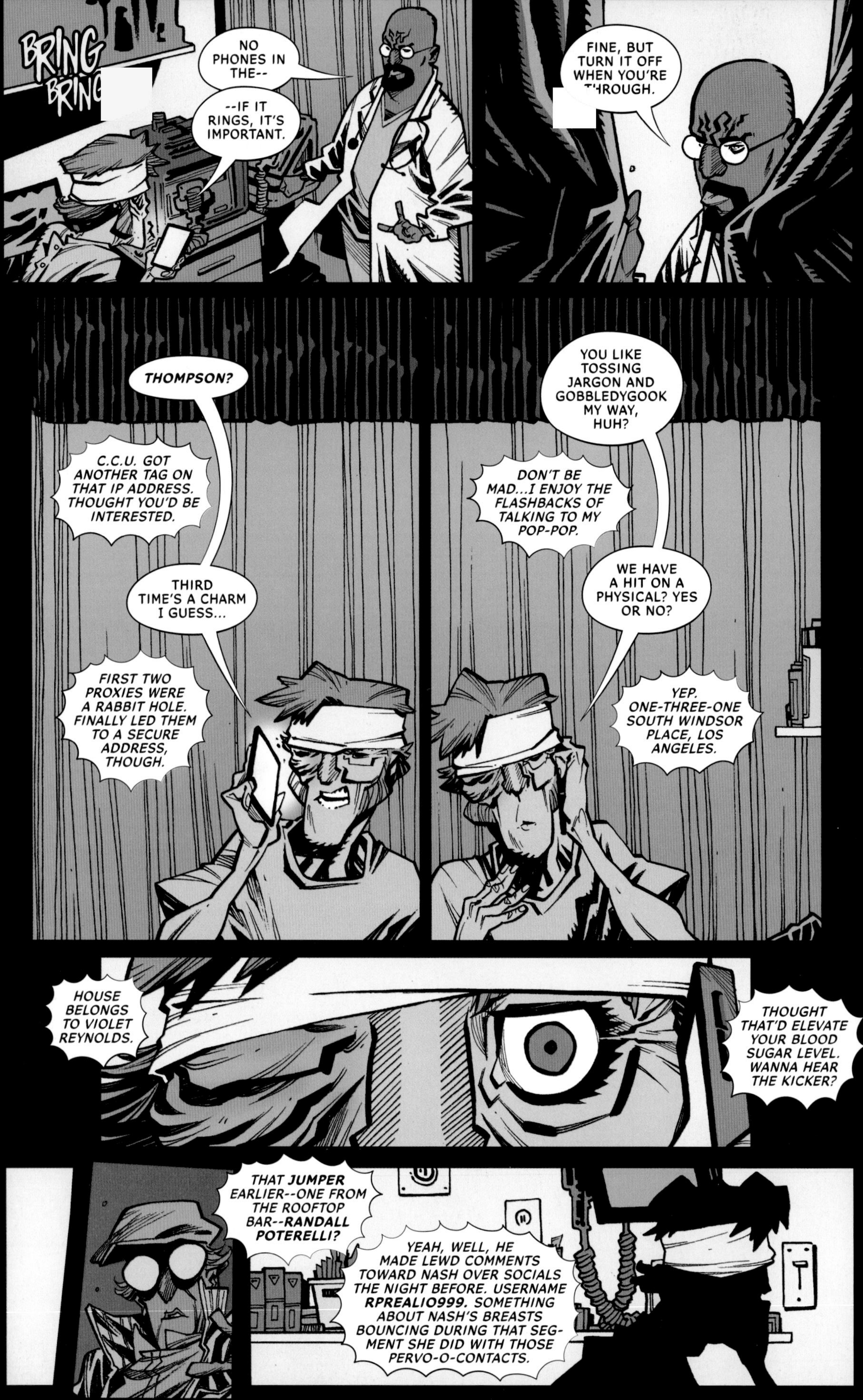
BRING
BRING
NO PHONES IN THE--
--IF IT RINGS, IT'S IMPORTANT.
FINE, BUT TURN IT OFF WHEN YOU'RE THROUGH.
THOMPSON?
C.C.U. GOT ANOTHER TAG ON THAT IP ADDRESS. THOUGHT YOU'D BE INTERESTED.
THIRD TIME'S A CHARM I GUESS...
FIRST TWO PROXIES WERE A RABBIT HOLE. FINALLY LED THEM TO A SECURE ADDRESS, THOUGH.
YOU LIKE TOSSING JARGON AND GOBBLEDYGOOK MY WAY, HUH?
DON'T BE MAD...I ENJOY THE FLASHBACKS OF TALKING TO MY POP-POP.
WE HAVE A HIT ON A PHYSICAL? YES OR NO?
YEP. ONE-THREE-ONE SOUTH WINDSOR PLACE, LOS ANGELES.
HOUSE BELONGS TO VIOLET REYNOLDS.
THOUGHT THAT'D ELEVATE YOUR BLOOD SUGAR LEVEL. WANNA HEAR THE KICKER?
THAT JUMPER EARLIER--ONE FROM THE ROOFTOP BAR--RANDALL POTERELLI?
YEAH, WELL, HE MADE LEWD COMMENTS TOWARD NASH OVER SOCIALS THE NIGHT BEFORE. USERNAME RPREALIO999. SOMETHING ABOUT NASH'S BREASTS BOUNCING DURING THAT SEGMENT SHE DID WITH THOSE PERVO-O-CONTACTS.

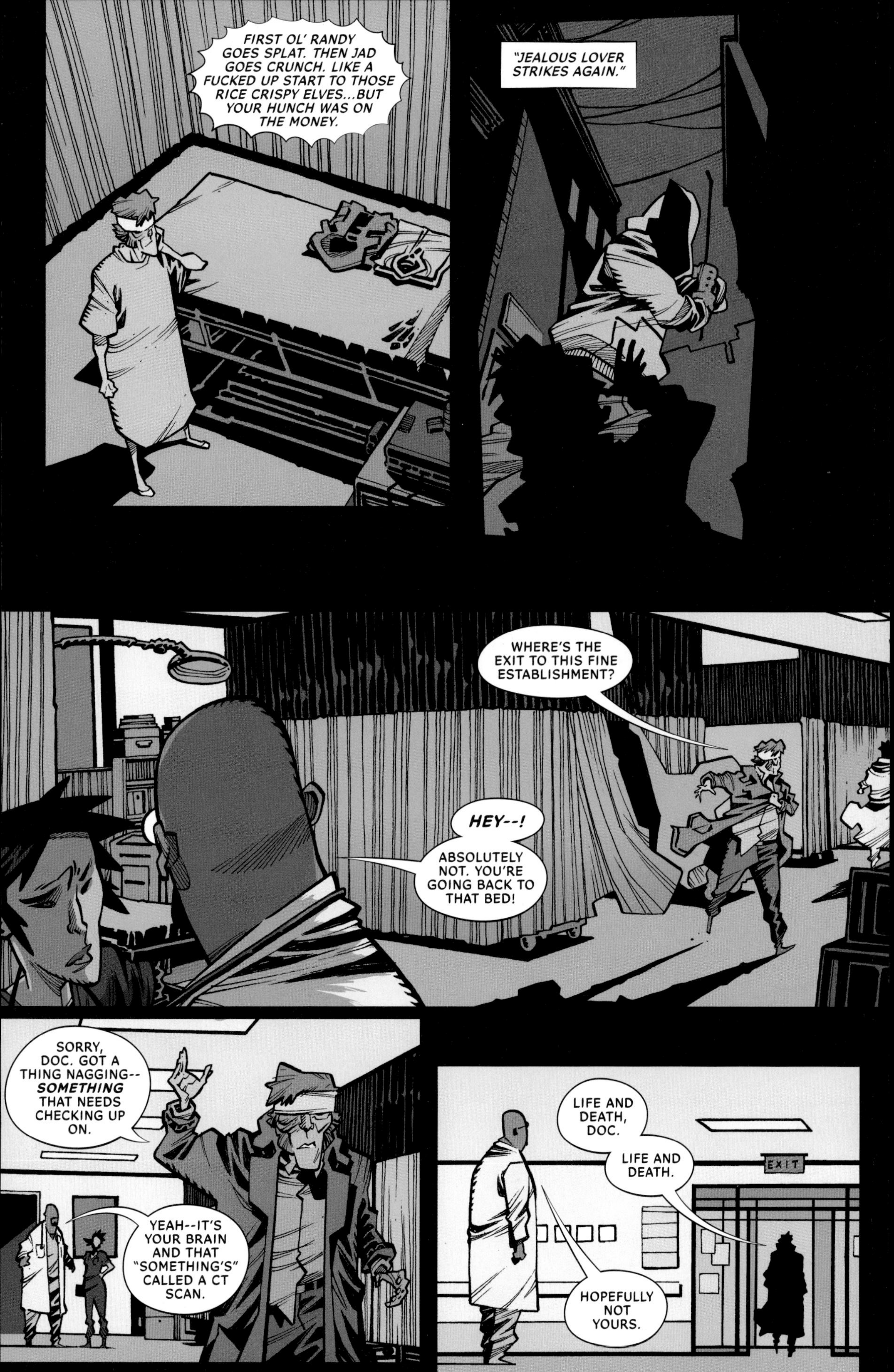
FIRST OL' RANDY GOES SPLAT. THEN JAD GOES CRUNCH. LIKE A FUCKED UP START TO THOSE RICE CRISPY ELVES...BUT YOUR HUNCH WAS ON THE MONEY.
"JEALOUS LOVER STRIKES AGAIN."
WHERE'S THE EXIT TO THIS FINE ESTABLISHMENT?
HEY--!
ABSOLUTELY NOT. YOU'RE GOING BACK TO THAT BED!
SORRY, DOC. GOT A THING NAGGING-- SOMETHING THAT NEEDS CHECKING UP ON.
YEAH--IT'S YOUR BRAIN AND THAT "SOMETHING'S" CALLED A CT SCAN.
LIFE AND DEATH, DOC.
LIFE AND DEATH.
EXIT
HOPEFULLY NOT YOURS.

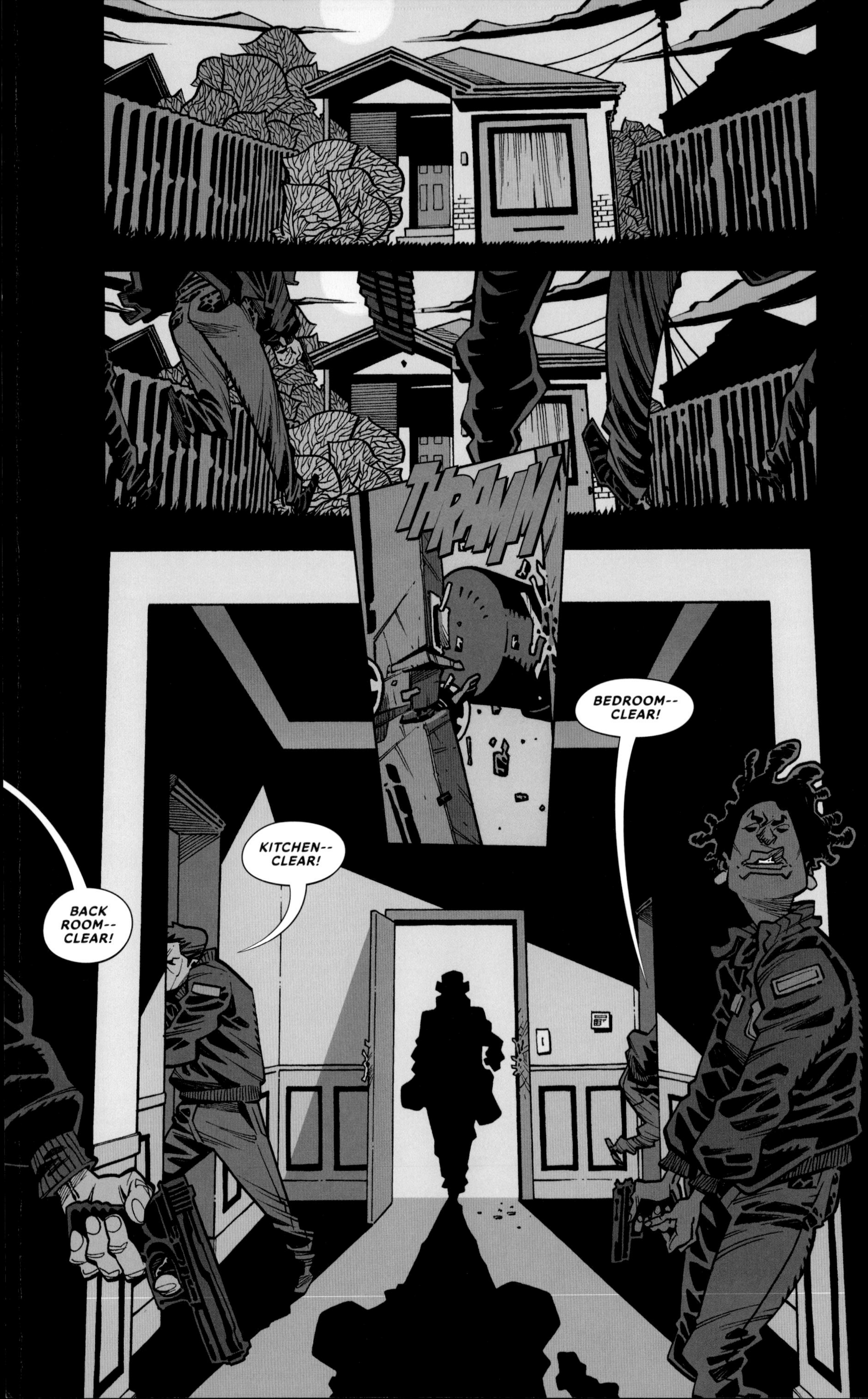

THRAMM
BEDROOM--
CLEAR!
KITCHEN--
CLEAR!
BACK
ROOM--
CLEAR!

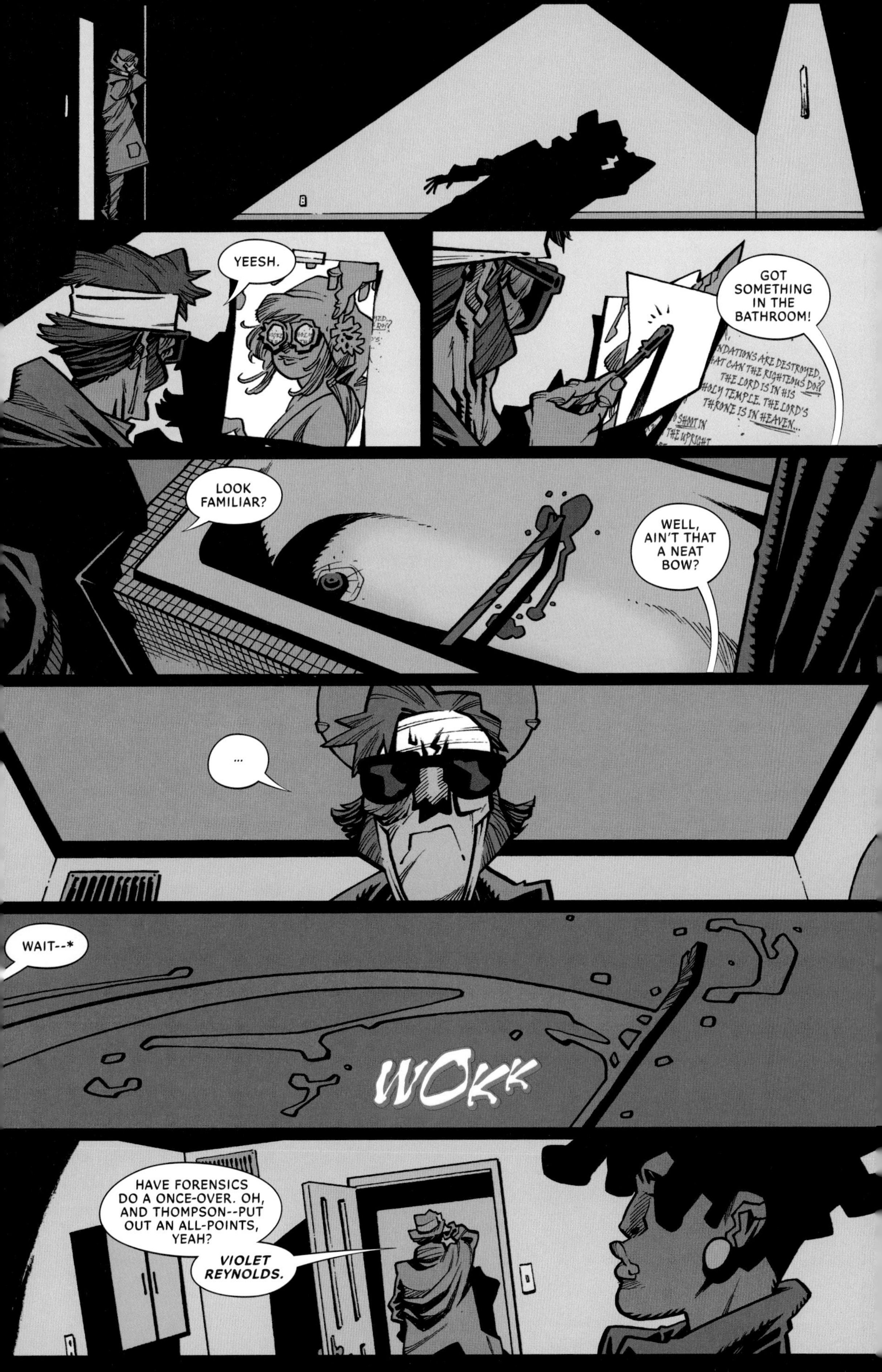

YEESH.
GOT SOMETHING IN THE BATHROOM!
THE LORD IS IN HIS HOLY TEMPLE. THE LORD'S THRONE IS IN HEAVEN...
LOOK FAMILIAR?
WELL, AIN'T THAT A NEAT BOW?
...
WAIT--*
WOKK
HAVE FORENSICS DO A ONCE-OVER. OH, AND THOMPSON--PUT OUT AN ALL-POINTS, YEAH?
VIOLET REYNOLDS.

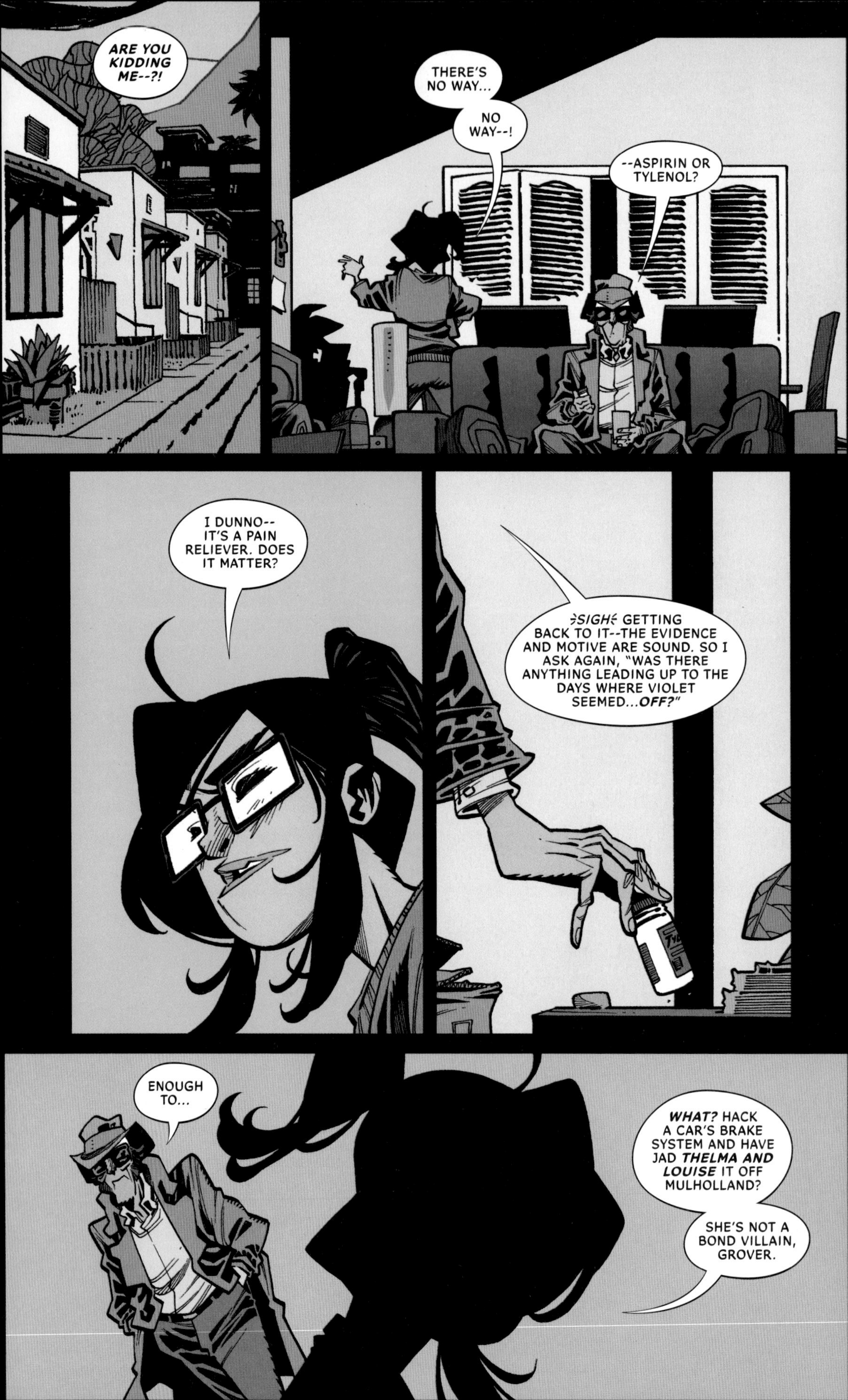
ARE YOU KIDDING ME--?!
THERE'S NO WAY...
NO WAY--!
--ASPIRIN OR TYLENOL?
I DUNNO-- IT'S A PAIN RELIEVER. DOES IT MATTER?
⩥SIGH⩤ GETTING BACK TO IT--THE EVIDENCE AND MOTIVE ARE SOUND. SO I ASK AGAIN, "WAS THERE ANYTHING LEADING UP TO THE DAYS WHERE VIOLET SEEMED...OFF?"
ENOUGH TO...
WHAT? HACK A CAR'S BRAKE SYSTEM AND HAVE JAD THELMA AND LOUISE IT OFF MULHOLLAND?
SHE'S NOT A BOND VILLAIN, GROVER.

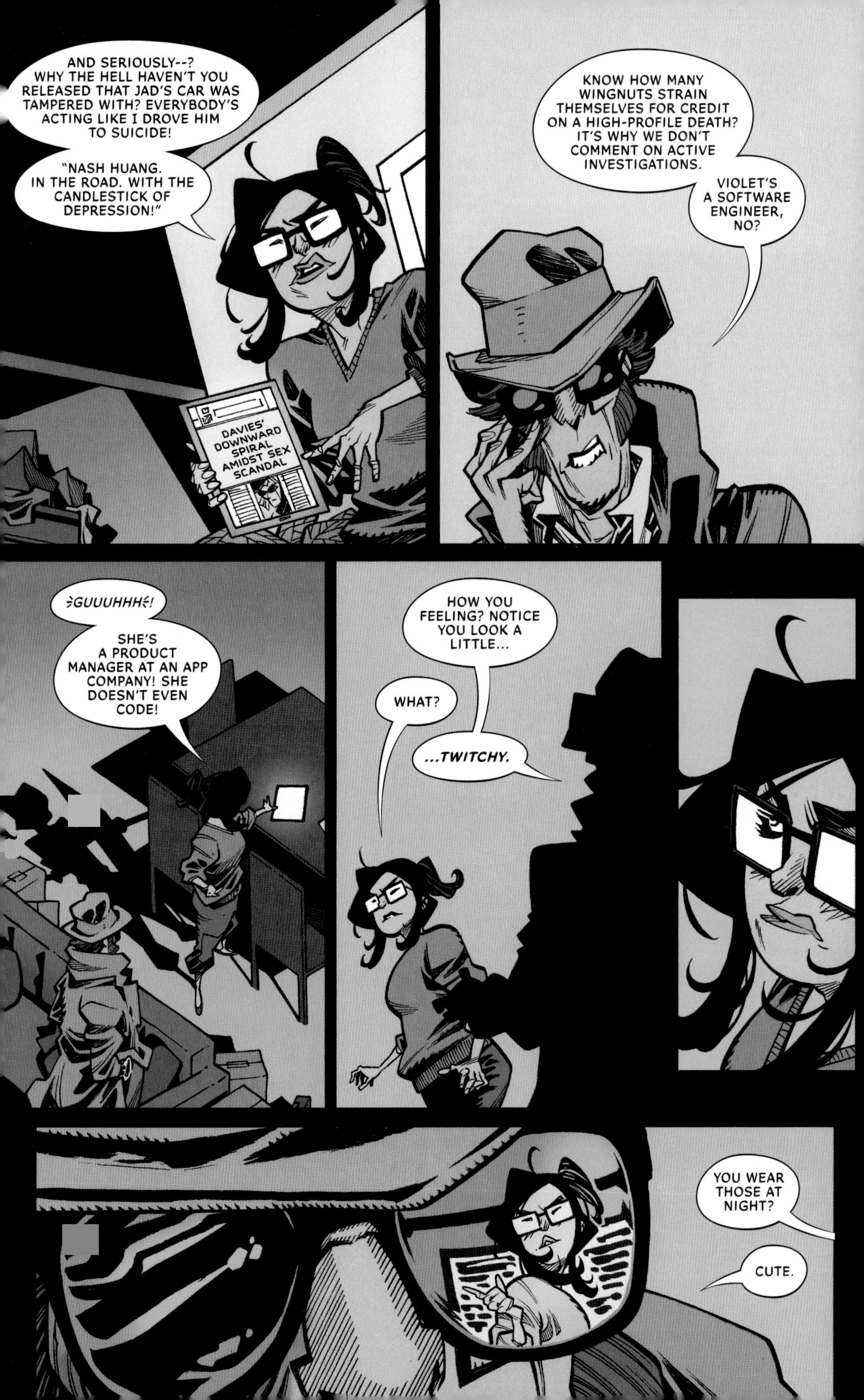
AND SERIOUSLY--? WHY THE HELL HAVEN'T YOU RELEASED THAT JAD'S CAR WAS TAMPERED WITH? EVERYBODY'S ACTING LIKE I DROVE HIM TO SUICIDE!
"NASH HUANG. IN THE ROAD. WITH THE CANDLESTICK OF DEPRESSION!"
DAVIES' DOWNWARD SPIRAL AMIDST SEX SCANDAL
KNOW HOW MANY WINGNUTS STRAIN THEMSELVES FOR CREDIT ON A HIGH-PROFILE DEATH? IT'S WHY WE DON'T COMMENT ON ACTIVE INVESTIGATIONS.
VIOLET'S A SOFTWARE ENGINEER, NO?
GUUUHHH!
SHE'S A PRODUCT MANAGER AT AN APP COMPANY! SHE DOESN'T EVEN CODE!
HOW YOU FEELING? NOTICE YOU LOOK A LITTLE...
WHAT?
...TWITCHY.
YOU WEAR THOSE AT NIGHT?
CUTE.

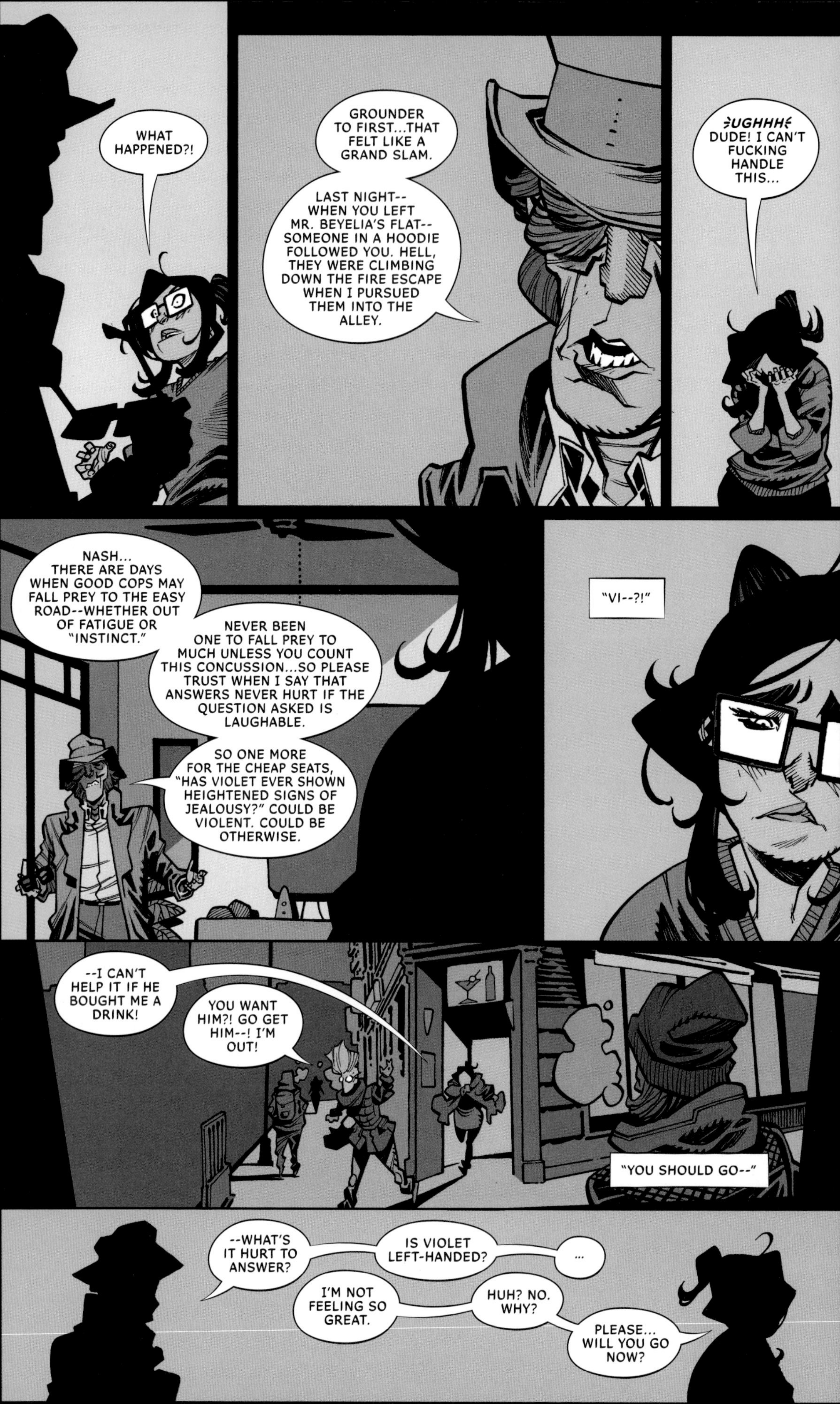
WHAT HAPPENED?!
GROUNDER TO FIRST...THAT FELT LIKE A GRAND SLAM.
LAST NIGHT-- WHEN YOU LEFT MR. BEYELIA'S FLAT-- SOMEONE IN A HOODIE FOLLOWED YOU. HELL, THEY WERE CLIMBING DOWN THE FIRE ESCAPE WHEN I PURSUED THEM INTO THE ALLEY.
UGHHH DUDE! I CAN'T FUCKING HANDLE THIS...
NASH... THERE ARE DAYS WHEN GOOD COPS MAY FALL PREY TO THE EASY ROAD--WHETHER OUT OF FATIGUE OR "INSTINCT."
NEVER BEEN ONE TO FALL PREY TO MUCH UNLESS YOU COUNT THIS CONCUSSION...SO PLEASE TRUST WHEN I SAY THAT ANSWERS NEVER HURT IF THE QUESTION ASKED IS LAUGHABLE.
SO ONE MORE FOR THE CHEAP SEATS, "HAS VIOLET EVER SHOWN HEIGHTENED SIGNS OF JEALOUSY?" COULD BE VIOLENT. COULD BE OTHERWISE.
"VI--?!"
--I CAN'T HELP IT IF HE BOUGHT ME A DRINK!
YOU WANT HIM?! GO GET HIM--! I'M OUT!
"YOU SHOULD GO--"
--WHAT'S IT HURT TO ANSWER?
IS VIOLET LEFT-HANDED?
...
I'M NOT FEELING SO GREAT.
HUH? NO. WHY?
PLEASE... WILL YOU GO NOW?

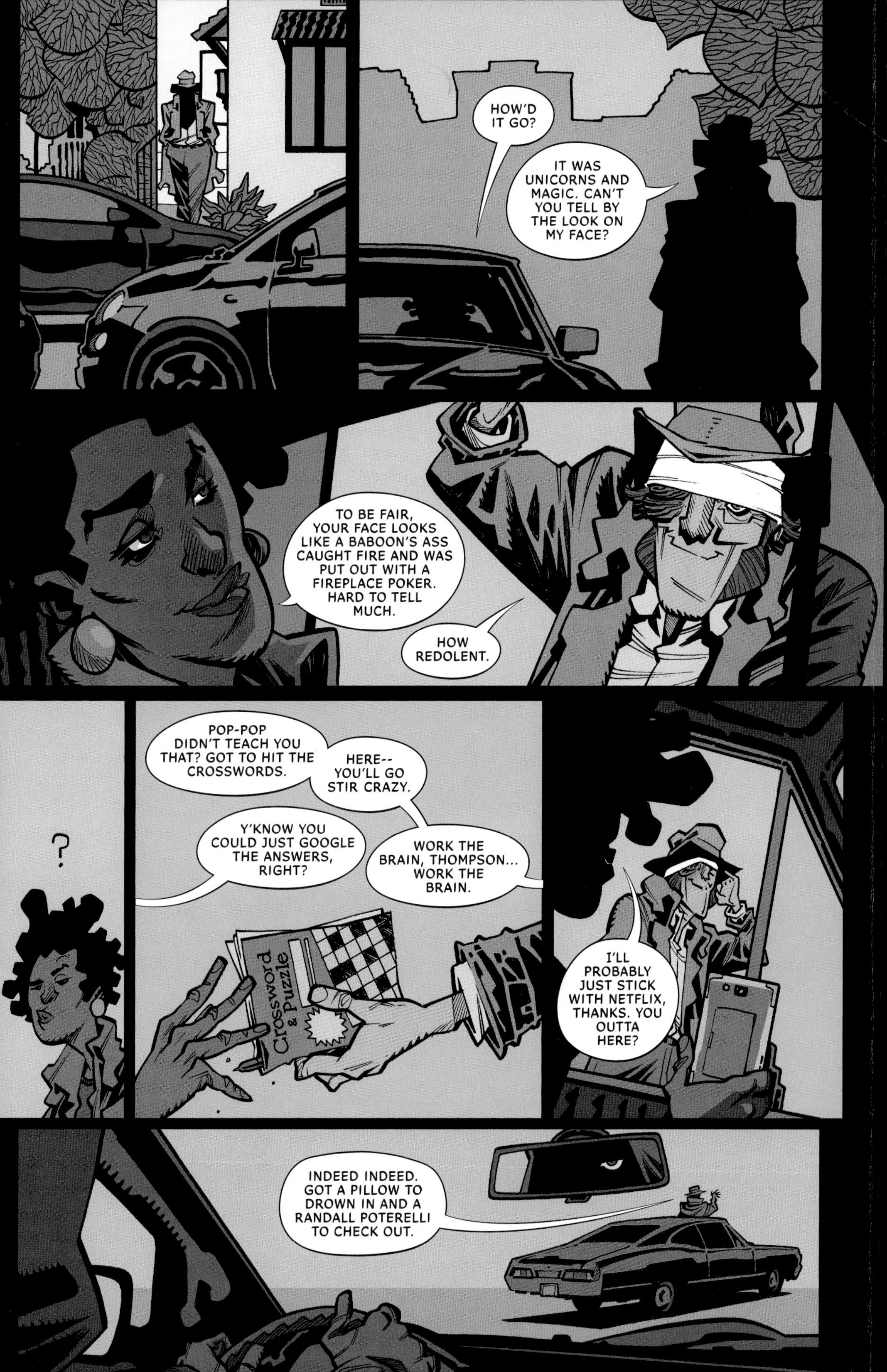
HOW'D IT GO?
IT WAS UNICORNS AND MAGIC. CAN'T YOU TELL BY THE LOOK ON MY FACE?
TO BE FAIR, YOUR FACE LOOKS LIKE A BABOON'S ASS CAUGHT FIRE AND WAS PUT OUT WITH A FIREPLACE POKER. HARD TO TELL MUCH.
HOW REDOLENT.
?
POP-POP DIDN'T TEACH YOU THAT? GOT TO HIT THE CROSSWORDS.
HERE-- YOU'LL GO STIR CRAZY.
Y'KNOW YOU COULD JUST GOOGLE THE ANSWERS, RIGHT?
WORK THE BRAIN, THOMPSON... WORK THE BRAIN.
Crossword & Puzzle
I'LL PROBABLY JUST STICK WITH NETFLIX, THANKS. YOU OUTTA HERE?
INDEED INDEED. GOT A PILLOW TO DROWN IN AND A RANDALL POTERELLI TO CHECK OUT.

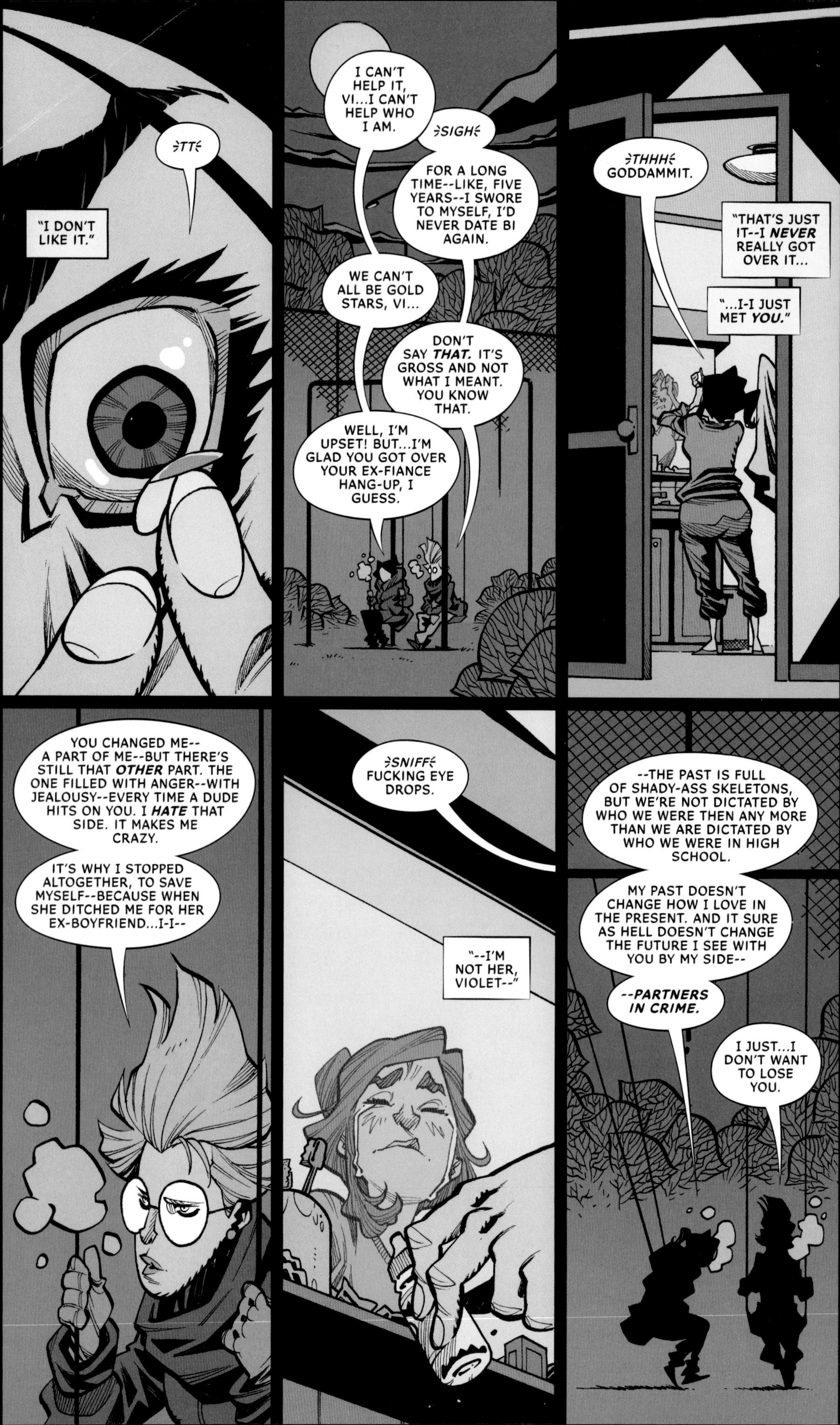

⋺TT⋹
"I DON'T LIKE IT."
I CAN'T HELP IT, VI...I CAN'T HELP WHO I AM.
⋺SIGH⋹
FOR A LONG TIME--LIKE, FIVE YEARS--I SWORE TO MYSELF, I'D NEVER DATE BI AGAIN.
WE CAN'T ALL BE GOLD STARS, VI...
DON'T SAY THAT. IT'S GROSS AND NOT WHAT I MEANT. YOU KNOW THAT.
WELL, I'M UPSET! BUT...I'M GLAD YOU GOT OVER YOUR EX-FIANCE HANG-UP, I GUESS.
⋺THHH⋹ GODDAMMIT.
"THAT'S JUST IT--I NEVER REALLY GOT OVER IT...
"...I-I JUST MET YOU."
YOU CHANGED ME--A PART OF ME--BUT THERE'S STILL THAT OTHER PART. THE ONE FILLED WITH ANGER--WITH JEALOUSY--EVERY TIME A DUDE HITS ON YOU. I HATE THAT SIDE. IT MAKES ME CRAZY.
IT'S WHY I STOPPED ALTOGETHER, TO SAVE MYSELF--BECAUSE WHEN SHE DITCHED ME FOR HER EX-BOYFRIEND...I-I--
⋺SNIFF⋹ FUCKING EYE DROPS.
"--I'M NOT HER, VIOLET--"
--THE PAST IS FULL OF SHADY-ASS SKELETONS, BUT WE'RE NOT DICTATED BY WHO WE WERE THEN ANY MORE THAN WE ARE DICTATED BY WHO WE WERE IN HIGH SCHOOL.
MY PAST DOESN'T CHANGE HOW I LOVE IN THE PRESENT. AND IT SURE AS HELL DOESN'T CHANGE THE FUTURE I SEE WITH YOU BY MY SIDE--
--PARTNERS IN CRIME.
I JUST...I DON'T WANT TO LOSE YOU.

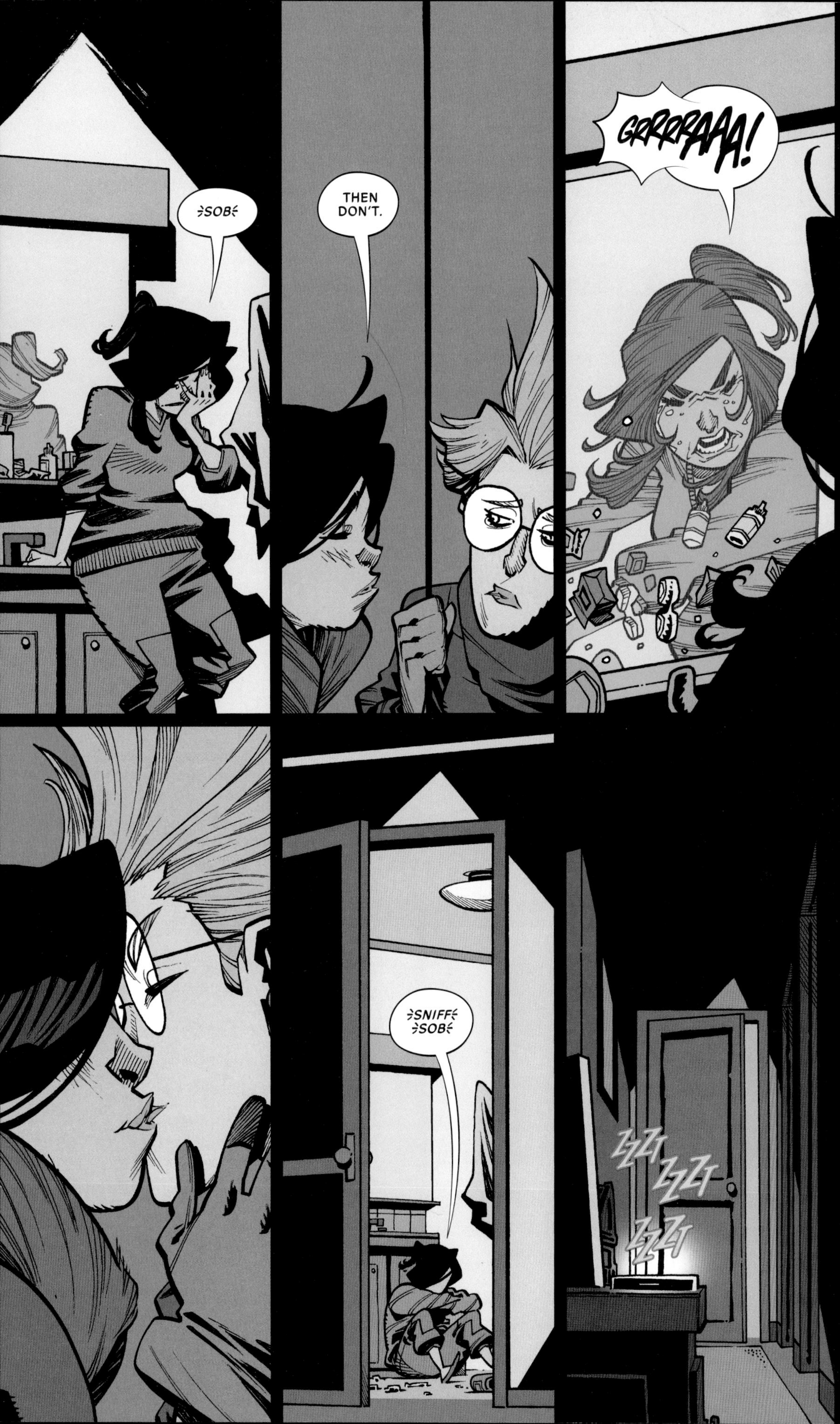

SOB
THEN DON'T.
GRRRRAAAA!
SNIFF SOB
ZZZT ZZZT ZZZT

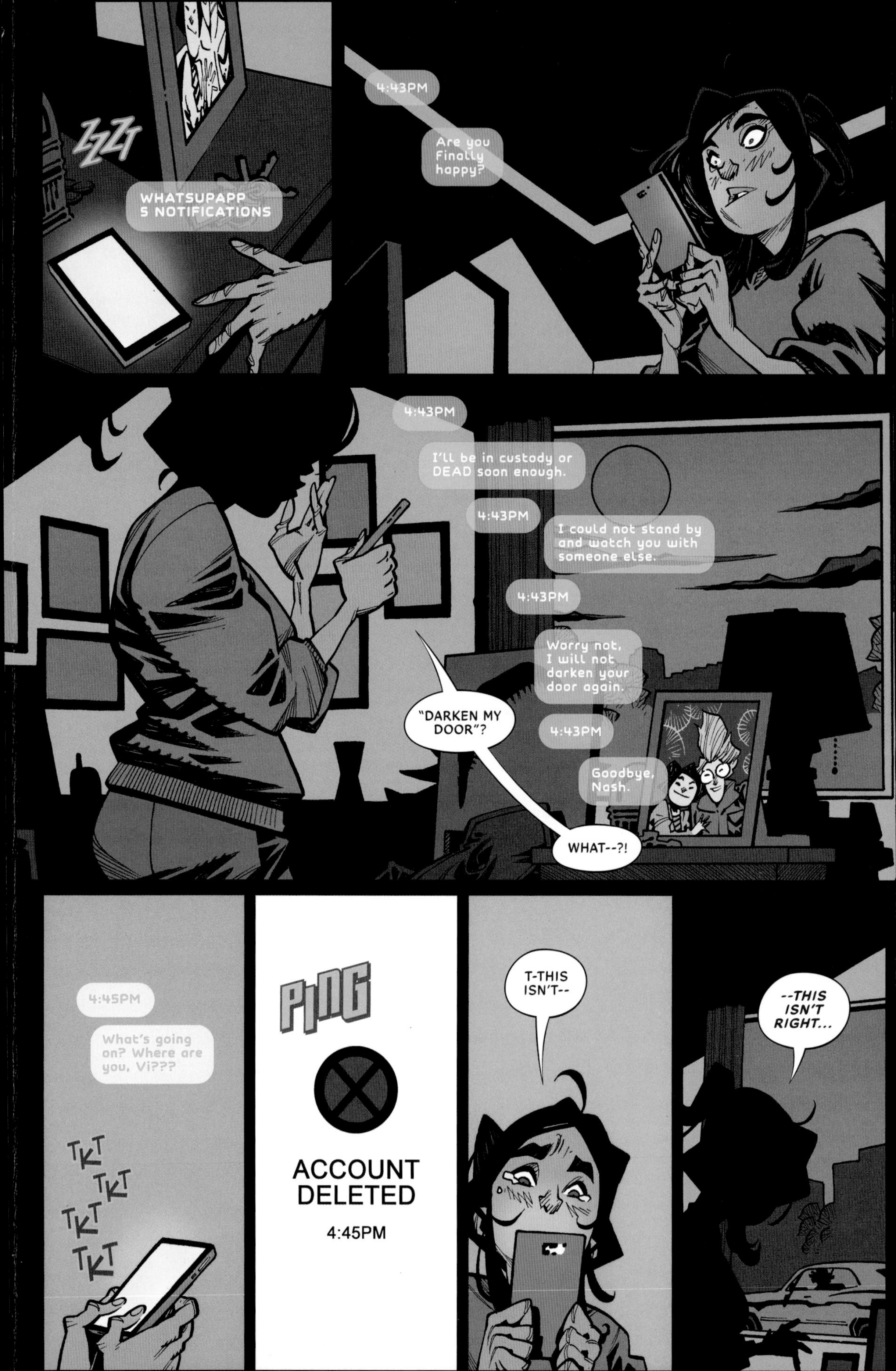
ZZZT
WHATSUPAPP 5 NOTIFICATIONS
4:43PM
Are you Finally happy?
4:43PM
I'll be in custody or DEAD soon enough.
4:43PM
I could not stand by and watch you with someone else.
4:43PM
Worry not, I will not darken your door again.
"DARKEN MY DOOR"?
4:43PM
Goodbye, Nash.
WHAT--?!
4:45PM
What's going on? Where are you, Vi???
TKT TKT TKT TKT
PING
ACCOUNT DELETED
4:45PM
T-THIS ISN'T--
--THIS ISN'T RIGHT...

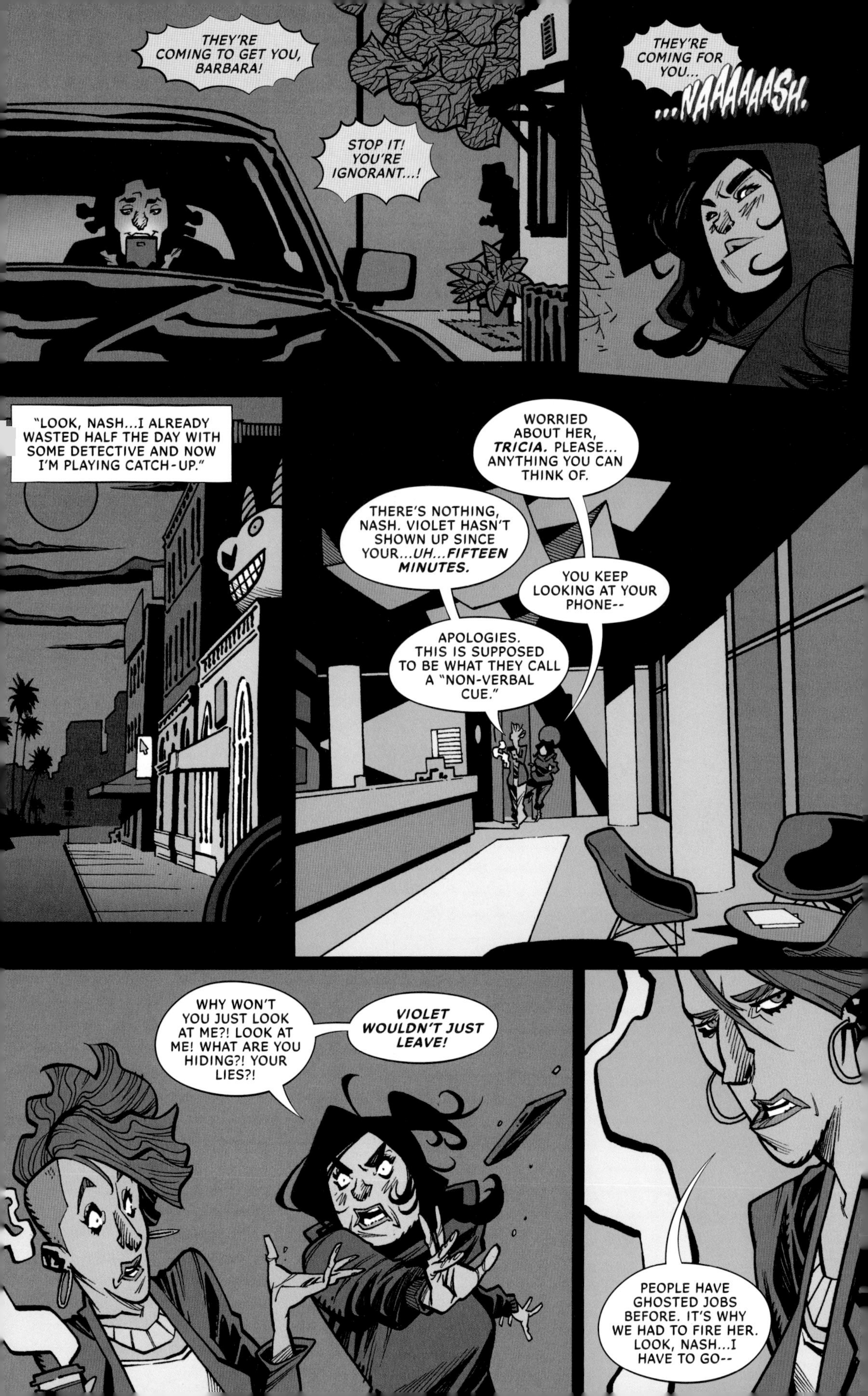
THEY'RE COMING TO GET YOU, BARBARA!
STOP IT! YOU'RE IGNORANT...!
THEY'RE COMING FOR YOU...
...NAAAAAASH.
"LOOK, NASH...I ALREADY WASTED HALF THE DAY WITH SOME DETECTIVE AND NOW I'M PLAYING CATCH-UP."
WORRIED ABOUT HER, TRICIA. PLEASE... ANYTHING YOU CAN THINK OF.
THERE'S NOTHING, NASH. VIOLET HASN'T SHOWN UP SINCE YOUR...UH...FIFTEEN MINUTES.
YOU KEEP LOOKING AT YOUR PHONE--
APOLOGIES. THIS IS SUPPOSED TO BE WHAT THEY CALL A "NON-VERBAL CUE."
WHY WON'T YOU JUST LOOK AT ME?! LOOK AT ME! WHAT ARE YOU HIDING?! YOUR LIES?!
VIOLET WOULDN'T JUST LEAVE!
PEOPLE HAVE GHOSTED JOBS BEFORE. IT'S WHY WE HAD TO FIRE HER. LOOK, NASH...I HAVE TO GO--

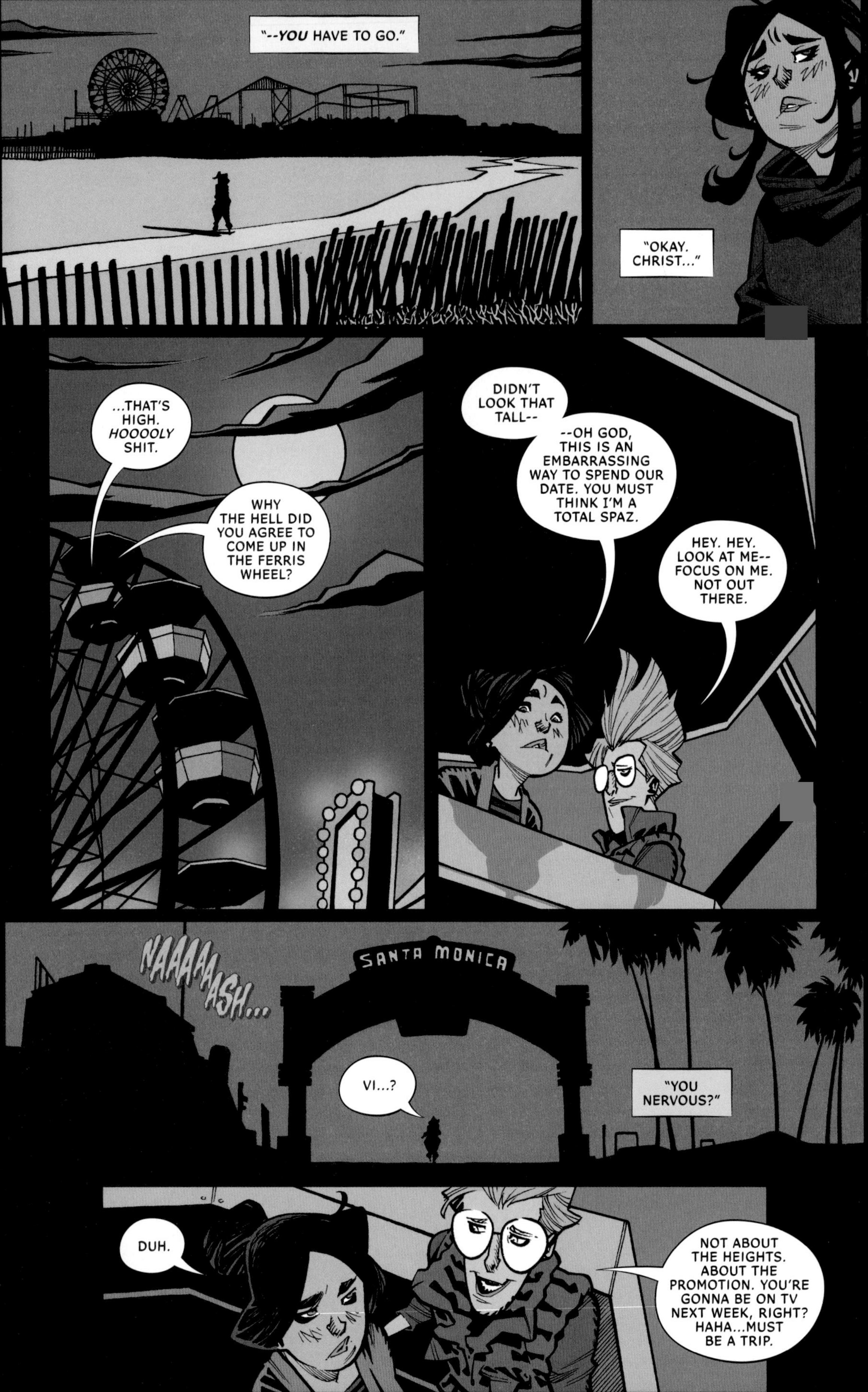
"--*YOU* HAVE TO GO."
"OKAY. CHRIST..."
...THAT'S HIGH. *HOOOOLY* SHIT.
WHY THE HELL DID YOU AGREE TO COME UP IN THE FERRIS WHEEL?
DIDN'T LOOK THAT TALL--
--OH GOD, THIS IS AN EMBARRASSING WAY TO SPEND OUR DATE. YOU MUST THINK I'M A TOTAL SPAZ.
HEY. HEY. LOOK AT ME-- FOCUS ON ME. NOT OUT THERE.
NAAAAAASH...
SANTA MONICA
VI...?
"YOU NERVOUS?"
DUH.
NOT ABOUT THE HEIGHTS. ABOUT THE PROMOTION. YOU'RE GONNA BE ON TV NEXT WEEK, RIGHT? HAHA...MUST BE A TRIP.

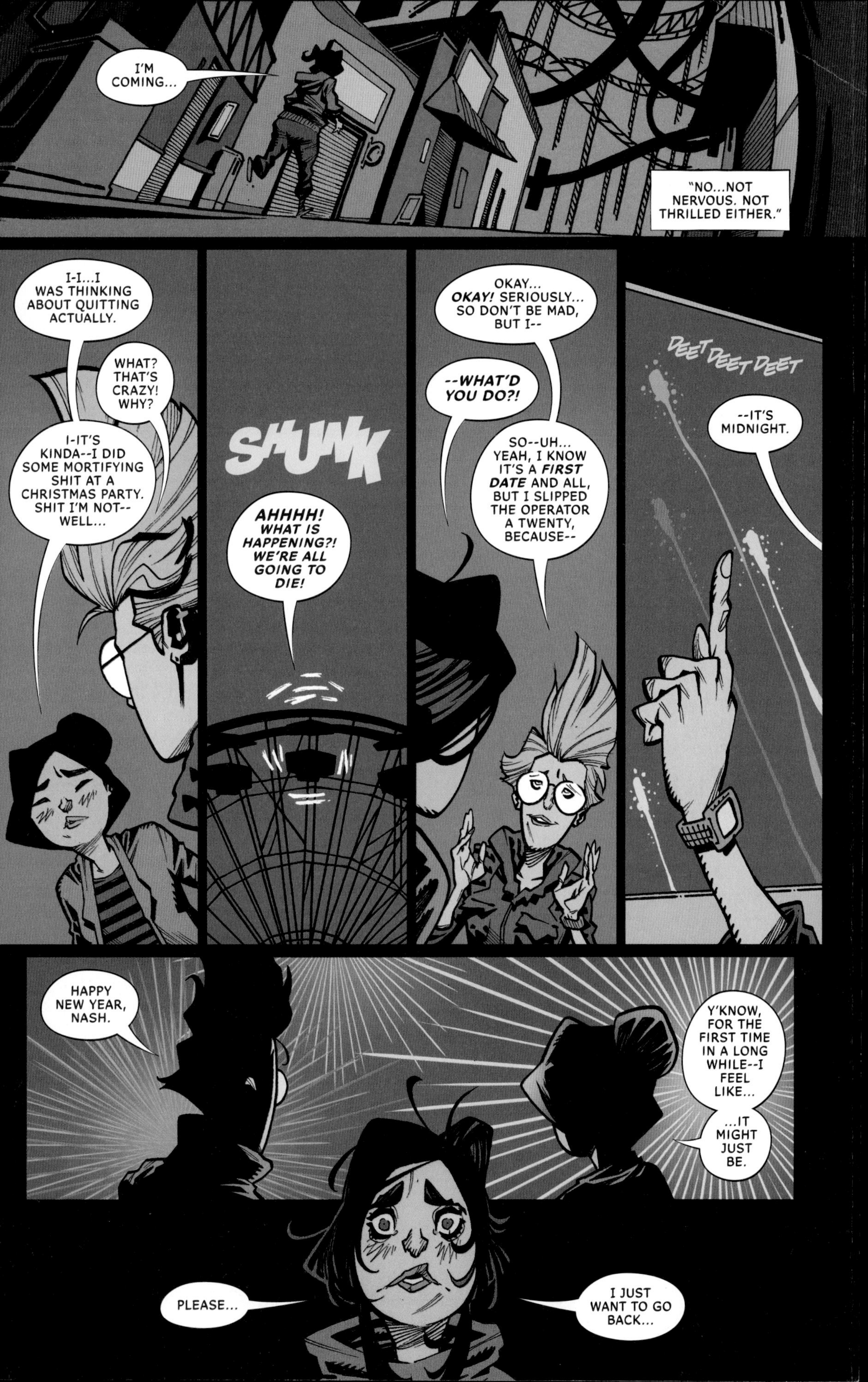
I'M COMING...
"NO...NOT NERVOUS. NOT THRILLED EITHER."
I-I...I WAS THINKING ABOUT QUITTING ACTUALLY.
WHAT? THAT'S CRAZY! WHY?
I-IT'S KINDA--I DID SOME MORTIFYING SHIT AT A CHRISTMAS PARTY. SHIT I'M NOT-- WELL...
SHUNK
AHHHH! WHAT IS HAPPENING?! WE'RE ALL GOING TO DIE!
OKAY... OKAY! SERIOUSLY... SO DON'T BE MAD, BUT I--
--WHAT'D YOU DO?!
SO--UH... YEAH, I KNOW IT'S A FIRST DATE AND ALL, BUT I SLIPPED THE OPERATOR A TWENTY, BECAUSE--
DEET DEET DEET
--IT'S MIDNIGHT.
HAPPY NEW YEAR, NASH.
Y'KNOW, FOR THE FIRST TIME IN A LONG WHILE--I FEEL LIKE...
...IT MIGHT JUST BE.
PLEASE...
I JUST WANT TO GO BACK...

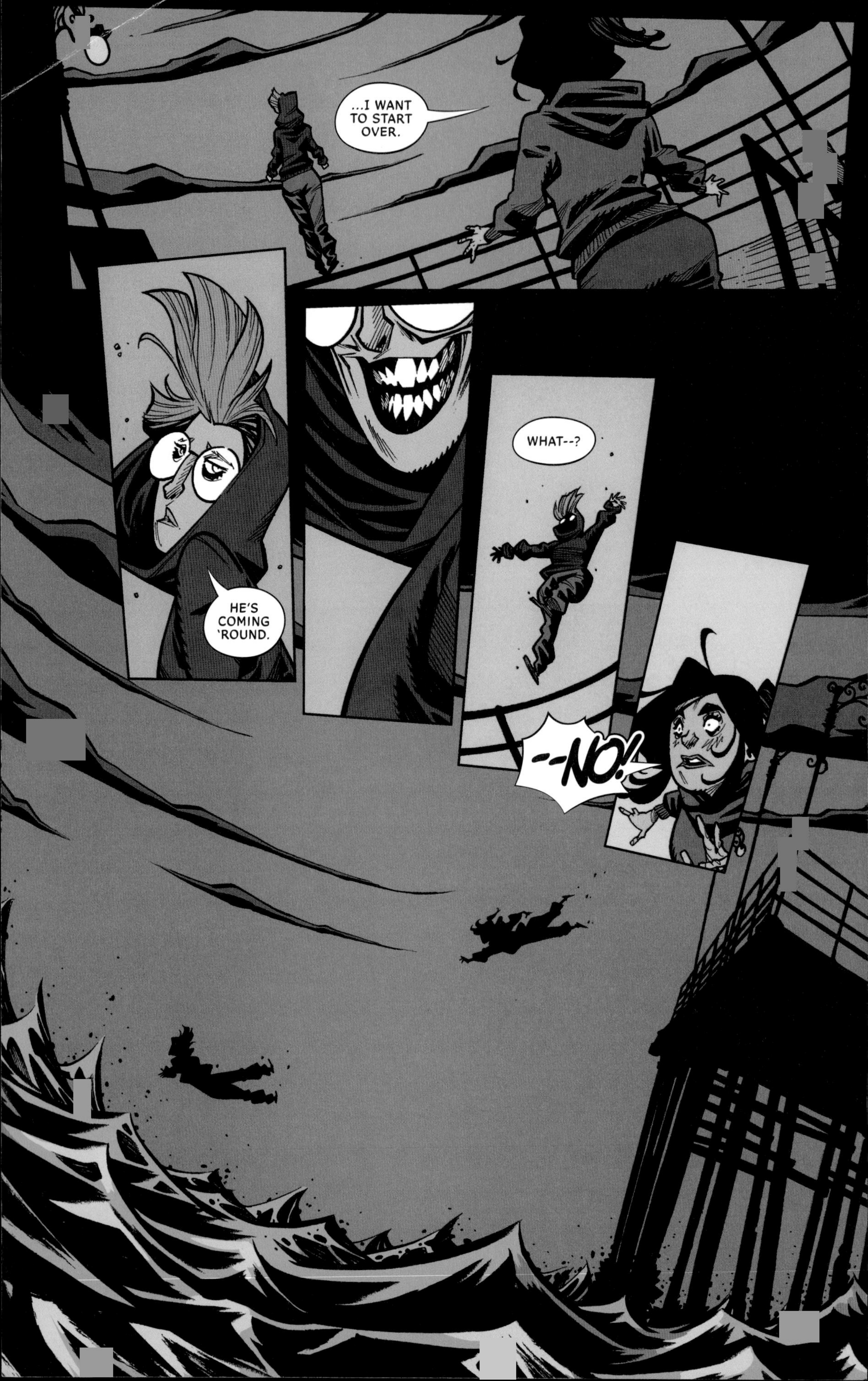
...I WANT TO START OVER.
HE'S COMING 'ROUND.
WHAT--?
--NO!

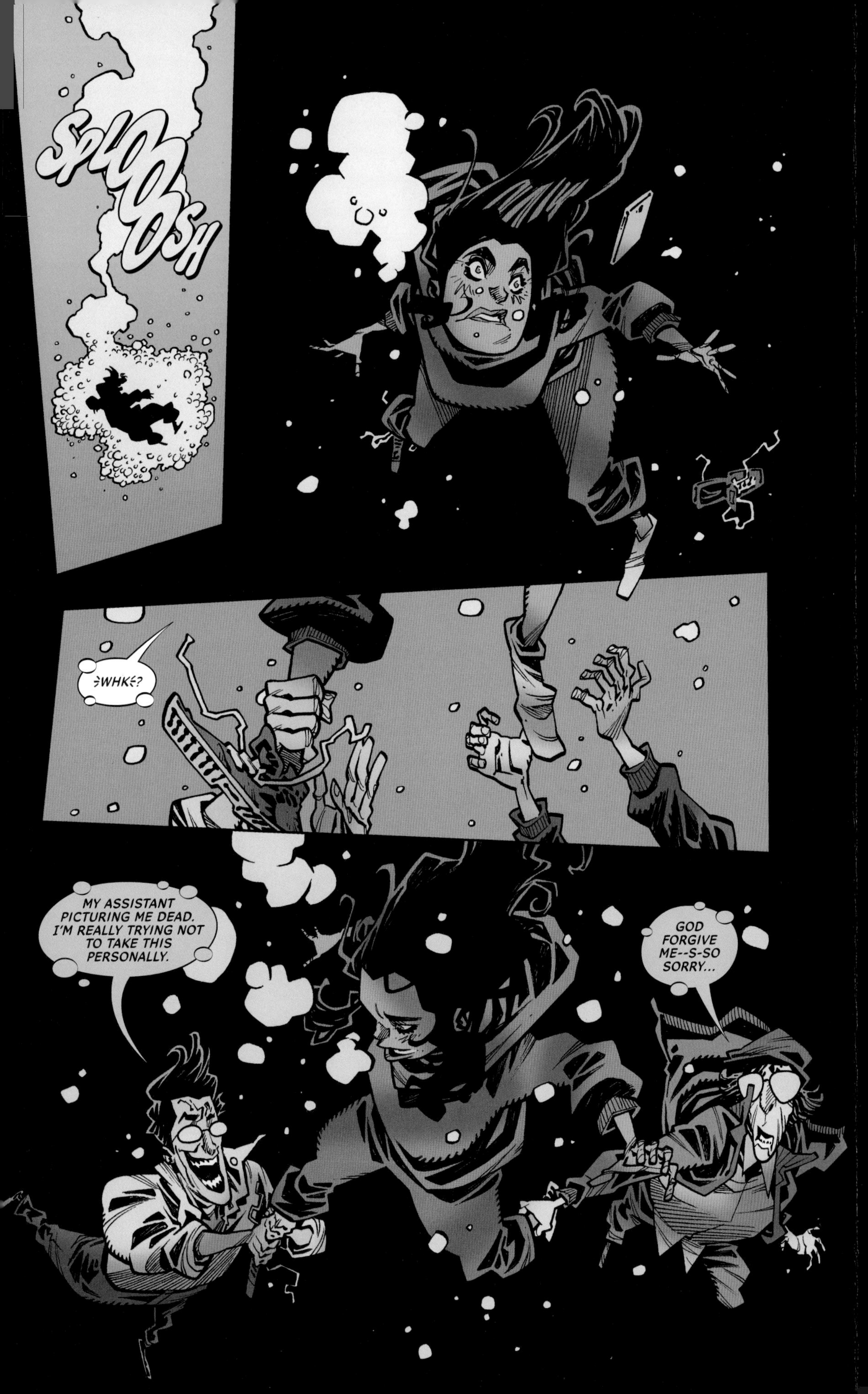
SPLOOOOSH
WHK?
MY ASSISTANT PICTURING ME DEAD. I'M REALLY TRYING NOT TO TAKE THIS PERSONALLY.
GOD FORGIVE ME--S-SO SORRY...

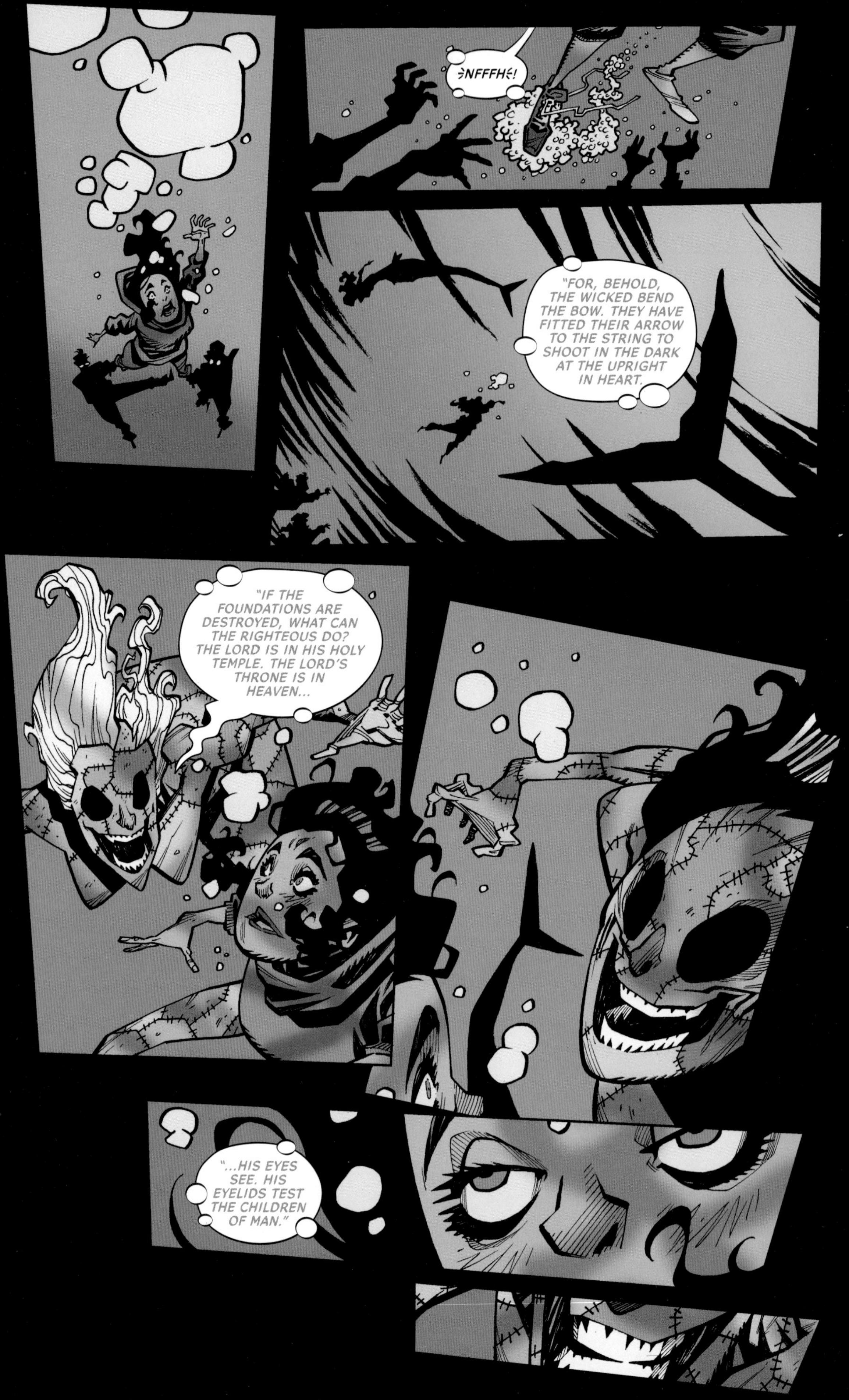

NFFFH!
"FOR, BEHOLD, THE WICKED BEND THE BOW. THEY HAVE FITTED THEIR ARROW TO THE STRING TO SHOOT IN THE DARK AT THE UPRIGHT IN HEART.
"IF THE FOUNDATIONS ARE DESTROYED, WHAT CAN THE RIGHTEOUS DO? THE LORD IS IN HIS HOLY TEMPLE. THE LORD'S THRONE IS IN HEAVEN...
"...HIS EYES SEE. HIS EYELIDS TEST THE CHILDREN OF MAN."

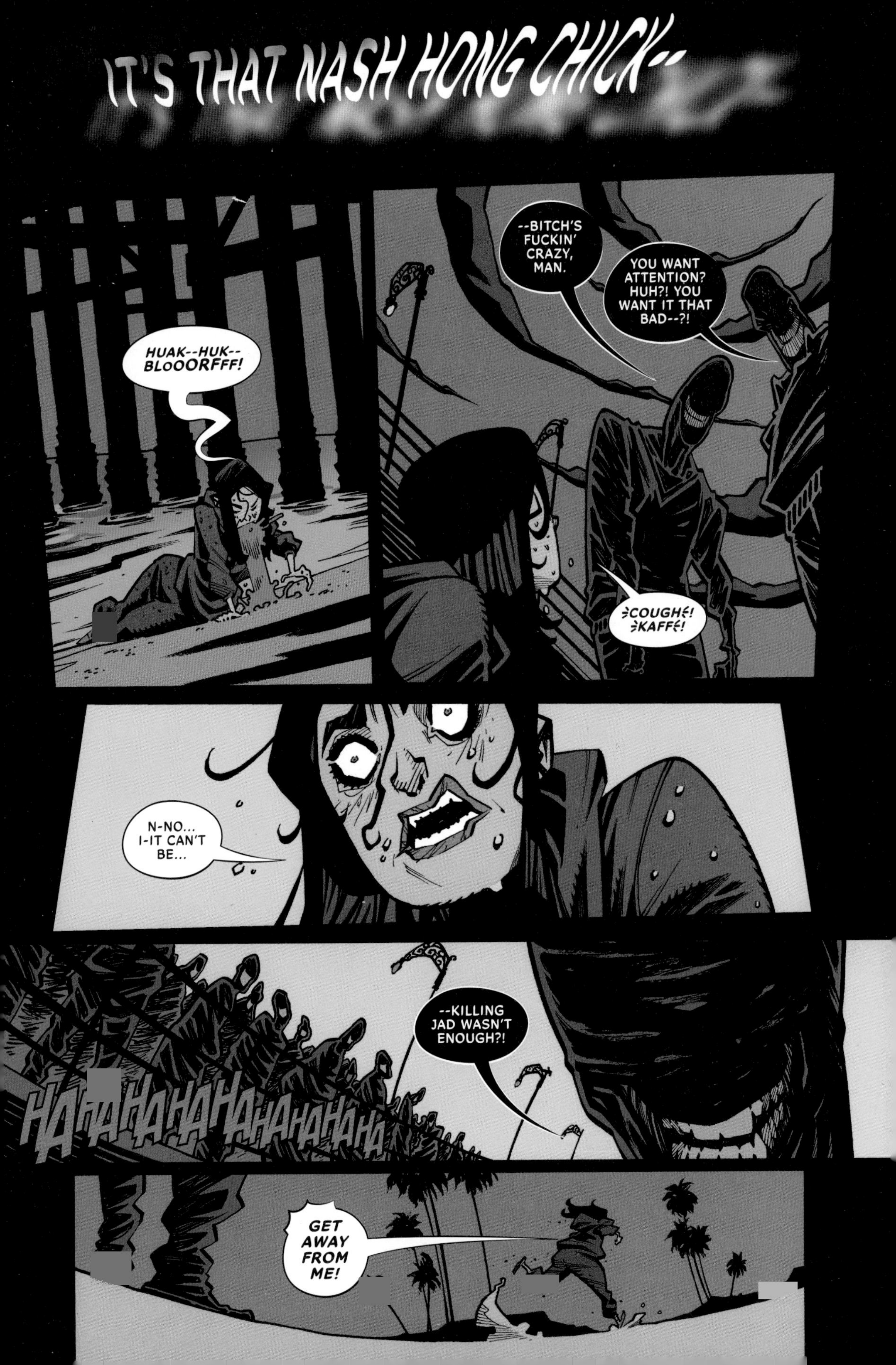
IT'S THAT NASH HONG CHICK--
HUAK--HUK-- BLOoORFFF!
--BITCH'S FUCKIN' CRAZY, MAN.
YOU WANT ATTENTION? HUH?! YOU WANT IT THAT BAD--?!
COUGH! KAFF!
N-NO... I-IT CAN'T BE...
HAHAHAHAHAHAHAHAHAHA
--KILLING JAD WASN'T ENOUGH?!
GET AWAY FROM ME!

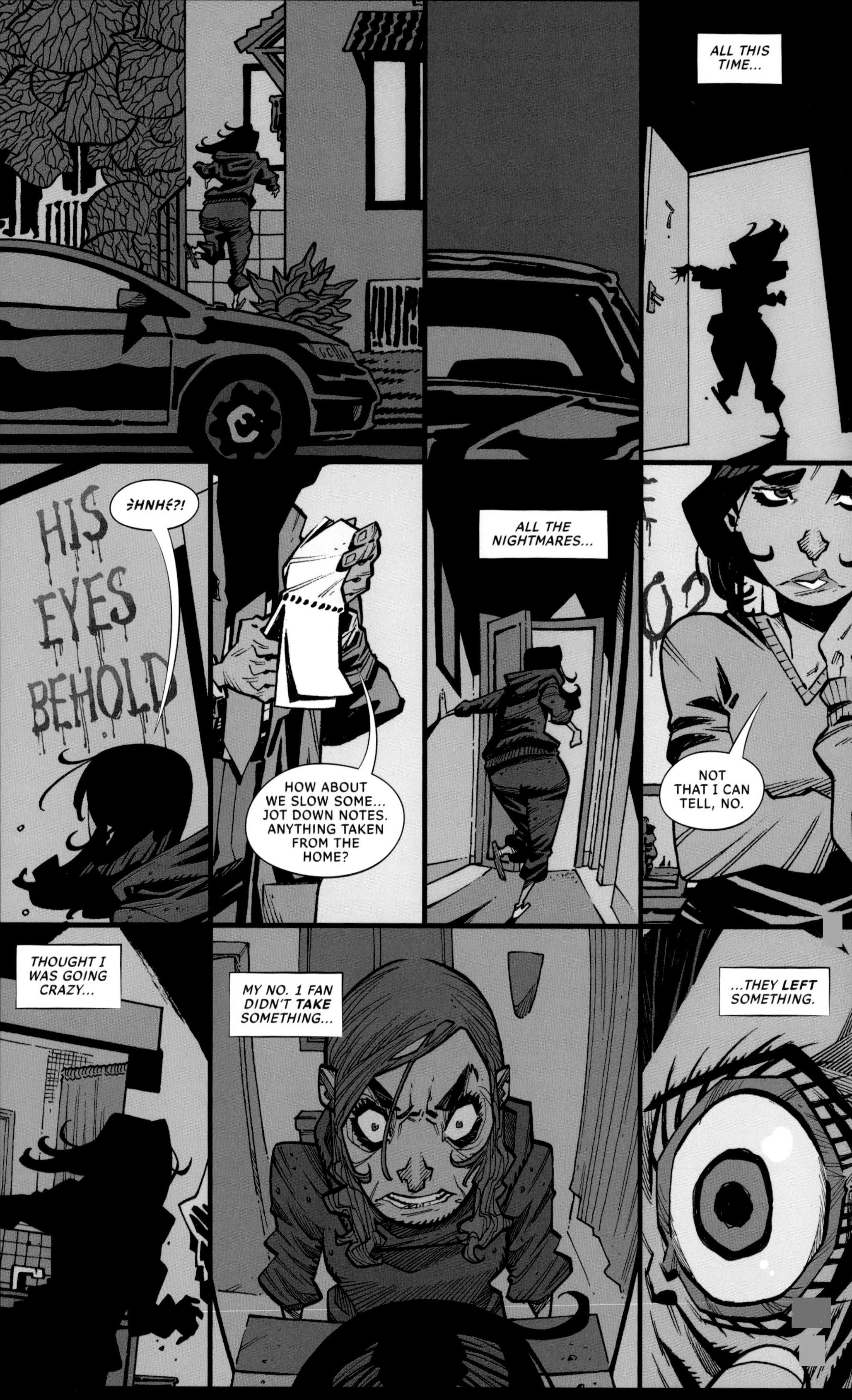
ALL THIS TIME...
HNH?!
HIS EYES BEHOLD
HOW ABOUT WE SLOW SOME... JOT DOWN NOTES. ANYTHING TAKEN FROM THE HOME?
ALL THE NIGHTMARES...
NOT THAT I CAN TELL, NO.
THOUGHT I WAS GOING CRAZY...
MY NO. 1 FAN DIDN'T TAKE SOMETHING...
...THEY LEFT SOMETHING.

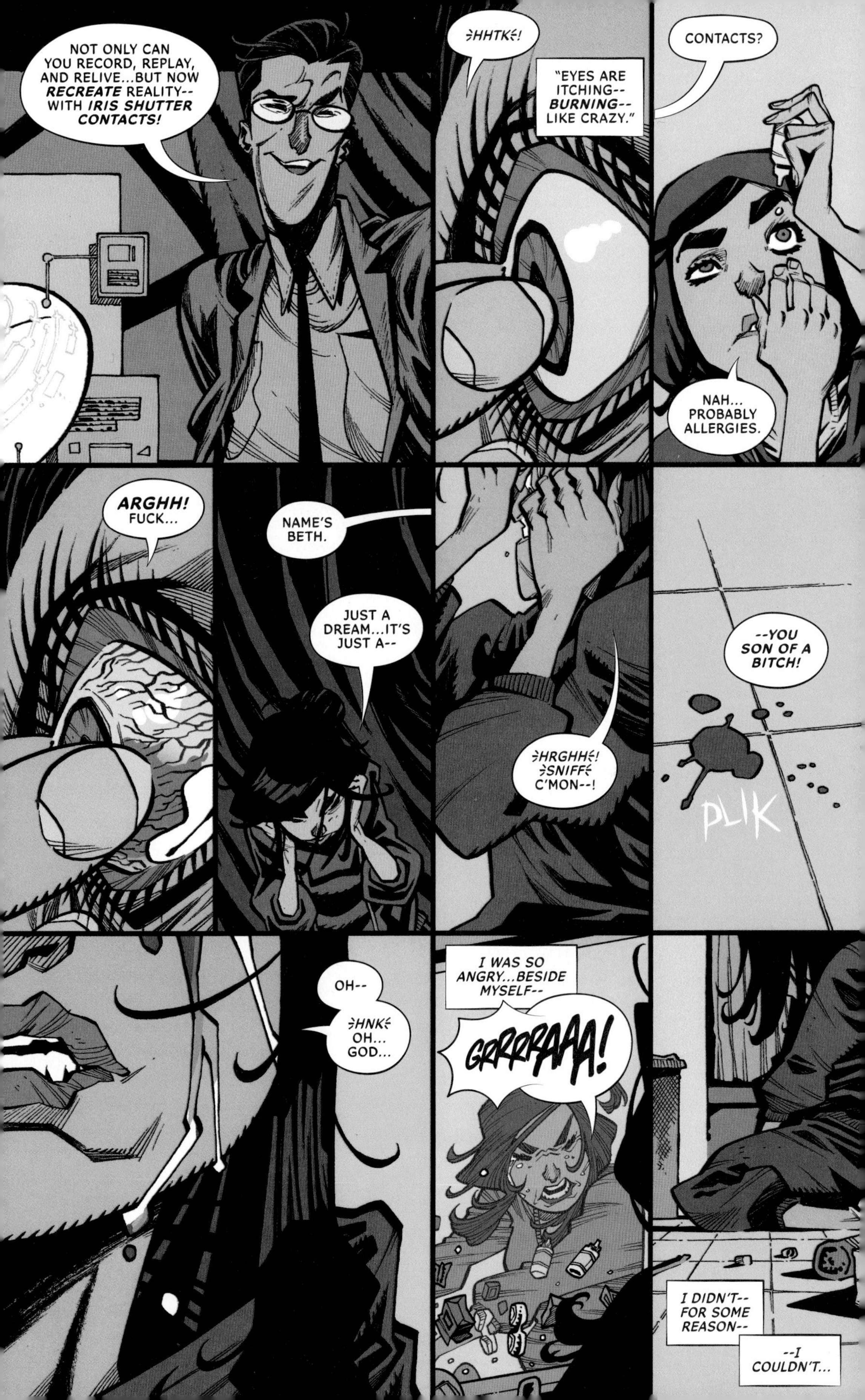
NOT ONLY CAN YOU RECORD, REPLAY, AND RELIVE...BUT NOW RECREATE REALITY-- WITH IRIS SHUTTER CONTACTS!
HHTK!
"EYES ARE ITCHING-- BURNING-- LIKE CRAZY."
CONTACTS?
NAH... PROBABLY ALLERGIES.
ARGHH! FUCK...
NAME'S BETH.
JUST A DREAM...IT'S JUST A--
HRGHH! SNIFF C'MON--!
--YOU SON OF A BITCH!
PLIK
OH--
HNK OH... GOD...
I WAS SO ANGRY...BESIDE MYSELF--
GRRRRAAAA!
I DIDN'T-- FOR SOME REASON--
--I COULDN'T...

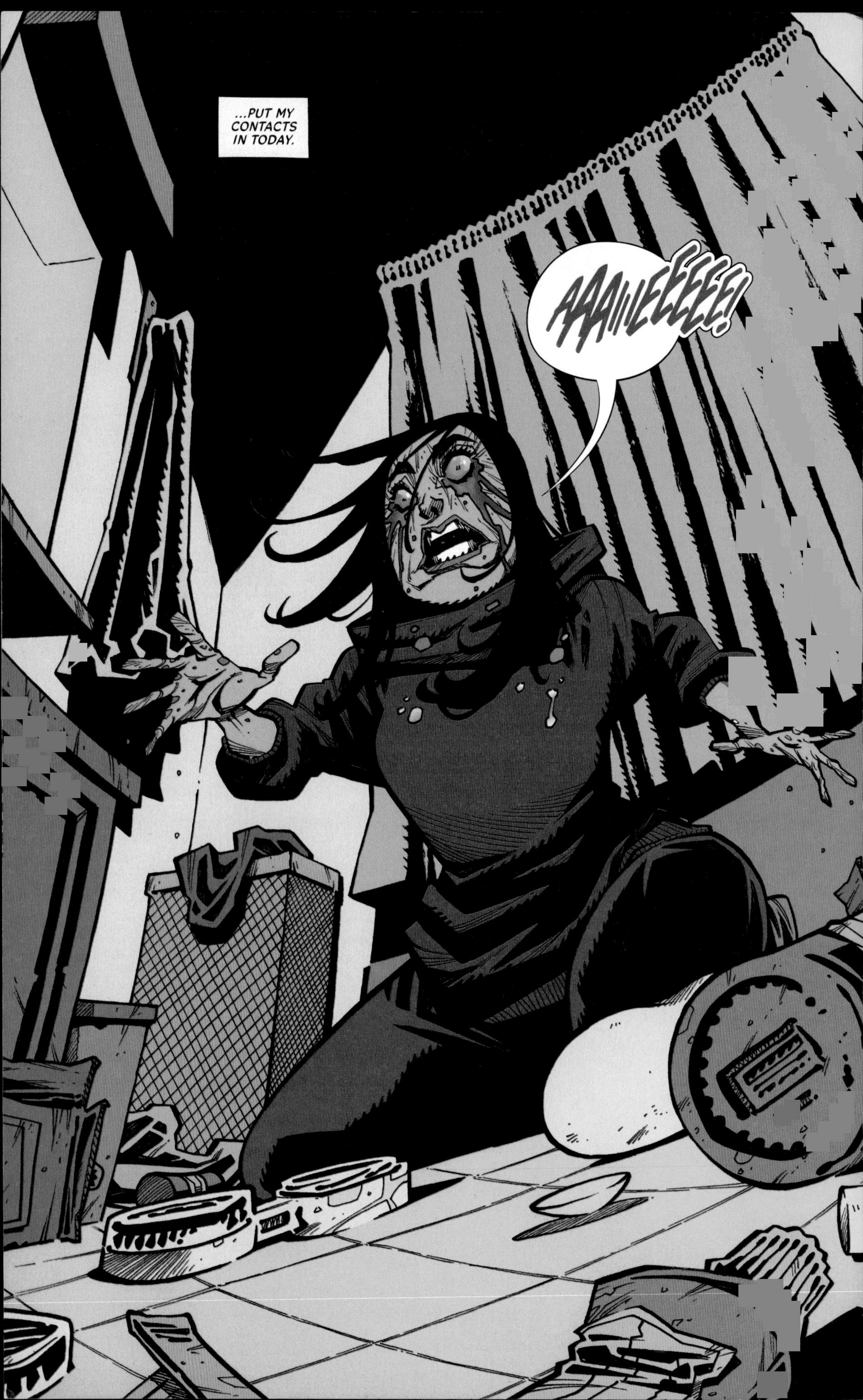
...PUT MY CONTACTS IN TODAY.
AAAIIIEEEEE!

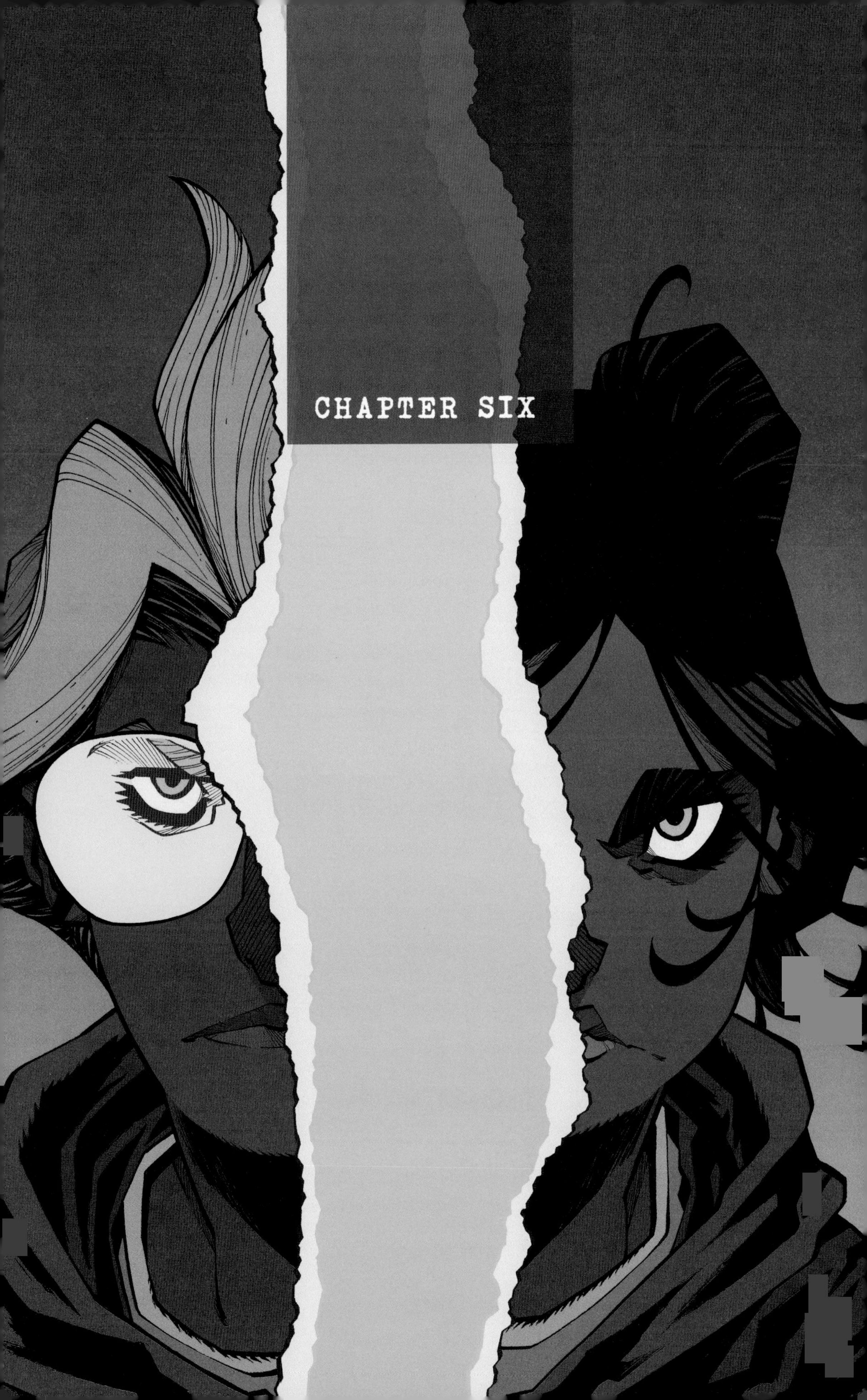
CHAPTER SIX

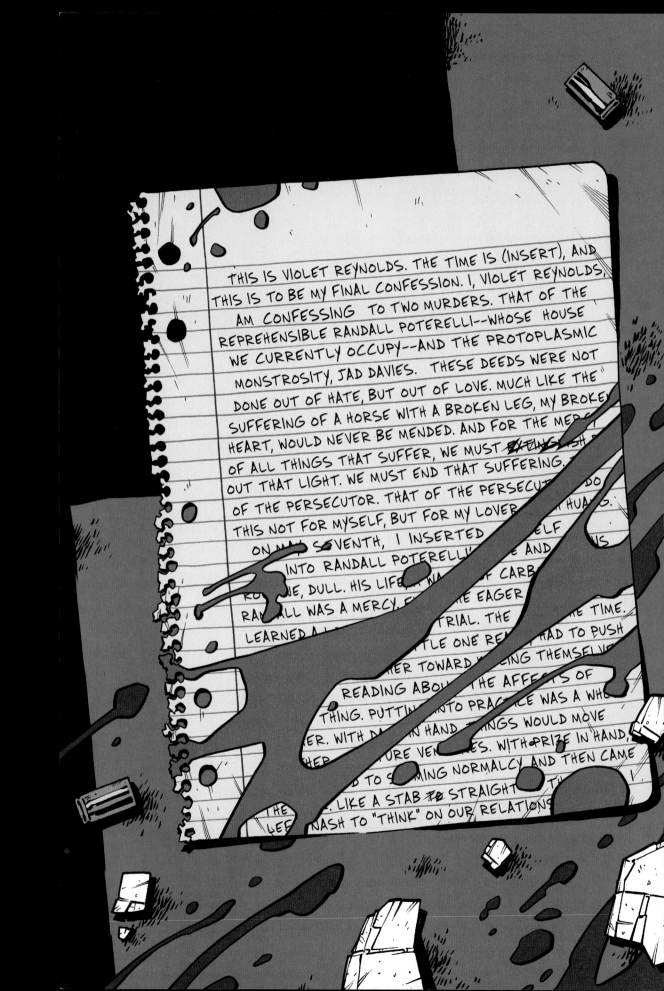

THIS IS VIOLET REYNOLDS. THE TIME IS (INSERT), AND
THIS IS TO BE MY FINAL CONFESSION. I, VIOLET REYNOLDS,
AM CONFESSING TO TWO MURDERS. THAT OF THE
REPREHENSIBLE RANDALL POTERELLI--WHOSE HOUSE
WE CURRENTLY OCCUPY--AND THE PROTOPLASMIC
MONSTROSITY, JAD DAVIES. THESE DEEDS WERE NOT
DONE OUT OF HATE, BUT OUT OF LOVE. MUCH LIKE THE
SUFFERING OF A HORSE WITH A BROKEN LEG, MY BROKEN
HEART, WOULD NEVER BE MENDED. AND FOR THE MERCY
OF ALL THINGS THAT SUFFER, WE MUST ~~EXTINGUISH~~
OUT THAT LIGHT. WE MUST END THAT SUFFERING.
OF THE PERSECUTOR. THAT OF THE PERSECUT___ DO
THIS NOT FOR MYSELF, BUT FOR MY LOVER___ HUA___.
ON MA___ S___VENTH, I INSERTED ___ELF ___S
___ INTO RANDALL POTERELLI___ E AND ___
RO___ E, DULL. HIS LIFE___ WA___ F CARB___
RAN___LL WAS A MERCY. ___ E EAGER ___
LEARNED A L___ ___TRIAL. THE ___ E TIME.
___TLE ONE RE___ HAD TO PUSH
___ER TOWARD ___ING THEMSEL___
___ READING ABOU___ THE AFFE___S OF
___THING. PUTTI___ NTO PRAC___CE WAS A WH___
___ER. WITH D___ N HAND ___INGS WOULD MOVE
___HER ___URE VEN___ ES. WITH PRIZE IN HAND,
___ TO S___MING NORMALCY. AND THEN CAME
___ LIKE A STAB ~~TO~~ STRAIGHT ___ TH___
___ NASH TO "THINK" ON OUR RELATION___

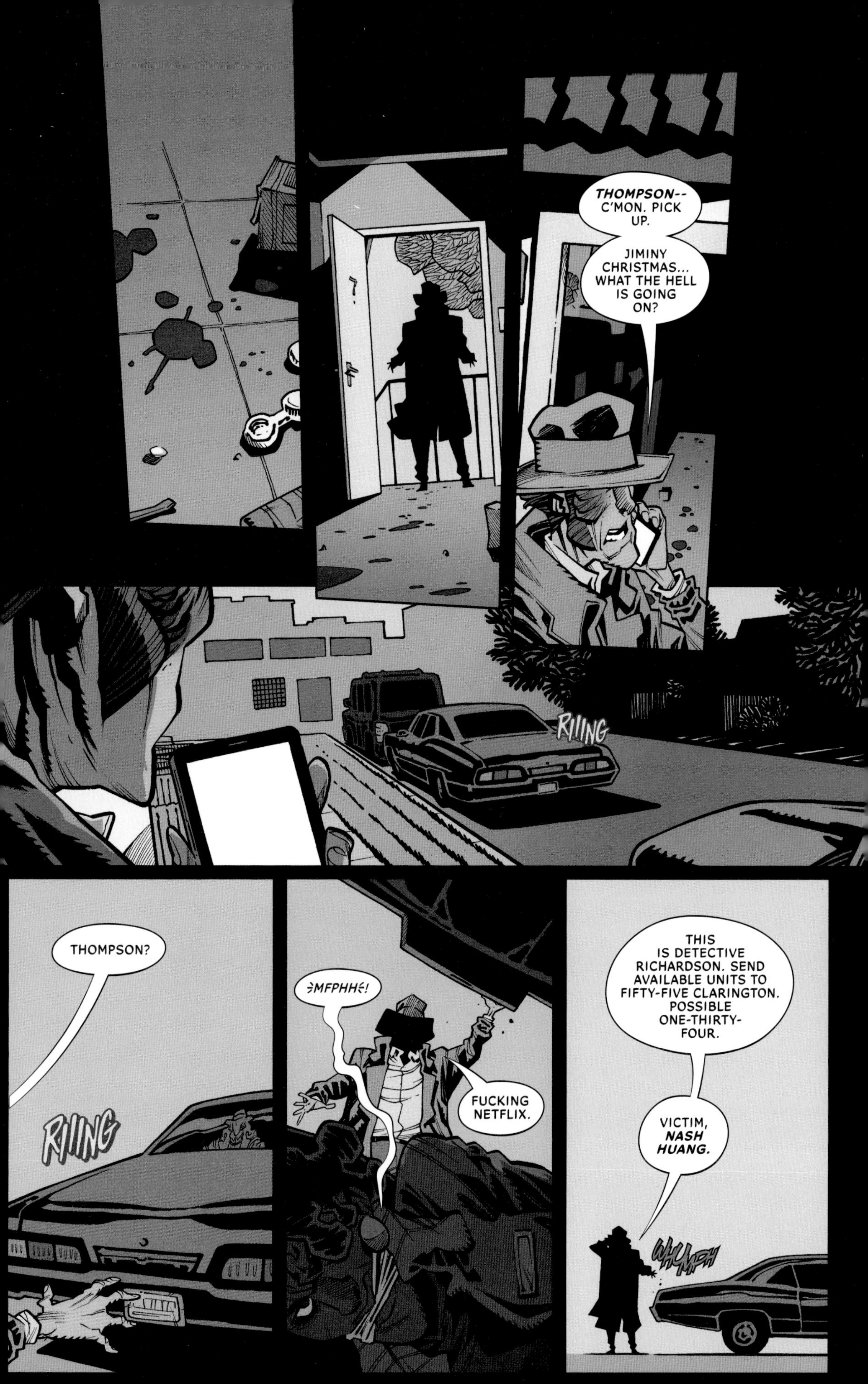
THOMPSON-- C'MON. PICK UP.
JIMINY CHRISTMAS... WHAT THE HELL IS GOING ON?
RIIING
THOMPSON?
RIIING
MFPHH!
FUCKING NETFLIX.
THIS IS DETECTIVE RICHARDSON. SEND AVAILABLE UNITS TO FIFTY-FIVE CLARINGTON. POSSIBLE ONE-THIRTY-FOUR.
VICTIM, NASH HUANG.
WHUMPH

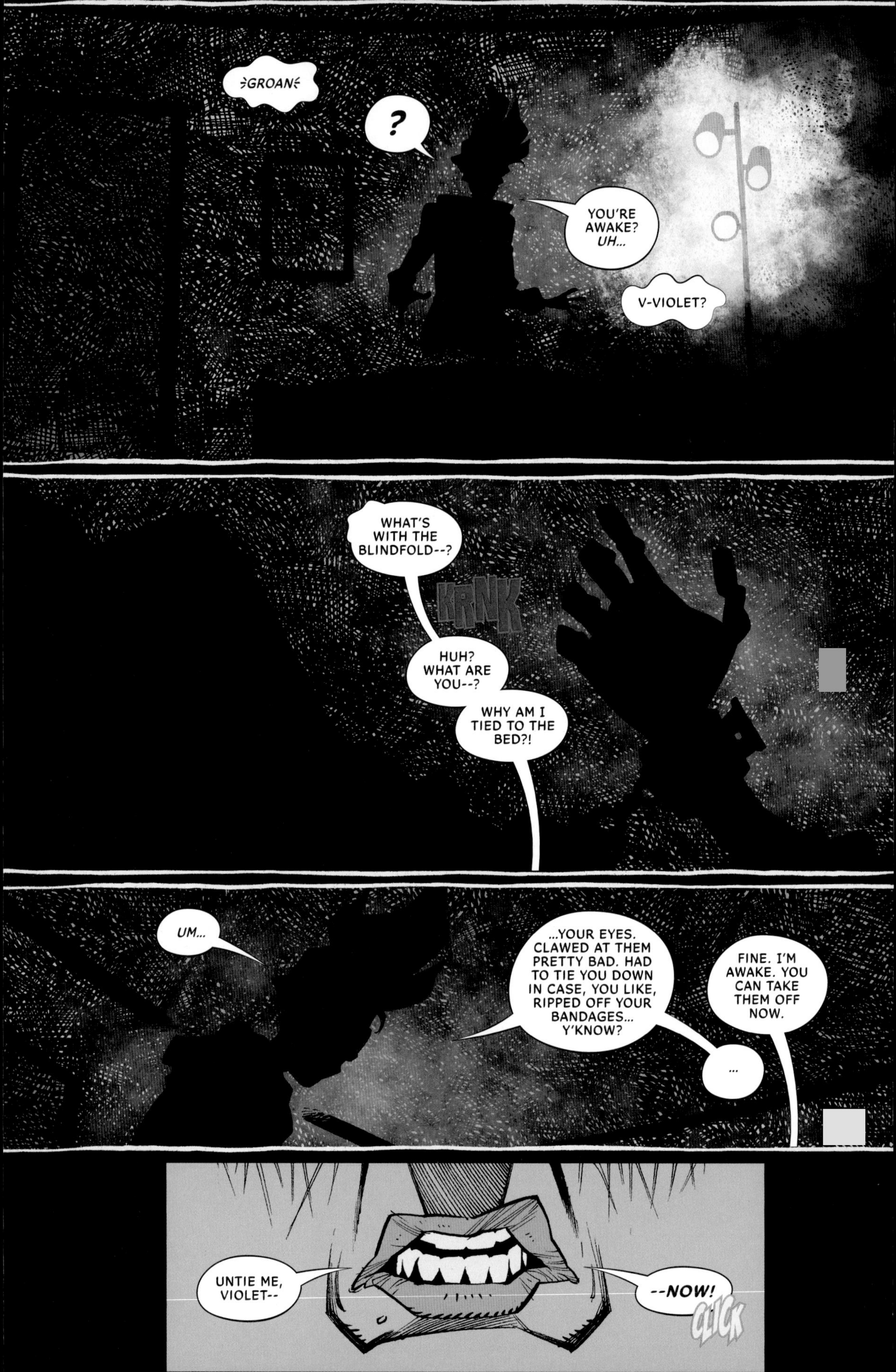
GROAN
?
YOU'RE AWAKE? UH...
V-VIOLET?
WHAT'S WITH THE BLINDFOLD--?
KRNK
HUH? WHAT ARE YOU--?
WHY AM I TIED TO THE BED?!
UM...
...YOUR EYES. CLAWED AT THEM PRETTY BAD. HAD TO TIE YOU DOWN IN CASE, YOU LIKE, RIPPED OFF YOUR BANDAGES... Y'KNOW?
...
FINE. I'M AWAKE. YOU CAN TAKE THEM OFF NOW.
UNTIE ME, VIOLET--
--NOW!
CLICK

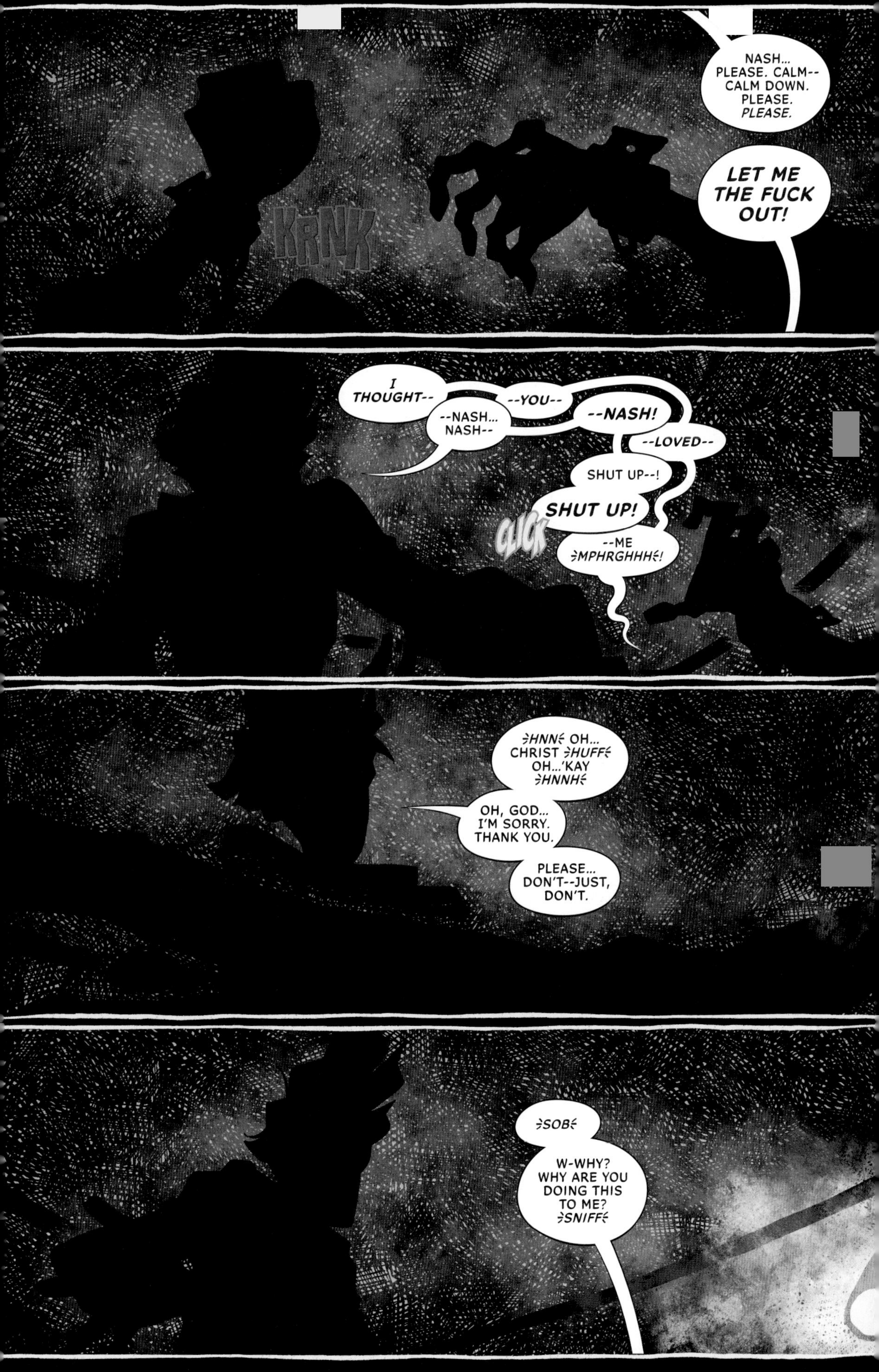

NASH... PLEASE. CALM-- CALM DOWN. PLEASE. *PLEASE.*
LET ME THE FUCK OUT!
KRNK
I THOUGHT--
--NASH... NASH--
--YOU--
--NASH!
--LOVED--
SHUT UP--!
SHUT UP!
CLICK
--ME MPHRGHHH!
HNN OH... CHRIST HUFF OH...'KAY HNNH
OH, GOD... I'M SORRY. THANK YOU.
PLEASE... DON'T--JUST, DON'T.
SOB
W-WHY? WHY ARE YOU DOING THIS TO ME? SNIFF

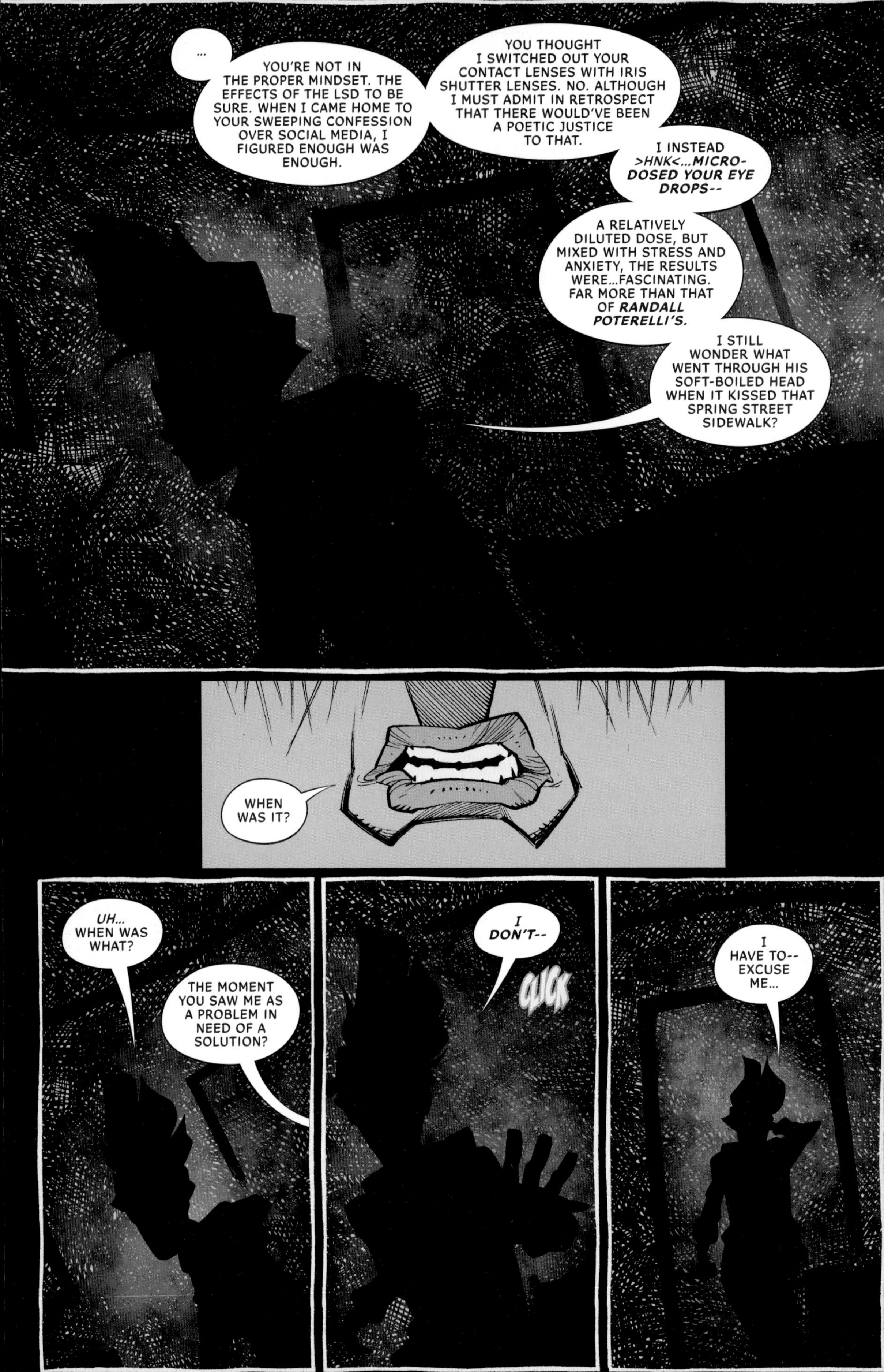
...
YOU'RE NOT IN THE PROPER MINDSET. THE EFFECTS OF THE LSD TO BE SURE. WHEN I CAME HOME TO YOUR SWEEPING CONFESSION OVER SOCIAL MEDIA, I FIGURED ENOUGH WAS ENOUGH.
YOU THOUGHT I SWITCHED OUT YOUR CONTACT LENSES WITH IRIS SHUTTER LENSES. NO. ALTHOUGH I MUST ADMIT IN RETROSPECT THAT THERE WOULD'VE BEEN A POETIC JUSTICE TO THAT.
I INSTEAD *>HNK<...* ***MICRO-DOSED YOUR EYE DROPS--***
A RELATIVELY DILUTED DOSE, BUT MIXED WITH STRESS AND ANXIETY, THE RESULTS WERE...FASCINATING. FAR MORE THAN THAT OF ***RANDALL POTERELLI'S.***
I STILL WONDER WHAT WENT THROUGH HIS SOFT-BOILED HEAD WHEN IT KISSED THAT SPRING STREET SIDEWALK?
WHEN WAS IT?
UH... WHEN WAS WHAT?
THE MOMENT YOU SAW ME AS A PROBLEM IN NEED OF A SOLUTION?
I DON'T--
CLICK
I HAVE TO-- EXCUSE ME...

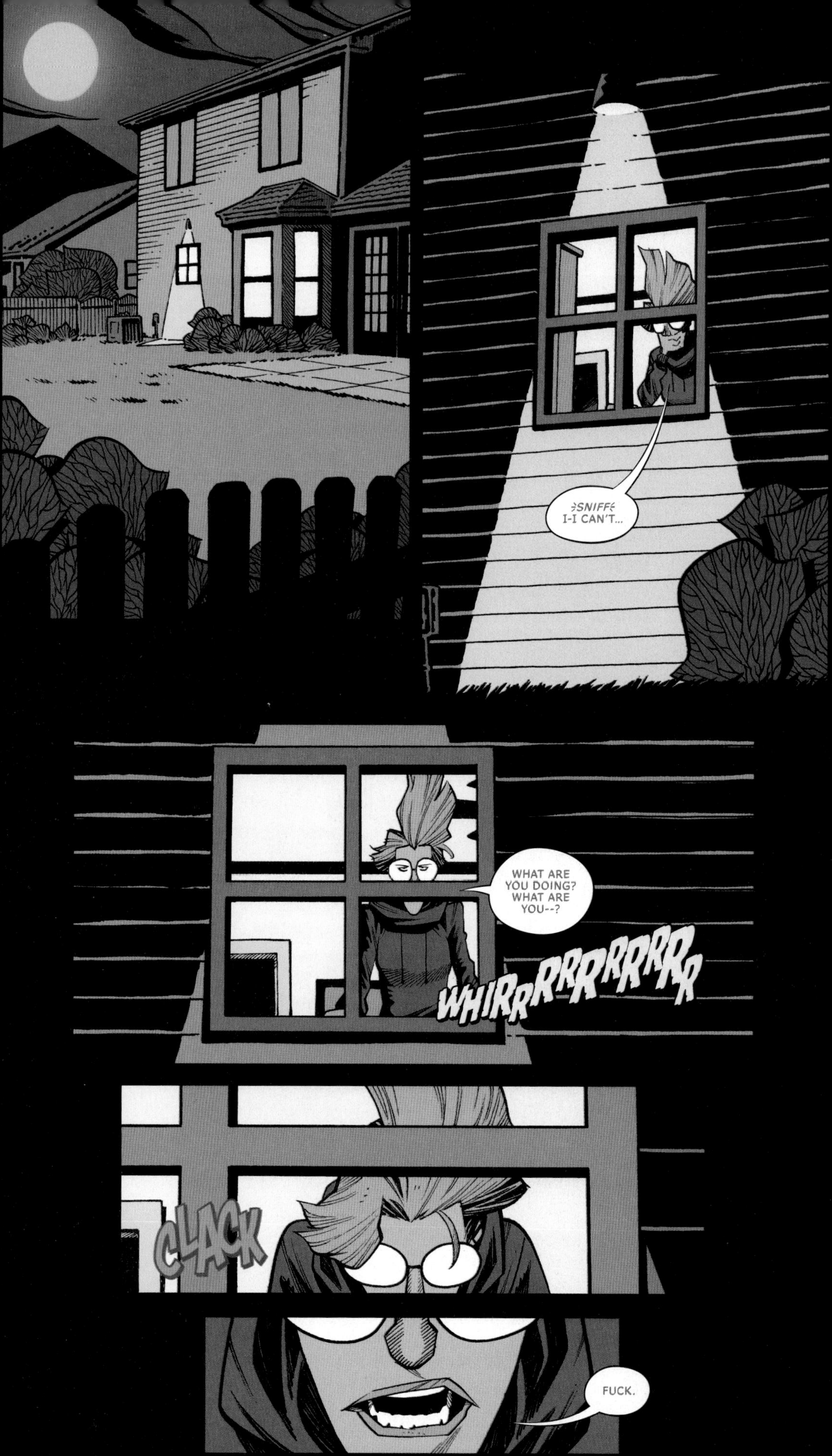
SNIFF
I-I CAN'T...
WHAT ARE YOU DOING? WHAT ARE YOU--?
WHIRRRRRRRRRR
CLACK
FUCK.

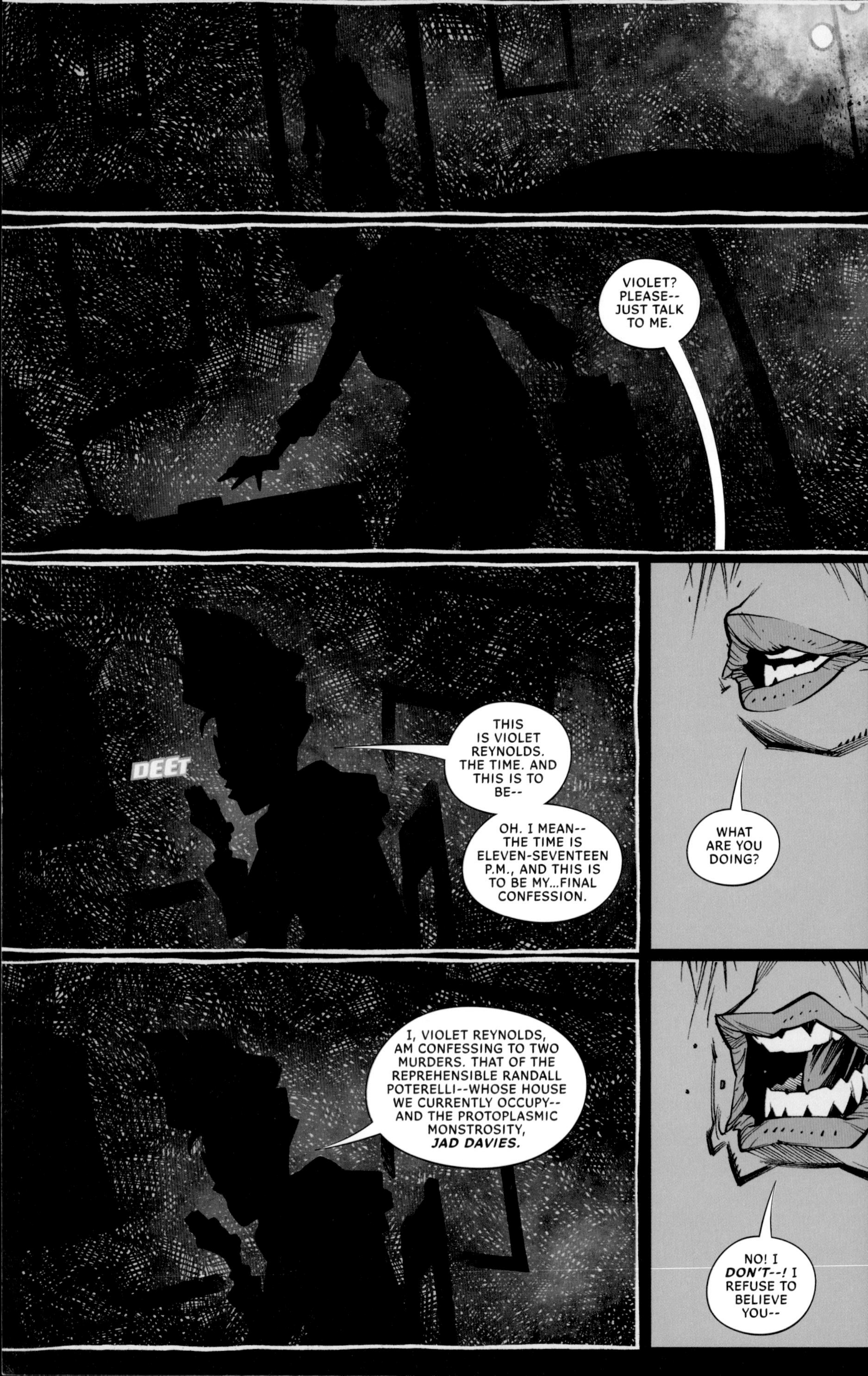
VIOLET? PLEASE-- JUST TALK TO ME.
DEET
THIS IS VIOLET REYNOLDS. THE TIME. AND THIS IS TO BE--
OH. I MEAN-- THE TIME IS ELEVEN-SEVENTEEN P.M., AND THIS IS TO BE MY...FINAL CONFESSION.
WHAT ARE YOU DOING?
I, VIOLET REYNOLDS, AM CONFESSING TO TWO MURDERS. THAT OF THE REPREHENSIBLE RANDALL POTERELLI--WHOSE HOUSE WE CURRENTLY OCCUPY-- AND THE PROTOPLASMIC MONSTROSITY, JAD DAVIES.
NO! I DON'T--! I REFUSE TO BELIEVE YOU--

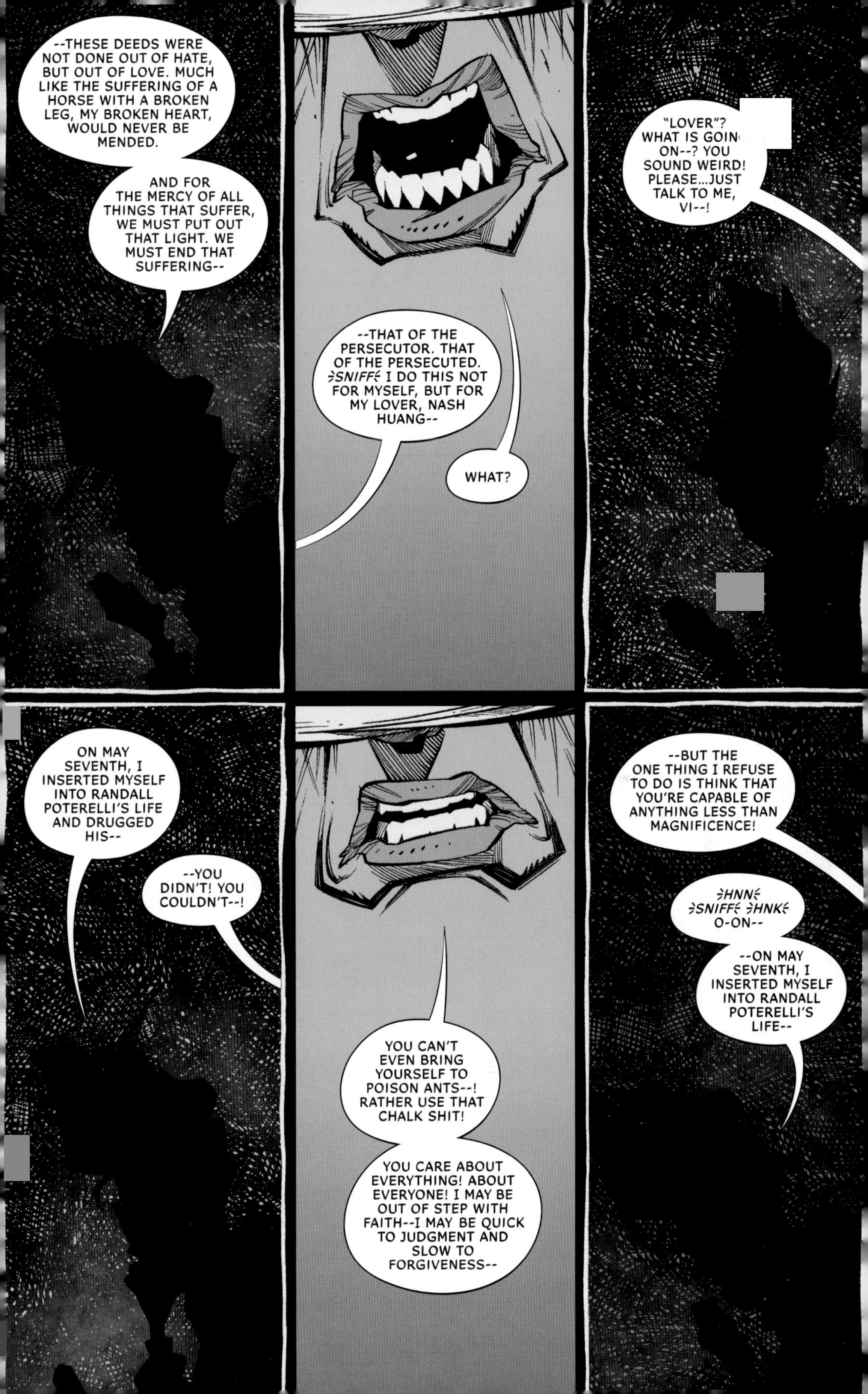
--THESE DEEDS WERE NOT DONE OUT OF HATE, BUT OUT OF LOVE. MUCH LIKE THE SUFFERING OF A HORSE WITH A BROKEN LEG, MY BROKEN HEART, WOULD NEVER BE MENDED.
AND FOR THE MERCY OF ALL THINGS THAT SUFFER, WE MUST PUT OUT THAT LIGHT. WE MUST END THAT SUFFERING--
--THAT OF THE PERSECUTOR. THAT OF THE PERSECUTED. *SNIFF* I DO THIS NOT FOR MYSELF, BUT FOR MY LOVER, NASH HUANG--
WHAT?
"LOVER"? WHAT IS GOIN ON--? YOU SOUND WEIRD! PLEASE...JUST TALK TO ME, VI--!
ON MAY SEVENTH, I INSERTED MYSELF INTO RANDALL POTERELLI'S LIFE AND DRUGGED HIS--
--YOU DIDN'T! YOU COULDN'T--!
YOU CAN'T EVEN BRING YOURSELF TO POISON ANTS--! RATHER USE THAT CHALK SHIT!
YOU CARE ABOUT EVERYTHING! ABOUT EVERYONE! I MAY BE OUT OF STEP WITH FAITH--I MAY BE QUICK TO JUDGMENT AND SLOW TO FORGIVENESS--
--BUT THE ONE THING I REFUSE TO DO IS THINK THAT YOU'RE CAPABLE OF ANYTHING LESS THAN MAGNIFICENCE!
HNN *SNIFF* *HNK* O-ON--
--ON MAY SEVENTH, I INSERTED MYSELF INTO RANDALL POTERELLI'S LIFE--

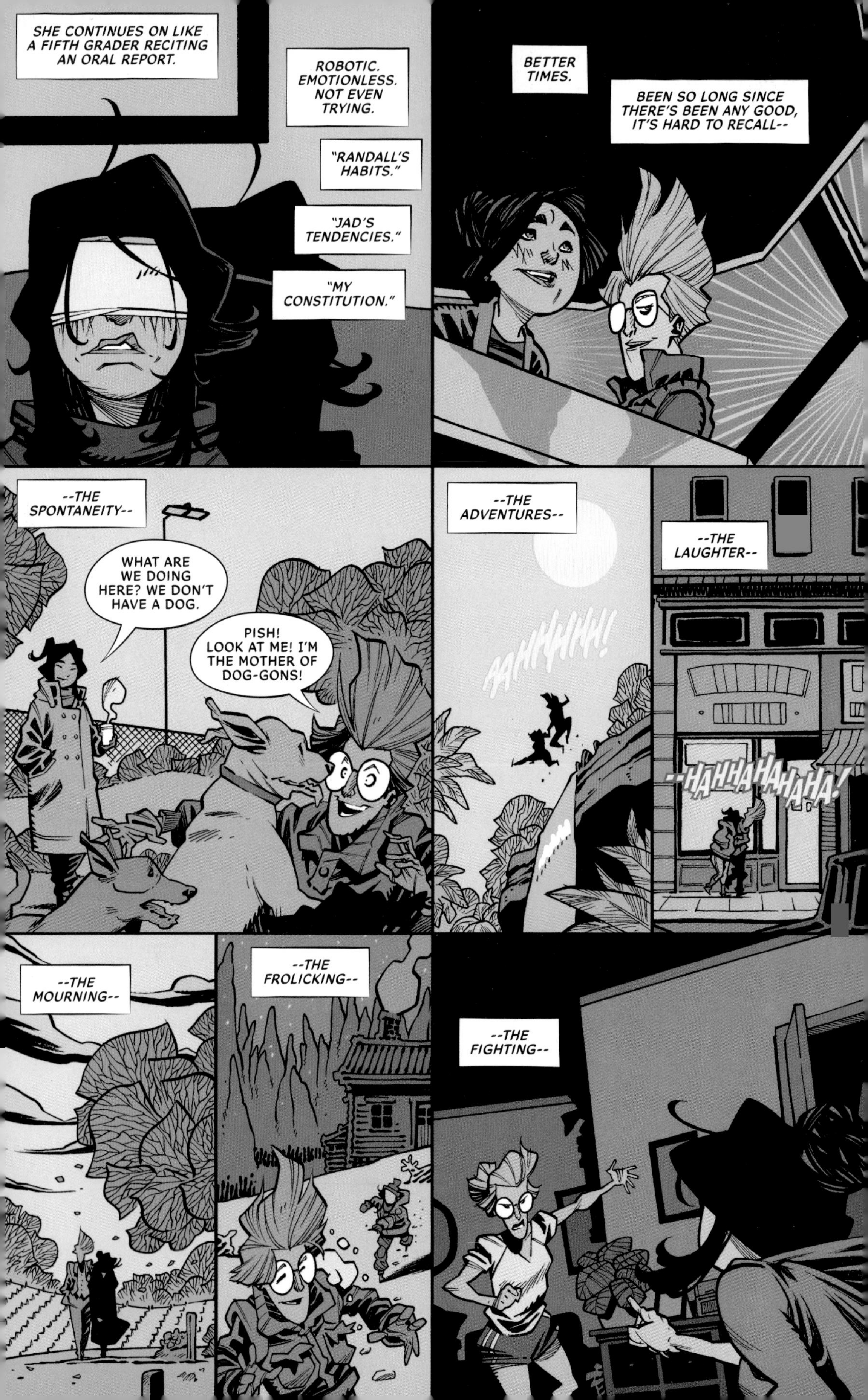
SHE CONTINUES ON LIKE A FIFTH GRADER RECITING AN ORAL REPORT.
ROBOTIC. EMOTIONLESS. NOT EVEN TRYING.
"RANDALL'S HABITS."
"JAD'S TENDENCIES."
"MY CONSTITUTION."
BETTER TIMES.
BEEN SO LONG SINCE THERE'S BEEN ANY GOOD, IT'S HARD TO RECALL--
--THE SPONTANEITY--
WHAT ARE WE DOING HERE? WE DON'T HAVE A DOG.
PISH! LOOK AT ME! I'M THE MOTHER OF DOG-GONS!
--THE ADVENTURES--
AAHHAHHH!
--THE LAUGHTER--
--HAHHAHAHAHA!
--THE MOURNING--
--THE FROLICKING--
--THE FIGHTING--

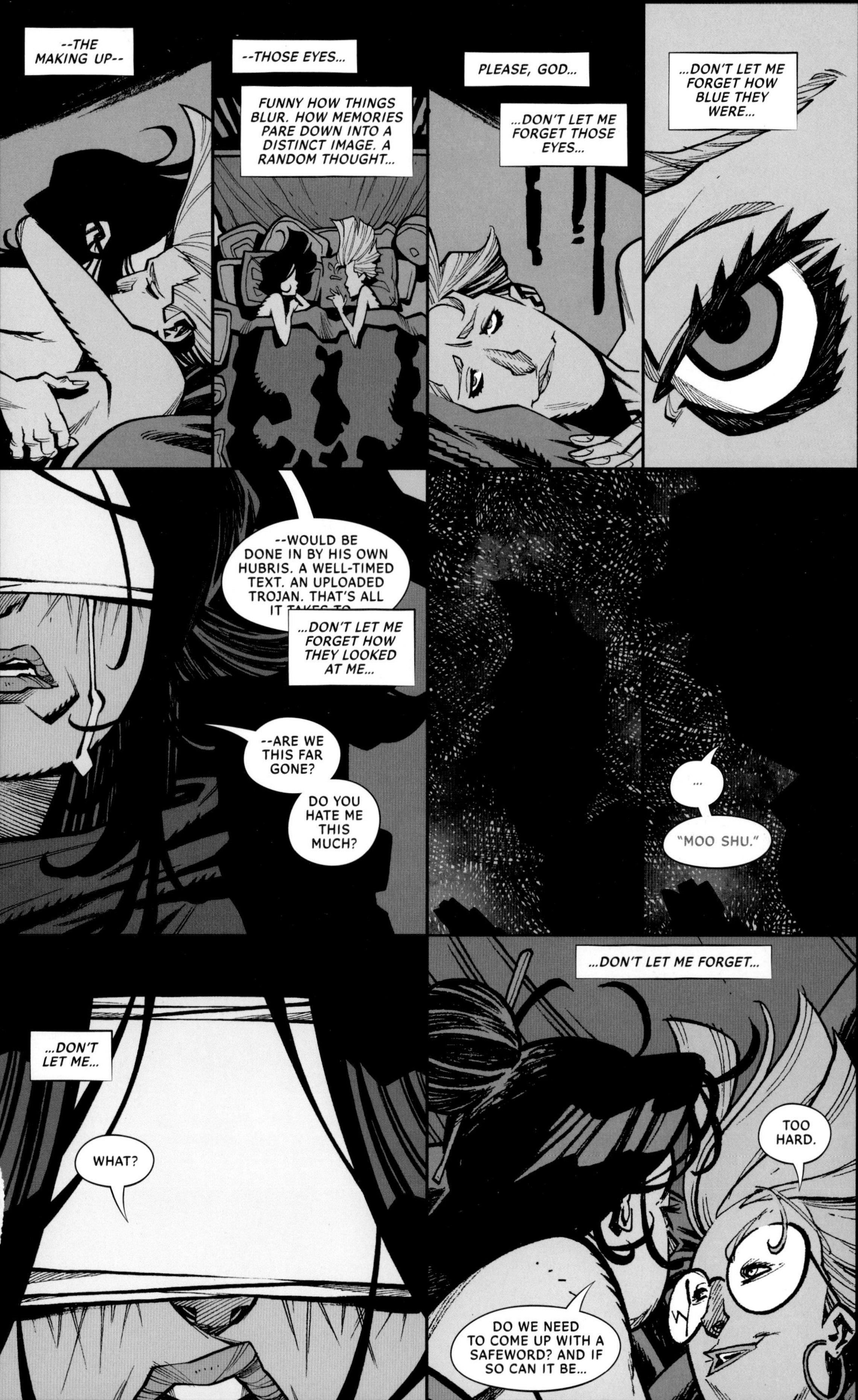
--THE MAKING UP--
--THOSE EYES...
FUNNY HOW THINGS BLUR. HOW MEMORIES PARE DOWN INTO A DISTINCT IMAGE. A RANDOM THOUGHT...
PLEASE, GOD...
...DON'T LET ME FORGET THOSE EYES...
...DON'T LET ME FORGET HOW BLUE THEY WERE...
--WOULD BE DONE IN BY HIS OWN HUBRIS. A WELL-TIMED TEXT. AN UPLOADED TROJAN. THAT'S ALL IT
...DON'T LET ME FORGET HOW THEY LOOKED AT ME...
--ARE WE THIS FAR GONE?
DO YOU HATE ME THIS MUCH?
...
"MOO SHU."
...DON'T LET ME...
WHAT?
...DON'T LET ME FORGET...
TOO HARD.
DO WE NEED TO COME UP WITH A SAFEWORD? AND IF SO CAN IT BE...

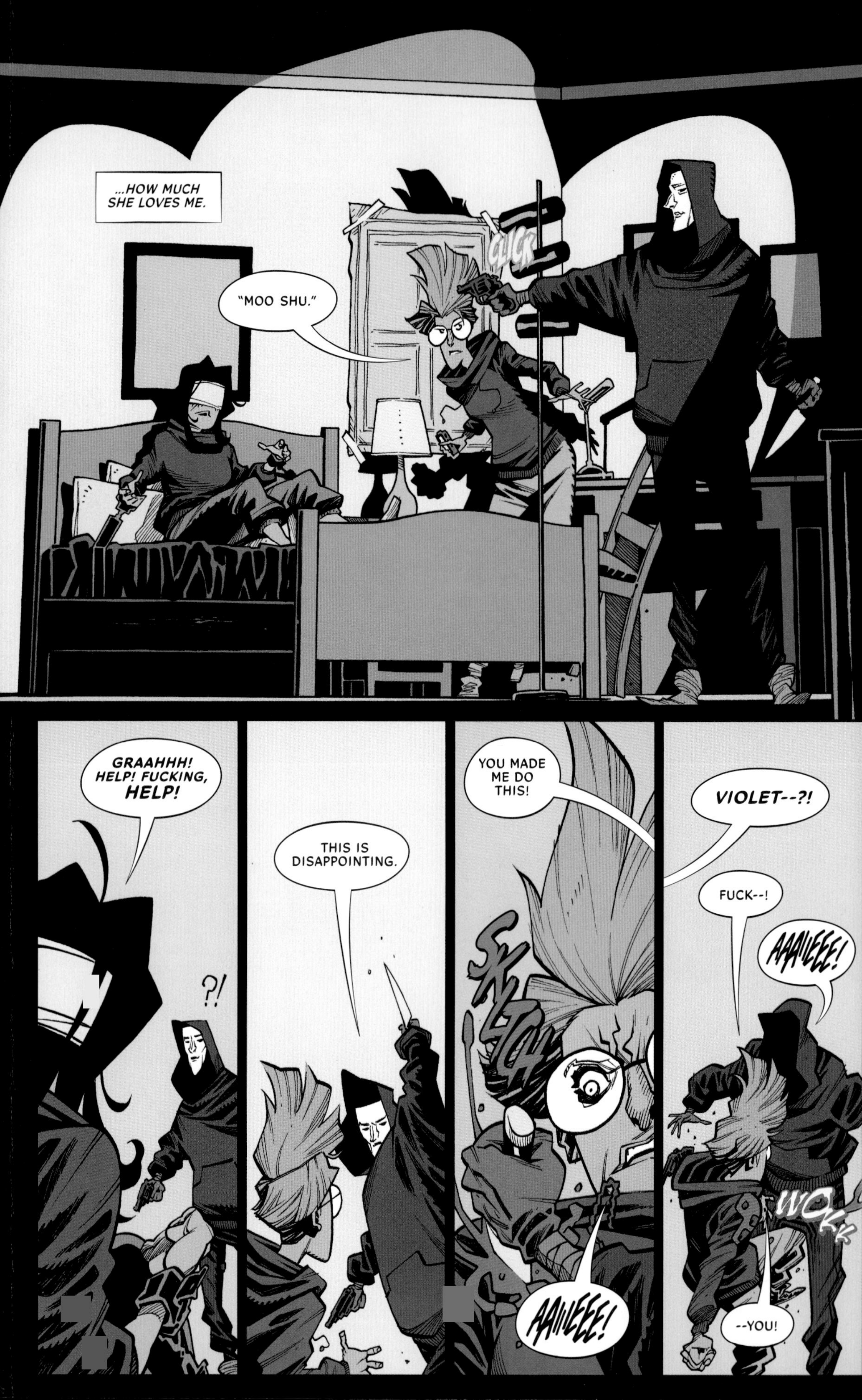
...HOW MUCH SHE LOVES ME.
"MOO SHU."
GRAAHHH! HELP! FUCKING, HELP!
?!
THIS IS DISAPPOINTING.
YOU MADE ME DO THIS!
AAAIEEE!
VIOLET--?!
FUCK--!
AAAIEEE!
--YOU!

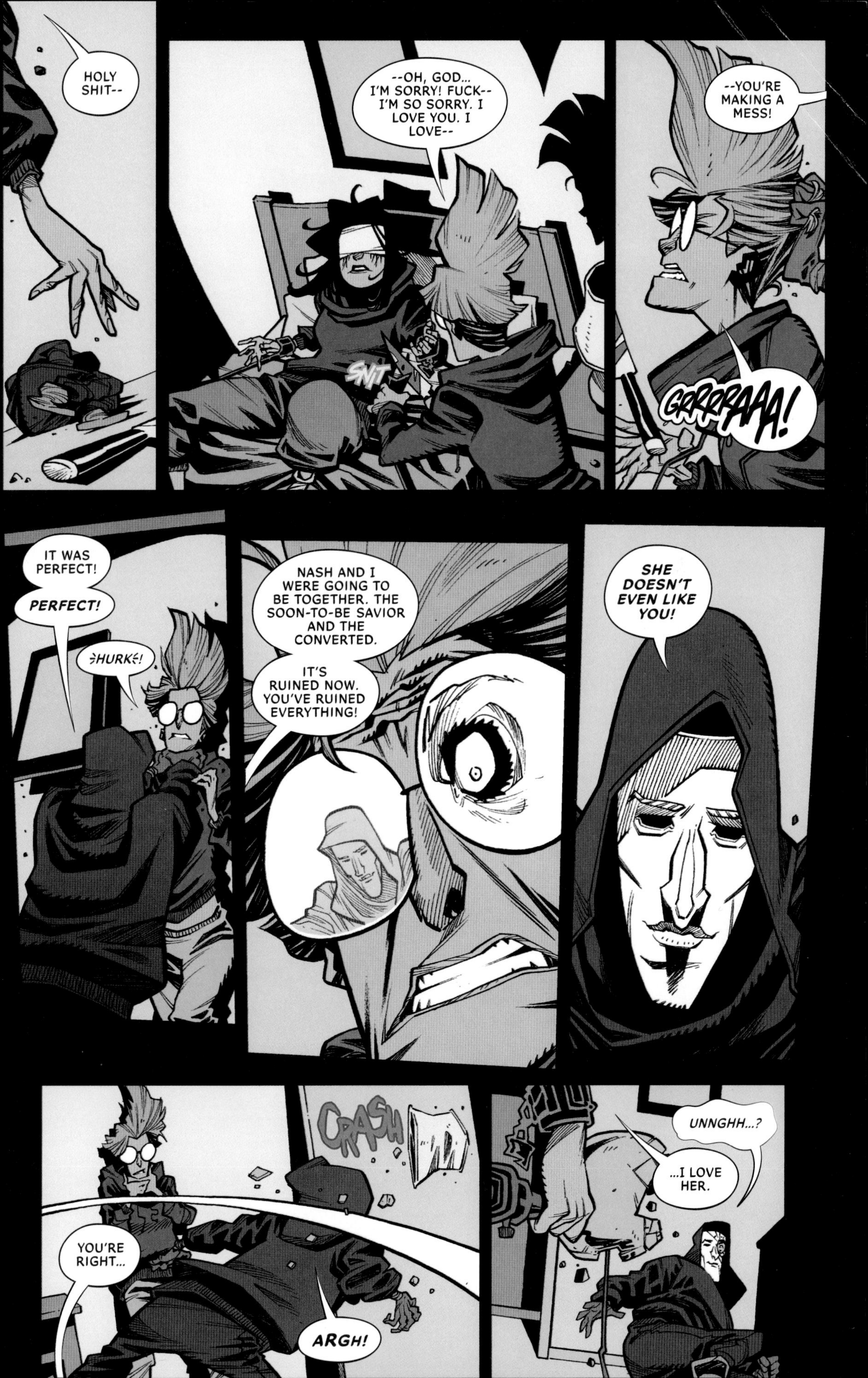
HOLY SHIT--
--OH, GOD... I'M SORRY! FUCK-- I'M SO SORRY. I LOVE YOU. I LOVE--
SNIT
--YOU'RE MAKING A MESS!
GRRRRAAAA!
IT WAS PERFECT!
PERFECT!
HURK!
NASH AND I WERE GOING TO BE TOGETHER. THE SOON-TO-BE SAVIOR AND THE CONVERTED.
IT'S RUINED NOW. YOU'VE RUINED EVERYTHING!
SHE DOESN'T EVEN LIKE YOU!
CRASH
YOU'RE RIGHT...
ARGH!
UNNGHH...?
...I LOVE HER.

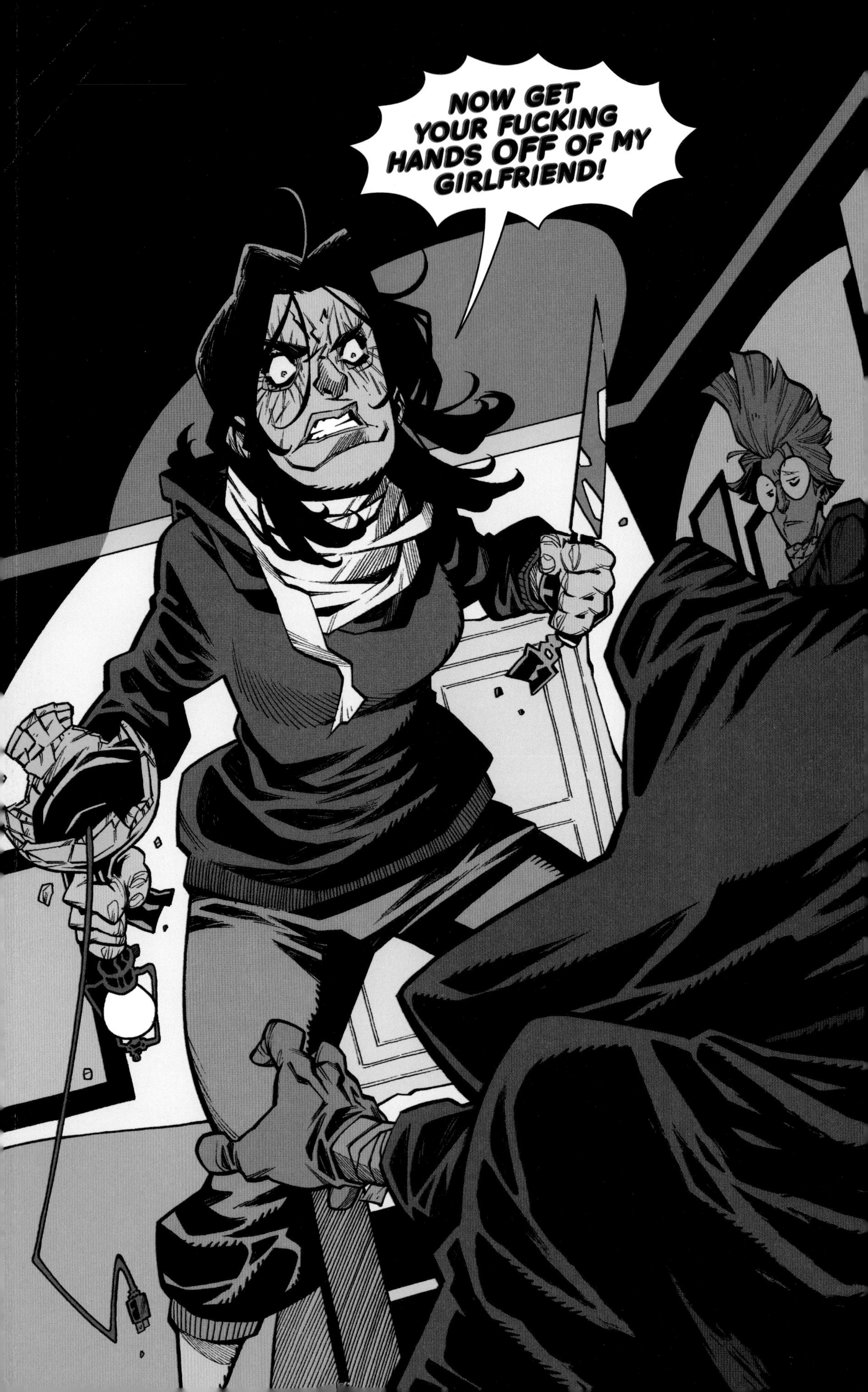
NOW GET YOUR FUCKING HANDS OFF OF MY GIRLFRIEND!

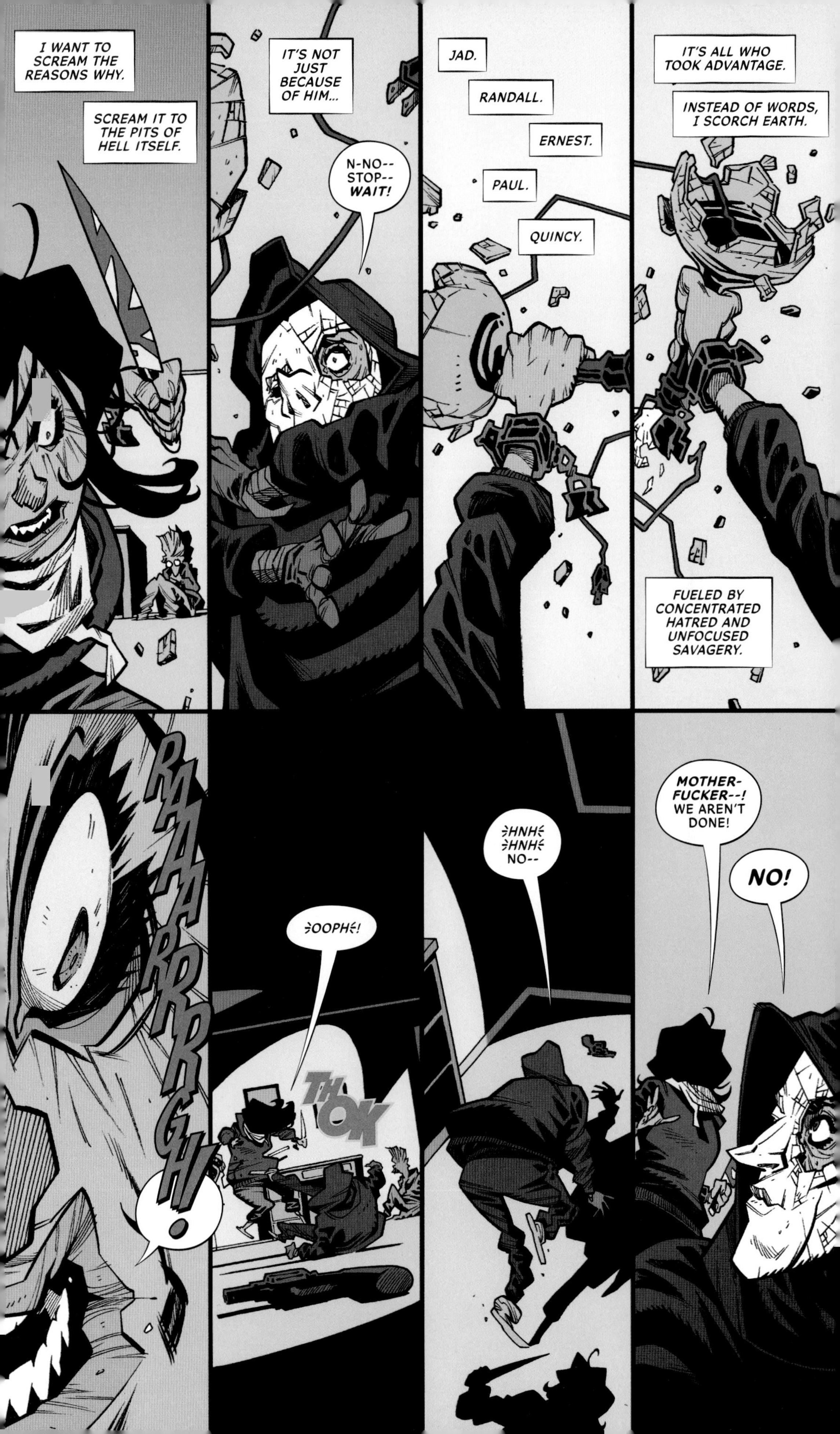
I WANT TO SCREAM THE REASONS WHY.
SCREAM IT TO THE PITS OF HELL ITSELF.
IT'S NOT JUST BECAUSE OF HIM...
N-NO-- STOP-- WAIT!
JAD.
RANDALL.
ERNEST.
PAUL.
QUINCY.
IT'S ALL WHO TOOK ADVANTAGE.
INSTEAD OF WORDS, I SCORCH EARTH.
FUELED BY CONCENTRATED HATRED AND UNFOCUSED SAVAGERY.
RAAAARRRRGH!
OOPH!
THOK
HNH HNH NO--
MOTHER-FUCKER--! WE AREN'T DONE!
NO!

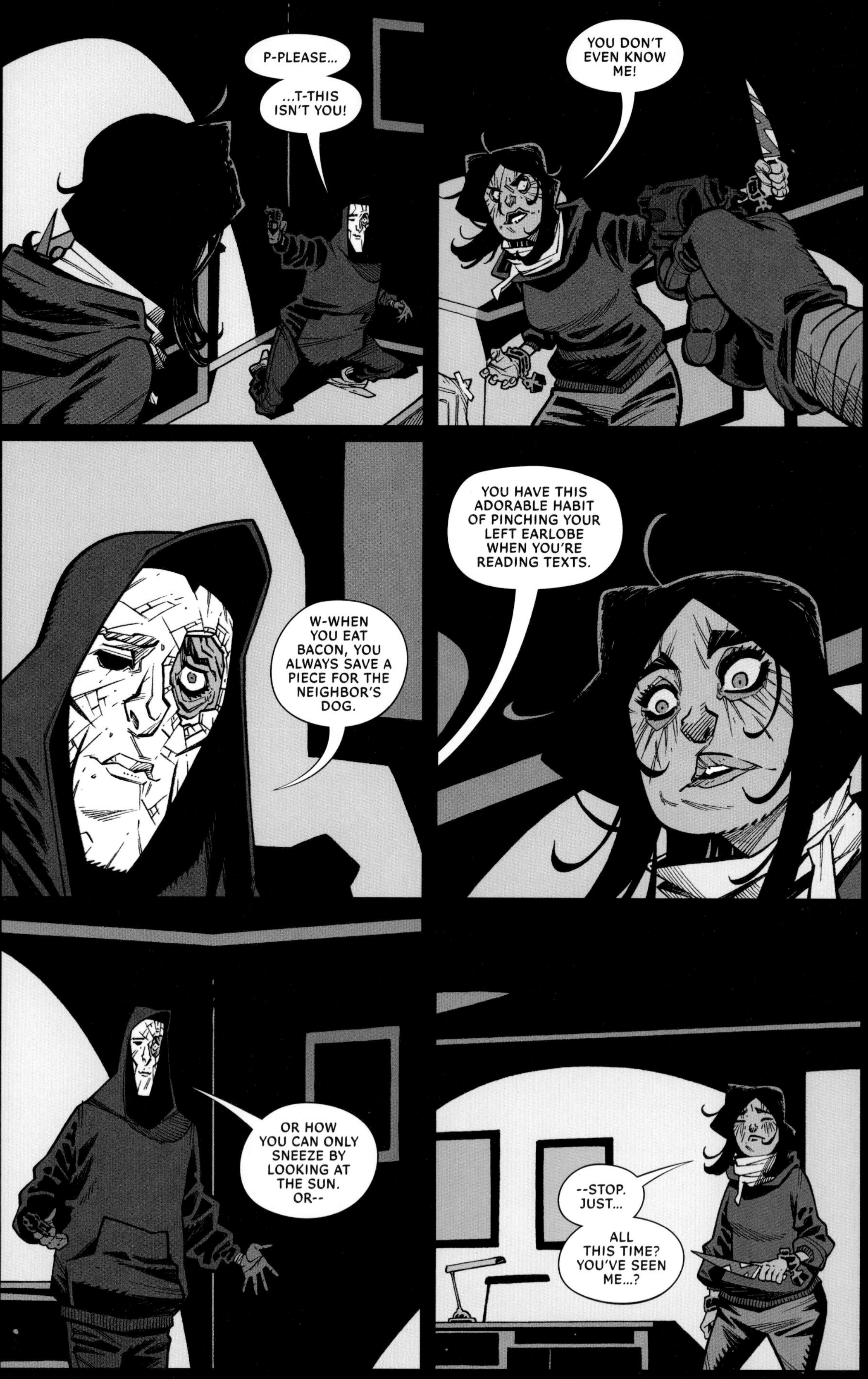
P-PLEASE...
...T-THIS ISN'T YOU!
YOU DON'T EVEN KNOW ME!
W-WHEN YOU EAT BACON, YOU ALWAYS SAVE A PIECE FOR THE NEIGHBOR'S DOG.
YOU HAVE THIS ADORABLE HABIT OF PINCHING YOUR LEFT EARLOBE WHEN YOU'RE READING TEXTS.
OR HOW YOU CAN ONLY SNEEZE BY LOOKING AT THE SUN. OR--
--STOP. JUST...
ALL THIS TIME? YOU'VE SEEN ME...?

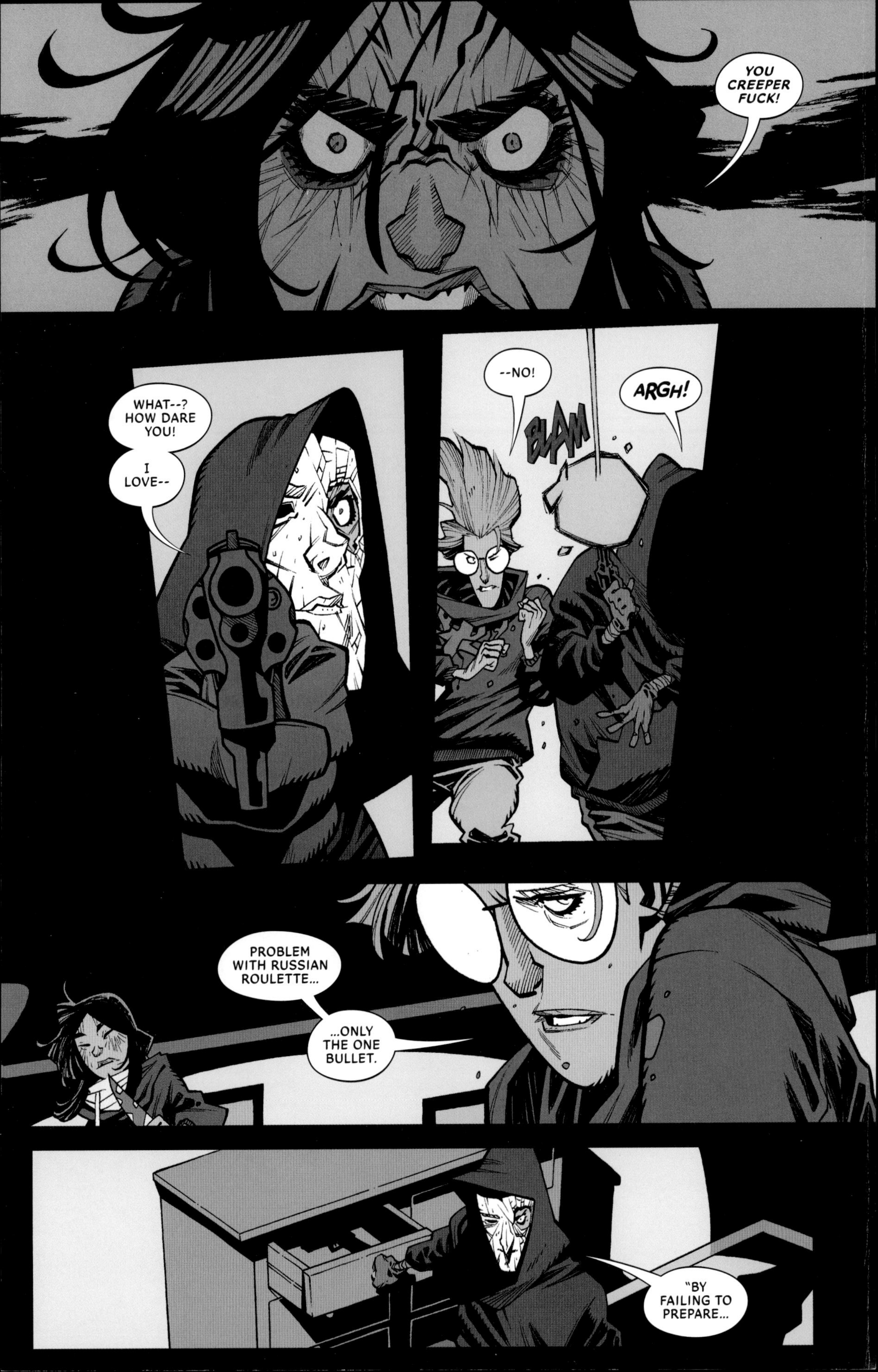
YOU CREEPER FUCK!
WHAT--? HOW DARE YOU!
I LOVE--
--NO!
BLAM
ARGH!
PROBLEM WITH RUSSIAN ROULETTE...
...ONLY THE ONE BULLET.
"BY FAILING TO PREPARE...

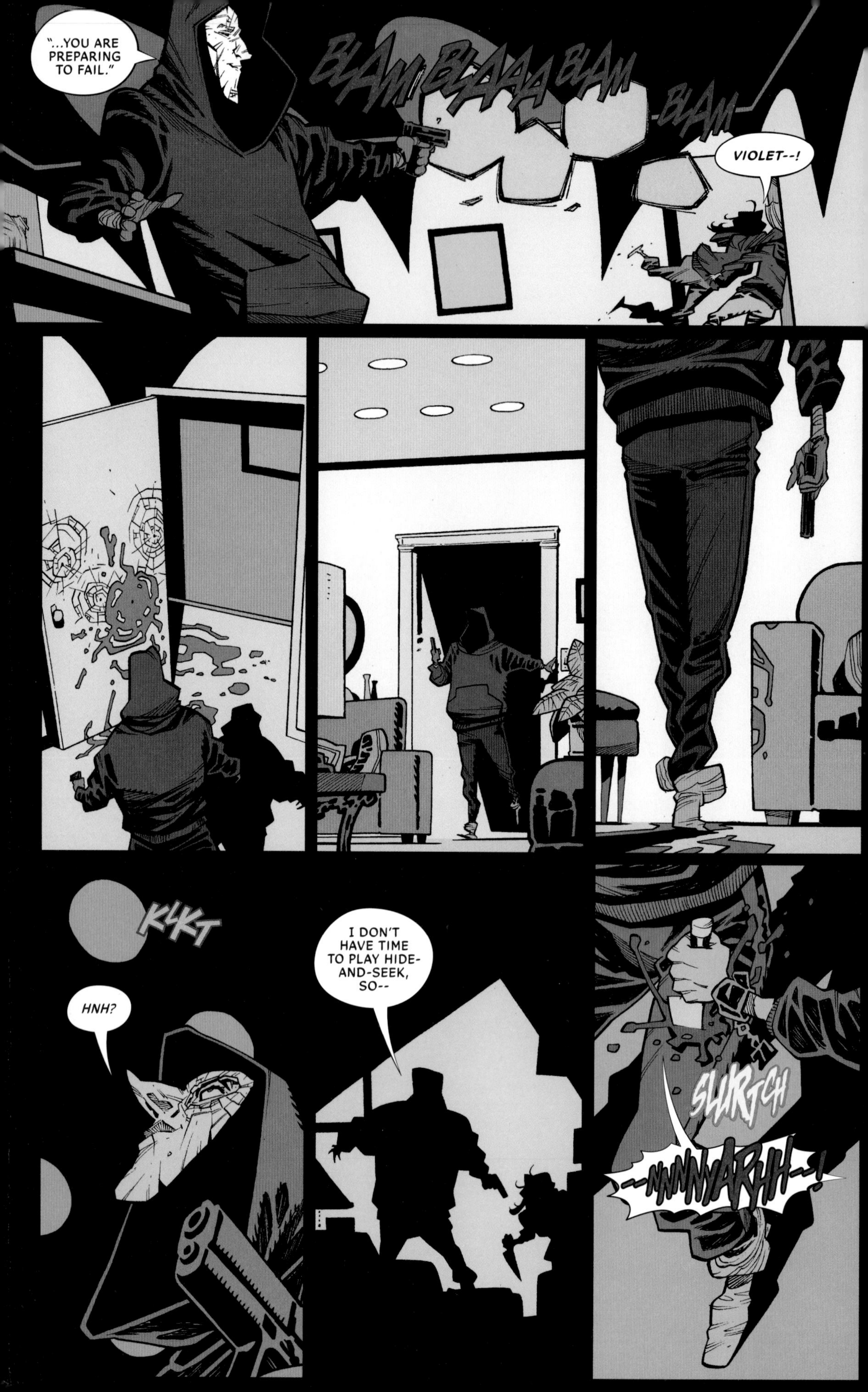
"...YOU ARE PREPARING TO FAIL."
BLAM BLAAAA BLAM BLAM
VIOLET--!
KLKT
HNH?
I DON'T HAVE TIME TO PLAY HIDE-AND-SEEK, SO--
SLURTCH
--NNNNYARHH--!

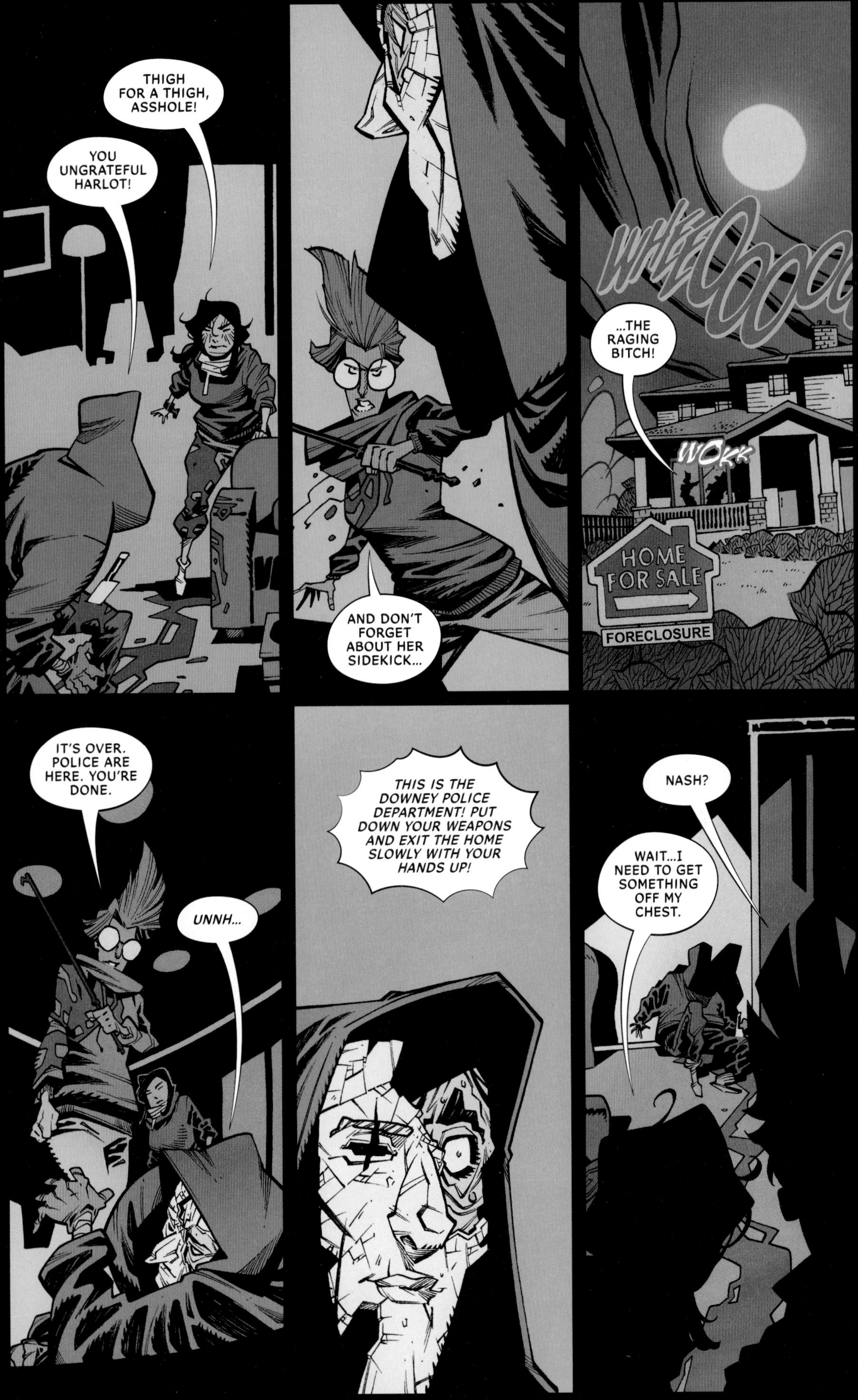
YOU UNGRATEFUL HARLOT!
THIGH FOR A THIGH, ASSHOLE!
AND DON'T FORGET ABOUT HER SIDEKICK...
WHEEOOOO
...THE RAGING BITCH!
WOKK
HOME FOR SALE
FORECLOSURE
IT'S OVER. POLICE ARE HERE. YOU'RE DONE.
UNNH...
THIS IS THE DOWNEY POLICE DEPARTMENT! PUT DOWN YOUR WEAPONS AND EXIT THE HOME SLOWLY WITH YOUR HANDS UP!
NASH?
WAIT...I NEED TO GET SOMETHING OFF MY CHEST.

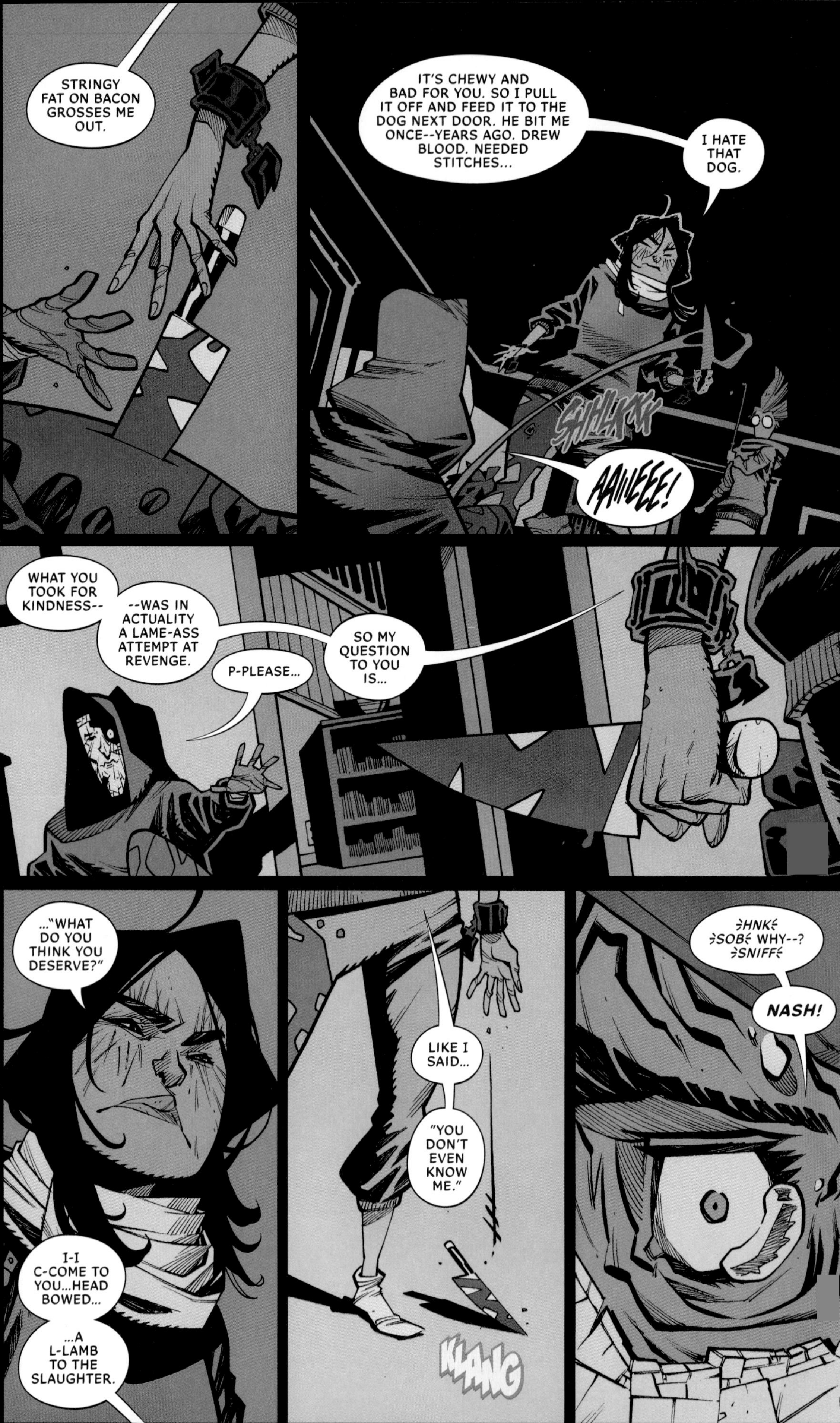
STRINGY FAT ON BACON GROSSES ME OUT.
IT'S CHEWY AND BAD FOR YOU. SO I PULL IT OFF AND FEED IT TO THE DOG NEXT DOOR. HE BIT ME ONCE--YEARS AGO. DREW BLOOD. NEEDED STITCHES...
I HATE THAT DOG.
SHHLKKK
AAIIEEE!
WHAT YOU TOOK FOR KINDNESS--
--WAS IN ACTUALITY A LAME-ASS ATTEMPT AT REVENGE.
P-PLEASE...
SO MY QUESTION TO YOU IS...
..."WHAT DO YOU THINK YOU DESERVE?"
I-I C-COME TO YOU...HEAD BOWED...
...A L-LAMB TO THE SLAUGHTER.
LIKE I SAID...
"YOU DON'T EVEN KNOW ME."
KLANG
HNK SOB WHY--? SNIFF
NASH!

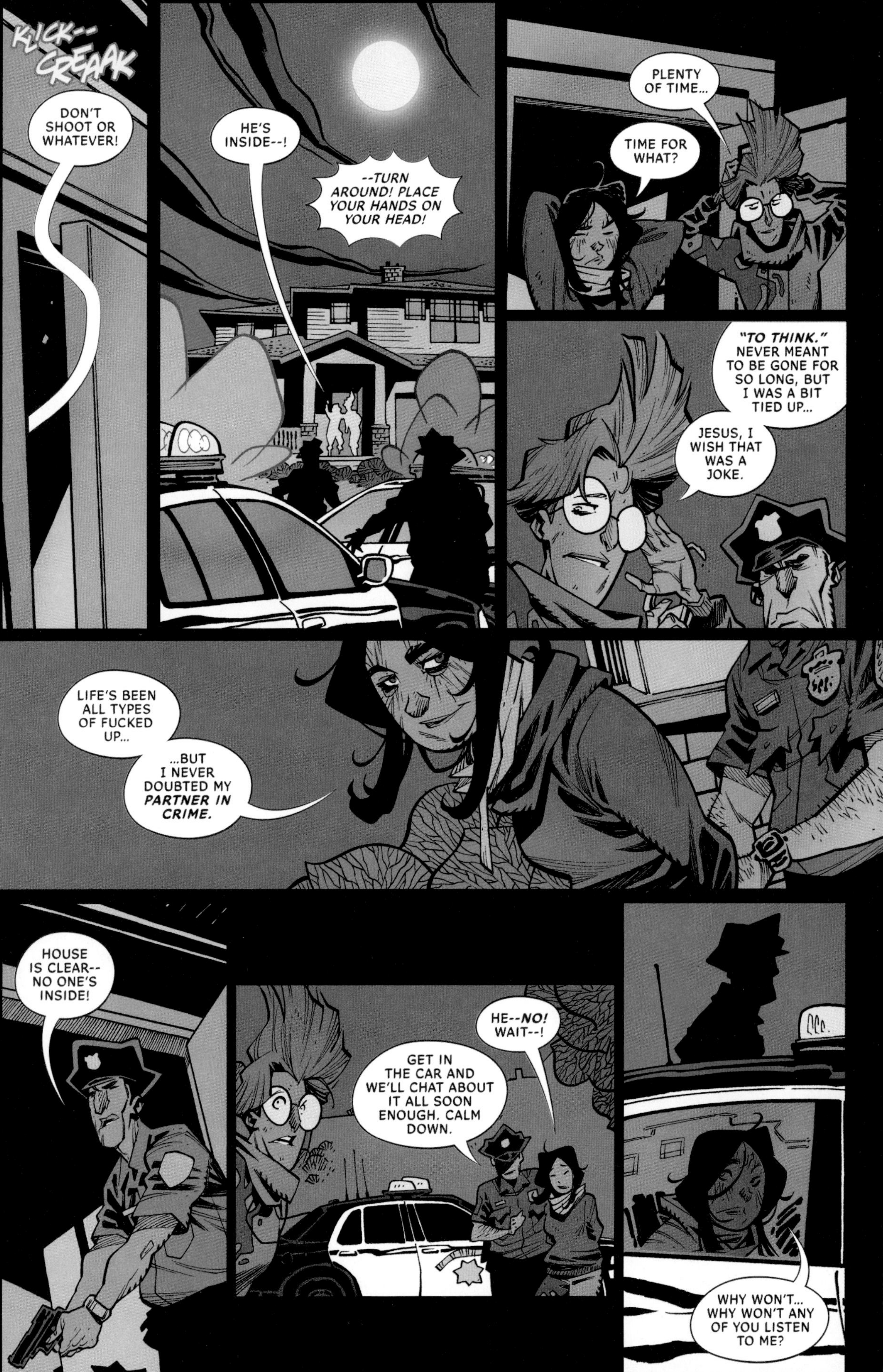

KLICK--
CREAAK
DON'T SHOOT OR WHATEVER!
HE'S INSIDE--!
--TURN AROUND! PLACE YOUR HANDS ON YOUR HEAD!
PLENTY OF TIME...
TIME FOR WHAT?
"TO THINK." NEVER MEANT TO BE GONE FOR SO LONG, BUT I WAS A BIT TIED UP...
JESUS, I WISH THAT WAS A JOKE.
LIFE'S BEEN ALL TYPES OF FUCKED UP...
...BUT I NEVER DOUBTED MY PARTNER IN CRIME.
HOUSE IS CLEAR-- NO ONE'S INSIDE!
HE--NO! WAIT--!
GET IN THE CAR AND WE'LL CHAT ABOUT IT ALL SOON ENOUGH. CALM DOWN.
WHY WON'T... WHY WON'T ANY OF YOU LISTEN TO ME?

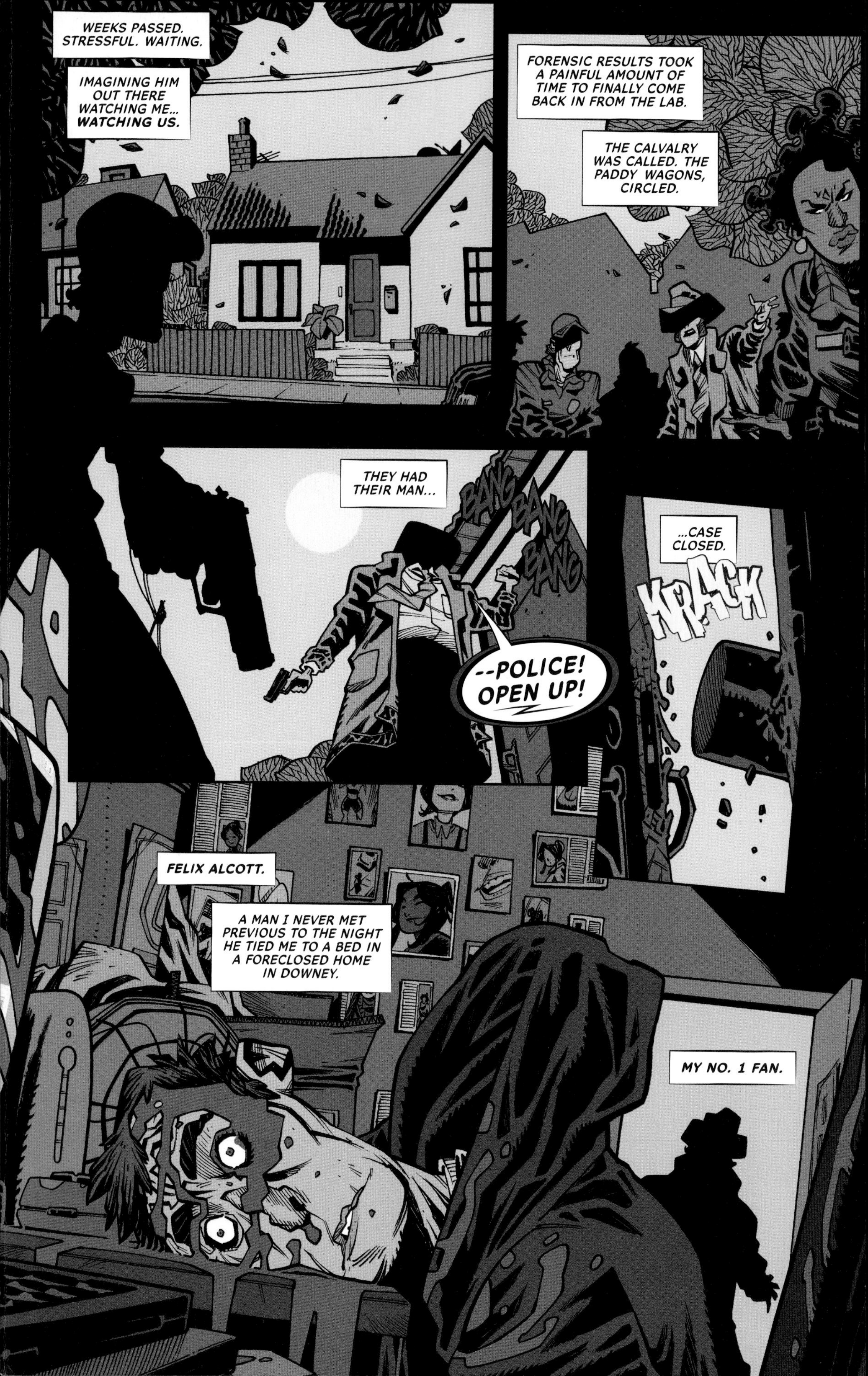
WEEKS PASSED. STRESSFUL. WAITING.
IMAGINING HIM OUT THERE WATCHING ME... WATCHING US.
FORENSIC RESULTS TOOK A PAINFUL AMOUNT OF TIME TO FINALLY COME BACK IN FROM THE LAB.
THE CALVALRY WAS CALLED. THE PADDY WAGONS, CIRCLED.
THEY HAD THEIR MAN...
BANG BANG BANG
--POLICE! OPEN UP!
...CASE CLOSED.
KRACK
FELIX ALCOTT.
A MAN I NEVER MET PREVIOUS TO THE NIGHT HE TIED ME TO A BED IN A FORECLOSED HOME IN DOWNEY.
MY NO. 1 FAN.

THE ARTICLES CAME. THE ARTICLES WENT.

NINETY PERCENT WERE FIXATED ON ALCOTT THE MAN. WHO *HE* WAS.

SOME EVEN WENT SO FAR AS TO SPECULATE ON WHO LEAKED THE SEX TAPE? THE VIDEO THAT EMBOLDENED ALCOTT TO INSERT HIMSELF INTO MY LIFE.

...TUAL TERROR:
...W WE NOW VIEW
...ONLINE SAFETY

"THE KENNEDY ASSASSINATION OF REVENGE PORN," THEORIES EXIST, BUT I CAN'T LET IT BE THE FOCUS OF MY LIFE ANYMORE.

AND WITH THE INTERNET BEING WHAT IT IS...ALL THAT SHIT FADED. I WAS FORGOTTEN.

AND YOU KNOW WHAT...?

...I'M OKAY WITH THAT.

Home

Delete Account

Nash Huang
Profile

Edit

YOU REALIZE THAT YOU'RE CURRENTLY MISSING THE GREATEST MUSICAL IN THE WORLD, RIGHT?

EASE UP, CAPTAIN HYPERBOLE. I'M SHUTTING DOWN.

I DON'T KNOW WHAT I'D DO WITHOUT HER.

MY MIND SHOULD BE LIGHT. MY EMOTIONS, SUNSHINE. BUT I CAN'T SHAKE THE NAGGING OF ONE SMALL THOUGHT.

"WHAT IF?"

GROVER ASKED IF VIOLET WAS LEFT-HANDED. DIDN'T UNDERSTAND IT THEN, BUT THINKING ABOUT HIS EYE--*THAT ANGLE*...HE WAS ATTACKED BY A SOUTHPAW.

BUT THIS ONE FACTOID FROM SOME FORENSIC SHOW I SAW YEARS AGO LOOMS LARGE--

--WHEN A PERSON TAKES THEIR LIFE USING A GUN, THE VICTIM ALMOST ALWAYS USES THEIR DOMINANT HAND.

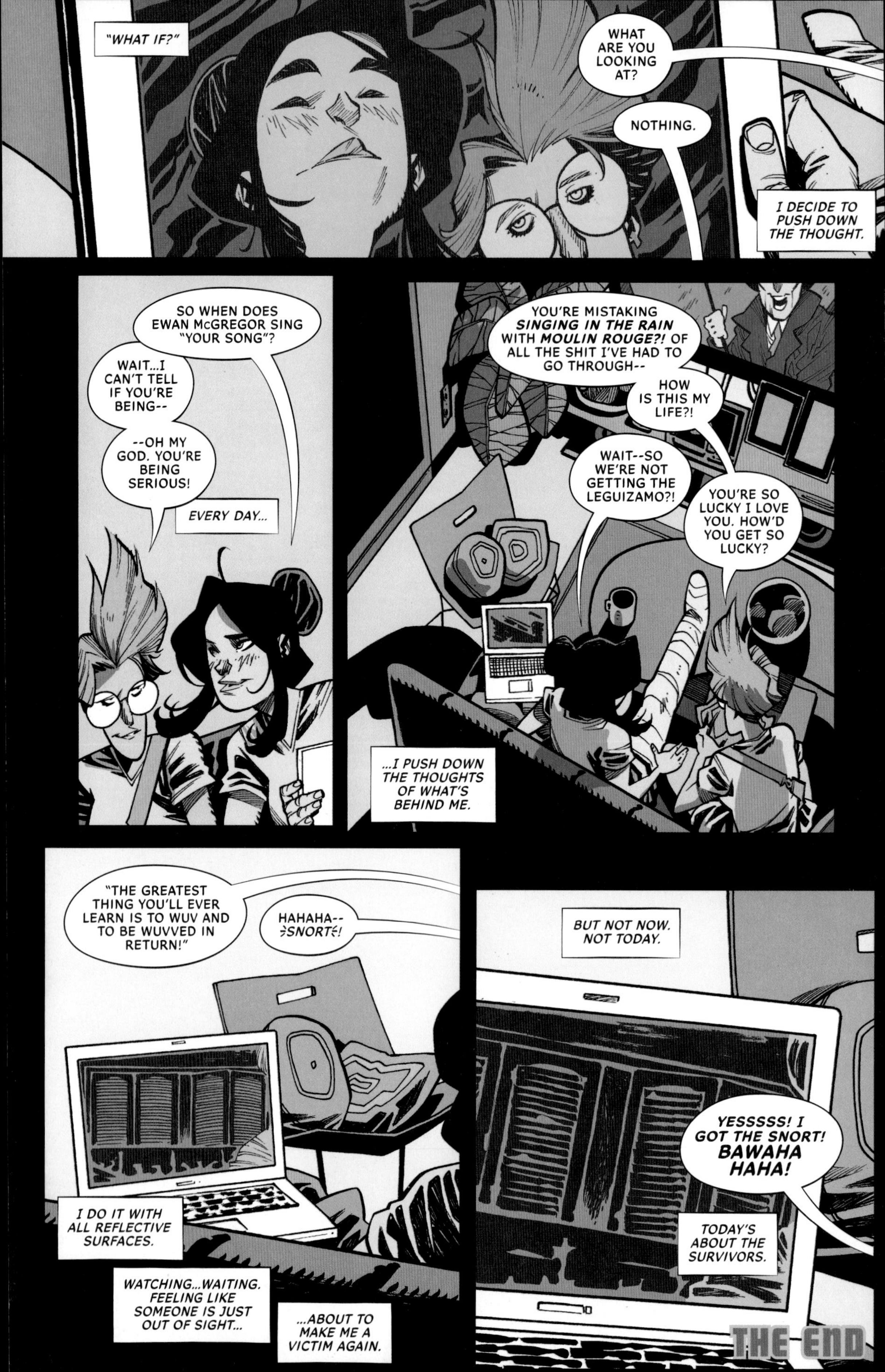
"WHAT IF?"
WHAT ARE YOU LOOKING AT?
NOTHING.
I DECIDE TO PUSH DOWN THE THOUGHT.
SO WHEN DOES EWAN McGREGOR SING "YOUR SONG"?
WAIT...I CAN'T TELL IF YOU'RE BEING--
--OH MY GOD. YOU'RE BEING SERIOUS!
EVERY DAY...
YOU'RE MISTAKING SINGING IN THE RAIN WITH MOULIN ROUGE?! OF ALL THE SHIT I'VE HAD TO GO THROUGH--
HOW IS THIS MY LIFE?!
WAIT--SO WE'RE NOT GETTING THE LEGUIZAMO?!
YOU'RE SO LUCKY I LOVE YOU. HOW'D YOU GET SO LUCKY?
...I PUSH DOWN THE THOUGHTS OF WHAT'S BEHIND ME.
"THE GREATEST THING YOU'LL EVER LEARN IS TO WUV AND TO BE WUVVED IN RETURN!"
HAHAHA-- SNORT!
I DO IT WITH ALL REFLECTIVE SURFACES.
WATCHING...WAITING. FEELING LIKE SOMEONE IS JUST OUT OF SIGHT...
...ABOUT TO MAKE ME A VICTIM AGAIN.
BUT NOT NOW. NOT TODAY.
YESSSSS! I GOT THE SNORT! BAWAHA HAHA!
TODAY'S ABOUT THE SURVIVORS.
THE END

No. 1 WITH A BULLET

artwork by JORGE CORONA

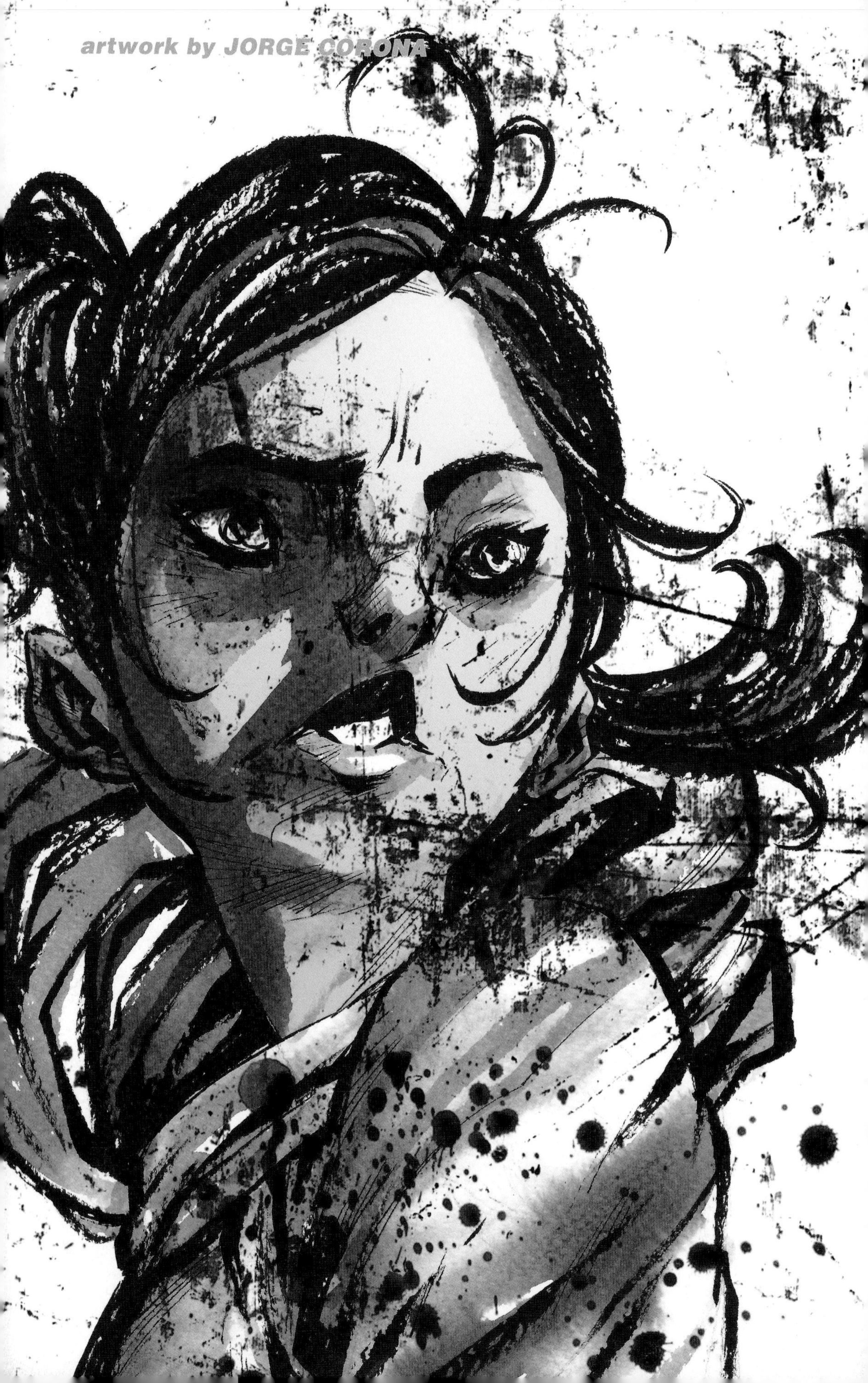

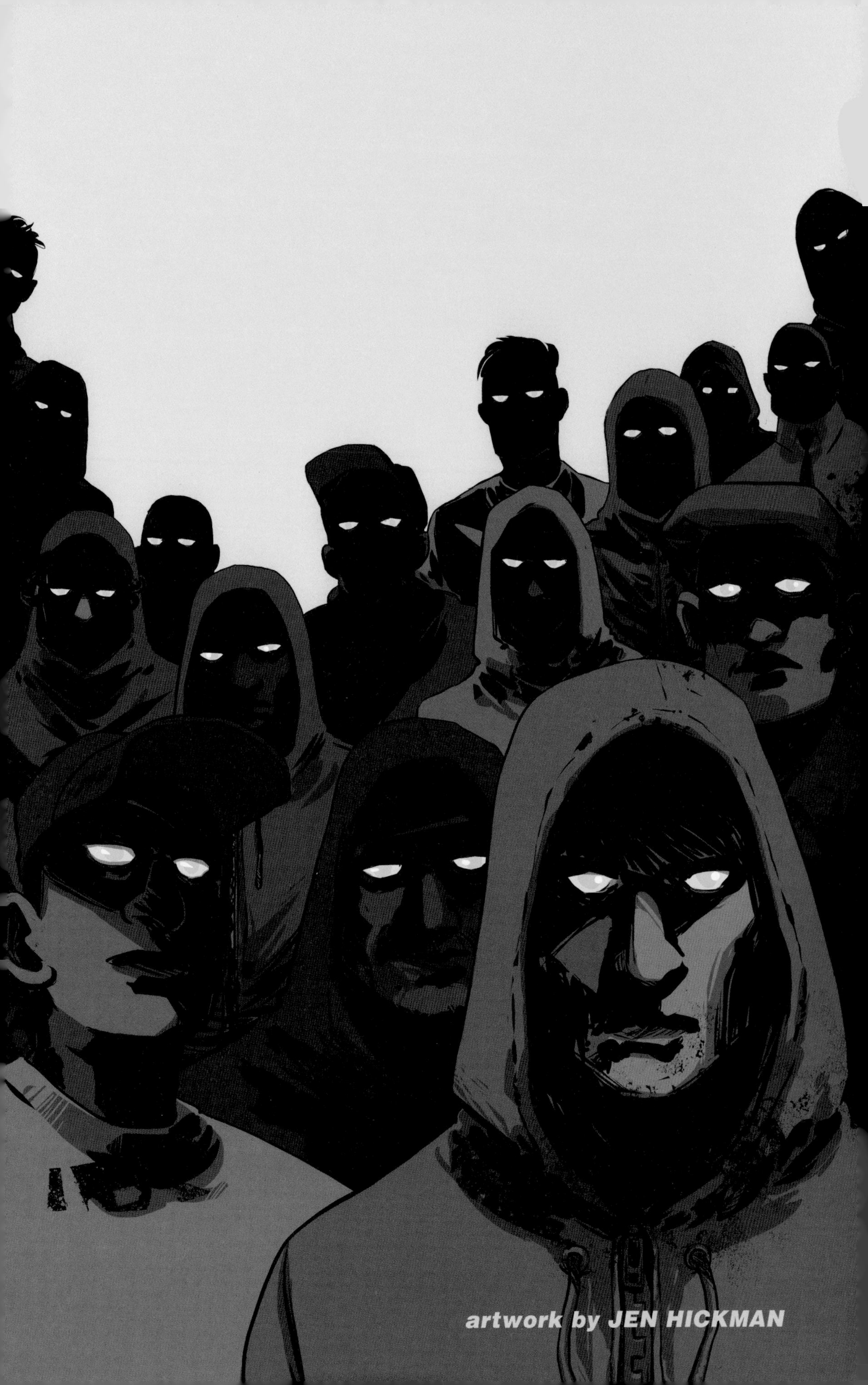

artwork by JEN HICKMAN

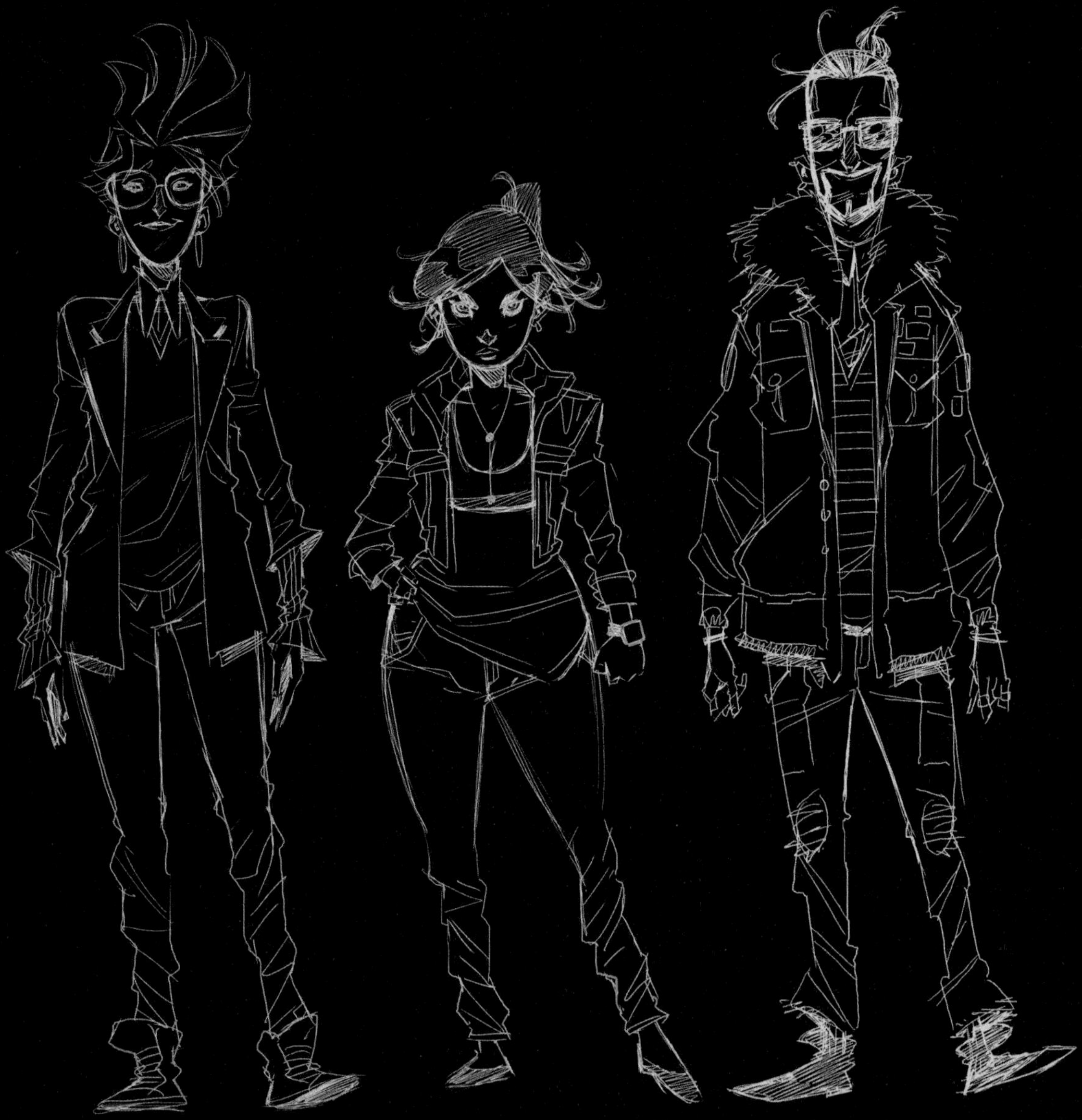

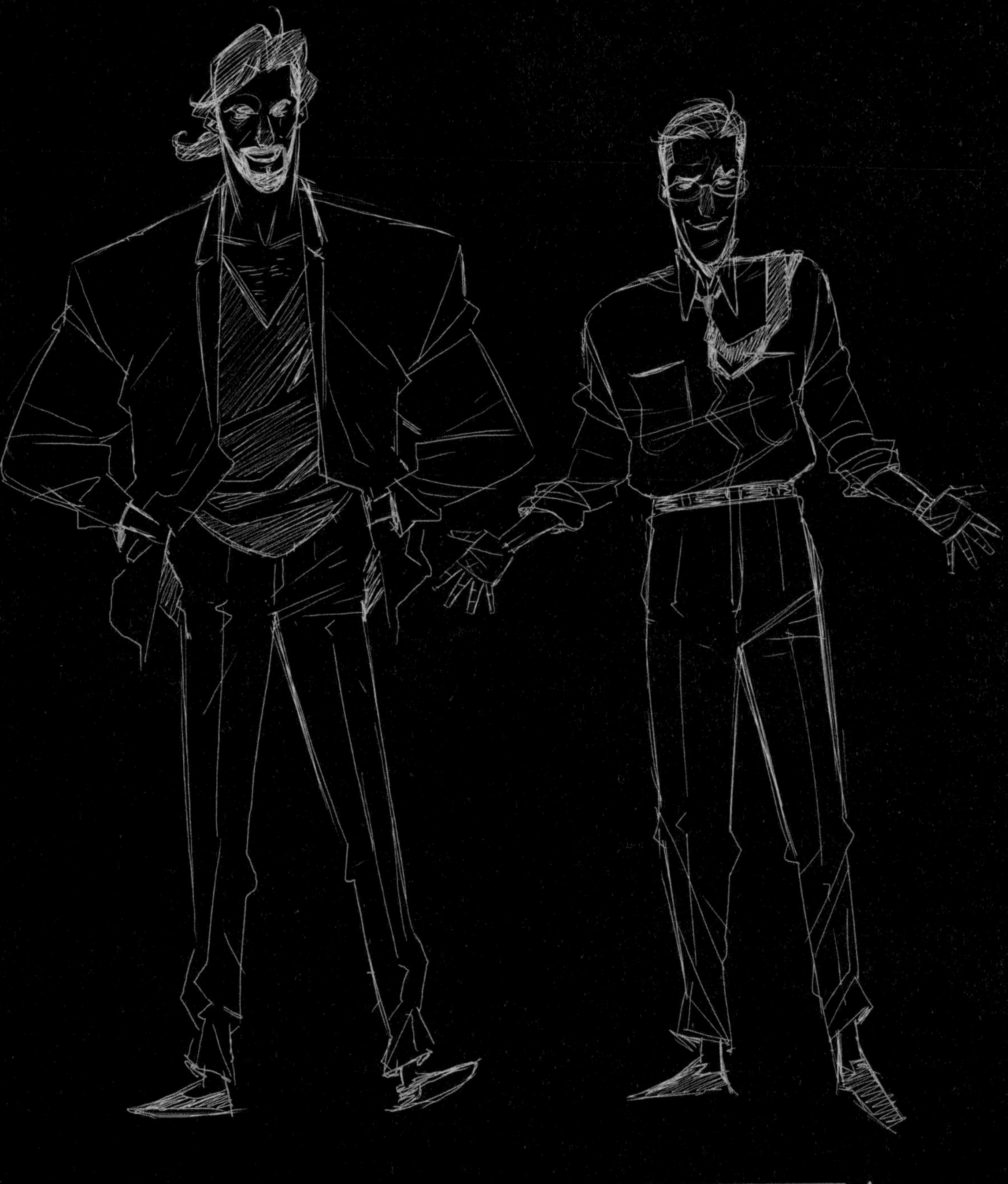

This comic is obviously a work of fiction, but it is based on our reaction to an unfortunate reality so many of our friends, peers, and co-workers have faced. Internet bullying, cyberstalking, and harassment are very real. In our book, we want to create space for victims of this behavior to have a platform to speak. Here you will find letters, interviews, and articles that we hope will continue and cultivate a healthy dialogue. One that lets others know that they are not alone.

Cosplay and the Creep
By Tini Howard (*Assassinistas*, *The Skeptics*)

Before I attended cons as a professional comic book writer, I attended them as a fan. Like many fans, I loved to cosplay. Long before cosplay was popular enough to be in TV, movies, and social media (hell, even before social media was a thing,) I was a cosplayer.

I've always loved dress-up, costumes, making stuff. To me, the fun part of cosplay was turning trash into treasure. Making a gravity-defying hairstyle out of a handful of clearance Halloween wigs and some extensions from the local beauty store. Turning dancewear sales into superhero garb. Painting a pair of twelve-dollar Wal-Mart boots with spray paint made for lawn chairs.

For me, it was as much about female bonding as anything. My girlfriends and I would send each other pictures and links to games, shows, comics, and books with pictures of characters we could cosplay all week long as. On the weekends, we'd hit the fabric stories and stay up late into the night working on our projects together, binge-watching nerdy television and pass out on each other's couches.
But entering conventions, primarily comics

and anime-themed affairs that were largely male-dominated, there was a sharp change in how I was seen.

The men at conventions largely did not care about the hard work I'd put into the costume, or how much I loved a character. They saw barely legal long legs in a sailor skirt, they saw girls eager to pose for pictures, they saw young women thirsty for attention.

And boy, did they have it to give.

I have endless stories about the weird in-person harassment I've experienced at conventions as a young cosplayer, but nothing beats the heart-stopping fear of hearing from a friend that your photos had been posted on 4Chan — the internet's own wretched hive of scum and villany. There's a specific sad sort of desperation to that prayer — make fun of my cellulite if you must, talk about all the depraved things you'd do to me, tell me I'm fat and busted, but please, god, let no one find out who I am.

"Use my image as you must for your own wretched needs but leave me alone."

This was my prayer. Not that they'd not befoul me but that I didn't have to know about it. These are the expectations I had.

I started cosplaying at sixteen.

The first time I ever felt truly violated were the messages. From one Twitter user in particular. This man; we'll call him Johnny. My best friend and I had dressed up as Sailors Venus and Mars, and in the interest of looking good in those little dresses, we wore tall, tall heels.

Johnny found the pictures. He searched for us. Found our faces. Found our cosplay profiles. He asked to buy our shoes, to buy our pictures, asked us about our feet in ways that my own podiatrist never would have.

He never pursued us, but he did find us. And that was the difference. I had accepted the fantasies and stares, the pictures that only made it into these men's private collections, the voices of the unwashed masses, but once I was found, I was effectively, done.

This is what harassment can do to a young woman.

I still cosplayed after that – monsters, or male characters, or masked things – but some of the magic had left me.

PAINTED INTO A CORNER
An Interview With Sara Charles

In late 2013, Sara moved to the San Francisco to work on some freelance projects and look for a full-time job as a reporter. As an avid gamer, she had made several close online friends over the years. In over a decade of casual gaming, she had had little personal experience of online creepers, perhaps the result of luck, and the small, close-knit communities she was part of; if someone was a creep, everyone knew who that creep was, and how to avoid them. Nonetheless, as with many online MMO communities, she found herself routinely deflecting questions about gender, and appearance, often preferring not to use popular voice chat programs while playing.

Even then, this is, and was, part and parcel of being a woman in a male-dominated space, enjoying a distinctly "masculine" hobby, despite several studies that have shown that adult female gamers in certain demographics outnumber men. Sara was happy and engaged with her online game community, often spitballing ideas and working on creative collaborations with friends during game sessions, confident and content that this was, for all intents and purposes, a safe space. That is, until G* came along.

How did you meet G?

G was an older guy who lived in Indiana, who played on a more competitive level than me – he took everything way more seriously. He had a good job, and a kid, and was recently-ish divorced. We got to know each other through a close mutual friend, after playing an MMORPG together for a few months.

What did he do to make you feel comfortable opening up?

So with any online community, you're going to meet some socially awkward people. Like, you may not be in the same room as them, or have a good sense of their physical idiosyncrasies, but you can tell from the way you speak to each other, that someone might be kind of "off," or shy, even if all you're going by is text chat. G was really open and candid from the start, and since we had a good mutual friend, I wasn't really worried about letting a few personal details slip about my job and city. He encouraged me to pursue creative ideas I had reservations about, and was supportive of my career. He paid a lot of attention to the fine details and asked for links to articles I had written. He had just gotten divorced and I guess his ex-wife hadn't had as many common interests with him as he'd thought, and we shared a lot of natural interest in tech development and weird gadgets and stuff. He made me feel confident and comfortable talking to him about things I was unsure of.

How/when did you realize this friendship was souring?

He started helping me with a writing project that I'd been having trouble with. He was interested in helping me with some technical aspects of storytelling, thanks to his computer science background, and I began to confide in him. After a few months of this, he began to act very possessive and demanding of my time. It started to become suffocating, because he was always completely focused on me, and he'd get pissy if I indicated that I just wanted to play the game and have fun and zone out after work. By this time, I had made the mistake of sharing my address so we could exchange chapbooks by mail. So he started sending me flowers, and random gifts, that seemed almost like inside jokes he had with... himself? Like a T-shirt with a Seinfeld logo on it. I had no idea what that was supposed to mean. He would Skype me relentlessly for 20 minutes, and if I didn't answer the call, he'd send messages until I did.

How/when did you realize the breaking point, that you might need to seek police or legal help?

I told G that I didn't feel comfortable and that I deeply regretted giving out my address. He thought I was being dumb. He made a donation to a Chinese panda reservation, in my name, and had the sponsorship gift package sent to me. I told him if he didn't stop, I would collect all the communication we'd had, bring it to the police, and get a restraining order. I didn't know if I could even do that, but I was scared and I knew it would make him pause. G became petulant, and then angry, and confused, and then more angry. I got kind of jumpy after that, because I was afraid he would show up on my doorstep. The last straw was when he sent me a replica oil painting from a professional online replica art company. It was gigantic and wrapped in brown paper. I refused to look at it; a friend came over to get rid of it, and informed me it was a painting of a classical nude. I lived in an apartment with a doorman at the time,

and I can't be more grateful for that. G would call me all night – dozens of calls a night, dozens of texts asking why I wasn't responding, and so on. It drove me insane and I had to block his number. He also kept track of my period by looking at tweets or public posts I made about feeling bad or cramping, and he would casually drop this information in conversation: "Oh, that's right, you're getting your period again."

How did it turn out?

I just kept saying no. I told G to stop talking to me, to stay away, and to stop sending me stuff, because it was getting way too much and I was uncomfortable and scared. He got especially angry about the painting, because he had pre-ordered it a while ago and accused me of tricking him into spending $200 on it. Eventually, after a lot of horrible emails and messages, he just stopped. Every once in a while, I'll get a weird message or a friend request from him on one of my social media platforms. The thing is, G is a dad. He has a teen daughter. I don't know how he can reconcile his behavior with the fact that his kid could one day be on the receiving end of intense and unwanted harassment. I don't think he ever will. He made me feel like it was my fault for leading him on to do all these things, and that my "no" was just me being confused, or playing "hard to get" or something. What helped were other female gamers I had befriended, who had experienced similar situations with online friends who had turned into overly entitled creepers. I knew I wasn't alone and they helped me stay sane.

Do you have advice for other women who might be facing similar problems (threats?)?

Stand your ground and don't be afraid to tell someone that they're making you uncomfortable, and to back off. I did a little research and learned that I had more than enough evidence to get a restraining order against him, even across state lines. I kept all of the insane messages and emails he sent me in a folder and kept a spreadsheet with dates and incident descriptions, when he mailed me things, in case I had to take legal action. I would stare daggers at the folder and hope it would never become necessary. I actually had a lot more recourse than I thought I did at the time, but at the time I was scared shitless and just wanted him to leave me alone. It's more common than you think, and it really shouldn't be.

Because It's Common Doesn't Make It Normal
An Interview with Jayinee Basu

Jayinee Basu is a writer and poet based in the Bay Area – she's also an instructional writer for anti-sexual violence programming. Here's what she has to say about online harassment, ways that we can help spread constructive solutions to the problem, and what you can do if you're being harassed or stalked.

What has your experience been like as a woman with a public presence online?

It's been generally positive – the people I interact with online have taught me a lot more about humans than I would have learned otherwise. I feel a sense of community and intimacy with people I've never met in person and it's cool to know that there are like-minded people scattered all over the country and world. It's kind of shrunk the world for me, in a good way.

It's also been bizarre. There's a guy who's been talking to himself in my inbox for several years even though I've never answered any of his messages. As far as I know he doesn't even know that I see them. Whenever I block him he makes new profiles to follow and message me with. He seems generally harmless so I ignore him as best as I can but it's definitely weird to have an active stalker. There's another guy who tried to get me to join his cult of eating menses (ew). That guy also told me I wasn't allowed to complain about IRL street harassment because I'm okay with people complimenting my selfies.

Your day job involves sexual violence prevention programming. Can you tell us a little about what that involves?

I'm an instructional writer at a company that makes interactive online courses for universities and corporations. The topics range from sexual violence prevention to data security to ethics. A lot of people have done training that's like "here watch this video and read this thing for 30 minutes about why you shouldn't grab your coworker's ass." We try to take a slightly more involved approach by trying to get into the historical and material reasons for things like sexual violence and also offer tangible solutions.

For example, we have a video interaction for university staff and faculty where a student comes up to the user and is about to disclose that they've been assaulted. The user has some choices on the language they can use to respond, and gets to see how the student might react to each response. When conceptualizing this interaction, we thought it was important for people to see all the ways this incredibly fraught conversation might go wrong. One example is that if you are a mandated reporter (like most staff and faculty are on campuses), you should definitely let the student know this before they tell you something they want to keep private, but you should also let them know that there are confidential resources for them and offer to help them access those resources. We hope that giving staff and faculty language they can use during those conversations will help to reduce incidents of re-traumatization. We also do focus groups with students on campus to make sure that we're not operating on assumptions, since the regulatory landscape and cultural understanding of sexual violence is so dynamic.

Can you tell us about a particular difficulty or challenge that you faced at work? How did you deal with it?

The biggest frustration for me in making these courses is that they're often associated with institutions who through their actions (as opposed to their rhetoric) show that they are not actually committed to the hard work of preventing trauma. Like the law mandates a lot of these trainings, but our country refuses to provide the resources that are necessary for them to actually work, like healthcare, or a functioning justice system. Like we as a country do not prioritize mental and emotional health. Access to mental health care is critical for people to help them access those resources. We hope that giving staff and faculty language they can use during those conversations will help to reduce incidents of re-traumatization. We also do focus groups with students on campus to make sure that we're not operating on assumptions, since the regulatory landscape and cultural understanding of sexual violence is so dynamic.

Can you tell us about a particular difficulty or challenge that you faced at work? How did you deal with it?

The biggest frustration for me in making these courses is that they're often associated with institutions who through their actions (as opposed to their rhetoric) show that they are not actually committed to the hard work of preventing trauma. Like the law mandates a lot of these trainings, but our country refuses to provide the resources that are necessary for them to actually work, like healthcare, or a functioning justice system. Like we as a country do not prioritize mental and emotional health. Access to mental health care is critical for people to be able to behave in pro-social ways. If someone is struggling to have their basic emotional needs met, they're more likely to behave cynically toward other people. This is obviously not to minimize the personal responsibility of someone choosing to commit a crime, but sexual violence is at its core a structural problem that requires deep structural solutions. It's great that there are resources for survivors, but we need preventative resources too. We need a system where sexually frustrated men don't feel ashamed to ask for help, and can actually access professional counseling instead of releasing their aggression on the internet among other sexually frustrated men.

I try to deal with this frustration by stressing intersectionality as much as possible in the courses, but that kind of content is highly political and adds a fair amount of seat-time. Most clients want their trainings to be as politically neutral and as short as possible while still hitting regulation benchmarks. This is a bad approach. Of course sexual violence prevention education is going to be political – it's trying to solve a problem by establishing a value system that isn't yet widely shared. People are going to feel uncomfortable with that if it goes against their current value system, but what's the alternative? Those people (i.e. men who hold rigid

positive beliefs about traditional gender roles) are at higher risk for committing sexual assault – they are the ones who need that messaging most. As long as it's evidence based, education needs more political contextualization, not less.

How do you think we can better combat/prevent online sex crimes (revenge porn, phone hacking and subsequent release of personal material and its ilk)?

We can combat online sex crimes by not finding coerced sexualized artifacts interesting in the first place. Obviously don't consume porn if it doesn't appear consensually produced, but if you do come upon it, make an effort to research its source and report something that looks suspicious. Hold people who circulate leaked images accountable in online communities. Most importantly, we need to prioritize victims and not do horrifying things like fire them from their job if a nude picture of them is leaked on the internet. Slut shaming is an intended part of the crime, and if you participate in it in any way, you are complicit in that crime. People and institutions should be held accountable for doing that.

Through the lens of someone who has written about the sensation of trauma, how do you think ever-expanding surveillance technology has had an impact on young women who have been victims? (think camera contact lenses, phone/cam hacking, location-based/tracking apps, rampant social media use)

I am still very much learning about trauma as well as surveillance technology so I'm not really sure whether I can answer this question. Some small thoughts: I think surveillance technology has the power to support survivors. Using social media to warn others of predators in the community is an example of responsible use, though of course there are issues with call out culture as it's sometimes practiced. And there's also something to the idea that while powerful entities have always had the ability to monitor and suppress threats to their power, the internet allows us to do the reverse panopticon thing (there's some word for it that I'm forgetting) to a certain degree. But I dunno, the fact that that kind of sounds like something a dweeby Anonymous person would say and the complete uselessness of things like body cams in holding police accountable probably means that I'm wrong about that.

Are there misunderstood or overlooked aspects of sexual assault prevention?

I think targeted messaging is really important. We tend to take a normalized, one-size-fits-all approach to messaging that uses academic language taken from sociology to discuss sexual violence, but for a lot of people that kind of language is an automatic signal to shut down and discredit it as academic bullshit. I'm actually pretty bad at this, but I think speaking to people where they're at is probably something we could be doing better.

Also one of the biggest reasons that people don't report assaults is because they don't think it's important enough to report. There should be stronger messaging that just because something is common does not mean it's normal. Sexual assault is incredibly common, but it is not normal. Not everyone who has been assaulted is traumatized by it or see it as assault, and that's totally valid and to some degree protective. However, unacknowledged assault is a risk factor for subsequent victimization. You don't have to tell the cops or anything, but consider telling someone.

Can you tell us about a significant accomplishment you might have had in the course of your work?

I wrote a post on the company blog talking about the phenomenon of unacknowledged rapes and why many victims minimize sexual violence. A couple weeks later one of my coworkers told me that a student had called the office wanting to thank me and tell me that the post helped her through a tough situation in her life. I don't have a phone at my desk so she was unable to reach me directly, but I was moved that she had taken the time to call and leave a message. It was also gratifying to learn that even if sometimes writing for a corporate blog feels like yelling into a void, sometimes it actually reaches people who need it.

How do you think society, as a whole, can get better at preventing and addressing sexual violence and associated behavior – especially when it starts online and creeps into "real" life? (not that online life isn't real)

I think the most effective form of sexual violence prevention is compassionate education that aims to eliminate all forms of structural oppression. We should be teaching concepts like consent, agency, and power starting when children are very young, and all throughout elementary, middle, and high school. Children should be receiving a lot more education on how to interpret images and analyze messaging, and also how to intervene or be defiant if someone around them is saying or doing something messed up.

Predators take advantage of people's natural tendency toward trust. There should be more education around being able to identify these people. "The Gift of Fear" by Gavin de Becker should be required reading for high school freshmen. If someone is not taking "no" for an answer, that person should not be trusted. I think this concept is very useful for all areas of life, but especially in intimate relationships. I say this with zero intentions of victim blaming – I understand that there is no way to fully protect yourself and also live a full, dynamic life.

Social Media. Social Expectations.

An Interview with Alexis Liistro

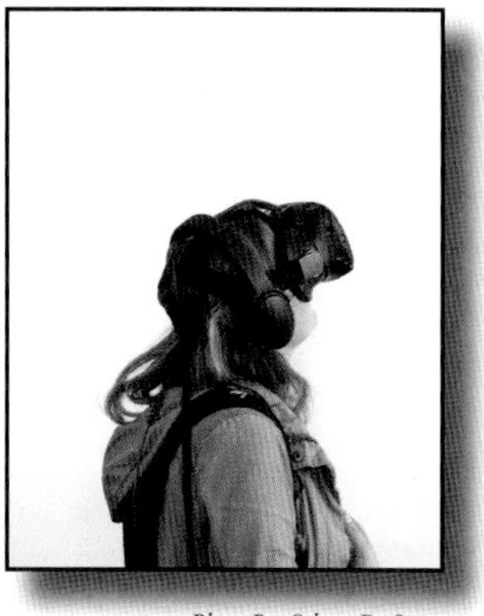

Photo By: Odette De Siena

For as long as she can remember, Alexis Liistro has been fascinated by digital technology and the business of "how things work." The Seattle-based attorney studied engineering and ergonomics at Tufts University, before going on to get her JD and enter the world of patent law. Today, she's working on her LLM – Latin Legum Magister, an advanced master's degree in law – that will allow her to teach law, with the goal of nurturing women in the field of patent law and intellectual property (IP). These fields have traditionally been the provenance of men, but as more women pursue STEM careers and become engaged with the technology that dictates most of our day-to-day lives, Liistro's passion has only deepened. We spoke to her about her thoughts on the current state of surveillance technology and its effect on women.

First off, let's talk about the elephant in the room: the #MeToo movement, which gained such incredible momentum online – do you think this "breakthrough" for women would be possible without social media?

Women have always gotten the short end of the stick, but technology has helped to increase awareness and exposure to the need for gender equality. But in this case, technology's impact really depends on the users, especially because social media is also home to trolls and bullies and bots. I guess my answer is yes, and no.

Can you elaborate?

For example, the "Me Too" movement was first started by a woman named Tarana Burke like ten years ago. She's still a social activist today. The phrase was co-opted by celebrities when the Harvey Weinstein scandal happened, but no one realized that this woman, Tarana Burke, had been doing this Me Too thing for so many years, until it got turned into a hash tag and really gained the traction it deserves. And now men are coming forward too, who have been abused or harassed, which is also a really important part of Me Too. Without social media and the hashtag, and subsequently the people who spread the word about Tarana Burke's work, we wouldn't know about it in the way we do today. I feel like tech aside, with our expanding social values and growing equality between the sexes, that women have been seeking a level playing field for a long time, and now we also have greater public dialogue on eliminating social stigma for male victims. I'm not saying that it would have happened without social media, but perhaps taken a longer and less immediately impactful route.

Tell me a bit about being a female patent attorney – is that rare in your world?

Being a woman in computer science patent law is pretty rare – there's actually a pretty fair 50-50 split between men and women in the biochem field. My undergrad degree was in computer science. When I was still prosecuting patent cases, I realized how unusual it was for me to meet other women in my field. I would go out of my way to try and meet other women who were in my field. In the past eight years, I worked at 3 different law firms and the third one sent me to Korea to work with a major tech company, and that was really eye opening for a lot of reasons.

Is that part of why you want to teach law—to help get more women in the field?

Yes, for sure. I think the key to getting more women into this field is nurturing them when they're in law school and helping them see the possibilities in the field when they're young and still learning about their own interests and strengths. Intellectual property law, and patent law in particular, requires a scientific and legal background – not just anyone can jump into it. It's a very specific skill set. So I think if women were given more opportunities to learn about practicing patent law earlier on in their law school careers, that would be a game changer.

What do you think about the argument that women should practice "self-surveillance" on the internet to stay safe?

I think everyone should practice self-surveillance on the internet, but also in life. Unfortunately, women have the added vulnerability of... being a woman on the internet. Being a woman on the internet is not fun. You can get a lot of unwanted attention and unwanted messages. I have a friend who used to be a semi-competitive online gamer. She chose a deliberately ambiguous username so you couldn't tell she was a woman, and she would stay silent during her gaming team's voice chats – she would listen, but only communicate by typing. For her, it was just easier to NOT identify herself as a woman to her predominantly male gaming team. Of course, this raises a lot of questions about being recognized on your own merit, and not giving people the benefit of the doubt to not behave like idiots. But she noticed that women who were "out" in that community received a lot more unwanted attention, and she just wanted to focus on the game. Actually, the demographic for the game she played showed that most new players were women in their 20s, so there must have been more women playing than she thought. Either way, it just seemed easier to never address the issue by staying quiet. It's a little bit funny, but mostly sad, to think that there were a bunch of women playing together and all staying silent about their identity because they all thought each other were men. Technically you could say that women have been trained to surveil themselves from day one: having to be smart about walking home alone at night, or going on blind dates, and so on. The way the Internet works now, especially social media, rewards people for sharing their lives online, so it creates a social expectation for you to be free and easy with information. Right now, this sucks more for women than men.

What's the next big thing that you think will have an impact on the social issues in tech?

I think the introduction of artificial intelligence into the world of IP has already been a game changer. It's going to be a challenge teaching IP law to students as it's still morphing and changing according to the latest tech. I also think virtual reality will raise a lot of interesting questions about intellectual property and identity. There was a short art film a few years ago about a couple who swapped genders in VR – a man and a woman who used VR to experience what it was like to be each other. I like the idea behind creating empathy and understanding with this project but we definitely have a long way to go, in the real world. Of course there is also the issue of virtual reality porn and content that allows you to "do" things to a person's image, which raises issues of ownership and consent about the use of their image. We live in a very interesting, but also scary time.

A Level Above.
An Interview with Leah Smith

Leah Smith has been working in games for a decade, and over the past few years, has watched her industry slowly but surely edge towards small positive changes for women. She currently holds a prominent position at a well-known startup. A big part of her job involves traveling the world to attend conferences, speak at major events, and spread the word about how she and her company can help creators achieve their goals. Of course, this is the same industry that spawned the societal tumor known as GamerGate; while society is doing the painful work of addressing, acknowledging, and trying to wrap its head around the forces behind GamerGate, Leah is one of the few living in the trenches. For those who have never experienced institutionalized harassment and/or even assault, it is one thing to read about the horrifying treatment of women working in games, and quite another to be a woman working in games. Here, Leah shares some of her experiences with us, and talks about ways in which the industry can help level the playing field and give women the respect they deserve.

Tell us a little bit about your background. What do you do?

My background is a little unique. I currently work in games although I studied something completely different in school. Video games weren't encouraged in our house, so I had to discover or secretly play games at friends' houses. I got into casual web browser games in high school and college, which helped me get my first job in games. I've now been in the industry for a full decade.

How did you get involved in the games industry?

I applied for a job online that sounded odd and too good to be true. They were looking for someone who wasn't deep into games and more on the casual side, which described me perfectly. I never thought working in this field was an option because not only had it never crossed my mind, but I didn't know a single woman who worked in games, so it was pure luck I broke into the industry.

What was the industry like when you first started working in games, compared to what you see and experience today? (e.g. in terms of gender visibility, did you have to go out of your way to see/meet other women in games, back then? Is there a noticeable difference today in terms of how/when and how often you meet women?)

When I started a decade ago the company I worked for was predominately male. I don't think I noticed it because every job I'd had up until then in various industries was always male dominated, so I didn't know anything different. When I left that company there certainly wasn't an even split of male to female, but more women were being hired each year to balance out the gender ratio. At my current job it's a 50/50 women/men split which is extremely rare in games, so I'm lucky. Conferences and events are a different story, but there are definitely more and more women attending events, and I know for panels there's a huge push to cancel panels at events if a woman/POC/other marginalized group is not represented for a well-rounded number of voices. I personally know cis white men who have refused to participate in panels or recommended a female colleague/friend in games to participate in their place. I don't know if that was happening 10 years ago.

Why do you think harassment and abuse are such prevalent issues especially in gaming?

It's a struggle to properly answer this question because I don't think it's as easy as pinpointing something specific. It's a combo, but I think the most simplistic answer is that it's easy to harass people on the internet. Mob mentalities are exceptionally dangerous, and if there's anything we've learned the last two years it's that folks want to be part of a community. Unfortunately with games, that community can easily be one of hate and vitriol, and to do so anonymously is so, so easy.

Have you experienced any type of harassment in the course of your work?

Absolutely. I haven't experienced it to the degree some of my friends or colleagues have, but I have definitely experienced it. The first time I was sexually harassed was at GDC in 2009, my first ever GDC. We threw a party and someone who was invited drunkenly screamed in my face about how much he "liked my boobs." I was shocked, and he was thrown out but didn't understand why he was in the wrong. Some of the more memorable things that have been said to me:

• "Can you sit in this meeting and just be there? You don't need to know anything about the project, it's just nice to have a pretty woman in the room." (Said to me by a male boss.)
• "But do you even play games?"
• "I don't know if you play games, but this is how a controller works."
• "Oh, are you here with your boyfriend?"
• "Is there someone higher up than you I can talk to who makes actual decisions?"
• "Why didn't you mention you're not single?" (This was literally said during a business meeting.)
• "You only got your job because you're hot."

These are the most overt, however there are smaller microaggressions that are just as frustrating. I've had lower level male colleagues cut me off or simply step in front of me while I'm talking to developers, explaining a process. Because I'm commonly the only woman in the room, I am ignored or not acknowledged in conversations, even on topics I am the most knowledgeable on. I once had a meeting with an extremely well-known and well-respected publisher who refused to look at me when I answered his questions, and instead only asked questions to the four men in the room. It was exceptionally awkward, to the point where my male colleagues were uncomfortable and weren't sure how to proceed. The absolute worst incident, however, was being grabbed by a stranger at an industry party where a strange man kept trying to forcibly kiss me. I had to push him off and run. That's assault.

What happened next? Did you take any action, and if so, what was that process like? Were the people you told responsive and supportive to your situation?

In the case of the man who commented on my body at our GDC party, he was immediately thrown out. I think it's important to have a zero tolerance policy if a guest insults or harasses one of the hosts of the party. I've learned to grow thick skin these last ten years and let a lot of things roll off my back. As women we are routinely subjected to street harassment, so it's conditioned in us to have our guards up at basically every moment, and unfortunately even in a work setting, I need to do the same. At the company I'm at now, I'm very open with my boss about things that are said to me or how I'm treated, and he takes any sort of harassment very seriously. I've learned to surround myself with people who don't engage with questionable behavior, and I have a wonderful group of supportive, smart, and strong friends in games. We find each other at conferences and look out for one another the best we can. I've also learned to pick and choose industry events, and to generally always have a friend or colleague with me if I attend any.

Does the games industry currently have a centralized body to deal with complaints and cases, or does it fall to each company and developer to handle these?

It falls to each company and developer. There is no "Time's Up" movement in games, no #MeToo. It really falls to the company and their harassment policies, but it's also kind of the general industry's responsibility. The industry has definitely gotten better at saying, "We are not okay with this," but we're years behind where we should be.

What are some ways in which the gaming industry could make events and workplaces more inclusive for women?

Required bias training, sexual harassment training, etc. And not just once, but once a year. We also just need more representation. We need to hire more women. We need to hire POC. We need to hire LBGTQA+ folks. We need to hire immigrants. We also need to hear those marginalized voices more at events at major panels and talks. It's great to have things like "The Women in Games Panel", but women shouldn't be pigeonholed into only talking about being a woman in games. We're artists, producers, programmers, designers, writers, and any other subset in the games industry, so we should have a voice in any facet of games.

What do you think the industry at large can do to improve the climate for women?

First, we need more men to step up and call things out when they see or feel like something is wrong. That has, without a doubt, started happening, but it needs to continue happening and it needs to happen more. Second, just hire more women. Third, women should be participating in every single panel or talk at any conference.

What do you think the industry at large can do to improve the climate for women who have difficulty reporting harassment?

I think it needs to start at the level of individual companies first. From there, every conference or event needs to have an anti-harassment policy clearly stated and implemented. PAX and ComicCon are great at posting signs that basically say, "Don't grab women in cosplay," which is fantastic, but those policies need to also have repercussions when the rules are broken.

What do you think are the top 3 things that need to change for women in games (and really any professional industry and life in general) to create a healthy, safe, and professional environment?

1. Believe women. We shouldn't need multiple women to say, "This person is harassing me" before women are believed.

2. Close the wage gap. If we're doing the same job as men in games, we should be paid just as much. Stop asking for salary history and pay us what we deserve. The pay gap is destructive because it silently tells women we're not as worthy as our male counterparts, while reinforcing that men deserve a higher wage simply because of their gender.

3. We need more men to speak up. Again, I've seen more of that in recent years, but it needs to not only continue but there needs to be more men not only speaking up when they see something, but they also need to listen to more women.

Online Harassment & What To Do Next

While the internet has certainly changed lives for the better (hello, cat videos), many of us have experienced the dark side of online communities. We've either directly been harassed or witnessed harassment to varying degrees, leaving us to wonder how a space for information exchange can turn into a place of abuse. *NO. 1 WITH A BULLET* is a fictional story but it's rooted in real life experiences, particularly those against women and LGBTQIA identifying individuals. You can put this comic down at any time and disengage, but we know for those of you who have experienced harassment, it's not that easy. In a survey conducted by The Center for Innovative Public Health Research in 2016, statistics around online harassment were gathered from over 3,000 Americans ages 15 and older.

• 47% of internet users have experienced harassment and abuse.

• 36% of internet users experienced direct harassment, including being called offensive names, being threatened, and being stalked.

• 30% of internet users experience being hacked, having information/images of the person exposed online without their permission, being impersonated, being monitored, and being tracked online.

• Four in ten young women say they have self-censored to avoid harassment online.

• Women are twice as likely as men to say they've been cyberstalked, with 10% of female internet users reporting that they have been repeatedly contacted in a way that makes them feel afraid or unsafe compared with 5% of male internet users.

So what can you do to protect yourself?
If you are receiving death threats, threats to your family/pets, or believe that you are in physical danger, call 911 immediately.

• *Self-Care:* Put your phone down. Close your laptop. Unplug from the negativity and spend some time repairing the damage. Get a snack, meet up with a friend, watch your favorite show, or read a book. Spend time doing something that makes you feel great, even if it seems silly. Your mental health is a priority and when you're exposed to harmful experiences, it's essential to recognize their impact and take steps to minimize the damage. Being a victim isn't your fault and you don't deserve to carry the weight of harassment. Help ease it with intentional, focused, healing time devoted to your safety.

• *Save, Block, Delete:* Ugh, who wants to keep nasty emails and comments? While it can be tempting to remove all evidence of harassment, you need to think long-term solutions. If the unwelcome conduct is pervasive, threatening, and persistent, you may have a legal case – which means it's essential to save copies of what happened. Reporting the conduct to your service provider can also serve to document the incident, even if they might not be able to do anything right away. After you've saved the receipts, block the offensive user and then delete anything you can't keep looking at.

• *Call the Police:* Laws around online harassment are still developing and while some states have certain protections, there isn't a clear legal route to take. That said, you should contact law enforcement to report the behavior and ask about options. Don't downplay your experiences – harassment is scary and you deserve protection.

• *Tell Someone Else:* Be public about what you're experiencing. Tell your friends, family members, or co-workers. If you feel you are in danger, let people know what's going on. Not only can this help alleviate the emotional labor of harassment, but it can provide a safety net. Ask people to look out for you, or to join you for outings, or to walk you to your car. You don't have to deal with this alone nor should you compromise your safety because it's "not a big deal."

• *Lock Down Your Private Info:* Update your passwords, consider two-step verification, and do a privacy check-up on all of your social media. You should also contact your bank to ask about identity protection, particularly if you're concerned about doxxing.

• *Know Your Resources:* Many employers offer some sort of employee assistance program (EAP) that can provide free counseling, legal advice, and financial guidance. Ask your employer what they offer and take advantage of it.